Storm in the Citadel

by the same author
THE PRODIGAL FATHER

Storm in the Citadel

KATE SAUNDERS

JONATHAN CAPE
THIRTY-TWO BEDFORD SQUARE LONDON

First published 1989
© Kate Saunders 1989
Jonathan Cape Ltd, 32 Bedford Square, London WC1B 3SG

Lyric from 'Brown Girl In The Ring' Traditional, music and lyrics arranged
by Frank Farian. Publisher: Far Musikverlag GmbH.

Lyric from 'Paint it Black' by Jagger/Richards © 1967 Westminster Music
Ltd, 19–20 Poland St, London W1V 3DD. International copyright secured.
All rights reserved. Used by permission.

A CIP catalogue record for this book
is available from the British Library

ISBN 0 224 02606 2

Printed in Great Britain by
Mackays of Chatham PLC, Chatham, Kent

For The Owners, with love

One

A thin, rasping wind, edged like a razor, made the whole steely city sing with frost. A colder wind was blowing directly into Cosmo Brady's heart, as he lay on his stomach in the hall, with his tears raining down into the doormat. Faith's departing footsteps were echoing away loudly along Corsica Street, as if she was walking in metal shoes across a great anvil.

Pilot, the black-and-tan springer spaniel, who had been shivering under the sofa during the worst part of the conflict, was circling Cosmo's body, brushing it lightly with his nose, as if puzzled by the unfamiliar smell of misfortune. Cosmo let the hard sobs in his chest explode one by one, until he had cried himself half blind. When he could draw a clean breath, he began to feel the bristles of the doormat stinging his salty cheek, and he sat up, treating himself with cautious tenderness. Changing position in this acid bath of humiliation made him feel momentarily worse. He rested against the wall among the coats and wellingtons, dropping tears across the smarting palm of his right hand.

Most of all, he was afraid of being left alone for ever. It occurred to him that he had run through the green inheritance of youth, and that, like everyone else, he was subject to the changes wrought by time. He was also afraid of death, since he was far enough past the beginning of the long journey to start thinking of its end. Like most men in their mid-thirties, he had begun to scrutinise his hairline and worry that his navel was moving further away from his backbone, but now he realised, for the first time, that there was a grave waiting for him somewhere. He dreaded it as acutely as if he had seen the strip of turf newly turned over in the churchyard, under the cypresses and yews.

It was four o'clock on a dark December afternoon, and Cosmo was due in the theatre at half past six. In the meantime, something had to be done about his face: raw, scarlet and pickling in brine. He was expected to strut and sparkle, and air his white-stockinged calves, in Molière's *The Miser* at seven fifteen sharp. Faith had told him that everyone else in the company knew. She had made a monumental fool of him and, despite his face, he could not help crying again. There are few things more gloriously ridiculous than a man whose girlfriend suddenly announces that she has been married to someone else for a fortnight. One hour before, his eight years with Faith had been enshrined in his imagination like a sweet bouquet. He could hardly believe that all he held now were ashes.

Shakily, he pulled himself to his feet, went into the kitchen and tore off a long strip of paper towel. While he mopped his eyes with it, and honked forlornly into its patterned border, Pilot nosed about in the dusty space between the refrigerator and the stove. The delicate clicking of his claws on the lino seemed to emphasise the abandoned vulgarity of Cosmo's grief. Cosmo believed he had a responsibility to maintain certain standards in front of Pilot, and he bent down to stroke him reassuringly. They had been walking in Highbury Fields that morning, and the skeleton of a leaf clung to the dog's curly ear. Cosmo gently removed it, and a sense of control returned to his hands. He made himself a mug of tea, slopping half of it into Pilot's bowl on the floor.

He was hollow and spent with emotion, but when he went into the sitting room it was so unnaturally quiet and tidy after the battle that he had to run back to the kitchen and cry into another wad of paper towel. Performing seemed out of the question when he had so little command of himself, and he wondered if he dared ring the Stage Manager to say he was too ill to go on. Unfortunately, the whole company would know that he was no more ill than Adam and Eve when they hid from God after eating the apple. And it was one of the great rules of his business that one must get on somehow, even at death's door. Getting on was supposed to be sufficient recompense for any amount of suffering, and often a cure for it. There was an ancient myth, believed since the days of Roscius, that an actor forgets himself on stage. 'Doctor Theatre' the older actors used to say, and they would recite tales of the lame walking and the blind seeing, as if the stage had been the pool at Bethesda.

Cosmo had secretly believed for some time that the old myth worked in reverse; that people became actors not to forget themselves, but to redefine themselves within the comfortable parameters of someone else's personality. When he was performing, he was aware of every breath he took, and that sense of self-control was the very thing he liked. In drama, unlike life, everything had a reason, and when he knew that people had paid to watch him he no longer needed to doubt his own significance.

He stopped crying and sat down on the sofa to drink his tea, with Pilot stretched across his knees. Now that the pain had lost its sharpest edge, he was gnawed by a familiar feeling of failure. Once again, his inability to read the signs had led him off the road. It was the old frustration – the sense of a door without a key, a vital question never asked. Obviously his eight years with Faith were not at all what he had assumed, for she had just supplied the missing part of the picture, showing him areas of himself he had never dreamed of. According to Faith, he was selfish, complacent and pitifully dense about things going on right under his nose. This was apart from his hang-up about God, with which, she added, she was bored to distraction. Cosmo had jumped with fright when she said it. For a quarter of a second, he saw his soul steeped in wickedness, like a pickle in vinegar, and almost believed again.

But his religious faith was undoubtedly gone. He had lost it years ago, while in a Dublin seminary, preparing to be a priest. Only the trauma of the actual loss remained, like the dried-up bed of a river. His thoughts tended to travel back to it auto-

3

matically, whenever anything in his life went wrong. He had made the mistake of assuming that the world would look rational without God. In fact, he had found it more confusing than ever, and a great deal less appetising without the saving blinders of Christian charity. His mother, his teachers and his contemporaries had all treated him with varying degrees of anger and scorn. They had not realised that, despite his militant unbelief, Cosmo was in mourning. He had left part of himself behind when he turned his back on the court of heaven, and all that royal circle of punishment and favour.

Faith had never understood that a man who has once believed in God is not the same as a man who has never believed in God. She was a born pagan, but Cosmo was an exile from a foreign country. His mind was still littered with the fallen columns of his religion and, whenever he searched it too deeply, admonitory fragments of scripture flew out of the ruins like malevolent bats. If a Jesuitical note slipped into their arguments, Faith screamed that she was not going to take any 'fucked-up Irish Catholic shit'. It never occurred to her that he could not help it.

Reeling from the shock of Faith's betrayal, Cosmo was certain that his wasted years in the seminary had led to the present disaster. He had emerged into the world too late, as naked in his ignorance as a shorn lamb, and there were some mysteries he had never understood. Now he thought he knew why Father Corrigan, his mother's parish priest, had looked at him with such infuriating pity. Cosmo had been armed to the teeth with theological arguments, but Father Corrigan had not bothered to wrangle over any lofty points of doctrine.

'Your mother's convinced there's a woman in it somewhere.'

'Typical,' Cosmo had said. 'She has a filthy mind.'

The memory of it still made him wince. Naturally enough, he had been a virgin when he left the seminary; mistrustful, opinionated, painfully shy, and so handsome that crocodiles of schoolgirls used to titter at him when they passed him in the street. Cosmo thought it was because he was somehow ludicrous, and wondered what he had to do to make himself like other men. Falling in love with Faith had not been the answer

4

– there was something he had failed to do. She would not tell him what it was, but she was very angry, and she considered herself perfectly justified in running off with someone else.

Sighing, he turned Pilot off his knee, and went upstairs to the bathroom to repair his wrecked face in front of the mirror. He had expected to see something tragic gazing back at him, but his face looked coarse and adenoidal – a blubbered mask with slits for eyes, and thick, shapeless lips. As he splashed and scoured with cold water, and dampened a flannel to apply in the car, he remembered that Faith was returning later with a borrowed van, to collect her belongings. This despoiling of his home was not suitable for a dog's eyes, so when he went out he took Pilot, bundled into the bosom of his tweed coat against the bitter cold.

Pilot liked the car, and he barked and slithered joyfully on the back seat, his muzzle wreathed in his own frosty breath. Cosmo's teeth were chattering as he coaxed the fretful engine and wiped the inside of the windscreen. It seemed a barbaric way to earn a living, driving out into a freezing winter's night, just as everyone else was going home. He should at least have had his work to comfort him but, although his job had the lustre of prestige, it failed to satisfy him at the best of times. Tonight, it was very poor consolation indeed.

The theatre where Cosmo worked was one of the Arts Council's 'Centres of Excellence', and acting there was a refined and serious occupation – graduates of Oxford and Cambridge, wreathed in laurels, lent their great minds to it. You would never see a common mountebank, or a cupboard full of tatty French's editions, or a pantomime horse inside that concrete palace. In rehearsals, the script was always referred to as 'The Text', a hallowed instrument, from which the correct resonances must be drawn with infinite care. To act in that theatre had once been the summit of Cosmo's ambitions, but when he got there he found that his frail sense of self-importance was lost among the draughty corridors and echoing fly-towers. As he saw it, any artistry or freedom in a finished production was swallowed up in the ravening maw of efficiency. Three plays had to go up and come down every night with impeccable neatness, in three different auditoria. One hundred actors sat down in the dressing rooms at the half, putting on wigs and false noses in the way that ordinary people opened briefcases or pounded typewriters. Black-shirted, beer-swilling technicians swarmed out of secret regions to shift the scenery. Computers supervised the lighting, and Stage Management teams supervised the computers. The actors – the only part of the process that could not be automated or modernised – were tolerated, but never deferred to. Perhaps, thought Cosmo, this was the reason why audiences were so chilly with him, and only one critic had mentioned him in a review. Even at six foot three, he was not big enough to project himself over such obstacles. He felt helpless and institutional-ised. There was a smell of canteen food backstage, which reminded him unpleasantly of his school, where the Jesuit Fathers had moulded Catholic men by whacking their ears with rulers.

The theatre loomed at him as he drove across the bridge, a modernistic slab, with the black water lapping at its foun-dations. It was not the sort of building you could possess by laughing at it. Some of the younger company members had tried to tarnish its newness by scribbling on the walls, and hanging chamber pots and pairs of knickers on its most inac-cessible reaches, but it grimly resisted affection. Cosmo made an effort to remember, as he entered the ringing dungeon of a car park, that any other actor would have been wild to step into his seventeenth-century shoes, but his success only existed in theory, and it was not nearly dazzling enough to make him forget his murdered innocence.

Pilot began to run about insanely as soon as he was released, yelping and barking, charmed by the echoes.

'Stop it,' said Cosmo. 'Stop buggering about.' He pressed the damp flannel to his eyes one last time, and checked his dim reflection in the rear view mirror. 'Pilot! Come back here!' His harsh voice bounced back at him, and he penitently stroked Pilot's ears when he clipped on the leash. Unhappy as he was, there was no reason to take it out on his dog. The impulse to do so raised a question that had troubled him since his priestly

6

days – why should the innocent suffer for the crimes of the guilty? Why should he and Pilot be the ones to bear Faith's awful sins?

Inside the stage door, there was a dusty heat and an odour of sausages. Cosmo heard feet running, the backstage lifts clanking, and the end of a thunderous message on the relay. After hastily initialling the register, he whisked Pilot past the security desk as quickly as possible. Dogs and other livestock were illegal in the dressing rooms. 'Card!' called the security guard, without looking up from his paper. Cosmo balefully whipped his identity card out of his wallet. Other actors, less important, simply walked past, but the man never seemed to remember him from one night to the next.

Beyond the fire doors, he undid the leash, and Pilot ran to sniff the cracks in the liver-coloured linoleum. The corridor was hot and windowless, its walls hung with photographs of past productions, to which people had added moustaches and bubbles of obscene speech. Out of sight around the bend, the next set of doors swung back on themselves. Someone was coming towards him, with very light, quick footsteps. When Cosmo saw that it was Hester Stretton from his own company, his sore hide smarted all over. He had never been able to talk to Hester. She was so beautiful that commonplaces were impossible. The details of her exquisite loveliness, the ornamental scroll-work added by nature, had always disturbed him. When he noticed the delicate fan of bones in her foot, the line of her fair hair when it was drawn away from her face, or the way her pearl earring rested on the lobe of her ear, he felt as if droplets of icy water were being shaken down his spine. If he contemplated the whole sum of her beauty, he felt oddly aggrieved. It was simply too much for him.

Hester smiled when she saw him. She was wearing jeans and a baggy grey jersey, and her magnificent blonde curling hair hung loose to her waist.

'Hello, Cosmo.'

Endless poetic sentences formed themselves in the pit of his stomach and died in his throat. He suddenly wished he had the right to confide in her, since she was the only person he trusted not to laugh at him. He imagined her to be as gentle and good as she was pretty, and as far above gossip as the angels. Despairing over his lack of grace, he walked past her without a word.

Hester called after him: 'You haven't seen Vinny, have you?'

'I've only just got in.' Cosmo was sorry he sounded so surly, particularly when he saw he had embarrassed her.

'Oh, all right. Sorry.'

He watched her hurrying away, and listened as she accosted the security guard on the other side of the doors: 'Sid, have you seen Vinny, by any chance?'

She left a faint, heavenly scent hanging on the air behind her, and when Cosmo inhaled it he felt that his overpowering loneliness made him as hideous as Caliban.

Two

'I see a red door and I want to paint it black,' sang Vinny, 'No colours any more, I want it to be black – ' Wrinkled white stockings sagged down his meagre shins. His skinny, grasshopper's legs were climbing into a pair of satin breeches.

'You'll be late,' said Cosmo. He was at the mirror, combing out the ringlets in his long wig, which had been sent down too tightly curled. 'We've had the quarter.'

'I'd have been fine if I hadn't stopped for a crap.' Vinny paused in his dressing to scratch his ribs. He was never in a hurry. However late he was, he always managed to get someone else to go into a frenzy on his behalf. 'Twenty minutes I sat there, and I couldn't shift a single thing. The food in this bloody place turns my guts to concrete – it was like trying to dump Stonehenge.' He pulled a frilled muslin shirt over his head, and his bright yellow hair emerged at the neck, standing on end like the clock of a dandelion. 'Are you all right, mate?'

'Fine,' Cosmo said austerely. Moving nearer to the glass, he examined the puffy ridges round his eyes. His make-up was spread neatly across a towel in front of him – two streaky sticks of brown base, a large tin of Cremine and a drum of powder. Vinny's sordid belongings were spilling into his territory from the next space along – smeared tissues dusted with ash, old cups of tea thickly-skinned like custard, and unmentionable morsels of food. Cosmo was used to the squalor, but

9

the misery of that afternoon had lowered his hale constitution, and as he pushed aside a repulsive-looking sausage wrapped in a paper napkin he felt queasy to the ends of his hair.

'Vinny, can you spare a cigarette?'

'Sure, help yourself. I thought you'd given up.'

Cosmo lit one from a shabby packet on the table. 'Can I chuck this away?'

'What, my sausage? Certainly not.'

'You're not going to eat it, are you?'

Vinny smiled, with good humour that only just stopped short of insolence, and put the sausage in his breeches pocket. He's planning to do something asinine with it, Cosmo thought, I shouldn't dream of asking what. But he felt excluded, all the same. There was an area of company life which was completely beyond his understanding – a collection of folkloric jokes, as mysterious as Sanskrit, whose origins he had somehow missed. Vinny Bliss seemed to be at the centre of it all. The two men were the same age, but Cosmo wore his years heavily, while Vinny kept the appearance and the dreadful energy of youth.

It seemed to Cosmo that Vinny's enormous power to charm lay solely in his being lazy and difficult to please. He genuinely did not care what other people thought of him, and those who did not bask in the warmth of his smiles shivered in the arctic circle of his indifference. He was one of life's easy winners, a perfect example of the Biblical maxim 'To them that hath shall be given'. Cosmo could not help brooding over their different positions. What had hurt him most about Faith's departure was her cruel rejection of his love. She had become quite savage when he pleaded that he loved her, and told him that it was not only irrelevant but downright insulting. Apparently, women did not care for men who gave them too much. One only had to look at the way Vinny managed his affairs. Every few months, his intemperate loins cut a swathe of disorder through his life. No trace of decency ever smirched the pure selfishness of his actions, and no woman had ever betrayed him – it was always the other way round. He was currently living with Hester Stretton, in her flat in Camden Town.

Hester loved Vinny with a devotion Cosmo thought absolutely beautiful, because it was lavished on someone so undeserving.

Sharing a dressing room with Vinny was like an arranged marriage. Since they had to strip to the skin together every night, they had an unspoken agreement to make the best of it, and politely refrained from treading on each other's corns. They were even able to keep up a show of intimacy, but there was no escaping the fact that they did not get on. The restlessness simmering beneath Vinny's languid grace set Cosmo's teeth on edge, and he was always aware that he bored Vinny. It had reached his ears that Vinny's brief flicker of interest in him had subsided as soon as he had hit upon a word to sum him up. The word was 'Dank', implying something closed and gloomy but not at all compelling. Possibly I am rather dank, Cosmo thought. 'Dank' was evidently what Faith had had in mind when she listed his hang-ups. 'You're hung up about God, your mother, the Catholic church ... ' A psyche like a rimy cellar, with these dull and unattractive obsessions stacked on cobwebby shelves.

Cosmo was now ready and, as he stubbed out Vinny's cigarette, he stared at his transformed self in the mirror, wigged and waistcoated, painted and curled; as outwardly brave as he was inwardly bitter. Then, sighing, he continued the routine he had evolved for himself during the run of the show. Gingerly, he picked Vinny's socks out of his size twelve boots, and shut them out on the windowsill, in the perishing night air. The dismal stench of Vinny's feet was no longer amusing, as it had been in the uneasy days of their honeymoon. Next, he righted a spilled ashtray and removed several squashed lager cans from the floor, where Vinny's aim had fallen short of the bin.

Pilot, leashed to the waste-pipe, lay sleeping under the sink, snuffling and moaning as he hunted in his dreams. Cosmo was hovering over him tenderly when Paul Fletcher, the director, shuffled into the room.

'Don't you ever knock?' Vinny asked amiably.

'Yes, yes, I know this is actors' territory, but you can't

intimidate me.' Paul sat down on the divan under the window. 'I was in last night.'

'Oh shit,' Vinny said.

'Yes indeed, well may you say Oh shit – seldom have I seen anything so funereal. You can count yourselves lucky I didn't call an extra rehearsal.'

'I suppose you were hoping to see us naked.'

'You really are extraordinarily vain. Isn't he, Cosmo?' Paul, as a figure of authority, enjoyed undiluted draughts of Vinny's charm, but it was Cosmo he loved. 'Ah, at last I can say I've seen your familiar spirit.' He leaned over to stroke Pilot's slumbrous head, and disgorged all the literary references his mind flashed up under 'Dog'. 'I am his Highness's dog at Kew – pray, tell me sir, whose dog are you? Horatia told me he was always running at your heels. You should call him Boy, you know. Prince Rupert had a spaniel called Boy.'

'His name's Pilot.' Cosmo was very stern, fearing ridicule.

'As in Pontius?'

'No. As in Sky-Pilot, because of the white band round his throat. See it?'

'How appropriate. I wouldn't have credited you with such a delicate sense of irony.'

'Nothing to do with me,' said Cosmo. 'It was Faith's idea.'

'Oh, how is Faith these days? Now there's a delicate piece of irony, while we're on the subject of names.'

Paul's love often took the form of needling. He was plumply handsome, with a flat epicene face and a receding fuzz of reddish hair. His eyes and mouth were wet and vulnerable, and he took a masochistic delight in flinging himself against Cosmo's flinty heart. Although he was capable of great generosity and kindness, his passion brought out the worst in him. The needling cost Cosmo untold torments, but he preferred it to the hideously embarrassing times when Paul became playful and begged to feel his biceps. He tried to prevent these moments by being as forbidding as possible.

'So, how's it looking out front, then?'

Paul applied himself to the piece of paper in his hand. 'You're all too slow on the cues. Particularly you, darling boy.'

His fingers closed round Cosmo's wrist. 'You're slipping back into those sultry Celtic pauses.'

'If I take it any faster, I'll lose the sense.'

'It's not "The Plough and the Stars", darling, it's a light comedy. All you have to do is think about what you're saying, and you can go just as fast as you like. Pace yourself more at the beginning – and please try to remember that you're supposed to be in love with Horatia.'

'You don't know what you're asking, Paulie,' said Vinny, 'Olivier couldn't do it.'

Paul ignored him. 'And why on earth did you pause like that after the lights came up?'

'She was late getting down to the apron,' muttered Cosmo.

'Never mind what she's doing. I've already spoken to her.'

Cosmo could no longer bear the gaze of Paul's wistful, salacious eyes. Twitching away his arm, he sat down in front of the mirror to look at him through the glass, like the Lady of Shalott. 'I'll see what I can do tonight.'

Paul followed him, placing his hands on Cosmo's shoulders. 'Are you all right? You look awfully tired.'

'I'm fine.' Cosmo tried to shake off the hands, but Paul had a powerful grip.

'Vinny, don't you think Cosmo looks tired?'

'Seems all right to me.'

'Oh, everyone seems all right to you, because you don't give a damn. Cosmo actually has some few rags of sensitivity still clinging to his soul.'

'I told you, I'm fine!' Cosmo said testily, shrugging himself free.

'Don't be so moody, darling boy. I only asked. You might be nice and smile at me. Oh, when Irish eyes are smiling, sure 'tis like a something something – '

But the Irish eyes were far from smiling, and Paul gave up, with a long sigh that sandpapered Cosmo's body with gooseflesh.

'Anything for me?' asked Vinny.

'What's the point, when you never listen?' Paul recovered his briskness. 'You might try acting better.'

'I might, I suppose,' Vinny agreed. 'Are you in again tonight?'

'Yes. I want five minutes off each half – that's a general note I'm giving to everyone.' He squeezed Vinny's arm affectionately, but looked at Cosmo. 'Have a good show.'

'Thanks, Paulie,' Vinny said.

As soon as Paul was out of the room, Vinny began to chant one of the company jokes, a song set to 'John Brown's Body':

'Cosmo Brady, keep your back against the wall,
Don't bend over when you're left alone with Paul – '

'Why don't you piss off?' For a moment, Cosmo felt a strong twinge of active dislike for Vinny. He hated this song, which floated at him down stairwells and around corners, and was intoned behind his back whenever Paul singled him out for favour or persecution.

Vinny got up to glue on his peruke. 'You'll never learn, will you? All that moody James Dean stuff turns him on. Why don't you play up to him a bit?'

'Because', began Cosmo, his indignation boiling over, 'I don't happen to – ' He was interrupted by a knock at the door. 'Who the fuck's that?' he demanded loudly. 'This place is like Victoria Station!'

After a short silence, the door opened, and Hester Stretton's radiant head appeared round the side.

'Is it all right to come in? I was only looking for Vinny.'

'Yes, come in, sweetheart,' Vinny said.

'Not if I'm in the way.'

'Of course you're not.' Vinny glanced reproachfully at Cosmo. 'Come in and shut the door.'

Cosmo was mortified that he had been rude to Hester, of all people, twice in one evening. Wishing he could express himself to her, he retired unhappily to the window, turning his back, and knowing he looked as if he was sulking. Reflected in the dark pane, he saw their two blond heads whispering close together.

The dressing rooms at the theatre were built to form a quadrangle round a strip of tarmac and a ventilator shaft. All the actors in the three companies were visible to each other, moving about behind their windows like creatures in an aquarium. In warm weather, they passed the long, light evenings leaning over the sills, having shouted conversations. The tarmac was permanently littered with cigarette ends and torn pages of script. Tonight, this rubbish was furred with frost, and the windows were sealed against the bitter cold. Cosmo watched his colleagues preparing for their various performances. Directly opposite him, Sir Freddie Brough was combing his beard over the sink, vivaciously conversing with an invisible dresser. In the room next door to him, poor old Alice Knowles, who had an alcoholic husband, was eating boiled sweets and knitting drearily. In her seventeenth-century costume, she looked like a Dutch painting in an incongruous aluminium frame. A couple of nuns from the *Measure for Measure* company lounged in their wimples, and a bare torso watered a cactus, its head cut off by a half-lowered blind. Several Edwardian characters from *The Winslow Boy* were studiously playing poker round a folding picnic table. On the ground floor, Cosmo's understudy, Simon Gartner, was putting the finishing touches to his white commedia dell'arte make-up, while Tommy Inchbald, who covered Vinny, did his exercises.

The long dressing room next door to Cosmo and Vinny, with windows at right angles to theirs, was shared by six women. Vinny often amused himself by exchanging bawdy remarks with his neighbours, and waiting to see if he could catch one of them in a state of undress. Cosmo spied more furtively. The idea of so many females in one small space made him nervous, and he disliked their hoots and whistles if he came out to answer the telephone without his shirt. Often they could be heard laughing raucously, and even singing. Tonight they were suspiciously quiet. Madge Worsnip was talking so hard that her buttocks wobbled beneath her ribboned dress. Madge was an arch musical comedy heroine, unfairly trapped in the bulky body of a forty-two-year-old spinster, and she thrived on gossip. As an audience, she had Kitty Ashbourne, who was pinning a wreath of silk flowers in her hair, and

Horatia, who stood with her hands on her hips while a dresser laced her into a corset. Horatia's sour black eyes turned eerily towards Cosmo, and she gave him a knowing half-smile. Immediately, he realised they were talking about him, and he hastily let down the venetian blind.

The Tannoy above the mirror gave its preliminary cough.

'The Miser company, this is your five-minute call. Five minutes, please. Thank you.'

Cosmo rudely pushed past Hester and Vinny, unable to bear seeing their lips touch. As he strode away down the corridor, he heard Vinny saying: 'What've I done now, for Christ's sake? He's been a right cunt all evening.'

Hester said: 'Don't you know? Faith and Dom have finally – '

Cosmo had been trying to put off telling Vinny, but he supposed he was bound to hear sooner or later. He went up to the stage, to take advantage of the monastic lull before Beginners. People were taking their seats, and there was a controlled roar of conversation in the vast, unseen auditorium. A bell was ringing front of house, and a dim, toothless voice announced that the performance would begin in five minutes. Backstage, the atmosphere was poised and quiet. Cosmo picked up his props – a silver candlestick and duster – and took refuge in the tiny, mirrored room used for quick changes. Sir Freddie's dresser had already placed there the great man's number two hat and his bottle of gargle.

Cosmo thought of all the capers his tired body had to cut over the next two hours, and was profoundly depressed. He had never liked Paul's production of *The Miser*, thinking it gutless and unnecessarily obscure. Audiences always thought they knew what was happening, until the commedia dell'arte danced on to move the furniture. Paul was obsessed with getting the furniture placed gracefully, and he had blocked the scene changes so that Harlequin, Columbine and Pantaloon reflected the action of the story. He had once directed a famous production of *Macbeth* at the Glasgow Citizen's Theatre, where the Thane and his wife had whispered of murdering Duncan while carrying off a large table between them.

'The Miser company,' said the Tannoy, 'this is your Beginners call. Your calls please, Miss Geldschmidt, Mr Bliss, Mr Brady, and all concerned in the opening of Act One. Thank you.'

Doors opened along the passages, disgorging a jumble of players as gaudy as parakeets. He would not be able to hide himself for long, as the satin pumps were thumping and swishing along the brown lino, and pressing up the ragged carpet on the prompt side stairs, past the notice which said: 'Silence! You can be heard on stage from here!' Tambourines trailed arcs of green and scarlet ribbon. Whitened faces, with eyes unnaturally quick and dark, wagged with gossip. Cosmo heard the seething whispers as they crowded into the prompt corner, and the hissing of the DSM telling them to be quiet.

'Well Cosmo, so here you are. I thought you'd be sulking somewhere.' Horatia Geldschmidt, wigged and tight-laced, swept her green brocade skirts into the room. 'You've been crying,' she observed. 'Really darling, she's not worth crying for.'

'For God's sake,' Cosmo said wearily, 'haven't I been shat on enough for one day?' He leaned his head against the doorpost, utterly desolate, but still professionally mindful of the glue on his wig.

'She must want her head examined.' Horatia winced as she settled her corset. 'I wouldn't risk my all for that ghastly Dom Shetoza.'

'It's nothing to do with him – ' Cosmo began, 'he happens to be a very interesting – '

'Honestly, just because he's black. You know you loathe him really.'

'It doesn't matter what I think,' he said. 'It won't make any difference.'

'Was today really the first you'd heard of it?'

'Yes.'

'Poor her! How on earth did she tell you?'

'How do you think?' snapped Cosmo. 'You've given enough people the elbow. You ought to know.'

'Yes, but I always drop a few hints first.'

'Well, Faith didn't.'

'Come on,' she coaxed, 'you must have had some idea what she was up to.'

'Not an inkling,' said Cosmo sadly.

'So you thought everything was fine, did you?'

'Not fine, exactly – '

'There you are then,' she said. 'You weren't surprised deep down. Neither was I, darling. It's been going on for ages.'

'But I was,' he insisted feebly. 'I was devastated.'

'I see. You're minding your own business, when in comes Faith. Cosmo, she says, I'm leaving. Dominion Shetoza and I have been at it like a pair of stoats under a hedge and, incidentally, we've just got married.'

'More or less,' said Cosmo, attempting to smile, 'except that she gave me a long list of all my faults before she went.'

'What a cheek. I hope you gave as good as you got. Surely you didn't just stand there, letting her walk all over you?'

He no longer had the stamina to resist her interrogation. 'I hit her.'

'You didn't!' Horatia's eyebrows rose, making a peculiar ridge in her forehead where her wig was glued. She seemed impressed.

'Don't you dare tell anyone. I just shot out my fist, and down she went on the carpet like a skittle. If you breathe a word, I'll kill you, Geldschmidt – I mean it this time.'

'As the tomb, darling, as the tomb. Was she hurt?'

'No, thank God. I wouldn't hurt her for the world. I didn't know what I was doing until I'd done it.' Two thin tears, the remainder of the day's sorrow and remorse, slid out of his eyes. Horatia hastened a handkerchief from her sleeve and gently dabbed his cheeks with it. Cosmo submitted, stunned by the scent of Bal à Versailles which she trailed about with her in choking clouds, as if she was a badger marking its territory. The whole room tasted of it.

'Don't spoil those pretty eyes, love,' she said, in what was, for her, a gentle voice. 'You'll soon find someone else.'

'It's not a question of finding someone else.'

Her face was moving towards him, to kiss him, as he suddenly realised. Rigid with embarrassment, he pushed her away, and the temperature dropped as Horatia withdrew her sympathy.

'Get into your bloody places and stop nattering,' whispered the DSM, appearing in the doorway girt about with earphones and walkie-talkies. 'The whole house can hear you.'

'Sorry, Malcolm.' Horatia gave Cosmo one of her vinegary looks, and he knew, with a thrill of panic, what a mistake he had made. By the end of the evening, the whole company would know he had been crying. She would put the story about the dressing rooms, ornamented with vignettes from his life with Faith which he had told her in the strictest confidence. They would all hear how Faith had coshed him with a Martini bottle on the first night of *The Duchess of Malfi*, and how she had once thrown yoghurt at him when he refused to get out of bed to fetch the papers. It was just possible she would keep back the part about him hitting Faith that afternoon, but only because she was saving it to use against him later.

Malcolm whispered into his mouthpiece, 'Okay, Harriet, house lights down,' and the tambourines began to whirr on stage as the commedia people ran on to set the chairs. Horatia took Cosmo's hand, not from any tenderness she had for him, but because he was hopeless about seeing in the dark. She always had to lead him through the velvety blackness behind the backdrop.

'Faith had to cheat on you,' she murmured, as he blundered against the leg of the prop table. 'It was the only way she could communicate with you – you'd never have let her get away on her own. I've seen it coming for a long time.'

'What?' he hissed. 'What are you talking about?'

'You can act the martyr if you like, but you're as much to blame as she is.' The backdrop lifted, the lights dazzled, and they ran out towards the huge, indistinct semi-circle of the audience. With the heavy task before him, Cosmo paused, trying to 'gather' his energy as he had been taught at drama school. A stinging pinch from Horatia on his upper arm recalled him, and he began, in his pleasing baritone, overlaid with a slight Dublin accent: 'My sweet Elise, how can you be melancholy, after all the pretty assurances you gave of your fidelity?'

He sang out his lines and struck his attitudes, opposite Horatia's charming and wholly unrecognisable stage personality, but it was a leaden performance. The more he wondered whether Faith really had been trying to get away from him for all those years, the more lost and bewildered he became.

Three

Most of Paul's painted, parti-coloured commedia troupe were among the crowd in the greenroom, giving that melancholy place a misleadingly Bohemian appearance, when Cosmo went in during the interval to buy cigarettes. The terrible effort of keeping himself covered with the tattered shreds of his vanity had worn away the top layer of his skin, and he was sure they were all laughing at him. He had read somewhere that the housemaids of Byzantium used to gossip about the nature of the persons of the Trinity. Among the understudies, the company equivalent of housemaids, sex was the common currency. They seemed to possess an almost supernatural knowledge of the goings-on in each other's bedrooms.

As he counted out his change for the cigarette machine, Cosmo felt their critical eyes staring at him, and imagined he heard mocking whispers. Of course, it was absurd that Faith had got herself married to Dominion Shetoza without telling him. It was also absurd, now he thought of it, that he had not linked the recent peculiar smell of Faith with the Dixie Peach Pomade which Shetoza used on his hair. A new scent, he had decided vaguely when he noticed it – a not terribly alluring new scent. Oh, the pity of it all. The African beads, which she fingered like a rosary, were also explained, as were the books about Nigeria. He was no detective, but trust had blinded him. Why should they laugh at him for that?

'Hello, my old cock.' Sir Freddie Brough, clad in a venerable, hairy dressing gown, stopped beside him, holding his interval glass of port.

'Evening, Freddie.'

'I don't know where that dresser of mine has got to – I told him to have my drink waiting when we came down. Not a sign of him. It's always the same, isn't it? You tip them a fiver after the first set of shows, and they never do a thing for you again. Didn't even get my wig until the quarter. They're all nice girls up in wigs, but they haven't a clue.'

'No,' said Cosmo listlessly.

'I say, Cosmo, I must apologise for that first scene of ours. Thanks for feeding me the line.'

'Don't mention it,' said Cosmo.

'Like a drink? Oh – no more money. Keep forgetting I'm not wearing my trousers. It was that fucking knee of mine, you see. As soon as I bent down, off it went like a gunshot. That's getting old for you. Every time you fart, another bit drops off.'

Sir Freddie began to move away, but something occurred to him, and he came padding back. 'I say, Cosmo – ' he lowered his voice to an intimate shout, 'sorry to hear about that girl of yours.'

Cosmo was caught off his guard, but he was surprised, rather than hurt. His misfortunes were apparently so famous that they had penetrated even Sir Freddie's leathery hide.

'Rather rough on you, I should think.' The old gentleman tilted back his head slightly. 'Your heart is burst, you have lost half your soul; even now, now, very now, an old black ram is tupping your white ewe.'

Cosmo was amazed that anyone could be so insensitive, and far too angry to reply.

'I know just how you feel,' Sir Freddie assured him. 'Good God, by the time I was your age I'd been married twice. When Cora left me, you know, when I was in Wolfit's company, I swore I'd never be unfaithful again, but, the truth is, women never understand how difficult it is for an actor, all those totties chucking themselves at your head. So you shouldn't think too badly of whatsername for wanting to

22

settle down. It doesn't matter how often you tell them a little jigging with the company tart doesn't mean anything – '

All parts of Cosmo were bathed in a scalding blush. The old fool had somehow got it into his head that Faith had left because he had been philandering. This was so cruelly far from the truth that his blood was slack with embarrassment during the next minute or so of Sir Freddie's reminiscences.

'. . . an enchanting little conjuror's assistant, staying in the same digs. But in the end, we went our separate ways, she to the Hippodrome, I to the Theatre Royal. No hard feelings either side.' He patted Cosmo's arm in a friendly, concluding way, and left him.

Cosmo lit one of his cigarettes. It was a shame he had started smoking again, but there it was, that was what love did to you. Vinny had disappeared as soon as the lights went down, and he had not dared to stay in the dressing room alone for fear of falling apart. Pilot was no comfort. He was still asleep under the sink, his jaw resting on one of Vinny's boots, which he had slightly chewed.

The greenroom was nothing more than a dingy bar, over-looking a partly-built office block and a stretch of river. It had once been scarred and battered, the sordid resort of all the theatre drunks, and the scene of frequent brawls. After a stabbing incident which got into the papers, the management had put a security man on the door, and had upgraded it with pink lighting and potted plants, but it had not quite shed its Dodge City image. The sweaty, immovable technicians were jammed in a solid line along the counter, the lords of the place. Their great bellies oozed through the interstices of their shirt buttons, and they spoke with the gangland accents of Shoreditch and Mile End. The actors were careful not to offend these goths and barbarians with their la-di-da vowels, for the Unions of the fly-tower and the armoury ruled the whole theatre, art or no art. The lifting of one of those chunky gold rings could darken every stage of the building in seconds.

Outside, a few small, starchy flakes of snow were falling, and a wintry moon looked through a jagged tear in the clouds. The noise became too much. Cosmo dropped his cigarette end into a tubbed palm, and went through the swing doors to read the depressing irrelevancies on the callboard.

Absolutely FREE! Two adorable fluffy kittens! contact Fiona Paige on Extn 467.

The Winslow Boy. Word run 2.30 p.m. December 19th. All Principals.

A letter from Sevenoaks, dated September: 'Dear Sirs, my wife and I have been on the mailing list for ten years, and it is our proud boast that we have never missed a new production – but "The Miser" was the best yet! The sheer high spirits and joie de vivre made it unforgettable. We fully expected it to be the smash hit of the season, so imagine our surprise when we opened our newspapers to read unfavourable notices. I can only assume that the London critics have lost their collective sense of humour, through seeing too many "kitchen sink" dramas!'

'Hello Cosmo.'
He turned warily, but it was only Kitty Ashbourne, waiting for permission to express sympathy.
'Oh, hello, love.' She was a nice little thing, he thought, wholesome as a hazelnut, and sweet to the very kernel. Her eyes, round and brown in her white make-up, reminded him of Pilot's.
'How's it going?'
'Could be worse, I suppose.' Cosmo took a step back. Kitty was unusually small, and her starved, childish figure aroused in him a peculiar mixture of tenderness and disgust. The vulnerability of her sparrow's bones gave him an alarming, delicious sense of his own physical power.
He had first discovered this one morning in rehearsals, during a tea-break. Kitty had been standing beside the urn, eating a biscuit (5p each, money in the jar) and listening to Madge Worsnip's parliament of scandal, which was in session near by. Cosmo had found himself fascinated by the dangerous nakedness of the blue veins in the back of her neck, where her

soft brown hair was shorn to a point. Without being fully aware of what he was doing, he had walked up to her, impulsively grabbed her under the arms, and tossed her high into the air. Her lightness and fragility had been intoxicating – his fingers tingled at the memory. Round and round he had spun her, at arm's length above his head, rejoicing in the strength he had so few chances to use. As he gathered speed, she weighed less than air, and seemed to draw him upwards into her spiral like a balloon. He had not realised how fast he was going until one of her shoes hurtled off and hit the wall with a violent smack. Then he had been terrified of hurting her, and still more terrified when for one moment he imagined he could not stop. Slowing down, he had held her above the floor and felt he never would forget her dizzy, puzzled face. It was a split second of physical intimacy, in which she had almost looked into his soul. The instant this thought occurred to him, he dropped her gently to the floor, and dived away to retrieve her shoe.

'I didn't hurt you, did I, sweetheart?' he had asked, tacking the 'sweetheart' on the end because he had forgotten her name.

'Oh no,' Kitty had assured him, in breathless delight.

Cosmo had hurried away, deeply ashamed. Even if Kitty had not been sixteen or seventeen years younger than himself, there was something about the notion of sexual contact with such an unfinished woman which made him feel slightly sick.

By now, his obscure pity for her had mellowed into a protective fondness. When he talked to her, he edited out the parts of himself which he considered unsuitable, and presented her with his impersonation of a thoroughly decent, harmless man. It was an effort, and he did not talk to her often.

'Not a bad house tonight,' he said.

'You're getting lots of laughs.'

'Oh no I'm not. I'm absolute shit.' Cosmo genuinely thought this, but he only admitted it to Kitty because he knew she would disagree.

'Nonsense.'

'Poor old Simon. He was probably hoping I'd slash my wrists or something, so he could have a crack at it.' Kitty's reverent manner had given him a thirst for feminine sympathy. She would provide it without throwing in any unwanted advice or philosophy.

'No Cosmo, honestly,' she was saying warmly, 'we're all so sorry about Faith. And anyway, he's very shaky on your lines.'

'I doubt if he'd be any worse than I am. I might as well go home.'

'You really mustn't say that. I thought it was marvellous, the way you prompted Freddie.'

He was suddenly irritated by her desperation to please. 'Well, it feels like having a tooth out.'

'Oh Cosmo – ' Kitty called to him, just as he was turning to go, 'Horatia asked me to look for you.'

The mention of Horatia turned him into an icicle. He was on his guard at once. 'Did she?'

'We were thinking of going to Francesco's tonight after the show, and she thought you might like to join us.'

'Oh, did she!'

'You'd be very welcome – ' Kitty sounded dismayed, and Cosmo tried to swallow his annoyance. She was not to know that the traditional wild horses would not drag him out to supper with Horatia in his present state. He could smell potential entanglements, even when the trap was baited with Kitty.

'Out of the question,' he said sternly. 'I'd be abysmal company.'

'That wouldn't matter – '

'I can't face it.'

'Poor Horatia, she'll be so disappointed.'

Cosmo uncharitably wondered if Kitty's guilelessness was actually a symptom of idiocy. Why else would she express such poignant regret for a serpent which was at that moment licking its jaws in anticipation? But she looked so disappointed herself that he was touched. 'We'll do it some other time, darling, when I'm in a better mood.'

He ducked away down the corridor, wondering whether he might have gone if Kitty had been on her own. He tried to imagine himself gazing at her across the romantic corner table at Francesco's, the one behind the trellis. She would ask nothing more than the privilege of listening to his sorrows, for Kitty was a famous listener, a pearl of rarity among actors. But she was so young and helpless, the romantic table would be wasted on them. He would feel like a vicar on a choir treat, encouraging her to eat up her ice cream and telling her he liked to see an appetite. In the hour of conquest after coffee, she would be nothing but a liability.

The door of his dressing room stood slightly open. Cosmo was forced to halt on the threshold when he heard Vinny and Hester talking inside. Angrily he waited, determined not to knock.

'Do tell me where you've been.' Hester was trying not to sound plaintive.

'Get off my fucking shoe, you little fart,' said Vinny. 'So help me, if Brady brings that dog again, I'll complain, I really will.'

No you won't, Cosmo thought furiously, or I'll tell how you snort cocaine to get yourself through matinées.

'Vinny – '

'My darling, I'm on in a minute, okay? I'll talk to you later.'

'But I've been looking for you everywhere!'

Cosmo, fascinated, challenged Vinny to resist that angel's harp of a voice.

'The thing is, I ran into Rosie Jaeger, and we went up to her dressing room.'

Vinny never lied to Hester, but he had a way of diverting her questions so that he was not forced to tell the whole truth. He was proud of never lying – 'being open', as he called it – and felt it allowed him to behave as he pleased.

'Oh,' Hester said bleakly.

There was no accounting for female taste. The morning when Vinny and his rucksack of dirty washing arrived on her doorstep had been the happiest of Hester's life. Cosmo had watched her gentle, withdrawn personality opening out, like the fleshy petals of an orchid in a hothouse, as Vinny hurried her emotions to the surface and rioted among them. His informal, slightly grubby lifestyle had put a little weight on her, which suited her, Cosmo thought. Her breasts seemed heavier, their shape rounder and more womanly.

'What were you talking about?'

'Look what is this?' demanded Vinny. 'I thought we agreed to give each other space. Would I have told you if I'd got anything to hide?'

'Sorry,' she said humbly.

'I mean, come on, Hessie. I've known the woman for years, and I've never had the slightest desire to throw a leg over. Some shit of a man's giving her a hard time and she needed to talk, that's all.'

'Oh darling, I'm sorry. I do so love you.'

They descended into billing and cooing. Cosmo heard the sounds of kissing and fondling, and felt shrivelled. Hester was all right for the moment, he thought, but even divinities had to learn some time that to love someone so completely could be as much a misfortune as a joy.

During the second half of the show, Cosmo discovered why Vinny had been saving the cold sausage. He was in the habit of whispering 'Feel my penis' at Horatia, when she ran past him upstage. Tonight, he thrust the sausage into her hand instead. In his debilitated state, Cosmo's concentration was unravelling thread by thread, and her stifled snorts of mirth nearly made him miss his next line. He snatched it desperately out of the air, after a pause in which his stomach somersaulted with fright. She gave way again during one of his best speeches, and he wrathfully turned his head, to see Vinny in the wings with the sausage poking out of his flies. The whole stage was convulsed by now, and Cosmo fought his way through a bewildering maze of words while the rest of the company watched Vinny taking down his breeches and pretending to have a crap on the fire bucket.

Cosmo never had the slightest inclination to giggle on stage himself, and he hated this kind of horseplay. When the commedia came on for the scene change, he registered a formal complaint with Vinny and Horatia. Vinny apologised, though not very sincerely, but Horatia lost her temper, and the two of them had a fierce argument, bobbing aggressively at each other, like Punch and Judy.

'I call it bloody unprofessional – there's people out there paying fifteen quid to sit through this shambles.' He spoke in a whisper, because they were at the top of the prompt side stairs, within earshot of the DSM.

'God, you can be a pompous old fart sometimes!'

'I'm sorry, Horatia, I just happen to find that sort of arsing about unforgivable. It shows nothing but contempt for the audience. We're not here to amuse ourselves – we're doing a job of work.'

He thought he had settled the matter, but in the last scene, when the whole company was assembled on stage, he was puzzled to hear splutters and giggles behind him, which swelled into suppressed hysteria whenever he opened his mouth. Only after the curtain call did he discover that Horatia had Sellotaped the sausage to the back of his hat.

He drove home to Islington in a stinging, despairing rage, and with a sad sense of being excluded and unpopular. Corsica Street was deserted when the wheels of his car made their frosty sweep across it. He owned the top two floors of a house at the end of a short terrace, divided by a weedy stretch of cobbled alley which led to a builder's yard behind. As he turned the key in his front door, the intense cold made the echoes resound right up to the eaves. Pilot smelt changes and began to yelp indignantly. Cosmo knelt down to soothe him, but his eyes were travelling round, making a rapid inventory of everything Faith had taken away in Dominion Shetoza's van while he was at the theatre.

She had had no difficulty separating their two lives. Everything missing was strictly hers – the dried bunch of shamrock in the kitchen clock, the framed poster of a play she had been in at the Royal Court, the works of David Hare and Howard Brenton. The stripped shelves and naked picture hooks gave the place a forlorn, lopsided appearance. Her doorkeys were in an envelope on top of the refrigerator, but he could not sit down to mourn over the finality of it all because she had taken both the bentwood kitchen chairs.

Instead, he looked for comfort in Pilot's round eyes, the colour of sweet sherry, which gazed at him over the tartan blanket in his basket. Cosmo filled his bowl with water and kissed him. He was always inventing expressions for those eyes, and they seemed to remind him now that he was loved. He went up to bed, tired and sick to the very core of his bones.

Faith had pulled out the drawers in the bedroom, exposing faded, outmoded garments he had worn in his student days. He shut them away, and closed the door of the wardrobe, which hoarded uncanny shadows in the corner, like a sarcophagus. A waxy film of cold lay over everything, and it occurred to him as he took his clothes off that he could now wear pyjamas. Faith had always objected to them, saying they made men look silly, and implying that he could not afford any extra silliness about his person. After a search, he found one ugly brown pair and put them on. It did not matter how foolish he looked when there was nobody there to see.

Sitting on the edge of the bed, shivering and winding up the clock, he thought about Horatia. She had used her unaccountable popularity to turn public opinion against him. He had no idea why. He was not sure how he had provoked her – he never was absolutely sure – but he wished now that he had managed to stay on her good side, for she was really the only person he could confide in. She prised his secrets out of their little shells with delicate precision as if she was eating winkles with a long pin. Two years before, they had had a brief, disastrous affair, while working together in Manchester. It had set up a sort of intimacy between them, but she seemed to carry about with her an atmosphere of love gone rancid, and he never could make up his mind whether to be fascinated or repelled. She was a blend of sterling qualities, such as intelligence, candour and determination, any one of which would have added the essential flavour to a personality. Mixed together, they made a moral cocktail almost too sour to swallow. He had admired her at first, because she had seemed to be the kind of woman he might grow into loving some day, when he was sufficiently mature. She was a dish for a discerning palate, but she was, as yet, too peppery for his own. He remembered lying beside her in a hotel room, full of guilt and self-disgust – it was the first and last time he ever cheated on Faith – too afraid of her to sleep. Horatia had always reminded him of some Old Testament heroine. Leah, perhaps, dressed in her sister's wedding veil, to fool Jacob into making love to her. Or Jael, who hammered a tent-peg through the temples of Sisera as he slept. Her parchment face, with those heavy-lidded, Hassidic eyes, made him imagine generations of aristocratic, high-nosed Horatias, stretching back to the courts of Solomon and David.

When Cosmo turned off the lamp and lay down, sleep would not come to him, although he was quite spent with wretchedness and humiliation. The same moon that bleached the piles of timber in the builder's yard below shone on Shepherd's Bush, where Faith and the Moor were making the beast with two backs. A spasm of erotic longing for her gripped his exhausted loins, and he found himself thinking, as he had not done for years, about the vexations of the flesh. He had once believed the flesh had a blighting, withering effect upon the soul, a curtain of muscle and bone which divided men from the angels.

As a young man, he had marshalled legions of saints to drive away the pornographic fantasies rising from the blackness of his soul. Remembering these nightly agonies, he eventually fell into a half-slumber, in which he began to dream. He was aware of being back in his old room at his mother's house in Dublin. The bed he slept on was the Islington bed, but as he lay face-down he felt with the back of his head that the rest of the furniture was changing round him. Without looking at it, he saw the varnished bedside table of his childhood, with a plaster statue of the Sacred Heart beside the night-light. Slowly, a drop of blood fell from one of its painted wounds, splashing hotly down on Cosmo's hand. Then the figure of Christ shook itself and came to life, laughing hideously and scampering across the table like a rat. It picked up the skirts of its robe and began to dance a sort of frightful can-can. Cosmo, stifled and half-choking, fought to free himself, but a sweet, evil lassitude had hold of all his limbs. Finally he woke, whimpering with

31

terror, to find his groin pumping out semen, making a blot on his pyjama trousers like a little map of Ireland.

Cosmo rolled over to switch on the lamp, with his blood vessels throbbing like drums and his heart knocking at his ribs. There was no night-light, no Sacred Heart – only the usual Habitat pine cabinet, with a novel by Alberto Moravia lying open beside the alarm clock. He considered his terrible dream, thinking it extraordinary that having rid himself of God he should still fear Satan after all these years. As he watched, still panting and twitching, the room assumed its normal proportions. He got out of bed, took off the pyjamas, and went downstairs to get Pilot out of his basket. At last, he was able to drift into sorrowful sleep, with the dog's untroubled heart beating against his own naked chest.

Four

The Miser gave way to *The Caucasian Chalk Circle* in the theatre repertoire. Cosmo spent his free days shut up in his flat like a shabby eagle in its eyrie, brooding over his parting with Faith. Cold, unshaven and dirty, he lived on sour tea and half-thawed meat pies from the freezer. When the television closed down, he watched his only video, *Sink the Bismarck*, over and over again.

On the sixth day, returning from a skulk round Highbury Fields with Pilot, he found a postcard on the mat from Horatia, inviting him to dinner. His first reaction was that he would certainly not go, when the woman had insulted him so grievously, but his extreme loneliness had already worn down his pride. The following night, he drove into town with Pilot, and a bottle of Sainsbury's Rioja in a paper bag.

Sitting in an armchair at Horatia's drinking gin, his eyes watering in the heat from the leaping fire, he decided that rich people had the means to stifle misery. Unable to stare them in the face, it had to seep through the cracks in a mighty shield of physical comfort. The new contentment creeping into his soul was entirely due to the ease of his body.

Horatia's mother was French, and had been born into a Jewish family of immense wealth in Paris. Her father was English, of German Jewish extraction, and had aristocratic connections with Mendelssohn-Bartholdys and minor Roths-childs – Horatia was fond of saying that her ancestors had

had the Oliver Messel Suite on Noah's Ark. Dissipation and world war had drained that great sea of wealth, but there was enough left for all the Geldschmidts to immerse themselves thoroughly.

'Don't,' Cosmo said softly to Pilot, who was tugging at the edge of a rug with his teeth. His voice had a muffled quality, deadened by the solid comfort of the room. He knew, because Horatia had told him, that the lease of the house had been a present from her parents, glad to get rid of her, so she said, at any price. She had created a sensation in her family, by refusing to live in either Kensington or Holland Park, and settling in three Georgian floors above a health food shop in Betterton Street, Covent Garden. While he waited for her to answer the door, Cosmo had looked through the steamy glass at two girls in striped aprons weighing out grain coffee among the garlic ropes and sacks of lentils. The shop windows were gallantly dressed for Christmas, and the tills were still ringing at seven thirty on that frosty night. Horatia said she liked to feel she was at the centre of things.

'Help yourself to another drink,' she called from the kitchen. 'There's a new bottle in the cupboard.'

'I'm fine,' Cosmo called back. The luxuries of the alcohol and the fire were sapping his self-will, and stilling any harsh or abrasive feelings. He had almost forgotten that she owed him an apology.

The larger furnishings in the room were cast-offs from various Geldschmidt residences, and over these Horatia's innumerable possessions swarmed. Cushions, tasselled and embroidered, lay in dazzling drifts upon the sofas and chairs. Carved elephants and china nymphs sported across small tables, shaded lamps threw circles of light on polished surfaces, the walls were choked with pictures. Most of the things she collected were flawed, as if she had tried to offset the smug excellence of her parents' furniture. Cosmo noted a nick in the raised ivory trunk of one of the elephants, and a discoloured seam in the leg of a shepherdess, where she had been glued together. The pictures were musty and speckled, in mouldy gilt frames. He sat opposite 'When Did You Last See Your

Father?', 'The Last Watch of Hero', and a gloomy illustration by Gustave Dore from Dante's *Inferno*: 'There stood I, like a friar that doth shrive a wretch for murder doom'd'.

'It smells wonderful,' he said, as Horatia whisked back into the room, although he could smell nothing except Bal à Versailles. As an afterthought, he added shyly: 'Not sausages, I hope?'

It was a very small sort of joke, but Horatia seemed to appreciate it. He had been trying to display the robust attitude she thought all men should have. Most of her disappointment with him had sprung from the fact that his courage did not match his size.

'Look, I am sorry about that. It wasn't fair, when you were so unhappy.'

'You've a real talent for making me look a prat,' said Cosmo. He began to laugh, fretfully at first, then more heartily, as the drink inside him restored his sense of proportion. He was not without humour, but he could not always risk letting it show. 'I suppose I've forgiven you now, haven't I? This dinner of yours had better be good.'

Horatia perched herself on the high brass fender, so close to him that her silken knee brushed his thigh. He shrank back into his chair defensively, but she appeared not to notice.

'We're having duck,' she said. 'Not terribly ideologically sound, I'm afraid, but there you are – I can't hope to compete with Faith. Soya mince and tofu never were much in my line.'

'Stop that,' Cosmo tried not to smile. 'I didn't come here to criticise her.' He had partly come to criticise Faith, but he wanted to do it himself.

'She took the wok, did she? Poor you.'

'I said, stop it.' He laughed again, and only had one pang of regret, not too severe, for Faith and her black-eyed bean stews.

'Oh, Cosmo, do you remember that night you brought her round here?'

'Lord, yes,' he said. 'Can I ever forget?'

'I took such trouble with her vegetarian slops, and then she wouldn't eat my Eggs Florentine, because she hadn't met the hen. I could have thrown it at her.'

'Vegan, darling – I told you she was a vegan.'

'Well, whatever,' said Horatia. 'She was terribly rude.'

'You needn't have served veal for everyone else,' Cosmo pointed out. 'You might have known it would upset her.'

'I'm simply not interested in animal rights. I don't want to know how my dinner gets injected with hormones before I eat it. Do you remember her saying how she wanted to get a horse into parliament?'

'She didn't, you're twisting her words,' Cosmo corrected her energetically. 'All she said was, animals would make better politicians than people.' He decided it was time to steer Horatia away from the subject of Faith, before she touched a raw nerve. 'Who else is coming tonight?'

'Only Kitty and Tommy.'

'Tommy Inchbald – Jesus Christ! I'll never know what you see in that idiot.'

'He's very sweet.'

'He's dead from the neck up,' said Cosmo. 'Nothing but a walking torso.'

Horatia said serenely: 'Stupid men have their own charms.'

'Such as what?'

'Well, they don't have any rubbish cluttering up their heads to interfere with the smooth working of their bodies.'

There was silence between them, while Cosmo chose his reply. When she spoke with that terrible fluency, he knew he had activated one of her rehearsed openings for an unpleasant subject.

'Does Tom know how much you want to get inside his trousers?'

'He'll know when I want him to,' said Horatia, smiling. 'Don't you go scaring him off.'

Cosmo handed her his glass to be refilled, thinking how odd she was about her love affairs. Like her blotched pictures, chipped lamps and cracked ornaments, all the men she chose were slightly flawed. At that moment, mellowed by hospitality and alcohol, he thought she deserved better. The lamplight softened her vixenish face and brought out the reddish tints in her short bobbed hair. She looked almost beautiful – a finely-textured, costly creature.

'Mind you,' she said, 'some quite clever men have a fatal lack of perception, which is a lot worse than being stupid.'

'You mean me, don't you?' Cosmo stretched out his legs comfortably. 'Can't I sit here for one evening without being lectured?'

He took his drink from her, certain that they would soon be talking, in blush-making detail, about his personal life, if he did not take care.

'Don't you want to know what went wrong with Faith?' coaxed Horatia.

'I know what went wrong, thanks. She married someone else.'

'No, I mean, surely you don't want exactly the same thing to happen with your next lady?'

'Horatia, can't you get it into your head? I'm not looking for a next lady.'

'Ah, but she may be looking for you.'

'Well, thank you very much, but I haven't the guts to start all that again. Women don't like lonely men. They don't like failures.' He could feel himself opening out to her, although a part of him, gagged by drink, knew this was unwise. The trouble was, whenever Horatia was in one of her sweet moods he was lured into believing she would be sweet for ever.

'Honestly, what an old misery you are,' she said. 'Living alone doesn't suit you, does it?'

Cosmo could not help filling in the space left by her question-mark. 'No, it's driving me crazy. I can't sleep, for one thing.'

'That's always depressing.' Her voice was soothing. 'You must miss having a nice warm body beside you, after all these years.'

'It isn't that,' said Cosmo. 'I keep having dirty dreams.' The admission came out of him like a bad tooth, and he was cross with Horatia for smiling. 'It's not funny.'

'Of course not,' she assured him. 'I just can't imagine it, that's all. I can't picture you doing anything so spontaneous.'

'Come and look at my sheets, if you don't believe me.'

Horatia could never hear of a problem, however remote

from her experience, without sticking her oar in. 'Why don't you masturbate?'

He flinched. 'Oh, for God's sake – '

'Well, what's the point of swigging Ovaltine and taking pills, when all you need to make you sleep is a good wank? If you were to make a point of masturbating every night, before you go to bed – '

'Horatia, do me a favour – '

'You're blushing, I've made you blush!' she crowed. 'I was forgetting about all those Catholic hang-ups. But seriously, darling – perhaps now might be the time to get all your sex problems out of your system?'

Too late, he felt the trap closing over his head, and knew that she was about to plough a furrow of torture in his self-esteem.

'I don't have any sex problems.'

'Oh, Cosmo, for goodness sake,' said Horatia, in a weary voice, 'you're talking to me, remember? More gin?'

'No!'

'There's no need to shout.' She undercut him with unpleasant mildness. 'You simply must learn to talk about these things without getting hysterical – that's half the battle. I ought to have made you discuss it in Manchester, but I didn't want to hurt your feelings.'

'Then why do you want to hurt them now?' he roared at her, choking with humiliation, and hating her sincerely.

Horatia tilted her head away from him, making a delicate face of disgust. 'Darling, please, please! If I don't help you, who will?'

Cosmo held on to the arms of his chair, breathing hard, as if he had been running. All six foot three of him was at her mercy.

'Since you were so set on staying with Faith, I thought I'd leave her to deal with your – well, let's give it the proper name, shall we? – your premature ejaculation.'

'It didn't happen with her,' Cosmo muttered.

'Really?'

Cosmo sighed. 'All right, all right, it did happen with her a few times. I will have another one.'

38

Horatia took his glass. 'Same again?'

'Yes.' His spasm of hatred for her had passed. Now that the dreadful subject had come up between them, he had a hollowed-out feeling of resignation. 'I did wonder whether I ought to see someone, but I think it had more to do with her attitude than mine. I mean, she isn't an easy woman to make love to.'

'One of those critical "Is that all?" types, eh?'

'Excuse me, darling, but that's a classic example of the pot calling the kettle black.'

'It takes one to know one,' said Horatia.

'You know, when we started working together again, with Paul,' he said hesitantly, 'I was afraid – I thought you'd tell everyone. It's been absolutely haunting me.'

'You don't think much of me, do you?' Horatia went on slinging ice calmly into his drink. 'I haven't even told anyone we had an affair, if you can call it that. And no lady discusses a gentleman's performance in bed.'

'You blabbed about everything else you had on me, though. Why do you do it?'

'I don't know.'

'Are you punishing me for something?'

'You sound totally pathetic, Cosmo. I didn't realise you minded so much. It's just a bit of gossip.'

'I hate gossip.'

She gave him the glass and sat down, putting her ringed claws on his knee. This time he did not recoil.

'So, when you shot off in three seconds, was Faith nice about it?'

'You weren't nice about it,' he said accusingly.

'I wasn't living with you.'

'She wouldn't let me mention it. I think it started when she went to work in Stoke, and met Dom. There was something different about her. Once or twice – ' he swallowed, and finished in a small voice, 'I couldn't get it up at all. And if you ever breathe a word, I'll wallop you.'

'What do you want, a written affidavit?' Horatia was nettled. 'Of course I won't.'

It was not usually given to him to read faces, but in the next few seconds he read hers. The bizarre flavour of his sexuality interested her, and she was considering his points, wondering whether to seduce him again. She was certainly vain enough to believe she could cure him. Cosmo was flattered, since she had already experienced his poor performance, but he was also alarmed. His will was nothing to hers.

'You need a sweet kittenish sort of woman,' she pronounced. 'The sort that thinks the sun shines out of your orifices, and never makes demands. Not like Faith.'

Or you, he thought. 'I'm getting too old to start screwing around again,' he said, smiling but meaning it. 'Look at my grey hairs.' He bent forward, rubbing a hand through his thick hair so that the silver threads in it caught the light.

'You're such a handsome man,' said Horatia decidedly. 'You'll age beautifully, if you don't get too fat. What's that smell? Is something scorching?'

'Pilot,' said Cosmo. 'He always gets too near a fire.' He nudged the dog aside with his foot. 'You make it all sound easy.'

'Once you've made up your mind what you really want, instead of what you think you want, it is easy.'

Cosmo wondered why she had never applied this excellent piece of wisdom to herself. 'I'm too scared,' he said.

'Nonsense.'

'Nobody', he said with bitterness, 'ever believes a man my size, when he says he's scared.'

The Entryphone buzzed, and Horatia rose to answer it. Cosmo realised that the interrogation was over. She had driven her tongue through all his sensitive places, cauterising his mental blisters. He felt limp and soothed, as if he had received absolution after a tough session in the confessional.

Kitty and Tommy had arrived on the doorstep together, and he heard the scuffle in the hall as coats were removed and kisses exchanged. When Kitty pushed open the sitting room door, she let in a complacent odour of roasting duck.

'Here's darling Pilot!' She was the sort of person dogs love, and Pilot rolled himself up off the hearth-rug to meet her.

Kitty knelt down, holding his paws and saying, 'Here's a good boy, what a lovely boy,' and other such doggish trivia.

'Here's darling Cosmo too,' said Horatia, leading Tommy in by the wrist.

Cosmo struggled out of his chair to receive the salute of Kitty. She brushed his cheek with lips as light as a moth. He kept his hands on her shoulders for a moment, looking down into her appealing face, and thinking vaguely, as he always did, what a nice little thing she was.

'For heaven's sake, tell her how I apologised about that fucking sausage,' said Horatia. 'She's been on at me for days.'

'I didn't think it was fair,' Kitty said seriously. 'I only laughed because the others were.'

Cosmo smiled. 'You're freezing, love. Take my chair.'

'No, honestly, I'd rather sit on the floor. I like to be close to the fire. So do you, don't you, boy?' she added, gathering Pilot into her lap. Cosmo sank back into his chair thankfully. Standing up had made him feel rather remote and unreal.

'Tommy,' said Horatia sharply, 'put down that hideous plastic bag, and stop shuffling about.'

'It's got my lager in it,' said Tommy. 'I don't like wine.'

'Well, let me have it, darling, and I'll get you a glass.'

'I don't need a – ' Tommy began.

'Yes you do.' She prised his fingers away from the bag, and took it out of the room. Tommy looked round, rattling the change in his pockets.

'Hi, Cosmo. All right?'

'Hello, Tom.'

'Posh here, isn't it?'

'Yes.'

'Not short of the folding, is she?'

'No,' said Cosmo.

'Jewish,' said Tommy sagely. His face, when animated by his limited militia of ideas, was somewhat coarse, but in repose it was blank, and perfectly beautiful. He began to comb his hair, perching on the edge of the fender so that he could see himself in the glass above the fireplace. When he had finished, he flicked his tie out of his jacket to show to Kitty. 'Like it?'

'Love it,' she said. It was bright green, knitted in the shape of a snake.

'Me mum got the pattern out of a newspaper.'

'Tommy!' called Horatia. 'Would you come here for a moment?'

He ambled off towards the kitchen. 'Where are you, gel?'

'I don't suppose her ladyship has ever been called "gel" before,' said Cosmo.

Kitty was caressing the top of Pilot's soft, round head. 'Oh, you are sweet.'

'He likes you,' said Cosmo, thinking how well they went together. 'Shove him on the floor, if you don't want him slobbering all over you.'

'I don't mind.'

Lazily, Cosmo considered Kitty. He had never seen her outside the theatre before, and had a desire to sketch in a background for her charming little figure.

'Where do you live, Kitty?'

'Highgate,' she said. 'Near West Hill.'

'Oh yes, I know it quite well. What road?'

'There isn't really a road, just a sort of cart track and then our house. It's called The Summer Garden.'

'That sounds lovely,' he said.

'I suppose so. I mean, of course, it is lovely. We're right on the edge of the Heath, so we look out across the fields – you'd never know you were in London. I should think it's worth a fortune now.'

Cosmo was amused. There was something sheltered and pastoral about her – even her name suggested green slopes, shaded by ancient boughs. It was beguiling to imagine her walking through life in a straw hat, with a basket of cut flowers over her arm. She had a watch on her wrist, which suggested birthday presents piled round the plate of a cherished daughter. Her eyes were dazzled by him, and he rose a little in his own estimation, for he saw himself reflected as a giant.

'It sounds delightful. Do you have brothers and sisters?' He was quizzing her indulgently, as if she had been a child.

'Two brothers, Ralph and Guy. Guy is still at school, and Ralph is up at Oxford.'

Cosmo imagined Ralph and Guy as Edwardian dream-children in a sepia photograph, the sort of flannelled, fresh-faced saplings who would have been killed in the First World War.

'What do your parents think about you being on the stage?'

She laughed shortly. 'Everyone seems to ask that. I must be giving the impression that they're awfully po-faced. They're not at all, it's just – well, you see, the trouble with living at home is that nobody's given you permission to grow up. My parents offer me gin nowadays, but that doesn't make me an adult. My childhood goes round in circles, getting a little better each time, and I know the real world isn't like that. I'm sort of on their level, but I haven't had a chance to go out and make mistakes. Do you think I ought to leave?'

'Why should you?' demanded Cosmo. 'Enjoy it while you can, that's what I say.'

'Did you find it hard to leave home, Cosmo, when you were my age?'

Cosmo magnanimously swallowed the implications of 'when you were my age'.

'It was all too easy. I couldn't wait to get out.'

'Yes, that's what most people say.' Kitty meditatively stroked Pilot's ears. 'I expect I'll just stay there, calm of mind, all passion spent, dusting the china, and turning into an old maid, like Madge Worsnip.'

He laughed unkindly. 'Take it from me, love, you'll never be remotely like Madge.'

'But how can I ever have proper affairs?'

Cosmo was rather shocked to think of such a tiny creature having proper affairs. 'You're well out of it,' he said. He indulged in enough melancholy to make his face look hand-some, and was gratified to see that her belief in him was absolute.

'Oh dear, I'm sorry.'

Entranced by his own stage effects, he was unexpectedly touched by a poignancy which all but brought tears to his eyes.

The restful thing about Kitty was that she expected nothing from him. Her sympathy was balm for the wholesome wounds inflicted by Horatia.

'It's ready,' said Tommy, coming to the door with an open can of lager. 'Come and get it.'

'Listen to the Admirable Crichton,' said Horatia's voice behind him. 'What he means is, dinner is served.'

As soon as Cosmo stood up, his drunkenness hit him on the side of his head like a hammer blow. He had been swilling gin on an empty stomach for over an hour, and he had forgotten the crippling effect of Horatia's hospitality. Part of him was detached, watching his own behaviour with amazement. He carried Kitty into the kitchen, with Pilot barking madly round his ankles, and actually tweaked Horatia's bottom while she was bending over to carve the ducks. She sat next to him, her bony knee jammed against his corduroy thigh, and her touch did not make him awkward at all. He played with her hand, twisting the rings round her fingers. Tipping back his chair to snatch the bottles off the dresser, he acted as wine-waiter, and huge quantities of food disappeared inside him.

Finally the ducks had dwindled into skeletons, the jar of stilton was empty, and he was smoking a cigar. His own voice rang in his ears, very loud and cheerful, with a strong Irish accent. Tommy got out of his chair to do his famous imitation of Paul Fletcher giving notes, and they all shrieked with laughter. He then did Hitler, with his hair brushed forward and the end of a comb across his upper lip. Cosmo, hungry again, ate water biscuits, while Horatia impersonated Madge Worsnip putting on her make-up and saying, as she always did: 'There's life in the old girl yet.' The whole picture was dissolving into a subdued warm glitter of candle flames reflected in glass.

He had one isolated moment of sobriety, standing in Horatia's lavatory, looking out of the tiny window at a man stacking empty kegs in the courtyard of the pub next door. A feeling of bewildered loneliness gripped him for a second, then passed. I'm drunk, he thought. He staggered against the cistern while he was doing up his flies, and yards of pink lavatory paper unwound all over the floor. He rolled it up again with exaggerated care, deciding it was time he went home. Horatia was pouring out coffee when he returned to the kitchen, and he stayed for another hour, drinking four large cups in a vain attempt to cast out the alien sot who had taken over his body.

The party broke up when the hands of the clock in the cooker stood at half past one. Horatia was wiping her eyes, and saying she hadn't laughed so much since she didn't know when. Cosmo picked up Pilot, who sagged over his arm, almost comatose after being fed under the table by four different hands. He suppressed a rumbling belch, and wished he could undo the top button of his trousers to release his stomach.

'I forgot what a complete lush you are when you get a glass in your hand,' said Horatia in his ear. 'You'd better stay here.'

'I'm fine,' Cosmo announced. 'I'm going to drive Kitty home.'

'He'll get breathalysed,' she said to Kitty. 'You know what the police are like this time of year.'

'Don't listen to her. I'm perfectly all right.' Cosmo mentally ordered his face to assume a brisk, competent expression and, several seconds later, it obeyed.

'It's miles out of your way,' hinted Kitty. 'Let me ring for a taxi.'

'Not out of my way at all.'

'You'll get stopped,' Horatia said, 'as sure as eggs.' She attempted to put an apron over the head of Tommy, who was washing glasses at the sink.

'Leave off,' he said. 'Fucking 'ell, you'll have me in a skirt next.'

'Well, thanks Horatia.' Cosmo kissed her cheek. 'See you Friday.'

'Drive carefully, darling, won't you?' She pulled him towards her, and whispered: 'You'd better not try anything with Ashbourne, or you'll have her father coming after you with a shotgun.'

'What? Eh?' Cosmo said loudly. 'Oh, don't be ridiculous.'

The stairs were uncompromisingly hard and formed themselves into peculiar geometric shapes beneath his springing feet. The withering cold brought him slightly back to himself. Pilot whined protestingly, and he folded him into the bosom of his coat.

'Hope he's not going to be sick,' he remarked. Kitty's innocent eyes reminded him that he had placed another creature under his protection. He offered her his arm and she took it gratefully, huddling her head against his shoulder. When they reached the car, he watched her shivering on the pavement, and wondered what she would do if he made a pass at her.

Handling the car was not as hard as he had expected. Extraordinary confidence in his driving ability welled up in him, and he was only mildly disconcerted to discover that he had twice hit the kerb in Long Acre. Kitty winced, but smiled at him trustingly.

'Well, Tom seems quite at home there, doesn't he?' He turned the corner flashily into Charing Cross Road.

'I can't imagine what it would be like, sleeping with Horatia,' said Kitty. 'I hope she's kind to him in the morning.'

Cosmo managed to stop himself explaining what it was like to sleep with Horatia. 'You're always worried about people being kind, aren't you, Kitty love?' He felt her muscles stiffen as he shot through a red light. 'Whoops. Horatia has many marvellous qualities, but she's definitely not kind.'

'You sound very sure – oh, Cosmo, do be careful!'

He swerved rather violently, to avoid a bicycle. 'Sorry, didn't see him. Being kind is useless in this life, darling. Gets you nowhere.'

The length of Tottenham Court Road was in front of him, intoxicatingly empty. He put his foot down on the accelerator and began to sing, beating time on the steering wheel. Out of the corner of his eye, he watched Kitty, and was delighted by her concealed panic.

> 'St Patrick was a gentleman,
> He came of decent people,
> He built a church in Dublin Town
> And on it put a steeple.

46

Irish songs – what a load of pony. Why are people always trying to get me to sing them? Well, I'll tell you. The general idea is, you press an Irishman's navel and out comes a lot of begorrah and bejaysus and Easter 1916.'

Kitty's laughter had an anxious note in it, and Cosmo exulted in his power.

> 'His father was a Gallagher,
> His mother was a Brady –

there you are, you're driving with a blood relative of St Patrick –

> His uncle was O'Shaughnessy,
> His aunt she was O'Grady –

watch what you're doing, you dick. Look at that silly cunt in the Volvo.'

'He's in the proper lane,' Kitty said, desperately trying to sound reasonable. 'It's you that's in the wrong one.'

'You're not scared, are you, darling?'

'Oh no, of course not.'

'Then let's stop all this crap about me being drunk. I know what I'm doing.'

'Sorry,' she said faintly. Outside Mornington Crescent station, he caught a glimpse of her frightened rabbit's face in the glare of passing headlamps.

'Paul Fletcher is always begging me for an Irish song,' he said. 'As if I was Val Doonican, or something.'

'But he likes them – ' began Kitty.

'Don't give me that – I know what he wants. Well, let me tell you, and anyone else that's interested: I'm not having any.'

'No.'

Cosmo glanced aside, hoping he had shocked her. She seemed puzzled and apprehensive, which was almost as good. For the rest of the way, he was grimly silent, making aggressive slashes on the tarmac with his tyres. Pilot, in the back seat, grunted nauseously. Kitty sat bolt upright, not daring to look at Cosmo.

The Summer Garden was still and silent in its frosty nest of evergreens when they halted on the gravelled drive. Kitty did look at him now, and he stared down into her wide, naked eyes. His heart was thudding heavily, and he had a yearning to act out his lost adolescence in a long snog over the dashboard. But a light suddenly snapped on in the house and shone directly into his soul, sobering him in a second. He had behaved appallingly, and talked of dicks and cunts to a gently-bred middle-class damsel, scarcely more than a child.

'It's Mummy,' said Kitty despairingly. 'I do wish she wouldn't wait up.'

He wanted to throw her back into the picture-frame of her English idyll as quickly as possible.

'Goodnight, love. Sleep well.'

'Thanks.' Kitty hesitated, then put her arms round his neck and kissed his cheek. 'I hope you get home all right.'

'I'll be fine.'

Cosmo drove back to Islington very slowly and carefully, immensely glad he had not done anything foolish with her. He could have wept to remember how gently she had kissed him, the poor little thing. *Time, you thief, who loves to get/Sweets into your list, put that in.* He imagined her lying asleep in her shaded arbour, while an angel with a flaming sword protected The Summer Garden from the likes of him.

Five

Hester switched on a lamp to dispel the thickening, brownish dusk, and went to the window with the string of Christmas tree lights in her hand, hoping to see Vinny dashing through the rain towards her. The porticoed houses opposite were half obscured by a glaucous downpour, through which the darkness spread like an inky stain and every gutter and drain gurgled in a frogs' chorus. The only person in Oakley Square was a woman struggling past the spongy, wired-in garden, as beaten and crushed as a dahlia after a summer storm. Hester turned back to the naked pine tree on the table, winding the lights round the branches in a spiral with an air of dogged concentration, as if she had been performing some necessary domestic chore. Coloured baubles and novelties lay in nests of tissue paper, their virgin surfaces bright and hard, ready to reflect and absorb years of family Christmases, and breathe out a hundred festive associations whenever they were taken from their box. Hester had bought them the day before, in a deliberate attempt to establish traditions in her relationship with Vinny. She was impatient for the decorations to assume scars and carbuncles, remembering the Christmas decorations of her childhood, which still lived in three shoeboxes in her mother's wardrobe, quite dim and shapeless with familiarity.

She blew imaginary specks of dust off golden apples, dropsical cherubs and tinselled stars, before placing them among the spicy boughs. Her face, reflected in the curved surfaces, was fascinated out of all proportion, for she was seldom called upon to create anything except her own beauty. She was working methodically to bind Vinny to her with innocent domesticity. The faintest shadow of a shadow lay between them, now that the white-hot temperature of their affair had dropped a degree or two. Sometimes she thought she detected in him an air of 'What now?' and, though she had given until she was exhausted, she drove herself to give more.

There were voices outside on the stairs, and the heavy trampling of people shaking moisture from their shoes. The doorbell rang and Hester went to answer it, knowing it was Vinny and that he had somebody with him. He always used his key if he was alone. She shut the sitting room door behind her first, to protect her tree from the frame of mind he put himself into sometimes when there was a third person present.

Vinny and Rosamund Jaeger gusted in like a blast of the bad weather, hilariously intimate. Hester was too clamorous in her greeting, forcing them to break off and take notice of her. The coat she took from Rosamund blew glamorous little zephyrs of Oscar de la Renta out of its wet folds. Vinny was furling her umbrella, allowing it to drip runnels of water all over the rush matting.

'Oh my God, what a filthy day.' Rosamund brushed Hester's cheek with her own. 'I hope you don't mind me crashing in like this. I'm on my way to dinner in Regent's Park, and he made me come up for a drink – you know how difficult he is to turn down.' Neither she nor Vinny seemed to think that any explanation was due to Hester. Vinny assumed that if Hester actually saw Rosamund with him, he was absolved of all guilt.

'Look at me, Bliss,' complained Rosamund, over Hester's head, 'I'm soaked, and you're as dry as a bloody bone. That's the last time I share a brolly with you, mate.'

She glanced round her curiously. Hester knew her flat was not comfortable or stylish. Before she met Vinny, she had only used it as a stopping-place, an anteroom to outside, and she had not had time to make it into a home worthy of him. It was just as she had bought it, with unimaginative, hard-wearing beige and oatmeal decor. Rosamund had a plaster-smelling house on the Hampstead borders, full of modern Italian furniture and dazzling abstract paintings. Every aspect of her seemed to emphasise Hester's inferiority. She was dressed in dark blue crêpe with huge, padded shoulders, and there was a discreet but hypnotic glitter of jewellery around her ears and fingers. Hester wore jeans and a jersey, and her face was unpainted. She was aware that Rosamund, although good-looking, could not compare with her own beauty, but the woman was elegant, clever and smart. Hester felt raw and clumsy beside her.

Vinny dropped his keys and hovered in front of the mirror for a second, pushing a damp skein of hair off his forehead with aggressive satisfaction.

'What've we got, Hess?'

'Wine, sherry, the whisky Daddy gave me – you must try some, Rosamund. I wouldn't let Vinny get at it until we had visitors.' She had not meant to parade her ownership of Vinny so soon, but was vexed at herself for having let out the reference to 'Daddy'. Rosamund, being much older, would have said 'my father', making the relationship sound sophisticated, almost like a joke.

Rosamund began: 'Oh, I don't want you to open it just for me – '

'Well, I'm having some,' said Vinny. 'I don't give a shite what you want. Get the bottle, there's a duck.'

'Okay,' said Hester flatly.

'What a rude bugger you are,' Rosamund exclaimed, apparently delighted.

'Come into the kitchen.' He propelled her towards a chair. 'Sorry about the dirty plates.'

'There aren't any dirty plates.' Hester felt she was howling at him across a chasm. 'I did them this morning.'

The kitchen, at least, was warm and cheerful, and there were some recent carnations in a jug on the table, another gift from 'Daddy'. Vinny shuffled his pine chair close to Rosamund, and Hester went to get the bottle and glasses from the sitting room, schooling herself not to descend into what Vinny termed 'paranoia'.

51

When she returned to the kitchen, he was saying: 'Are you really sure about the book?'

'Don't be silly,' said Rosamund. 'Why are you making such an issue of it? It didn't cost much, God knows. If you insist on paying for it, you can damn well pay for the coke you've been snorting all afternoon.'

'Well thanks, it's really sweet of you.'

'Think of it as a Christmas present.'

Hester asked: 'What's this?'

Both pairs of eyes, when they turned to her, took a moment to focus.

'She's been lecturing me about "Ulysses",' Vinny explained radiantly, 'And she finished it off by dragging me into a bookshop and buying me a copy. How on earth did we get on to the bloody subject in the first place?'

'It was: "I asked him with my eyes to ask again yes".'

'Ah, yes,' said Vinny. 'Yes, my mountain flower.' He fingered the book idly. 'And his heart was going like mad.'

Hester lowered her eyes, conjuring up a strong physical memory of Vinny in bed with her the night before, making love tenderly, savagely, and with lingering relish. Watching him now, with all his attention tunnelled towards Rosamund, she loved him with such heart-rending eroticism that she wondered if she was going to die. Life could not be carried on indefinitely at such a peak of emotion. She was running through her whole three-score-and-ten's allowance of passion, and would drop painlessly into her grave, bleached and spent, like a sucked orange.

'Have you read "Ulysses"?'

Hester took this question as a direct insult. She was sure Rosamund could tell, just by looking at her, that she had read nothing during the past year except *Scruples* by Judith Krantz.

'No,' she said. On the table the new paperback, with the squiggly drawing on the cover, looked hostile.

'I couldn't make head or tail of it when I was your age,' said Rosamund placatingly. 'I was very intellectually impatient when I was at Cambridge. I only liked books I could swallow in a single gulp.'

'So what made you read it, finally?' asked Vinny.

'Well, I was stuck in a hotel room in Arizona, with nothing to read except a Gideon Bible, so one of the grips on the film crew lent me "Ulysses", and I was totally enthralled.' Her taut, tanned skin, stretched across prominent bones, made her face seem like the mask of an animal. 'Conventional novels are full of self-imposed barriers – you won't understand until you read it. Joyce daubs words about like an impressionist painter.' She clasped her brown hands on the table. 'There's only one writer you can compare him with, in my opinion, and that's Dickens, oddly enough.'

Hester poured generous amounts of whisky into the tumblers, and placed them in front of Vinny and Rosamund with martyred efficiency.

Vinny was making an intelligent face. 'Oh, come on, he was nothing but a cheap sentimentalist – '

'Don't confuse sentiment with sentimentality,' Rosamund interrupted crisply. 'Sentiment is what you'll find in "Ulysses". Wait till you get to the bit where Bloom sees Stephen Daedalus after he's been beaten up, and has a vision of his dead son – I bet you cry.'

'I don't cry over books,' said Vinny lazily. 'I'm not a fairy.'

'Look mate, you don't have to be a fairy to express your emotions.' Rosamund bared her large, perfect teeth and narrowed her tawny eyes, smiling at him. Hester had plummetted far below the level of the conversation, and was confused when Rosamund turned back to her.

'This whisky is gorgeous. Your father must be a peach.'

'Yes, dear old Sir Oswald,' Vinny said tiresomely. 'We ought to drink his health.'

'What was he knighted for?'

'Banking,' said Hester tersely. She loved her parents, and ached protectively when Vinny teased her about them.

'Rolling in money,' he said, 'with a fucking great mock-Tudor hacienda in Chobham and a Bentley, and a paddock for Hessie's pony – '

'Look, if you don't marry her, Vinny, then I will.'

Hester laughed uneasily, and they both looked at her as if she were a child of ten, wearing her gymkhana rosettes.

'He's never even met my parents,' she said. 'They'd adore you, darling, they really would.'

She had slender, secret hopes of taking him home for Christmas, and imagined him sitting at his ease in her father's study like a streak of brilliant light – mercury among the solid, consequential furnishings.

'I'd have to borrow a tie from somewhere,' said Vinny.

This was so true that Hester was angry. The death knell of her hopes for Christmas was rung a moment later, when Rosamund said: 'Are you two around on Christmas Eve? I'm having a drinks party.'

'Sorry,' Vinny tilted back his chair. 'Hess has to go back to Chobham, and I'm off to my mum's.'

Hester struggled to conceal her surprise and her nagging desire to bombard him with questions. She had never met Mrs Bliss, a widow living in Dorchester, and was only aware of the lady's existence through the large parcels of hand-knitted jerseys she periodically sent to Vinny. Hester was wearing one of these now – an elaborate affair in cable-stitch, rather spoiled by a noticeable mistake in the neck. It was a new one, straight from the parcel, and smelt of Youth Dew, Morny guest soap, and the crumby interior of a knitting-bag. It had never occurred to her to consider the woman as a rival. Vinny's attitude to her seemed lackadaisical and distant. Unconsciously, Hester had decided that Mrs Bliss expected very little from him. She pictured her as an ordinary woman, in awe of her shimmering son, taking gratefully the crumbs of regard which he threw her in recognition of the months when he had glittered in her prosaic womb. Yet here he was, cheerfully undertaking a dismal provincial Christmas, and even telling Rosamund he was looking forward to it. She subsided, mortified, as Rosamund embarked on a long story, full of weighty names, about a film deal she was discussing. Leaving the listening to Vinny, she drew the new book towards her. When she glanced at the first page, she was frightened. It did not seem to be in English at all, but Rosamund and Vinny understood this sinister

54

gibberish, and it was something between them she could not share.

The idea of Vinny withdrawing himself into this unknown region made her guts turn. She thought for a moment she would rather see Vinny dead than loving someone else, before descending into bathos as she pictured the horror of him dying. Absurd fantasies of herself in old age, tending the flower-studded plot where his earthly dust reposed, flitted through her mind, bringing an odd sort of comfort. At least his death would not have the sting of desertion. If Vinny's body died, his love for her would be immortal, instead of going to someone else. She mulled over her own mad state forlornly, only shrugging when Vinny asked her if she would like some ginger ale in her second glass of whisky. He went to the sitting room to get it, and Rosamund arched her eyebrows inquiringly.

'Hester!' Vinny shouted from the next room. 'Hessie!'

'What?'

He lunged back into the kitchen, clinging to the door-frame and swinging himself backwards and forwards. 'When did you put up the tree?'

Afraid of mockery, Hester replied carefully: 'Just now. Do you like it?'

'I love it. You're a real artist.'

'Oh, a Christmas tree? May I see it?' Rosamund stood up, and Hester checked her for satire, but saw none. It was extraordinary how even grown-ups like her took Christmas seriously.

'Of course.'

'Hang about.' Vinny snatched up *Ulysses*. 'I ought to put this underneath it.'

'Honestly, you are silly.' Hester laughed, warmed by the light of his attention. Rosamund, suddenly in the shade, laughed too.

'You've done it beautifully,' she said, when she was walking round the tree with her glass in her hand, making the needles shiver with the movement of her skirt. 'I always get things like this wrong. Too arty-farty, I suppose.' When she smiled at

Hester, she seemed younger and less remote. 'Look at this adorable little angel.' She imprisoned it for a moment with her scarlet nails.

Vinny examined each ornament closely, causing Hester to giggle by manipulating a tin dog so that it sniffed up the skirt of a fairy. He put out his arm, and Hester pulled it round her waist. They were a couple again, gazing out at Rosamund through the same pair of eyes.

'You're the only woman I've ever lived with who's thought of putting up a Christmas tree,' he announced. 'All the others spent their time whingeing at me because I wouldn't spend Christmas with their fucking parents.' He placed the book on the table under the tree.

'Give it to me,' said Rosamund. 'I'll write in it. No, I will. Have you got a pen?'

Vinny, without taking his arm from Hester's waist, dug in his pocket for a mutilated stump of pencil. Rosamund's rings flashed in the coloured lights as she wrote in the fly-leaf: 'To Hester and Vinny, Merry Xmas. Love from Rosamund.'

When she had departed for her dinner in Regent's Park, leaving the flat smelling of Oscar de la Renta to its uttermost corner, Hester said: 'Vinny – '

'What?' He was peering at the first page of *Ulysses* with an intellectual crease between his eyes.

'Does it bother you that I don't read much, or – or talk about art and things?'

Vinny glanced up. There was a short silence before he spoke. 'Of course not. Why should you?'

'Well, I don't want you to think I'm stupid. I'll try, if you like.'

He pulled her towards him, pressing his pelvis into hers. 'All right love, I'll get you a couple of Noddy books.'

'No, seriously – '

'Seriously, Hessie, do I want to live in a bleeding seminar? You're not stupid. Your cleverness goes into all the right areas.'

He put her hands underneath his leather jacket, to caress his bony back. Her stocks of common sense, although much reduced, were not quite gone, but she ignored the inner voice which told her that 'all the right areas' meant the area of Vinny, and that if she failed to please him her cleverness was useless.

Six

Ordinary people can afford to be sparing with their charms, but actors are used to making the most of every shred they possess, and their pleasing qualities are continually hung out for inspection. Even with tousled, wig-flattened hair and smuts of make-up behind their ears, Paul Fletcher's company managed to give a collective impression of glamour and bold presentation. Kitty had never been to a company party before, apart from sessions in the pub at drama school, where ambitions had been harped upon over beer and sausage rolls, and she hovered beside the door, a little frightened by the ferocious compulsion her colleagues had to entertain one another. It was the Friday before Christmas, and they had all crowded into Francesco's after their last performance of *The Miser* until the middle of January.

A long table had been laid for them, but they stood in the centre aisle of the restaurant with their drinks, unwilling to commit the political act of sitting, for fear of who should plump down beside them. Discreet calculations were already being made by people who realised they were standing in the wrong groups. Those who were unpopular, or known to be tedious when drunk, were beginning to find themselves drifting inexplicably away from the nucleus of the action. Kitty hoped she would not be stuck next to Sir Freddie Brough, whose idea of amusing a young girl was to fold his napkin into bunny's ears and make it speak disagreeable intimacies to her in a squeaky voice. As she took her coat off, she heard him declaiming, 'This is Melissa, my number five!' and saw to her relief that he had his fifth wife with him – a gentle, willowy creature, like a portrait by Gainsborough. Standing with her hands nervously folded, Kitty looked around at the terracotta tiles and tuscan fishing-nets, trying to find faces she knew among the signed photographs on the walls. A softened Horatia smiled above the till, with her eternal gratitude to 'Francesco, Paolo and all the boys' scrawled across her chin. Sir Freddie, also grateful, hung above the door to the gentlemen's lavatory, ten years younger, wearing fur robes and a crown. Grateful for what? Kitty wondered. It wasn't as if Francesco let them eat there for nothing. She went to the table to take a glass of wine from the tray, making herself as insignificant as possible so she wouldn't end up sitting next to Madge and old Alice Knowles.

'I asked Simon if I could sit next to him,' Madge was shrilling into Alice's flaccid face. 'I mean, I asked him if he was bringing anyone, and he said no, and he sort of looked at me – you know – ' Madge's hopeless, heroic pursuit of Cosmo's understudy Simon Gartner was the last resort of the company when other sources of gossip ran dry. It was an epic as endless as the voyages of Sinbad, since Madge never came near to catching her prey.

'Shall we sit down, dear?' asked Alice, whose ankles gave her trouble. 'I can't really hear you.'

Madge turned up the volume until she could be heard above everyone else, like the garbled foreign voices that intrude on a badly-tuned radio. 'I've got to spend a few days with my parents – poor old things – and then I'm off to Lancaster, to see Beryl playing a fairy godmother. Oh, you know who Beryl is, Alice. I told you. Yes, I did. She's the one who fell down those steps. Perfectly all right now, of course, or how could she appear in a puff of green smoke, singing "You'll never walk alone" like she's supposed to? Mind you, they had to lengthen her frock to hide the knee-bandage.'

Horatia squeezed herself in beside Kitty and began to scoop raw vegetables from a saucer of crudités.

'Hello,' Kitty said, brightening. 'Where's Tommy?'

Horatia rudely ignored her, reaching out to touch the arm of someone behind her. 'Francesco – this is kind of you – don't let us wreck the place, now will you?'

Francesco, a stocky Italian businessman with flashing gold cufflinks was winding his way through the crush, tenderly placing his hands on people's shoulders, to move them aside.

'Forget it, Horatia, I don't mind doing my friends a favour.'

'Six quid a head,' said Horatia. 'They are a stingy lot of bastards.'

'That's only for the food, and a dozen bottles of wine.' Francesco pointed out. 'By half past two, they'll have drunk every drop in the cellar. If I didn't know about company parties, I couldn't afford to put my kids through school.'

Kitty smiled timidly, feeling this cast rather a wintry shadow across Francesco's kindness.

'How are the children?' Horatia asked politely.

'Wonderful – wonderful – taking them all skiing in the Dolomites for New Year – my eldest starts at Downside next September – '

'Francesco!' roared Sir Freddie. 'Don't ignore me, man! Come and meet my fifth!'

'Coming, Freddie.'

'What about you, Alice?' began Madge. 'Are you and Colin going anywhere nice for Christmas?'

'Well,' said Alice flatly, 'it all depends whether they let him out of the clinic.'

Her spent, placid voice fell into a conversational lull, and caused a second or two of foot-shuffling. It was difficult to know how to react when Alice refused to leave her sordid troubles at the door. She met their embarrassed gazes, drab and defiant. Paul released Tommy Inchbald, whom he was fondling, and embraced her shapeless body, while Madge hastened to refill her glass. She accepted these attentions with grey indifference.

'How can you bear him pawing you about?' demanded Horatia, drawing Tommy towards her.

'I can look after myself,' he said loudly. 'What if he does fancy me? He's not going to do anything.'

'He doesn't fancy you, you idiot – can't you see him goggling at Cosmo?'

'Fuckin'ell Horatia, you get right up my nose sometimes, you do, gel.'

Flames leapt up in front of Kitty as a waiter poured alcohol on crêpes suzettes, and Cosmo's frowning face appeared to her, through bars of fire. He was talking to the assistant director, Paul's nail-bitten Grand Vizier, who was known among the actors, for some forgotten reason, as 'Patsy'. As Kitty approached them, she was aware of all her deficiencies: the coy girlishness of her velvet dress, the antiseptic neatness of her unpainted face, the fact that she smelt wholesomely of cold cream instead of alluringly of scent. Only the thought of weeks without seeing him gave her the courage to accost him. Cosmo had not spoken a word to her since he had driven her home. If they met in the theatre corridors, he looked at the walls, the names on the dressing room doors, anything but her. Kitty had thrashed her sturdy optimism until it came up with the theory that perhaps Cosmo was shy, because he was interested in her. However, this did not seem very likely now, when he skimmed his darkling eye across her as if she had been a shadow. He leaned against the trellised partition, spiking a couple of grey hairs on a plastic vine leaf.

'So it's definitely not King John?' he asked doggedly.

'I haven't the faintest idea,' said Patsy. 'There's no point asking me about the casting when we don't even know what the play is.'

'But I heard – '

'I don't think it'll be a Shakespeare.' He smiled nervously at Kitty, 'Paul's awfully bored with the English Renaissance.'

'Now look, Jim, I understood there would be a notice about the next production on the board by this afternoon – '

'Do let me refill your glass, Kitty,' said Patsy eagerly. 'Cosmo, what about you?'

'No thanks. Look, Jim – '

Patsy snatched Kitty's glass and hared away towards Paul.

Cosmo sighed down at his shoes, and Kitty waited for him to look at her, suddenly confident and contented because she was with him. He cleared his throat, and his neck, above the collar of his jersey, turned the colour of salmon.

'Kitty – I'm really sorry about – that night. I was disgustingly drunk. I wasn't fit to drive.'

'You don't have to apologise,' said Kitty, adding sadly: 'I thought you were lovely.'

'Did you? God almighty, funny taste you've got, if you think it's lovely driving with a maniac.'

'But I like you when you're a maniac.'

He shrugged, and Kitty was chilled with disappointment, until he looked up and she saw how sad his eyes were. Cosmo's eyes were always full of veiled, mysterious sadness to Kitty, no matter how cross or bloodshot they appeared to anyone else.

'Your singing was hilarious,' she said.

'Oh Christ, my singing!' Cosmo exclaimed harshly. 'What did your mother say about me ploughing up her drive?'

'Nothing. I told her you were like St Patrick.'

'Eh?' He drew back suspiciously, but Kitty recognised the early rustlings of his sense of humour, and persevered.

'I said you were a gentleman, and came of decent people.'

'Oh, I see.' He warmed her with a rare, brief smile.

People were beginning to scramble for places at the table. Cosmo took formal responsibility for Kitty, tucking a chair under her and shaking out her napkin with rather cumbersome politeness. Madge had managed, after all, to cram herself in next to Simon Gartner, and she squawked out her triumph quite openly. Vinny, very loud and red, was throwing pieces of breadstick at Bill Duckworth, while Hester, arranging her hair beside him, laughed with her mouth full of tortoiseshell comb. Paul and Horatia were on either side of Tommy, shrieking at each other across his blond scrubbing-brush of a head, and bewildering him with their patronage.

'We need some more white up our end!' shouted Vinny.

'You've had the twelve bottles you ordered,' said Francesco, grinning at Horatia, to show that he was teasing.

A great gibber of outrage rose from the table, topped by Vinny: 'Sod the twelve bottles – bring us some more!'

Laughter, and somebody trying to initiate a round of applause. Francesco nodded to his major-domo, who was already waiting behind the partition with a corkscrew, and orders were given.

'A cinzano and lemonade – '

'What's in the seafood spaghetti?'

'Seafood, you plonker.'

'I know, but what kind – '

'Is there anything for vegetarians?'

'Make that five lasagnes – sorry, six – '

The frenzied babble died down, leaving only Sir Freddie's loud voice hanging on the air, saying deliberately: 'And if I eat mussels, darling, I get the runs for a fortnight.' He nudged Patsy beside him. 'Have to keep my bicycle clips on, ha ha ha!'

Patsy laughed with a brave face. He was wedged in rather tightly between Sir Freddie and Alice, who was a silent woman when at the trough.

Madge was just getting her camera out of her handbag when Simon said artlessly, 'Oh, are we starting?' and climbed out of his chair. 'Do excuse me, Madge.' He had been in base collusion with Vinny, who was saving him the seat next to Hester. Madge's face dropped, and there were female murmurs of reproach.

'You'll spend Christmas at home with your parents, I suppose?'

Kitty was gratified at the way Cosmo bent his head to listen to her. 'Oh yes, we'll all be gorging ourselves with mince pies and mulled wine. They really do Christmas terribly well.'

She tried to sound urbane, to cover a sudden surge of childish happiness. Sitting under the buttress of Cosmo's shoulder, she seemed to realise the very essence of Christmas – carols from King's College on the radio while the icing was slapped round the flanks of the cake; the elves and snowbabies who frolicked on the cake's surface, their feet blotched and mouldy with last year's marzipan; the frosted quiet outside; the coals hissing in the grate; the sense of being under siege, with pies and hams enough to last until spring.

'Do you go to Midnight Mass?'

Kitty thought she detected a note of wistfulness in the question. Cosmo's lost faith puzzled her, since she belonged to a world where people who ceased to believe simply phased out going to matins and carried on as normal. She could not help wondering why, if Cosmo's apostasy had been so distressing to him, he had not been able to persuade himself to go through the motions until belief came filtering back.

'Yes,' she said gently. 'I couldn't miss that.' She saw the pew in her mind's eye, and herself, standing between her brothers, warming her blue fingers in the crooks of their elbows, and smelling the yeasty alcohol on their breath. She wished she could convey to Cosmo the peculiar quality of that night, with the choir and servers shivering in their robes, the holly and mistletoe above the radiators crackling in the patches of heat, the way the dim electric light fell upon the yellow sandstone walls, the candles flickering in the chancel, the smell of incense and waxen winter flowers, the procession down to the crib, with the Vicar holding a plaster image of the infant Jesus in a lace handkerchief, and the poignant flavour of singing 'Yea Lord, we greet thee, born this happy morning'. She doubted Cosmo would understand her, for she imagined that the Roman Catholic church was far less comfortable: a heavy, gloomy affair, all musty dark wood, repentance in sackcloth and furtive murmurs in the confessional.

'Will you be staying in Islington?'

'I wish to God I was.' Cosmo scored the tablecloth with his knife, choking on his deep depression. He had placed himself beside Kitty because he imagined she would have the good sense not to flirt with him, and because the territory of her prettiness was so very clean and safe. Hopefully, by clinging to her, he would be able to endure this horrible party. The next day, he was taking the plane to Ireland. In the first terror of his loneliness without Faith, he had agreed to spend the holidays in Dublin with his mother, and he knew now that he had made a ghastly mistake. Pilot was to stay with his friend Bill Duckworth, where he would be made much of, but Cosmo hated leaving him behind.

'Cheer up, Cos!' yelled Vinny, throwing a pellet of bread at him.

Icily, Cosmo fished it out of his wine glass. Vinny's high spirits had been grating on him all day, making him feel full of absurd dignity, like an unpopular schoolteacher.

'Give him some more wine,' Horatia called down the table. 'Get him sloshed.'

'Give him a sausage,' said Paul. Nobody had yet dared to tease Cosmo about this episode, so the shrieks of laughter were out of all proportion. Cosmo managed to smile, but he was furious, and his limbs stiffened into a rigor mortis of shame.

'Don't be so horrid, Paulie!' said Horatia. 'I'm trying to forget about it.' She spoke as if they had all been laughing at her.

Paul meanly ignored this. 'You don't mind, do you, darling boy?'

Cosmo refused to look at him. He loathed being called 'darling boy', feeling that it was ridiculous for a man of his age.

'What's fagioli?' asked Tommy, poring over the menu.

'Shall I tell him, Paul?' Horatia neatly raised another laugh, to obscure the sausage, and Cosmo's agonised muscles relaxed.

Paul's arm crept round Tommy's shoulders. 'White beans, darling boy. Italians are mad about them.'

Tommy looked suspicious. 'I dunno – '

'You're in an Italian restaurant,' Horatia said severely. 'Do try to subdue your hankering for steak and chips.'

'Don't you patronise him.' Paul gave Tommy's thick neck a squeeze. 'That's tumbril talk, isn't it Tommy?'

'Am I in time to order?' Malcolm Snelling, the DSM, came to the table with his coat still chilled from the night air, and settled himself in the vacant seat next to Madge. She brightened as attention focused on her corner, and picked up her camera again with renewed heart.

'Smile, Paul!'

Paul smiled, heaving Tommy into the picture with him. More shouts went up as the waiters arrived, balancing plates up their sleeves like jugglers.

'Jim, did you order tagliatelle? Then whose it is? Listen! Whose is the other tagliatelle verde?'

'Is it vegetarian?'

'Yes, sir.'

'Well, it's certainly not mine.'

'Pass the sauce.'

'Some one pass Alice the sauce.'

Forks scraped across china, spoons dug into the flesh of avocados, mouths sucked up soup. It became hot, and candle-flames illuminated the sheen on scarlet foreheads. Several of the men pulled jerseys over their heads, and Madge, who was tipsy, cried: 'Get 'em off!'

Francesco walked round the table, keeping an eye on the amount of wine being consumed. He decided it would not be long before someone thought of champagne – having wide experience of company parties, he already had the £13.90 bottles on ice in the cellar. Sir Freddie, determined to estab-lish himself as a popular figure, boomed: 'Give the boys a drink on me!'

Francesco made a graceful speech of acceptance, and said something to the waiters in Italian. Then he turned back to the table. 'I'd like you all to have a glass of champagne, with my compliments – ' He flapped his hands to beat down the chorus of thanks, certain that they would be greedy enough after the first taste to order two more cases. 'Merry Christmas.'

When the second-course plates were removed, everyone had a damp, crumpled look. Collars were opened and belts undone. Belches were stifled, teeth picked, and cramped legs fought to stretch out under the table. The cloth was a derelict landscape of empty bottles, dim glasses, scrofulous crumbs and blots of tomato sauce. Cigars were brought round in a polished wooden box, and Sir Freddie gravely sniffed them and listened to them, before selecting one and veiling himself in blue smoke. Cigarettes were lit, and dozens of earnest con-versations tussled for airspace. Francesco went the rounds again, snapping his gold lighter and watching the bottles being banged down in pairs. Sir Freddie's wife, still gentle, but flushed and smiling, was leaning towards Kitty, telling her all the ways she had tried to give up smoking.

'I threw packets and packets away, but the least crisis had me burrowing through the dustbins like mad. I even went to a self-help group at the town hall.'

'I'm so glad I never started. I've never even been tempted.'

'Oh, wait till you're married – '

Sir Freddie broke into a terrifying laugh, displaying teeth liberally blobbed with spinach. 'What's this, what's this? What are you telling the poor girl?'

Horatia, with one hand on Tommy's knee, was talking across several heads to Patsy. The wires crossed and tangled.

HORATIA: Why? why should I like Donatello more than Bernini? Who says so?

PATSY: Because Donatello's use of imagery –

SIR FREDDIE: – just because I wouldn't go to her mother's for Christmas. Honestly, darling, a mother-in-law, at my age.

HORATIA: And he never did anything to match Brunelleschi's Calvary –

PAUL: Why won't anyone talk to me?

PATSY: The intense purity of line in his Magdalen, for example –

ALICE: Pass the sugar.

PAUL: ... Left and abandoned of my velvet friends ...

PATSY: – but everything in the Museo del Duomo was terribly badly hung.

ALICE: Pass the sugar.

HORATIA: Ye gods, Alice, how much sugar does it take to satisfy you?

ALICE: They never give you enough.

PAUL: Oh Alice, how like life. There's never enough sugar on that, either.

VINNY: Who's badly hung?

PAUL: Horatia, I insist on joining in. I want to disagree with you.

HORATIA: When do you ever do anything else, you nasty little man?

VINNY: Look, what's going on over there?

'Sorry,' Patsy said, with an educated smile. 'It's awfully difficult to talk about Florence without getting into Art.'

'Well, why the fuck do you have to talk about Florence?'

Hester smiled at Vinny uncertainly. She was having a difficult time next to Simon Gartner, who was usually the least difficult of men. He had not spoken much since his escape from Madge, but he had, without attracting attention, managed to drink a great deal. Unnoticed, the bottles had meandered to his part of the table and lingered there. Gradually, he became loquacious and, as the alcohol overcame his better self, he became convinced that of all the actors – or indeed, men – in London, he was the most ill-used. It had started mildly enough, with a few muttered sarcasms. Hester had nothing to do at first except assume a sympathetic expression and occasionally nod, but she was getting worried as Simon showed signs of working himself up into a crescendo. Furtively, she glanced round to see if help was at hand, but not a single face was turned towards her. Simon was now enlarging upon the theme of Madge Worsnip.

'If I go for a leak, she follows me to the door,' he was saying indignantly, 'and she's waiting for me when I come out. Wherever I turn, there she is, pressing that great pair of tits against me, with a predatory leer on her face like a hyena.'

'We all think you're so patient with her, poor soul,' Hester said soothingly.

'I'll tell you what – she's cracked. She ought to see someone. It's not natural for an old bag like that to persecute someone like me – I'm ten years younger than her, for fuck's sake, and does she know what she looks like? I mean, all right, I'm only an understudy, but I've still got my pride.'

'She'll hear you!' Hester was shocked by the phrase 'old bag'. She was fond of Madge, and it was company policy to protect her.

'Let her hear.' Simon smacked his hand down adamantly. 'It's about time she did. I've had enough.' Belligerently, he lolled back in his chair and took a mouthful of brandy.

Hester sought Kitty's eye for help, but Kitty was leaning on Cosmo's arm, whispering urgently into his ear. She turned back to Simon, rather desperately bright, wondering what to say. Living with Vinny, her tolerance for the problems of other people had widened, and she found herself sorry for Madge. She knew what it was to have one's self-esteem hanging by the thread of someone else's mercy.

Simon had now become eloquent. 'She's always lecturing me about her diets, as if I cared, and she ruins everybody else's appetite at supper by eating slimming biscuits out of a box, and she's still fat. And why is her hair always untidy at the back? Why can't she brush all of it? As for her clothes, talk about mutton dressed as lamb – '

Hester was helpless here, for these details, brutally as they were pointed out, were not untrue. She was slightly impressed that Simon had noticed them, as she did not credit men with such powers of observation.

'Well, perhaps if you dropped her a few gentle hints – '

'Do you think I haven't tried?' Simon's voice rose an anguished decibel or two. 'I've been dropping hints like fucking great anvils! She's too stupid to take them. You know what, Hester – '

'What?' asked Hester limply.

'My biggest problem is that I can't speak my mind. This is a symptom. If you don't tell the truth, you get dumped on. Honesty,' he said in a lugubrious voice. 'Let's both make honesty our New Year's resolution.'

'All right.'

'Honesty in everything. Do you promise?'

Hester was amused. 'I promise. If you see me slipping, you can tell me.'

'Don't lie to people about your feelings, Hester, because you think you've got to be nice.'

'Oh Simon, you are funny – '

'Right. I'm starting now. Cosmo Brady's acting – '

'You mustn't!' Hester began in alarm.

'Just because I'm his understudy, everyone assumes he must be better than me – I let them assume it. Listen, love, if I could

69

get one chance to play that part, I – if he'd just unclench his buttocks, it'd be a start. It's meant to be a comedy, but every time he opens his mouth the punters cough like a TB sanatorium. You don't think I'm being vain, do you?'

'No.' Hester dropped her voice to a whisper, hoping he would follow her example. She had never seen Cosmo in a real rage. Like most large men, he was mild-mannered, but his great fists, lying on the cloth like two canvased Virginia hams, made her nervous.

'I mean, we all know why Paul hired him. Fancies him rotten.'

She had begun to shake with laughter. 'Shut up, can't you?'

' – thinks it doesn't matter that he can't act his way out of a paper bag.'

'He'll hear you!'

'Just name me one person – one – who thinks he's any good – '

'Vinny!' Hester jogged his elbow.

'What is it, sweetheart?'

She hid her hysterical face in her napkin, hardly able to get the words out. 'Make him stop!'

'What's he doing?'

'He's insulting Cosmo.'

'Can anyone play?'

'Oh, no!' Hester almost screamed.

'He can't hear,' Vinny said reasonably. 'He's pissed out of his mind.'

Distorted images and scraps of noises loomed at Cosmo through the murky fog of his intoxication. He was struggling to express himself to Kitty. 'You can't explain to a dog that you're only going away for a few days. He'll think I've betrayed him.'

'But Cosmo, dogs live from day to day, and they don't feel things like humans. He'll miss you, of course, but – '

'Don't you tell me he hasn't got feelings!' interrupted Cosmo sternly. 'That dog worships me. What's more, that dog is a Christian.' His Irish accent thickened. 'Some people say dogs don't have souls, but that's a lot of crap. Pilot is fitter for

70

heaven now than any human being I can think of. Even that one – ' he indicated Hester across the table, 'even that Divinity. There's a little angel inside my dog Pilot's skin. If anything happens to him while I'm gone, I'll never forgive myself. A dog's love is a tragedy, you see, Kitty. An absolute tragedy.' He nearly wept as he said this. 'I'm not nearly good enough for love like that.'

'You are,' Kitty murmured. 'I love you. I love you ten times more than that.' She knew he was not listening.

'An angel,' said Cosmo. He lifted his heavy head to stare at Hester, and the liquor inside him conjured up a chiaroscuro round her silken head, like a halo. Her beauty seemed to remind him of some scrap of poetry in his soul, which he must give voice to or perish. It burst from his lips, surprisingly, in a bubble of song. Straightening his sagging back, he began to sing:

> 'My gentle harp, once more I waken
> The sweetness of thy slumb'ring strain,
> In tears our last farewell was taken,
> And now, in tears, we meet again – '

Cosmo had a singularly attractive singing voice – light, sweet and full of melancholy. Strain after strain of 'The Londonderry Air' issued from him with soaring ease and, drunk as he was, he forgot none of the words. They were stored in some inviolable cell of his brain, which no amount of debauchery could damage. One by one, the revellers round the table fell silent, listening to this unaccompanied partita in disbelief. It appeared that though Cosmo lacked any sort of social grace, there was one hidden recess in his personality which had the power to charm. Kitty shaded her eyes with her hand, and two sizzling tears dropped into her palm. By the time he had got to

> 'Alas, the lark's gay morning measure
> As ill would suit the swan's decline,'

the party had shifted into the past tense. The waiters came out from behind the partition in overcoats, swinging their car-keys and yawning.

71

'For how shall I, who love, who bless thee,
Invoke thy songs for freedom's strains,
When e'en the wreaths in which I dress thee
Are sadly mixed, half flowers, half chains – '

He was deathly tired, and all power seemed to have left his limbs. Slowly, he collapsed like a deflating balloon, with his head buried in his arms. The last thing he registered before his memory-bank shut down for the night was Hester, leaning across the table, still cloaked in radiance. Then his wits descended into a black chamber of echoes.

'I don't know what's happening to him,' said Horatia. 'He never used to get so pie-eyed before that frightful woman left him.'

'What a gift!' Sir Freddie was saying, to anyone who would listen. 'Never underestimate a gift like that. Why doesn't he use it? He ought to make a good few bob out of a voice like that.'

Paul blurted out tearfully and incoherently: 'That proves my point – that's just what I've been saying – you actors can never call yourselves real artists, because your best work involves the loss of innocence, the blunting of perceptions – you think it's so bloody clever and professional to look at personal beauty in terms of buying and selling – the moment you see one part of a soul that's uncorrupted, you can't wait to get your filthy hands on it and take it to market.'

Everyone who was sober exchanged significant glances. Sir Freddie, apparently far gone in this kind of corruption, was cheerfully pulling on his coat, deaf as usual to anything abstract. Malcolm Snelling put on his glasses and did long division on the bill. It was settled with remarkably little squabbling.

'Come on, Paulie,' Horatia said, 'I'll drive you.'

'Somebody ought to go with Cosmo,' he began wistfully.

She laughed. 'Not you, darling. He'd think you'd been tampering.'

'Give me his doorkey. I'll look after him,' said Francesco. 'Islington, isn't it? It's right on my way.'

'You're very kind,' Kitty said. 'You really are. Could you set

72

his alarm clock? He has to be at Gatwick by half past ten tomorrow morning.'

Horatia was still laughing. 'I can just see his face if he woke up and found you there.'

Hester and Vinny had to walk back to Hester's car, which was parked outside the theatre. It was three in the morning, wickedly cold and profoundly dark. They passed the battered hulk of Waterloo station, their feet cracking the frozen puddles on the pavement.

Hester's voice pierced the unnatural silence. 'I suppose you really have to go?'

'I promised.'

'But why tomorrow?'

'I can't let her down now. I do little enough for her.'

'Can't I come with you?' she begged.

'I've told you, love. You'd be bored out of your mind, and my mother would look daggers at you and refuse to speak to you directly. It'd be "Does she like mince pies" and "Does she know we don't keep late hours" – I swore last time I'd never do it again.'

'Which woman did you take?'

Vinny was inwardly calm from being well-fed and slightly drunk. He did not mind being interrogated. 'Can't for the life of me remember. Could have been Alison. Or was it Sarah? I'll have to ask Mum. I dare say it's pretty well engraved on her heart.'

There was a light under one of the arches of the railway bridge. A great fire was blazing in a choking vapour of smoke, spitting out sparks like bullets which spiralled upwards and perished against the brown London sky. Silhouetted against the flames were the forlorn, shuffling figures of the tramps who were building the fire, breaking up packing-cases and rotten planks. Others were huddled against the icicled wall, drinking from bottles wrapped in paper bags. They turned opaque and tremulous eyes upon Hester and Vinny as the two of them paused to warm themselves. Vinny drew Hester close to him, touched to see how chilled and weary she looked.

'What's the matter, my darling?'

73

'I'm afraid if you go away you won't come back,' she said flatly.

'Oh, that's it, is it?' He gave her shoulders an affectionate shake. 'Now, will you stop all this? Of course I'm coming back. Aren't you my girl? I don't know why you put yourself through all this agonising.'

One of the tramps suddenly spoke, in a soggy Glaswegian mumble, and they stared at him with pained, apologetic faces. His hand, creased with grime and shaking uncontrollably, was reaching out to touch the hem of Hester's coat. Vinny pulled her away, and gave the man a pound. He saw Hester as she must appear to him, so beautiful and graceful that he had to touch her before he could believe his eyes. He had a strange pang of remorse, which was almost like foreboding.

What a shit I am, he thought.

Seven

Vinny's sister was an effigy of himself, inflated around the midriff and dressed in a skirt and glasses. Her long hands, his own with rings on, greedily cut squares of turkey and bathed them in gravy. The high colour of her youth had flared up into two purple wedges on either side of her nose. Her hair, once as butter-yellow as Vinny's, had resolved itself into a reddish Brillo pad, streaked with grey. She reminded him that though his beauty was only just past the high noon of its splendour, it was not indestructible. He felt like Ebenezer Scrooge, with the Ghost of Christmas Yet To Come: 'Why show me this if I am past all hope? Oh, tell me I may sponge away the writing on this stone!'

He smiled and pulled crackers with his nieces, but this was the point where the energy he had been suppressing broke its banks and whirled across his vision. Sitting at Christmas dinner in the frigid lounge of his mother's bungalow in Dorchester, he was cruelly aware of the dullness and vulgarity of his family. They were as painful to his senses as pulsating, bloody lumps of raw meat. Only by the grace of God had he been spared their depressing, good-natured coarseness. They expressed their emotions in a sort of warm-hearted, gutter-press morse code, and lord how they loved him.

The net was nearly over his head now but years of practice had made him adept at wriggling away. He escaped on the 27th, and his mother, who had been one bland curve of pride during his visit, sagged back into her usual forlorn parameters.

'Must you go so soon?'

'Got to, Mum. We're doing a show tomorrow.'

This was a lie, but it never occurred to Mrs Bliss to check up on him in the entertainments page of the *Daily Telegraph*. Like other women in Vinny's life, she mistook the radiance of his conviction for truth. Once free, he sped back to London, with his familiar feeling of wanting to throw himself on the fire like a stick of dynamite, and renew himself in the explosion. Afterwards, he sometimes regretted these orgies of destruction, but he had learned that trying to avert them was a waste of time. One just had to brazen it out when other people's feelings were hurt. Sooner or later, the fuss always died down. It was possible to get away with almost anything.

His family had heavily overworked the moral lobe of his brain, so he shut it down, letting his instincts lead him, and at ten in the evening he parked Hester's car outside Rosamund Jaeger's house in Gospel Oak. The long drive from Dorset had cramped his legs, and he tottered on the pavement for a moment, savouring the damp London air, which smelt of diesel and front gardens. The handsome red brick houses all had the wilted, tawdry appearance that sets in at the fag-end of the year, when festivities are on the wane, and everyone is thoroughly bored with the cosy trappings of winter. Rosamund's house alone looked tidy and rational. Grey blinds, suffused with lamplight, were drawn across the bay window. Her one concession to the season was a wreath of evergreen, tied to the doorknocker with a red ribbon. Dancing up the path, Vinny barked his shin severely against a large tricycle chained to the gatepost. He swore in violent whispers, sending moist clouds of his breath towards the sky: 'Oh fuck, she's got someone with her – what sort of arsehole rides a tricycle?'

Massaging the bruise, he thrust his nose through the letter box, smelt the food, and heard a rumbling male voice. Cello music was playing somewhere, giving the inaudible conversation a Socratic weight it probably did not deserve. Cockily, he rang the bell in rhythm – pom tiddly om-pom, pom pom!

– and a moment later he saw Rosamund through the frosted glass panels, walking unhurriedly, dressed in white.

'My God, it's Vinny!'

Seeing that she smiled, and stepped aside for him to enter, Vinny said: 'I haven't come at a bad time, have I? I'll go if you want.'

'No, don't you dare go. Come in at once. What are you doing here? I thought you were in the country.'

'I was, but my family started getting up my nose, and I couldn't stand it any longer. You've no idea, Rosie – all microwaved mince pies and Hergé's 'Adventures of Tin-Tin'. I've watched enough telly to last me for years. And I couldn't even masturbate, because Mum kept bursting into my room with mugs of Ovaltine.'

Rosamund laughed and closed the door behind him. She seemed in no hurry to get back to her guest. 'Poor you. Did you have a go at "Ulysses"?'

'I tried.' Vinny handed her his scarf. 'I'm afraid I was immeasurably bored. Spent the whole time riffling through for the dirty bits.'

'You didn't try at all, Bliss, you're such a lazy shite,' said Rosamund. 'Give me a kiss, then.'

He kissed her, pulling her towards him so that he could feel her breasts squashing against his ribcage. They were brown and freckled, like free range eggs. When he drew away, a musky scent wafted up from inside her clothes.

'God, you look lovely.' He tried her with one of his thrilling, poignant looks, something he had never done in all the fifteen years he had known her.

'Oh, go on,' she said. There was no answering pathos in the ruthless shallows of her eyes. She was not the poignant type.

'That white thing makes you look sort of innocent, and rather wistful – '

'Save all that garbage for Hester. Does she know you're back, by the way?'

'No,' he said, 'why should she?' He was noticing her feet, bare in gold sandals. Each of her curly toes was tipped with coral, and the whole effect was exotic and inviting. Dim possibilities began to drift just beyond the range of his conscious mind, and the area of his groin which he referred to as his heart became deliciously charged.

'Are you hungry?' she asked.

'Starving.'

'We've finished, but I can put the casserole back in the oven.'

He followed her, looking round with alert satisfaction. Rosamund lived among white walls, sanded floorboards and elegant, hard-hearted abstract paintings, with ceiling spotlights trained upon their vicious colours. The whole of her ground floor had been knocked into one huge room, and there was a spiral staircase, hung with ferns in baskets, upon which she had recently been photographed for a women's magazine: 'Actress Rosamund Jaeger, in the vanguard of the anti-chintz brigade, lets simple textures speak for themselves in her North London home.'

'Derek, you know Vinny Bliss, don't you?' She led him through the folding doors to her kitchen. 'You must have seen each other at the theatre.'

At the black oval table, looking disgruntled and suspicious, sat Derek Hooey, the radical playwright.

'Hi,' said Vinny, shaking his clammy paw. Hooey's bicycle clips lay on the table beside his plate, like the picked bones of some new kind of meat. He was a seedy man, with a pubic beard and a head like a musty, ill-formed potato.

'I'm doing Derek's new play at the Studio,' Rosamund explained, with forced brightness which told Vinny immediately what sort of evening she had been having.

Hooey said: 'You're in Paul Fletcher's company, aren't you?' He had a slushy, accusing voice, which put Vinny in mind of slops in a bucket.

'Yes, that's right.' He sat down, and Rosamund handed him a glass of red wine. 'Here's to you, lovey,' he said.

'Here's to you, ducks,' replied Rosamund. 'Vinny and I were in the ADC together at Cambridge. We go back further than I care to remember.'

'Oh,' said Hooey.

She bent to shut the oven door, and Vinny eyed the movement of her buttocks. They quivered slightly, but he did not care for hard-fleshed women.

'I saw you in "The Miser",' Hooey said.

'Oh? You should have stayed for a drink afterwards. It might have broken the monotony.'

'I'm no good at greenroom chit-chat. I can't say Darling you were marvellous, when I don't mean it.'

'Hmmm,' said Vinny pensively. An actor in one of his plays had once punched Hooey on the ear, and it was possible to see why. 'You don't necessarily have to say we're marvellous.'

'We can take criticism sometimes, you know,' said Rosamund, sitting down beside Vinny. Hooey looked from one to the other with sulky hostility.

'No subtext,' he said. 'Played too much like a comedy.'

'It is a comedy,' Rosamund observed.

'It's a satire.' He pronounced it 'shatire'. 'Fletcher has taken the balls right out of it. What that play needs is a structuralist interpretation – I don't give a fart what Molière was thinking at the time. It could have so much relevance now. The corruption of wealth is always relevant.'

Vinny made a thoughtful, non-committal face. He did not want to argue. It was evident that before he came Derek Hooey had been in high hopes of throwing a leg over his leading lady. Well, I'm sorry for you mate, Vinny said to himself, so you needn't look at me like that. Rosamund, he knew, would sooner have slept with a warthog. But playwrights, playwrights – you fed them on toadyish admiration during rehearsals, and they became impossibly vain.

'Maybe some of Paul's ideas did fall a little flat,' he said.

'We've only just begun to get to grips with Derek's piece,' said Rosamund. 'It's unbelievably tricky.' She leaned against his arm, and Vinny inhaled the almond-sweet breath of her tanned skin.

'Having fun, are you?' he asked.

'Oh no. Nobody has fun working with Derek.'

Clearly, Hooey could no longer bear the languid, airy presence of Vinny without fighting back. 'You're not paid to have fun,' he said fretfully. 'You're paid to bleeding well work. If you were slaving away in a biscuit factory, you wouldn't go round saying Doing the Garibaldis now, darling? Having fun?' He assumed a foolish, mincing voice in the last phrase, and Vinny thoroughly understood the dislike of him which ran through the whole theatre like a bad drain. Scared of actors, he decided. The resentment caused by actors had often puzzled him, for where could one find a more harmless collection of people? Telling outsiders what one did invariably became a kind of confession, which spiked the atmosphere with hostility. Complete strangers smilingly accused one of shallowness and irresponsibility. Almost in the same breath, they often revealed that they had played Pooh-Bah at their local Am-Dram, to hysterical acclaim. There was, they implied, nothing to it. Only their innate humility prevented them from storming the boards professionally themselves. An uncle of Vinny's had been unable to look at him for years without muttering darkly about National Service, and the 'nonsense' such ritual humiliation would knock out of his sleek head. It was odd, Vinny thought, that a nation so terrified of people who 'get above themselves' should produce actors of such distinction.

'I wanted amateurs for "Don't Know Nuffin",' Hooey stated. 'Or rather, what you lot call amateurs. I call them real people, who know what I'm on about. I try to convey the problems of a redundant working class, and some public school fairy ponces in and throws the whole lot out of the window.'

Vinny was bored. This unoriginal spurt of aggression reminded him of fights he had had in pubs, provoked by people who assumed you were a woofter because you worked in tights. Really, it was too pathetic. The curiously light weight of Rosamund's bones against his shoulder began to stir his blood. There was a pleasing tightness round his testicles, and he was getting an erection. He lolled back in his chair so that Rosamund could see it.

'"Don't Know Nuffin" is about class,' Hooey continued. 'Class and education – like all my plays. This government has a deliberate policy to keep the lower classes ignorant. Education equals discontent, equals the demand for change, equals the collapse of capitalism.'

'Oh, I agree,' said Vinny, and he mostly did, but his penis had taken control of his consciousnes, and that organ was capable of only limited political thought.

'God yes,' Rosamund said, brushing Vinny's thigh with the ends of her fingers, and sending electrical sparks up his spine.

'Basically, it's about a university lecturer married to a Labour politician, who gets kidnapped by a group of unemployed kids in Peckham.' Hooey was scarcely able to contain his fury. 'She thinks she's on their side, but she hasn't a clue.'

'That's my part,' said Rosamund.

'You actors always think of plays in terms of "My Part",' Hooey complained. 'Anyway, her husband's family owns this department store, and she helps them break in, when she's really on their side. She gets the key. The locked door is a metaphor for society, of course – she has the means to let them into society. Pretty bloody obvious, but why should I be subtle? In the last scene, she's being beaten up by the police, but she's in ecstasy.'

'Into the old S and M, is she?' asked Vinny.

Hooey snorted, and slopped more wine into his bleared glass. 'No, it's her redemption. She has to experience the pain of the oppressed.'

'It's high time that theatre put on a really strong piece of polemic,' said Rosamund, assuming her Girton voice, but still stroking Vinny's thigh. 'It'd be nothing but "Rookery Nook" and coach parties, if the governor had his way.'

'Don't make it chic!' bayed Hooey. 'None of your Designer politics!'

'I'm on your side, Derek, so stop worrying. Your point comes across like a sledgehammer. Nobody's going to get you mixed up with Alan Ayckbourn.'

Her hand crept to Vinny's flies and caressed the rod-like projection underneath. His arms fell limply to his sides, and his eyelids drooped. Hooey could not see what Rosamund was doing, but he could hardly miss Vinny's tumescent rapture. He glared at them, daring them to get rid of him.

'Look at the time!' exclaimed Rosamund. 'Oh Derek, I am sorry. You have to be up early tomorrow, and I completely forgot.'

'I'm in no hurry.'

'But you'll miss your plane.'

Hooey drew his fungous brows together. 'I'm not a heavy sleeper.'

He had lost. Rosamund was taking his leather jacket off the back of a chair, and holding it out for him.

'He's going on holiday, Vinny, to Albania.'

Hooey's departing grunts were such music to Vinny's ears that he sacrificed the pleasure of asking: Are the beaches nice? Instead, he said: 'That should be fascinating.'

There were ten more minutes of Hooey bobbing to and fro like a jack-in-the-box, while he delivered final thoughts about the Albanian system of education, but at last he was mounted on his tricycle in the street.

'Thank God you came when you did, Vinny,' Rosamund called from the front door. 'Thank God, thank God! The things an actress has to do for her art!'

Vinny had left the table and was standing on a violently coloured Provençal rug, unbuckling his belt. Rosamund pushed his fingers away and did it for him. They were both laughing. Reflected in one of the glazed exhibition posters, Vinny saw his face flaming into demonic ecstasy as she took his swollen penis into her mouth. They cast off their clothes, and after sweaty coupling in a variety of positions Vinny achieved a roaring climax, thrusting into her from behind, while she leaned across a small chest of drawers. He squeezed her breasts as his spasms died away, and then he fell out of her. A dribble of warm semen splashed on the rug. He rolled his foreskin back into place, and smelt his fingers appreciatively.

'Jesus,' murmured Rosamund. She turned to face him, with the perfect impression of a drawer-handle stamped upon her stomach, and they both laughed uncontrollably. 'Your dinner,' she said. 'It went right out of my mind. Do you still want it?'

'Yes. My vital juices need replacing.' He took a cushion off the sofa, and stretched himself on the floor. 'That was brilliant.'

'It was, wasn't it? I like men who come loudly. I always thought you would. Do you want another drink?'

'Not half.' Vinny watched, slack with contentment, while Rosamund moved about in the kitchen, wearing nothing but her gold bracelet. Doing something as ordinary as ladling out vegetable casserole, her nakedness was unexpectedly touching. He had forgotten what it was like to have brutal, unromantic sexual intercourse. Hester's love-making was pastel-shaded, and flowed to its conclusion like a tasteful fade-out in a film. It was deeply restful not to have to rack his brains for new protestations of undying love. Each one had to be more sincere than the last, and his inventiveness was running dry. Often, all he wanted to do was roll over and go to sleep. And Hester had an uncanny habit of tenderly recalling fucks far back in history, the details of which Vinny had long forgotten.

'It's somewhat crinkled and elderly,' Rosamund said, bringing in the tray, 'but still viable. Just like me, in fact.'

'Oh, bollocks. Don't put yourself down and expect me to contradict you, because I won't.'

She laughed, as if there was a joke he could not see. 'No, I know.' Stretched out on the floor beside him, supporting herself on her elbow, she gazed at him, amused and thoughtful. 'I like the way sex doesn't turn you silly.'

'Why should it?'

'Well, exactly. Why should we change to another script, just because we've seen each other's bums? We're actually fine as we are.'

'Yes,' Vinny said, turning the idea over, 'we've always got on well, haven't we? As friends, I mean.' He settled his back against the sofa, positioned the plate near his lips, and forked the stew energetically into his mouth.

'Love the table-manners,' said Rosamund

'Sorry. Sex makes me ravenous.' Drops of red juice spattered his bare chest.

'Vinny.'

'What?'

'This doesn't mean anything, got it?'

'Suits me,' said Vinny, with his mouth full.

'I'm not in love with you.'

'All right. Not compulsory.'

'Rather a relief for you, I should think.'

'You're right there, girl. I've got as much love as I can handle.'

'Good,' said Rosamund. 'I don't mind a friendly screw, but I could never bear the indignity of becoming one of your women.'

'You're too smart for that,' he said. 'But we can see each other sometimes, can't we? Just for a laugh.'

'Maybe. We'll see.'

He put down his empty plate, forced a belch, and contentedly shifted his weight to scratch his buttock. 'That was terrific.'

'You get a kick out of cheating on women, don't you?' demanded Rosamund.

'No, I just hate complications. Pass me my trousers, will you?'

She passed them. 'That's rich. You have the most complicated life in the world. Is this the first time you've cheated on Hester?'

'Oh come on, what do you think?' Vinny opened his tobacco tin, to roll a joint.

'I don't know what to think, Bliss, I'm sure. Do you love her?'

'Yes, I do. I love her a lot. And if you must know, this is the second time I've been unfaithful to her.'

'Do you tell her?'

'Of course not. She wouldn't understand.' There was a minute's silence as he finished making the joint. He lit it, dragged at it until he turned scarlet, and handed it to Rosamund. She began again.

'You should be more honest with her, you know.'

'Women expect to be lied to.'

'Rubbish,' she said briskly. 'You're going to get yourself into trouble one of these days.' She crushed out the joint on Vinny's stained plate and straddled his legs. 'You eat like a pig, too. God knows what they all see in you.' One by one she licked the gobbets of sauce off his flesh.

Presently, he said: 'I'm getting another stonker.'

'You're not.'

'I bloody am. Can we do the encore in bed? There's a shocking draught on this floor.'

Eight

'Apparently we've all survived it,' Alice Knowles said, in her slow cow's voice. 'The day itself is never as ghastly as you think it's going to be. Our son did come round for Christmas lunch after all, and no blood was shed.'

'Did Colin speak to him?' The muscles in Madge's face were fixed in a sort of rictus of sympathy, the only possible expression when listening to Alice's troubles.

'On and off. Pass the butter. That sort of thing.'

'Better than nothing,' hinted Madge.

'I suppose so.'

They were sitting in Alice's small, squalid dressing room on the top floor, eating chocolate biscuits and drinking watery tea from a thermos. Over the Tannoy, they could hear the distant, muffled chatter of the audience filtering back to their seats as the interval ended. It was the first performance of the New Year. Madge, who had suffered and pined for gossip during the break, was on a round of visits, pollinating all the dressing rooms with the latest news. Alice reached clumsily for another biscuit, scattering crumbs across her knitting.

'So what's going on, dear? You always seem to know. What about this "Otho the Great"?'

Madge brightened. 'Yes, it's definite. Paul's going to do it late nineteenth century, sort of Prussian, at a stuffy German court.'

'Why?'

'Simon says it's an excuse to get the younger men into uniform.'

'Oh,' said Alice. 'Have you any idea what it's about?'

'Not a clue. Nobody has. Sir Freddie will play Otho, of course. He's on a play-as-cast contract for the next nine months, and they've got to find stuff for him to do. None of the other parts are cast. Cosmo Brady wants to do the lead dreadfully, but I'm afraid he won't get it unless he's nicer to Paul. We all keep telling him.'

'Anything for us?'

'Not a sausage. We'll probably be ladies-in-waiting.' Madge always understudied Alice, and kept a jealous eye on her status in the company.

'Never mind,' Alice said. She was an actress of distinction, whom age and strife had withered early, but if she minded the prospect of a bad part she did not show it. She was squeezed quite dry, and had no more passion to spare for trivialities. 'Could you fancy a pork pie?'

'Oh Alice, you've only got the one.'

'Don't worry about that. Could you fancy a gherkin?'

'Lovely.'

Alice wearily drew the bottle of pickles out of her drawer and dabbled her fingers in the vinegar. She unwrapped the pork pie with hypnotic slowness, and Madge tried not to mind when she sawed it in half with a comb.

'May I use one of these tissues as a plate? This frock shows every spot.'

'Do, dear,' said Alice, whose own costume was stained and daubed with samples of the canteen menu, despite the efforts of her dresser.

Madge giggled. 'I'm supposed to be on a diet. I put on half a stone over Christmas.'

Alice froze the smile on her face with a stony, portentous gaze. 'Have you got anything to get slim for? I haven't.'

'You musn't give up', she said, 'just because of Colin. How has he been?' She could not help lowering her voice to a respectful whisper, as if she had been in church. Alice's married life was so turbulent that it fully restored her appreciation of spinsterhood.

'He lobbed the poker at me last night,' said Alice calmly.

'Did it hit you?'

'No.' Alice took a mouthful of pie. 'It broke the kitchen window.'

'Oh, how awful. Have you managed to get it mended?'

'Colin tried. But the new pane fell into the area.'

'You'll have to get someone in,' said Madge helpfully.

'I suppose so.' Alice looked grey at the mere idea. 'I should have brought some mustard,' she said. 'I meant to.' They chewed silently for a moment. Madge mentally rehearsed the tale of the poker. Kitty and Horatia, for their different reasons, were always interested in these vignettes from Alice's life.

'So that's our new play,' said Alice, ' "Otho the Great". Is it really by Keats, or did I dream it?'

'No, it's by Keats. Paul says it's beautiful.'

'Then why isn't it done more often, I'd like to know?' Alice was always slightly less bovine when talking about work. 'I hoped it would be "Woman of No Importance". There's a lovely part in that for us.'

'Well, you can't win them all. Perhaps next time.'

'I can't think that far ahead, dear.' She picked the crumbs off the table with the ends of her fingers.

'Goodness, that's the front of house bell – ' Madge stood up, brushing her skirts, 'I'd better pop downstairs for another dab of lipstick.'

'I meant to catch up on all the news,' complained Alice. 'I never hear anything. Is Cosmo back with his girlfriend yet?'

'No, I told you. She married someone else.'

'So you did. The Indian.'

'African. Alice, I must go.'

'Why was Vinny kissing that Rosamund Jaeger woman?'

Madge was electrified. It took her a couple of seconds to digest this snippet – it was such an unexpectedly prime cut. 'Kissing Rosamund? When was this?'

'Just now,' said Alice. 'I saw them at it in the corridor. Has he left Hester?'

'No, no – ' Madge was in delicious bewilderment, 'he's still crazy about her. Was it real kissing? You know – were they – '

'Tongues, you mean,' said Alice sadly. 'Oh yes, it was tongues all right. They'd both have been reported to the stage manager in my day.'

'How dreadful! Poor Hester, she must never know – I'll warn the others not to drop the smallest hint. How she worships that man. I was the first person to predict that it wouldn't last. I wish I'd been wrong. What did he do when he saw you?'

'Nothing, dear. I don't think he noticed. Wasn't that your call?'

'My – oh God, I'm late – where's my tambourine?'

Madge, who hated being late, dashed down to the stage, through the maze of stairs and corridors. She was so great with news that she did not care about the dishevelment of her wig, or the fact that her wreath of silk flowers was slipping drunkenly over one eye. All she could think of was the sensation she would create. She arrived in the slips just in time, with her bows and ribbons sticking out like porcupine quills and her massive bosom heaving breathlessly. As she fought her way up the line to her place, the other commedia people stared at her curiously, knowing something was up. Madge was usually on her mark fully five minutes before the off, fiddling with her make-up and worrying the DSM. The lights faded, the first bars of music played, and they all craned their necks forward to hear her whispering into Kitty's ear: 'Guess what – '

Vinny had not expected to fall in love with Rosamund Jaeger, but after sleeping with her once he could not get her out of his mind. He had underestimated her. She had a lovely house, too; a thousand times more comfortable than Hester's poky little flat. He would have been living there now, if the other woman in the case had been anyone except Hester. He thought of the strain he had sung once, when playing Macheath at the Connaught Theatre in Worthing: 'How happy could I be with either, were t'other dear charmer away.' Whenever he was most fascinated by Rosamund's enamelled self-possession, his drift towards her would be suddenly arrested by some deeply touching quality he noticed in Hester. In the same way, when most bound up in Hester's gentleness and effortless loveliness, he would feel a throb of attraction towards Rosamund's calculated glamour. He could not decide which he preferred, and the situation was becoming troublesome. The worst of working in a large company was that secrets were impossible. Sooner or later everyone would know what he was up to, so he did not even bother to be discreet. Alice Knowles had seen him necking with Rosamund, as he very well knew, and he was not surprised by the meaningful glances he got during the curtain call. They were all on Hester's side, naturally. He wondered how long he dared to leave it, before the poor girl heard of his betrayal.

Keeping up with two women at the same time curtailed his freedom, and taxed his imagination. He constantly had to invent fantastic lies for the one and plausible excuses for the other, and his double sex life kept him in a state of nervous exhaustion. During the first act, he had dozed off in the wings, and would have missed his entrance but for Malcolm Snelling thumping him between the shoulders with his torch. The decision had to made, and made with the minimum of fuss.

At home that night he made love to Hester, and was made miserable by her youth and serenity as she slept. Her clinging depressed him sometimes, but he did not see how he could ever bring himself to walk out on her – he was not such a shit as all that. Her beauty was the sort one never got tired of, and she adored him. Regretfully, he made up his mind never to desert her, and fell asleep with his face against her warm shoulder.

The next day, however, while having supper in the canteen, he saw Rosamund, and was annoyed to discover that one look from her was enough to set the debate in his body raging all over again. His blood began to heat as he imagined what she would do to him when they were alone, and there was Hester, right beside him, eating rhubarb tart and custard. He forced his eyes away from Rosamund, and gave his attention to the discussion at the table. Paul was casting *Otho the Great*, and there was the usual frantic speculation about who would get what. Like everyone else, Vinny had laid hands on the play and combed it for opportunities. Generally, he approved of the choice. Paul had a genius for directing romantic tragedy, and the company needed a success after the lukewarm reviews for *The Miser*. The London critics were going through an anti-intellectual phase, and they had taken great exception to the fey antics of Paul's commedia dell'arte.

'I really don't think I can bear Cosmo's agonies of suspense much longer,' Horatia was saying. 'I wish Paul would make up his mind. He enjoys keeping the poor man dangling, that's the trouble.'

'I hear you got Erminia,' Simon Gartner said to Hester. 'Nice part, love, congratulations.'

'It's what Paul calls a Frock Part,' said Hester placidly. 'He doesn't rate my acting, but I light well.'

Everyone laughed, except Vinny. He suddenly realised how inconvenient it would be if he left Hester and then had to rehearse with her for five weeks.

'Don't let him put you down,' he said. 'You're starting to believe him.'

'Oh darling, let's face it, I've read the thing twice and I can't make head or tail of it.'

'I'm coming round to the piece,' announced Horatia. She had plotted and schemed to get the part of Auranthe, until she wore down Paul's resistance. 'There are some good moments.'

Vinny said: 'Keep on at it, Hessie. It really does have its points.'

'You could always ask Rosamund Jaeger for a few tips,' suggested Horatia blandly. 'She has some marvellously intelligent ideas, doesn't she, Vinny darling?'

Vinny masked his annoyance with a smile. This sort of needling was only going to get worse until he solved his dilemma one way or the other.

Kitty poulticed the smarting silence. 'The play has the advantage of being completely obscure. Nobody will be able to say the RSC did it better.'

'Just like Paul Fletcher', said Simon, fiercely lighting a cigarette, 'to pick something nobody's ever heard of.' Simon had every reason to be bitter, because he had read for the part of Albert, 'A Knight favoured by Otho', and Paul had turned him down. He was stuck with his lowly position until his contract expired, and that one brief gleam of hope made it now all the harder to swallow. The hierarchy in that particular theatre was extraordinarily rigid, and the understudies led a dog's life. Once a peasant, always a peasant. Nobody ever rose from the ranks. Any actor who started at the bottom stayed there, and watched his aspirations becoming fainter and more absurd with each production. He could move from play to play for years, in ever-increasing obscurity, dressed from the bottom of the costume-basket, and wearing wigs with strange knobs and bumps in them because they had been made for someone else's head. Simon's ambition, instead of sustaining him, was beginning to corrode his essentially kindly nature. 'And Brady's a cert for Ludolph,' he added, 'so I can't think why we're all talking about it. It's always the bloody same. If you've got a good leg in tights and the director fancies you, you're made. If not, don't bother.'

'Well, I hope he's keeping a soft corner in his little heart for me,' said Vinny, 'because I want to do Conrad. I'll be parrot-sick if I get landed with Albert.'

'It'll be an interesting challenge for you, playing such a two-faced villain,' remarked Simon. 'However will you do it?'

Vinny made every possible allowance for the man's disappointment, but was still amazed that he dared to drop such a hint in front of Hester.

'He's bound to get it,' she said. 'We're counting on working together again.'

'Nice and cosy,' suggested Horatia. 'Just like Michael Denison and Dulcie Gray.'

There was another barbed silence. Vinny felt the reproaches, and told himself again that Rosamund must, unfortunately, be the one to go. He did not know how he was going to explain this to her, since she had already wound him in a web of unspoken obligations.

'Darling, that's you.' Hester was tugging at his sleeve. 'You're being called – I know you've got it – good luck – '

He heard the end of a metallic message over the relay: 'Vincent Bliss, Bill Duckworth and Cosmo Brady, please call four-six-eight.' Another piece of his future was about to be decided. With each new part, there was always the possibility that it would cause him to be perceived in a new way. Vinny's personal difficulties receded as he realised how intensely he wanted to play Conrad. There was no way of knowing how Paul's capricious mind would work. Like most directors, he was quite capable of exercising his power to drop a former favourite, as punishment for some obscure offence. As he went to the door of the canteen, Vinny searched his memory, and wondered uneasily whether Paul would hold his current imbroglio against him.

Bill Duckworth had beaten him to the telephone. 'Paul's office,' he said, replacing the receiver. 'The royal summons.'

In the office on the fourth floor they found Paul himself, his assistant director 'Patsy', and Cosmo. Cosmo was standing by the window, drinking coffee out of a plastic cup and gazing out at the lights dancing on the surface of the river. When Vinny and Bill came in, he turned, and they saw a wild gleam of triumph on his solemn face. His eyes were quite unfocused with happiness.

Paul lounged in his swivel chair with his hands folded across his chest. It was a small office, and Patsy was squeezed in beside the filing cabinet, clutching a pile of Keats-related literature. Paul's thesis at Oxford had been about Leigh Hunt and the *Examiner* as a Forum for the Romantic Poets, and he was in his element. The birth of his productions always had an academic flavour, and the sight of the books made the actors rack their brains for suitable remarks, as if they had been cramming for an examination. Paul and Patsy had, as usual, worked themselves into a state of romantic intoxication over the piece, and were in the honeymoon period of possibilities.

'I've just told Cosmo', said Paul, 'that he's to play Ludolph.'

'Nice one, mate,' said Vinny. He felt he ought to say

something, as Cosmo's body expressed his smug radiance so eloquently.

'Thanks.' Cosmo smiled, with such pleased naiveté that Vinny was almost charmed out of his normal indifference to the man.

'Sorry to summon you all like this,' said Paul, who was not sorry, 'but the governor wants the cast list up by tonight, so I've no time for the niceties.' He took a digestive biscuit from a plate that stood on a pile of pictures of Prussian uniforms. 'Bill, I'm offering you Gersa.'

'Wonderful,' said Bill, who had been expecting no less. 'Thanks, Paul.'

'You have the most marvellous entrance,' said Patsy, hanging over the open text. 'You're led on in chains.'

' "Plucked like a red stag from the fallow herd of prisoners".' Paul quoted, with dreamy relish. 'Possibly with a little wound on the side of the head – what do you think, Jimmy?'

'Absolutely,' said Patsy. ' "Slow, in the demure proudness of despair".'

'Short but sweet.' Bill nodded once or twice in approval. 'I can do something with that.' Bill was forty-two, but his style of acting belonged to an older generation. He was handsome though balding, spoke excellently, and could be relied upon to set his performance like granite in the early days of rehearsal, never to vary it again. Ten years before, he had been a beautiful young man, and Paul liked to use him now that his charms had faded, as if he was showering gifts upon a once-loved mistress who recalled a golden epoch.

'Now Vinny, my dear boy.' Paul swivelled round. 'I had to ponder rather hard about you. I've decided I want you to play Conrad. Do you think you can manage it?'

'Yes, of course I can,' said Vinny, relieved.

'Your recent moral development makes you entirely suitable.' Paul looked meaningly at the others. 'I think we all know why.'

Vinny did not like this line of conversation, but accepted the aggravation as the price he had to pay for the part he wanted. 'I'm getting too old for juvenile leads,' he said.

'No, no – I didn't mean that,' Paul's eyes glazed senti-mentally. 'The years haven't condemned you yet, darling boy. You must have a portrait hidden in the attic like Dorian Gray, which bears the ravages of your wickedness. You don't look a day older than twenty-five under the lights. Does he, Jim?'

'Thirty, perhaps,' said Patsy.

'The interesting point about Conrad', Paul continued, 'is that he's a thorough villain, but with devastating charm. He has people eating out of his hand and utterly believing in him, until his villainy is impossible to ignore. I think there's an interesting relationship to be highlighted between Conrad and his sister. A whiff of incest, don't you think, Jimmy?'

'Absolutely,' Patsy riffled through the pages of his anno-tated Keats. 'There has to be sexual jealousy in the way he tor-ments Auranthe about her affair with Albert.'

'So you see', said Paul maliciously, 'it seems to fit you pretty well. Not that I'm accusing you of sleeping with your sister – it's just that I've always thought your particular brand of charm rather deadly.'

There was no possible reply to this, so Vinny wisely kept his mouth shut. He had learned that there was no way people could get at you if you refused to feel guilty. He knew that Paul was enjoying his dilemma over Rosamund and Hester. Paul, he suspected, like so many other directors, did some-times arrange the casting of his plays to get the maximum amount of amusement from the actors' private lives.

'I've been looking through some heavenly pictures,' he said. 'You're going to have a waxed moustache, a monocle and an amber cigarette holder.'

'Are you serious?'

'Perfectly. I want you to suggest decadence.'

'So terribly Almanach de Gotha,' murmured Patsy. 'You have to imagine one of those petty German courts, in the twi-light before the First World War.'

'Like Saxe-Coburg or Hesse,' said Cosmo intelligently.

'Exactly. There's a book of contemporary photographs I think everyone should see. Do you all have scripts?'

Patsy took three typed copies of *Otho* from a pile on the

cabinet. 'This is the final version. We've made a few small cuts.'

'You might read Robert Gittings's marvellous biography of Keats, too,' said Paul. 'Lord, how I wept at the end. "Here lies one whose name was writ in water." He said he felt the daisies growing over him, poor boy. And the tragedy of it is that the man who wrote so poignantly about sex died a virgin.'

'He never did it with Fanny,' Patsy stated.

'Quite right too,' said Paul. 'Sex ruins everything, don't you think, Vinny?'

'Oh, for heaven's sake,' interrupted Bill, 'of course it doesn't!'

'Ah but Bill, it's different for you. You met your wife, you married her, you gave her children, and you'll stick to her till the end of your days.'

'Well, what the hell's wrong with that?'

'Nothing, nothing – it's just another kind of pathos altogether. Vinny knows what I mean. It's obsession with the forbidden that makes the true romantic. I've always maintained that the key to Keats is masturbation.'

'Byron called his poetry "brain-frigging",' supplied Patsy, who was to Paul what the dry footnotes are at the bottom of a flowery dissertation.

'But we'll go into this properly at rehearsals.' Paul looked slyly round at Cosmo, to make sure that he was blushing. 'You'd better go and get some supper, Cosmo darling. It's nearly the half.'

'Yes, I will,' said Cosmo. 'Thanks – thanks a lot, Paul.' As he left the office, he even smiled.

Paul tipped his chair back against the window sill. 'Isn't he bliss, the way he goes scarlet when you say "masturbation"? It works every time.'

When he stood with Bill on the other side of the door, Vinny said: 'Well, you and me are sorted, eh?' He thought about his monocle and his amber cigarette holder, and what he could make of them, and his euphoric feet automatically took him to Rosamund's dressing room, where he knew she would be smoking a joint before the evening performance of *The Winslow Boy*. Vinny's triumph weakened him, and it suddenly did not seem so easy, or so necessary, to give Rosamund her marching orders. Later, when he was back in his own dressing room, hastily washing the lipstick off his genitals at the sink, he decided he might be better off with Rosamund after all.

Nine

Love is, of course, the best emotional food. Ambition is to love what thin gruel is to roast beef, but Cosmo was emotionally starving and ambition was the only diet available. As soon as he heard Paul was casting *Otho the Great*, Cosmo prepared to sweep together the splinters of his shattered faith and disappointed love, and use them as bricks and mortar for building his failures into Art. With the part of Ludolph, he knew he could touch the subconscious of the audience as subtly as a hand playing a harp, bringing out their buried regrets and associations, making them hang their own phantoms round his shoulders. Ludolph turned to pure poetry the areas of himself he was sorriest for. His self-pity had all sorts of exquisite hues, and was capable of expressing itself on stage with great poignancy and depth of feeling.

His surge of happiness when he was given the role took him by surprise, and made him reel like a drunkard. He did not even mind Paul's fingers clamped across his forearm, nor was he afraid that the director's sharp tongue was about to slide from professional matters into something more intimate and disagreeable. During that evening's performance of *The Miser*, he found the courage to swagger, to push himself out beyond the embarrassed faces in the front three rows, and he got real confident laughs from the audience, instead of the usual scattered titters. Afterwards, sitting at home in Corsica Street, he nursed his euphoria, and mulled over this sudden change in his fortunes. Faith's departure had set him on a downward curve which had reached its nadir in Ireland, where he had so unwisely spent Christmas with his mother. From his new vantage point, he began to think that this demoralising experience had been necessary, if only to bring him face to face with his dreams, and force them either to take flesh or disappear.

Like the man in the gospels whom Christ raised from the dead, he was the only son of his mother, and she was a widow. Mrs Brady had been deserted by her husband when Cosmo was only five months old. She had brought him up under a strong impression that his father was a bad man, but that God would punish him – her God was a horrible creation, who existed to justify her meanness. Sure enough, in Cosmo's ninth year, they heard that Mr Brady senior was dead, having fallen off some scaffolding in Liverpool while drunk. Cosmo remembered a suitcase containing his belongings arriving, with a small cheque from the building company. He had been vaguely moved by the meagreness of his father's worldly goods, but his mother was triumphant. 'Only money I ever got from him,' she said. 'I ought to frame it.' When Cosmo lost his faith, one of the first things he admitted to himself was how deeply he disliked the woman. She was bigoted, she was vindictive, she was spiteful. She had driven away her husband and rejoiced in his untimely death. She had constantly told her only son that his painful birth had robbed her of her health – she knew how to make such clichés powerful and offensive.

He found that his mother's house, the location of all his worst nightmares, had become shrivelled and meagre. It did not have the lurking sense of evil he gave it in dreams, but there were threatening aspects he had forgotten. Everything in the place mocked his last few tatty shreds of self esteem. He had arrived at rock bottom, with a piercing hangover from the party at Francesco's, and he realised, before he had been there one hour, that it was possible to go lower still. He had had to choke back panic when he took it all in – the close rooms, the mean staircase with its trodden red linoleum, the antimacassar on the television, which hung down a few inches over the screen, giving every newsreader a lace bonnet. The cheap picture inscribed 'Priez pour nous, Notre Dame de Lourdes', the tea-towel commemorating the Pope's visit to Knock, the prominently placed *Universes* and *Catholic Heralds*. The same old sour smell clung to everything, having its centre in his mother's room, where her rosary drooped in its familiar place, across the mirror of her dressing table. Not being vain of her appearance (and having no reason to be), she presumably needed the mirror to check the stages of her deterioration. She had a morbid fondness for decay, and took great pride in her infirmities. Cosmo checked his own deterioration in the glass in the bathroom and decided he had no more pretensions to youth. Under the naked bulb, his dark hair was crumbling into ash. There were fine lines in the soft flesh round his eyes, and his stomach, though not spreading badly, had a spongy, over-ripe look.

On his first night, sleep was out of the question. He lay on his back in his old bed, staring at the wrinkles in the ceiling paper, while his stomach squirted painful gouts of acid on the food he had just consumed. The statue of the Sacred Heart, newly dusted for his arrival, cast an immobile shadow on the wall. Half ashamed of himself, Cosmo watched the bland smirk on its face, to see if it conveyed any threats about what it would do when he closed his eyes.

He suddenly remembered that as a child he had been afraid of his dressing gown at the end of the bed, because its folds had a sinister habit of drawing themselves into the figure of Jesus Christ, praying in the garden of Gethsemane. In his devout days, he had pitied Christ at that part of the story, when He prayed the cup might be taken from His lips. Cosmo had been one of the disciples sleeping for sorrow, and the reproachful voice had said to him: Could ye not watch with me one hour? Even now, Cosmo could not help retracing that shape, and shuddering at the face his imagination gave it – horribly eerie and full of the tomb. Cosmo's childish sins had, so his mother said, lacerated that Sacred Heart. If ye love me, keep my commandments. Cosmo feared Christ far too much to love Him.

In his infancy, he had been told charming tales of flowers

that were blue because the Virgin had brushed them with her cerulean robe, of asses with crosses on their backs, because Christ had ridden one into Jerusalem, of robins whose breasts were scarlet because a biblical ancestor of theirs had been splashed with blood from the Cross.

When he was older, however, people had been keen to impress upon him the fewness of the saved. To attain heaven was virtually impossible. The willing spirit was hampered at every turn by its coarse robe of flesh. Perhaps, he thought, my faith was taken away because I was not to be one of the saved. Cosmo at this point switched on the radio to dispel these cowardly meditations, and wore away the rest of the night on the threshold of consciousness, lulled by the BBC World Service. To compensate, he fell into a surreptitious doze the next afternoon, after lunch, and his mother was furious to find her mountainous son asleep in the daytime. Generally, she treated him like a prisoner who has inexplicably escaped the gallows. She got plenty of mileage out of Faith's betrayal, and Cosmo was goaded into painting his miserable existence in defensive colours which were far too gaudy. He was aware that she was praying for him and, since he considered her prayers equivalent to a voodoo curse, it made his flesh creep. She treated him like Count Dracula, placing crucifixes and copies of the *Universe* where he might stumble across them and recoil. Communication between them became steadily worse.

On Boxing Night, Father Corrigan came round to eat chicken sandwiches and pull crackers. He was very much disposed to be jolly, chipping away at Mrs Brady's granite disapproval with numerous little jokes, and he wore a purple tissue paper crown across his grizzled brow. Presently, Mrs Brady took away the tray and shut herself in the kitchen, with three of the crones and harpies who made up her social circle. Behind the door, their hen-like squawks and shrieks served to emphasise the masculinity of Cosmo and Father Corrigan. Cosmo began to nerve himself for something unpleasant. The stuffy room was too small for both himself and a man of God.

Two tumblers had been ceremoniously placed in front of Father Corrigan. He took a half-bottle of whiskey from his jacket pocket. 'Mary's a good woman,' he said, 'but she carries her horror of alcohol a little too far, I sometimes think.'

Cosmo knew then that something was coming. He recalled perfectly the technique of setting his mother aside, to encourage him to speak freely.

'My dad drank,' he said. 'I expect that's why.'

'Shouldn't be surprised.' Father Corrigan handed him a glass. 'Your health, Cosmo, and plenty of success to you.'

'Thanks.'

'You seem to be doing pretty well at this acting lark.'

'It's not too bad.'

'Have you been busy since you got back?'

'No.'

'Plenty of people to catch up with, I suppose?'

'Not really.'

Father Corrigan laughed. 'You don't have to be so defensive. I'm not going to ask why you weren't in church.'

'Good.'

'I can't be pushing my product all the time.'

'Good,' Cosmo said again, knowing it was rude but unable to help himself.

'Your mother tells me you've broken with that girlfriend of yours.'

Cosmo winced. 'Yes. She – she left me a few weeks ago.'

'Never mind, never mind,' said the priest. 'Plenty more around. There can't be a shortage of nice girls in your line of work.'

He smiled slyly, as if implying that Cosmo was a pimp, or a white slaver. Cosmo was irritated.

'I'd better be honest with you.' Father Corrigan deliberately put down his glass and folded his knotty, freckled hands. 'Or we'll get nowhere. Your mother won't give me a minute's peace until I've spoken to you.'

'I thought that was it,' said Cosmo grimly.

'I told her, Cosmo, I wouldn't dream of lecturing you. She thinks you're a boy, and here you are, looking forty in the face. I can't exactly put you across my knee and tan you with my belt.'

'You'd better let me have it, Father,' said Cosmo. 'It's the only way I'll find out what's on her mind.' The situation was foolish, but he could not help looking at the priest with the eyes of a whipped cur.

'Bad as that, eh? All right, it's this girlfriend of yours that's bothering her.'

'What? She's left me – how can she be a problem now? It's what the old cow's been praying for, isn't it?'

'Steady now, steady. We don't call our mothers old cows. Give the poor soul a bit of respect. She says she was hoping you'd settle down with this girl and get married. She wants grandchildren.'

'She's lying,' Cosmo cut in promptly. 'She's always hated me having girlfriends. She's only saying that because she knows how unhappy I am without Faith, and she wants to rub my nose in it.'

Interestingly, Father Corrigan said: 'Oh I know. That's why I didn't want to mention it.'

'I'm a disappointment to her. I've failed her.'

'Nonsense,' said Father Corrigan. 'She expects too much from you, she always did. I kept telling her, leave the lad alone. Would she listen?'

'Father, I've tried and tried to please her. Nothing works.'

The priest patted Cosmo's arm consolingly, and refilled his glass. 'If you'd been a saint, she'd have found something to carp about. Don't waste your time trying to satisfy her – satisfy yourself first.'

Cosmo could no longer remember what it would take to satisfy him, or even what the state of personal satisfaction felt like. Still, he breathed a little easier, probably because of the drink. Mrs Brady kept a dry house, and his capillaries had been parching for want of alcohol. He worked loose the knot of his tie.

'She's never forgiven me for not becoming a priest.'

'No,' said Father Corrigan. 'She'll probably never get over that. She doesn't like men – your poor father was enough to put anyone off – and she got this idea that if you put a man in a cassock and clap a biretta on his head he'll become a sort of honorary woman. I said to her at the time, God makes priests, not Mary Brady.' He chuckled. 'Oh, she was furious.'

'I thought she'd put you on to me to hook me back into the fold.'

'You wouldn't be far wrong. Do you want me to try?'

'No,' said Cosmo.

'That's that, then. Stop feeling so guilty.'

Cosmo shifted into a more comfortable position in his chair, which was, like everything else in the house, too small for him. 'I was born guilty. I always seem to choose the hardest way of doing things. Why do you think I lost my faith so suddenly? Could there be any particular reason?'

'I'm sure I couldn't say,' said Father Corrigan.

'But didn't you think it was odd at the time? It strikes me as odd now.'

The priest looked bored, but resigned. He wore his pastoral face, the face with which he kissed his stole.

'Listen Cosmo, you're not unique. People lose faith all the time these days. I've heard every possible reason, from space rockets to filth on the television.'

Cosmo laughed, though he was slightly annoyed not to be considered unique. Father Corrigan had always been a master of the prosaic.

'But it can't be natural, the way I'm haunted by it,' he persisted. 'I keep having nightmares – incredibly macabre nightmares – all about God and Jesus, and the saints – '

'And you can't sleep, and you play the radio all night long and drive your mother berserk,' Father Corrigan finished for him.

'I didn't know she could hear. Why to God couldn't she tell me herself? But seriously Father – ' he hurried on, afraid of being laughed at, 'I can't help wondering what it all means. How would you explain it? Are the nightmares meant as a punishment, or are they meant as a sign, sort of, to bring me back?'

'Are you telling me you still believe?'

'No, no – ' Cosmo was dismayed that it could be taken that way.

'Well, if you don't, it can't mean anything, can it?'

'No, I suppose not.'

Father Corrigan refilled the glasses and became jolly again. 'You always were the boy for asking me stiff questions.'

Mrs Brady came in with a fresh tray of tea, followed by a caravan of harpies bearing sandwiches and scones. The talk once more became harmless, and Cosmo felt foolish about nagging Father Corrigan for some heavenly explanation of his disturbed dreams. He began to drink his way through the rest of the bottle. By the time Father Corrigan was saying his goodbyes, the drink had taken effect. He did not feel the old priest's gnarled handshake until he had gone, and then the impression lingered on his palm, refusing to go away. He was slumping. The inadequate armchair creaked beneath his weight. He ate cakes and sandwiches with his head back, covering his bosom with a bib of crumbs. His mother glared at him over the papery white heads of her friends.

'He's the image of him, Mary,' said one of them. 'He's his father all over again.'

They departed in a gaggle, a dowdy Greek chorus in headscarves, hobbling towards the bus stop with their vinyl shopping bags. Cosmo did not rise to see them out. He had finished the bottle.

Mrs Brady stood in the doorway, holding the ashtray she had taken away to wash. She was very angry, but the barrier between herself and her son forced her to circle him charily, like a boxer in his first round waiting to see where he should plant his blow.

'What were you laughing about?'

'When?' Cosmo dredged up from somewhere a slurred, piggy voice.

'You and Father. I heard you laughing.'

'Oh dear, were we laughing? Oh dear oh dear I'm immensely grieved, do forgive me, that wasn't what you wanted at all, was it?'

'What did he say to you?' she asked suspiciously.

'Oh dear, wasn't your satellite dish trained to the right

station? What a shame. You missed a treat. We were laughing at you.'

He raised his head and they stared at each other accusingly. Mrs Brady straightened a lamp with a plastic flower imprisoned in its base.

'This room smells like a distillery,' she said icily. 'You're drunk, Cosmo. You're filthy drunk. You did it on purpose, didn't you?'

'That's right,' Cosmo shouted, 'I never make mistakes, I always do everything on purpose.'

'You know I won't have drink in the house. If it had been anyone but Father Corrigan bringing it in – '

'You'd have had them flogged at the cart's tail and burned at the stake. Oh, I know.'

'And there's smoke everywhere – '

'He told me not to take any notice of your nagging, because you're frigid, you don't like men – '

She turned on him. 'Don't you tell me lies.'

'He says you're a warped old woman.' Cosmo liked the phrase, and mouthed it to himself in the twilight: 'Warped old woman.'

The sour smell round Mrs Brady intensified. 'Oh yes, you're the image of your father, all right. I'll say you are, sitting here dead drunk and yelling abuse at me.'

'Ah, shut up!' Cosmo bellowed at her. 'Whenever you want to rubbish me, you say I'm like him. Well, I'm bloody glad I'm not like you.' He heaved himself to his feet, and the room shrank accordingly.

'I'm not surprised that woman left you,' said Mrs Brady inexorably. 'I should think she'd had just about enough of you. It must be in the blood. You're weak and stupid and disgusting, just like he was. Don't imagine you'll find another woman to put up with you for eight years, or even eight minutes – '

Cosmo's insides became light as air, freeing his limbs. He wanted to sweep her out of his consciousness.

'I'm weak, am I? This is weak, is it?' He shot out his arm and swatted her heavily against the door. She clutched at the post to steady herself and put one hand to her cheek. Her wedding ring glinted feebly. Her eyes were triumphant beads.

'Yes, go on, you hit me. You'll have to do it harder than that if you want to be like him. He used to knock me about when I was carrying you – great gashes and bruises, I used to have. It's a wonder you were born at all.'

Cosmo was trapped again. His frustration almost choked him. 'I didn't ask to be born.'

'And I didn't want you,' she said. 'If you hadn't been on the way, I wouldn't have had to marry him, would I? It seems to me I've been punished enough for one little slip. I had to have the forceps – you nearly killed me.'

This was a familiar saw, and Cosmo replied, as he had often secretly yearned to: 'I wish I had killed you. I wish to God I was an orphan.'

'I did my best for you. I don't know what else you expected.'

They gazed at each other, more interested in each other's state of being than they had ever been. The dislike between them was so intense that its expression was like a powerful love-scene. Inside, Cosmo was screaming that he had been cheated of his birthright and punished for something he had not done. The words would not come out, although he was desperate to know why it was impossible to love him.

'I'm going to bed,' he said.

'Please yourself.' She stood aside to let him pass. 'If you're ill tomorrow, you won't get any sympathy from me.'

'I don't want your fucking sympathy.' Cosmo blundered up the narrow stairs, muttering to himself: 'Honour thy father and mother. Honour thy fucking mother. The old bloody old witch – ' His hand smacked at the walls of his room, trying to find the switch. It had moved, or vanished. He stumbled across to the bed in inky darkness, throwing himself down fully clothed on the mattress and upsetting the bedside table. The first things he saw when he unglued his eyes the next morning were the two halves of the Sacred Heart, split right across the middle, lying on the floor. Its core was plaster, white plaster, of the cheapest possible kind.

Ten

Poor Hester Stretton's last moment of happiness was really no more than a comfortable state of blindness, and the ordinary warmth that comes from being wadded in thick layers of assumption, but she remembered it afterwards as Arcadian bliss, never to be regained.

She was dashing across Oakley Square, in the fine, sharp January sunshine, all milky-white and innocent, like a curly lamb to the slaughter. Very carefully, in both hands, she carried a cake-box tied with a silver ribbon. Inside it was a flan she had bought from an Italian bakery in Frith Street, a bilious-looking affair made of collapsing pastry and syrupy pears. Her only care in the world was to keep it in one piece going upstairs to her flat. It had already rocketed off the seat of a taxi at a red light and, although it had sustained no serious damage, it was not hardy enough to bear another knock. There was a greasy stain on the white cardboard where a blot of custard had seeped through, like blood from an internal wound. The whole point of buying such a thing was to produce it after supper in pristine symmetry, with the glazed pears in perfect, concentric rings.

She slammed the front door behind her with her foot and sang out: 'Vinny!'

And Vinny's voice unmistakably said: 'Shit.'

Hester hurried the box to the kitchen table, listening to the puzzling silence which followed. 'Darling?'

She heard his feet shuffling uneasily, but he did not reply. The atmosphere seemed peculiar, and Hester glanced round with the beginnings of suspicion. Something was not quite right. Most unusually for him, Vinny had swept and garnished, as carefully as a holidaymaker quitting a rented chalet. The cups, plates and saucers from breakfast lay face-down on the draining board, long beads of water sliding away from their rims.

'Where are you, sweetheart?' She opened the box, and absently nibbled a loose fragment of pastry.

Vinny flung her in at the deep end of an incomprehensible explanation. 'Listen, I wasn't expecting you back so soon – '

'Where are you?'

She pursued his voice to the bedroom, and he sprang out to block the doorway. 'Don't look – '

But she had already seen the bed, and was drawing in a long breath of horror. His only piece of luggage, a shabby nylon rucksack, yawned on the duvet, half-inflated by a tangle of his clothes. Some books, a dented alarm clock, a can of shaving foam with no lid and the Player's Navy Cut tin in which he kept his dope were scattered near by. These were the possessions he had brought with him four months before, all he cared to own. He plunged his hands into his pockets.

'Oh shit, you weren't meant to see this. I worked it all out, and then you had to come crashing in an hour early. What a fucking farce.'

Hester did not understand. She had hoped for a harmless reason for this, and now she knew she was not going to get one, that was all. Her stomach turning, she picked up the cigarette tin, as much a symbol of Vinny's residency as the flag above Buckingham Palace, and gazed blankly into the jaunty face of the sailor painted on the top. Vinny prowled, ready to rise to anything she threw at him, jingling the change in his pockets and pursing up his lips, as if he meant to whistle.

'Let's have it, then,' he said eventually. 'Let's have the scene and get it over with.'

Hester stammered: 'What – what are you doing?'

'Come on, love – what does it look like?'

'I don't know.' It was still not too late to reassure her. Her eyes implored him to do so.

'Well, I'm leaving, aren't I?'

'But where are you going?'

'I was going to write you a letter.' This phrase hung in the air between them, so incredibly feeble that he added: 'And then I was going to ring you. Oh Christ, this is ghastly.'

'Vinny, where – '

'Well, I mean, it's bleeding obvious, isn't it?' he demanded fretfully. 'I'm moving in with Rosamund. Where else would I be going?'

'But you can't be – you said she was just your friend – ' Hester was still desperately trying to prompt him into a reasonable explanation.

'Look,' he said briskly, 'I'll go down on my knees and emote a bit if you like, but there wouldn't be much point. I freely admit I'm a turd.'

Hester turned white and supported herself against the bedside table.

'Vinny, you – oh, you can't mean you've slept with her!'

'I don't believe this,' Vinny said, to some invisible third party. 'This is a fucking nightmare. Of course I've slept with her. Are you doing this on purpose, to give me a hard time?'

'When?'

'Hessie, please don't look at me like that. You know I can't take histrionics out of office hours.'

'More than once?'

He raked his fingers roughly through his hair. 'Obviously more than once. Oh, Jesus Christ, girl, use your brain.'

'How long has it being going on?'

'Look, what is this – the Oxford Book of Clichés? You can chuck something at me if you like – you'd be well within your rights – but do let's get this over with.'

Hester realised she was still holding the cigarette tin, and looked from it to Vinny in pathetic confusion.

'You can call me anything you like, from soup to nuts, and I'll probably agree with you,' he said, turning pink with exasperation, 'but don't expect me to do a big number about my soul being torn in half – because it isn't. I know where I'm going, and no amount of hysteria will make me change my mind.'

She was icy and trembling. 'But what have I done? Why are you so cross with me?'

'I'm not,' he said impatiently. 'It's got nothing to do with you.'

'Then why – '

'Hester listen, listen, just try to see it from my point of view. This is the biggest thing that's ever happened to me – I've got to be with her. I'm not complete without her.' He was eager. 'Haven't you ever had the feeling that there's a part of you missing that you're always searching for, and then you meet a particular person and it all falls into place – ' He seemed to realise, though Hester said nothing, that he was turning the dagger in the wound, and he hastily changed direction. 'I've known her for fifteen years, and we've always had this amazing rapport, but I've only just discovered that there was something missing – not just sex, but love. We were meant to fall in love, and now that we have it's incredible – we read each other's minds in a way that's virtually supernatural. You know I don't believe in suppressing emotions like that. I did try, Hester, because I'm so terribly fond of you, but it simply wasn't healthy.'

Hester tried to listen to all this, with her head spinning. All she took in were Vinny's favourite words, 'rapport', 'suppressing emotions' and 'healthy'.

'She's old,' she faltered stupidly.

'She's only my age,' Vinny pointed out. 'That's another problem, Hess – you're too young for me. You're a Thatcher-baby, and all your dreams are about possessions and commitments. The sixties and seventies are just a big joke to you. Dope and flared jeans and the Rolling Stones – you think it's hilarious, and it makes me feel a hundred. You were a little thing in short white socks when Rosie and I were barricading the Union together. How can you possibly relate to the experiences we've shared?'

'You said you loved me,' Hester whispered.

III

'Sweetheart, you kept saying Do you love me? And I kept saying Yes. There's a big difference.'

'But you said it last night when we were making love, and you seemed to feel it so deeply – '

Vinny said, 'Oh Jesus,' and blushed until he was puce.

'You don't know what you're doing, Vinny. You'll only regret it if you leave me now.'

'I was saying goodbye to you, I was trying to be nice so we could end with good memories. I'm not chucking what we had into the dustbin – I'm really grateful. We're going to be friends – '

'No!' shouted Hester. 'You do love me! She'll never make you happy, because she can't possibly love you like I do! You're the only man I've ever, ever loved. I've said things to you no living soul will ever hear from me again – oh darling, if you'd only try staying with me for another month, another week, even – '

Vinny was tired of having this violin solo played upon his heartstrings. They were tough old guts, and he lost his temper.

'You love me too much!' he yelled at her. 'I've had you up to here! You're like a bloody ball and chain!'

Hester erupted into a violent fit of sobbing and incongruously hugged the cigarette tin to her bosom. Vinny repented almost at once. It was not his policy to be needlessly cruel. He strode about the room, wrestling with his patience until he had got it under control. 'I never promised you anything,' he began, trying a 'kind but firm' line of argument. 'You can't say I'm breaking my vows to you, or crap like that, can you?'

'I'm going to die!' Hester wept. 'Oh, I can feel it, I'm dying!'

'I told you ages ago, I can't be tied down. Didn't I tell you? Stop that caterwauling – the neighbours will think I'm killing you.'

'You are killing me!'

'Bullshit. Did I or did I not tell you?'

'Oh yes, all right, you did.'

'You ignored it, didn't you? You've been thinking of me as a permanent fixture, haven't you? You women, you live on fucking fantasy – I'm constantly amazed.'

'Yes, but Vinny, I ignored it because I fell in love with you – you wanted me to love you, and I couldn't have unless I ignored the things you said about being tied down – ' Great whooping sobs demolished the rest of the sentence.

'Oh God, never mind, never mind.' He plucked the tin out of her numb fingers and put it in his rucksack. This done, he took her resignedly in his arms. Hester clung to him as if she would squeeze the bones out of his body and crush them to powder. She could already feel how the quality of his embrace had changed.

'This won't do,' said Vinny. He glanced at his watch. 'I'll make you some tea. Come on.'

Hester allowed him to lead her by the wrist into the kitchen. He was treating her abominably, she was sure, but it was difficult to pinpoint exactly how. She saw now that he had laid down a deliberate get-out clause, even when he was most in love. It was only too plain that he had played dozens of variations on this theme. She was no longer Hester, but a compound of all the women he had ever deserted. With all the resolution of Mary Poppins saying she would leave when the wind changed, he had lectured her about his hatred of being tied down. Just as determined, she had shut her ears. Despair settled heavily on her throat and chest. Cold and still, she watched Vinny moving about the kitchen. He put a mug of tea down in front of her, and she curled her fingers round the handle, though she did not mean to drink it. Vinny slurped his tea thirstily and waved a knife above the pear flan.

'Mind if I have some of this? I'm ravenous.'

'I bought it for you,' said Hester dismally.

'It's a beauty. Shall I cut you a slice? Might make you feel better.'

'No.'

'Suit yourself.' He impaled the pears with the end of his knife and took the glacé cherry out of the centre, effectively destroying the whole design and reducing the sweetmeat to so much sticky rubble. 'I expect you think your heart is broken,' he said, 'but you'll get over this, you know. People always do. I'm certainly not vain enough to imagine I've ruined your life, or anything like that. You're a raving beauty, Hess. You'll find someone else like a shot.'

There is an unwritten book of law about sexual relationships. Women frequently read each other excellent pieces of advice from this book, but seldom take it themselves. According to its wisdom, Hester knew she should have pitched Vinny out with a frying-pan wrapped round his head, but it was no use. She was even rather grateful to him for postponing the great love of his life for another quarter of an hour, to comfort her.

'I'd better be off now, sweetheart. It's always a good idea to do these things cleanly.'

Hester trailed after him to the bedroom, watching as he stuffed the last of his belongings into the rucksack. He slung it over his shoulder and faced her, ready to walk out just as he had walked in, like a film played in reverse. She grabbed a fistful of his jersey.

He kissed her cheek. 'Take care of yourself, love. I'll see you at the theatre, and you can tell me how you're making out. All right? I know it seems tough, but you've got to learn that your notion of love is hopelessly unrealistic. You just can't possess a person body and soul. Let go of me.'

'No!

'Don't be silly. Let go.'

'No! You can't do it!'

But he could do it, and he did. The flat petrified the moment it was bereft of his energy. Hester was dizzy in the roaring silence that came crashing down. She ran to the sitting room window in time to see him turning the corner without one backward glance, fresh and hopeful, ready for the next adventure.

How was she to cope, or even begin to cope, with such a catastrophe? The room grew dark while she tried to digest it. Eventually she realised she was far too helpless to spend the night alone. She picked up the telephone.

'Mummy? It's me – can I come tonight? Mummy, Vinny's left me ...' She burst into tears again, and wailed childishly into the receiver while her mother made distressed and soothing noises. This did not remove the sting in the way Hester had expected. For the first time her mother, that fount of protection, was useless. She could go home and sleep in her old room, surrounded by old dolls and mementoes of dead ponies, but she could never get back to the creature she had been before she met Vinny. She had been reared in a carefully controlled environment, like a nectarine in a greenhouse. Vinny had smashed the glass, and now, in the first freezing blast of adversity, she was withering away.

Eleven

There was a damp, dismally-lit concrete stairwell leading from the dressing rooms to the bowels of the theatre. It smelt of the mouldy exhalations of the river, and was so close to the foundations that one could almost hear the sulphurous tide mud oozing. In this dungeon, among the chained bicycles, Hester was crying. Two paper tissues lay in sodden fragments at her feet, and she was smearing gluey mucus all over her face with her hands.

Vinny had been living with Rosamund Jaeger for a month, and he was so loudly, indecently happy that the other actors were beginning to relax their disapproval of his villainy. Hester, knowing that possession of happiness is nine-tenths of the law of popularity, did her best to appear cured, but she suffered agonies in private, and wondered sometimes if she would ever get over it. A performance of the *The Miser* had come down half an hour before, and Vinny's charm had poured over her in such torrents during their counterfeited love scenes that she could not face the desert of her bed, or the predictable misery of another night without him.

'Hester?' A hand lightly touched her shoulder.

She jumped, and her sleeve flew to her nose, making a snail's track across her cuff. Cosmo Brady stood on the step behind her. From her crushed position at his feet, he was a mountain of tweed and corduroy, with a distant face at the summit almost as startled and embarrassed as her own. If she had considered, she might have guessed that she would meet him here. This staircase was the resort of the isolated, the cussed and the meek; anyone who wanted to sneak away after the show without having to pass the foyer or the stage door.

Cosmo sat down on the step beside her. It was a tight squeeze, and Hester shrank nearer the bannisters to avoid touching him. A bicycle basket with a waterproof cover dug into the small of her back. He coughed and hemmed, until he managed to say, his face red with effort: 'What is it, love? What's the matter?'

Hester foolishly replied, 'Nothing!' in a primal shriek which amazed her.

'Can't I do something?'

'Go away.'

'I can't just leave you here, can I?'

She supposed he could not. He wore his habitual suspicious frown, and she thought he looked rather angry, as decent people are angry when they find a smelly old drunk on the doorstep and feel they are forced to do something humanitarian.

'Have you got a hanky?' she asked.

'Here.' He shifted his weight to reach into his pocket, and as soon as the warmth of his body fell against her, Hester relaxed. The contact was not so dreadful after all. He was so close that she could see the black dots on his chin where he shaved, and she registered how large and solid, and how undoubtedly handsome he was. He gave her a creased handkerchief, with a man's smell of sweat, keys and leather wallets. She sobbed into it extravagantly, too far gone to care what he thought. Cosmo made no effort to soothe or caress. He simply waited, his hands resting on his knees, until she was ready to speak again.

'Thanks, I must look a wreck.'

'You don't,' Cosmo said seriously. 'You look – ' He did not finish, but he stopped frowning, and several years lifted off his brow.

'You don't have to stay, Cosmo. I'll be fine now.'

'Do you want me to leave you alone?'

He asked this so wistfully that politeness forced her to say: 'Oh, no.' But she did not know what to do with him, and she doubted whether he knew what to do with her.

'I hate the idea of you sitting here, all by yourself,' he said.

'I don't care. I'm so miserable, I just wish I was dead.' She ended on a whimper, and Cosmo made a move as if to put his arm round her. He changed his mind and patted her sticky hand instead.

'Is it because of Vinny?'

'Yes, of course it is,' she said irritably. 'And don't tell me I'll get over it. So what if I do? I'm miserable now.'

'I shouldn't dream of saying anything of the kind.' His voice was mild and encouraging. 'I know how you feel. It happened to me too, don't forget.'

'I'm trying so hard to be normal,' she sobbed, 'because that's what everyone wants me to do, but it's not fair, Cosmo, it really isn't. They're all used to Rosamund now, and my feelings are just a nuisance because they have to be considered all the time, oh, I wish I'd never set eyes on him – '

'He's a shit,' said Cosmo. With a thrill of satisfaction, Hester watched one of his great hands curl into a fist.

'Look at this,' she said tremulously. 'Read it.' She pointed to a copy of the *Evening Standard*, which lay folded on top of her bag.

Cosmo picked it up. It was open at the Londoner's Diary.

'Read it,' she repeated.

'Oh.' He saw at once the picture of Rosamund and Vinny, clasped affectionately, laughing like hyenas at something out of the frame.

Among the revellers tasting the sphincter-scorching delights of Fulham's newest Indian restaurant were bluestocking actress Rosamund Jaeger and the new man in her life, tax-payers hearthrob Vincent Bliss, who is currently causing heavily-subsidised swoons in Paul Fletcher's *The Miser*. Cambridge-educated Rosamund, last seen as Dorothea Brooke in TV's *Middlemarch*, told me: 'I've never been happier. Settling down really suits me. We're talking about starting a baby next year, and it could be the toughest role I've ever tackled.

Hester studied Cosmo's profile as he took the piece in, seeing him more clearly every second as the mists lifted from her eyes. The edges of the vague being, distinguished only for sharing a dressing room with Vinny, were drawing together into a man, and (she noticed again) a very handsome one. Hard as she looked, she could not find a thing wrong with his face.

Throwing the paper aside, he said very gently and kindly: 'Oh darling, what a horrible thing for you to have to read.' With one unhesitating movement, he put his arm round her and drew her head down to his shoulder. Such sympathy made Hester feel stronger and behave weaker. As soon as her cheek touched the rough fabric of his jacket, she began to cry again, clutching his lapels in anguish. His arm lay heavily across her back, and the relief of his strength was inexpressible.

'You go on and cry,' he said, 'you've every right. He is a cruel bastard, carrying on in front of you the way he does. I ought to go straight up to the greenroom and beat the shit out of him this minute.'

'Don't – you mustn't be angry with him – he doesn't know he's doing it – '

'Like fuck he doesn't.'

'No, he doesn't! You can't judge Vinny like other people. He never understands women being sad about him.'

She felt a grudging laugh rumble in Cosmo's chest. 'I wish I had someone who'd stick up for me like that,' he said.

'You think I'm stupid.'

'Of course not.' Cautiously, afraid of taking liberties, he stroked the back of her head. 'I know what it's like. People just cut you off unless you start being brave – it's the "Ridi Pagliacchi" syndrome. You take ages to get over it, but if you still look pitiful after three days they all turn round and kick your arse.'

The ringing bitterness in his voice interested Hester. It had not occurred to her that he might have been just as harrowed as she was now when Faith married Dominion Shetoza. In retrospect, she was mildly guilty. Vinny had been one of the principal arse-kickers, and she had thought it a great joke at the time. Cosmo's personality, formerly shadowy, began to take flesh.

'How did you manage?' she asked.

He sighed. 'I don't know. I hung about at home like a bad smell, trying to be adult and reasonable, and secretly wishing someone would drown Dom Shetoza in a vat of boiling oil.'

'Well, I've never been able to stand Rosamund,' Hester stated. 'She's a nasty old thing, always looking down her nose. And she's been under the sunlamp so long she looks like a fried banana. But I can't be angry with Vinny. I love him too much.'

'That's always the way,' said Cosmo sadly. 'We never blame the person who deserves it most.'

'Would you ever take Faith back?'

'Not in a million years,' he said fiercely. 'She could beg till she was blue in the face.' He sighed again. 'She never will, so it's all rather academic. Look, what am I going to do with you?'

'I – I don't know.'

'You can't sit here all night. I could buy you a drink – the bar's still open.'

Hester slumped against him, totally passive, waiting for the decision to be made for her. 'I can't go up there. Look at my face.'

His muscles stiffened. 'I could drive you home.'

She began to choke again, and her voice came out in a weary whine. 'I don't want to go home. It's freezing cold and there's a man upstairs who plays Scottish reels all night really loud and I hate it without Vinny.' Cosmo's arm tightened round her, and he laid his cheek against her forehead. His skin was a shock, but not unpleasant. It was smooth because he had shaved before the show.

'I won't make you go home, darling.' He pushed her away from him, so that she was forced to see his face. It was pale in the gloomy, greenish light, and he was breathless. 'Hester, if you come back with me, I'll look after you. You'll be quite safe – what I mean is, I won't touch you, unless you want me to.'

Hester listened to her own name, reverently uttered as if it was poetry, and was surprised to be the cause of so much agitation. His hands grasped her shoulders so tightly that they almost hurt, and for a moment she was flustered. Here was a man she hardly knew – working with him for six months had made no difference. Handsome he might be, but he was touchy and cross, and his life was so supremely dreary that she was afraid it might be catching. It was his desperation that grabbed her. His unguarded eyes were moist with eagerness. She suddenly had an eerie idea that she could not refuse him even if she wanted to. Her fate was poised, ready to swing wildly on her yes or no.

'All right. If you really wouldn't mind.'

He conjured up a shy, rather sweet smile, the sort surly people often surprise with. 'You can drown your sorrows in a bottle of whisky if you like,' he said. 'It feels like hell in the morning, but it takes your mind off being lonely.'

Loneliness, that was it. It was the creeping tentacles of his loneliness she feared. Once he smiled, the odd feeling vanished. She blew her nose.

'Come on, then.' He pulled her to her feet easily, as if he was hardly aware of her weight.

'Shall I follow you?'

'Leave your car here,' he said. 'I'll drive you.'

'Okay.'

Strong-minded colleagues had often lectured Hester about her liking for male domination. They could not know how disagreeable she found independence and self-assertion. In her present state of helplessness, she would have submitted to much worse than the protection of Cosmo Brady.

He led her out of the fire doors into the drizzly February night, his arm clasped so firmly round her waist that her feet scarcely touched the pavement. As soon as Cosmo had strapped her into the passenger seat, her perceptions shifted gear and she was trapped in a web of unreality.

The first part of the journey, the roundabout, the bridge, the underpass coming out in the middle of Kingsway, was the same route she took herself on the way home to Camden

Town, but it looked different from the windows of his unfamiliar car. Panic stifled her when they veered away at Holborn towards the Angel, and her newly-formed vision of Cosmo began to fragment. She saw him only in bits and pieces. He was a pair of large hands on the steering wheel, a pair of massive brown brogues on the pedals, an elbow that brushed her occasionally when he swatted the gears. What he was doing seemed far too dainty for his physical capacity.

Hester gazed out at the landmarks she recognised, as if imploring them for help. They drove down Upper Street, towards Highbury Corner, and passed one of Vinny's favourite pubs – 'The Hope and Anchor', known affectionately to him as 'The Dope and Wanker' – shut up now, of course, with the grille pulled across the doors and the lights extinguished. When had she been there last? Mid-December, wheezing in the smoke, half deafened by the band, but nourished and sustained by Vinny's smiles when he bought her spritzers and bags of Scampi Fries. She had one of her dislocated moments, when yearning for him made her as limp as a rag doll. A twinge of pain clawed at her breasts. At the traffic lights, she made herself look at Cosmo.

'Nearly there,' he said, and the words mercifully drew him together again. They swung round the green bump of Highbury Corner into Corsica Street. She studied the dark, shuttered buildings, apparently mostly small factories and workshops, rather troubled by the gloom. The headlamps snagged a row of concrete nymphs in a mason's yard, all contemplating the gravel with their sightless eyes, urns slung upon their shoulders.

In front of his short row of houses Cosmo stopped and parked badly, jerking them both forward. They sat in silence, until the last murmurs of the engine had died away. Hester watched two cats circling and fleeting in the alleyway. The springs twanged mysteriously in the seats. Cosmo's breathing was feather-light and apprehensive.

'Well.' He gave her what seemed to be a wary, calculating look. Hester got quickly out of the car. While he locked it, she examined the front of his house. She knew it was his because

Pilot's head was silhouetted in one corner of the lighted first floor window. He could be heard barking sharply.

'Come in, then.' Cosmo sounded hostile, and Hester realised that his bashfulness was making him resent her. Feeling suddenly confident that she could manage him, she tucked her hand into his arm as he turned the key. He pressed it firmly against his body. Whenever she was not touching him, she felt awkward and responsible. Feeling his arm underneath his sleeve brought back the sensation of protection. It had to do with physical strength rather than personality. There was a reassuring stillness in his body, the exact opposite of Vinny's mercurial energy. To touch Vinny was to feel the blood rushing in his veins, and his nerves dancing.

With Pilot cavorting round his feet, he showed her into the sitting room. Hester decided that nothing in it particularly surprised her. The Habitat sofa, pine table and chairs, sanded floorboards and cheerful ethnic rugs were all entirely expected. It was a little too bare, owing to the spaces Faith had left. The shelves on either side of the chimney breast were only half full. There were a couple of bare picture hooks, one wrapped in a froth of cobweb. Above the mantelpiece was a handsome poster from the Chichester Festival Theatre, framed and glazed, with Cosmo's name at the top of an alphabetic cast list. Hester read the titles – *A Winter's Tale, The Duchess of Malfi, Daphne Laureola* – wondering which parts Cosmo had played. Vinny said it was naff to frame your old posters. He said only queeny old actors with cartwheels in their front gates did things like that. Vinny was a terrible snob in his way.

Cosmo threw a pile of the previous Sunday's newspapers and magazines on to the floor, and dropped his keys on the table. Seeing him in the setting he had made for himself was extraordinary. Men's homes diminished them, somehow. A large part of Vinny's attraction had been his floating freedom. Did Cosmo clean this place himself? What on earth did he look like with a Hoover? His eyes seemed to expect to be hurt by her. Hester caught the end of his smile when he glanced up from caressing Pilot. The dog clearly derived the same reassurance from his touch, stretching out under Cosmo's hand in mindless adoration.

'You don't mind him, do you?'

'No, no, how could I? He's terribly sweet.'

Hester sat down on the sofa, to make things less stilted. Vinny, of course, would never be lost for words in a situation like this.

'Drink?'

'Thanks, Cosmo. I'd love one.'

'Wine or whiskey?'

'Whiskey, please.'

Once he and the dog were out of the room, Hester sighed, stretching out her legs. It was blissfully warm – Cosmo was not mean about his heating bills. Vinny, oddly enough, was always switching off lights and turning down radiators, even though he never paid for anything. He was gone – it was no use thinking about him. Hester searched her bag for cigarettes and a lighter. She had been clutching the bag like an anchor. Now, she dropped it and lit a cigarette, letting herself drift about the room. There was a marble vessel on the table which she used as an ashtray, hoping it was not supposed to be an ornament. She scrutinised the cork notice board on the wall opposite the fireplace. There were two National Portrait Gallery reproductions on it, appropriate to the work of the moment: Lord Byron in his Albanian costume and John Keats, chin resting on hand, rather rabbity and callow, Hester thought, for such a romantic figure. Cosmo had pinned up his birth certificate and his degree from University College Dublin, as if he needed proof of his own existence. There was also a photograph of himself and Faith, both younger and hairier, which Hester examined curiously. She collapsed back on the sofa finally, exhausted by new impressions.

Pilot returned, his nails rattling on the bare boards. Hester regarded him without emotion as he sniffed her shoes. In Cosmo's absence, she did not have to put on any show of being a dog-lover. Pilot raised himself on his hind legs, resting his front paws on her knees. Thrashing his feathery tail he stared at her eagerly with round brown eyes. Hester smiled slightly at the pressure of his little pads against her skirt. Those eyes, so easy to please or hurt, could not fail to remind her of Cosmo.

'You really are quite sweet,' she whispered, stroking one of his ears. She patted her lap, and was gratified when he jumped on the sofa and laid himself across her thighs. His heart fluttered on her leg like a piston.

Cosmo brought in a bottle of Jamesons and two glasses. His shirtsleeves were rolled over his mighty forearms.

'You're honoured. He likes you.'

'Doesn't he like everyone?'

'Certainly not, he's very discriminating. Pilot's no flirt.'

'Who doesn't he like?'

After making sure she was not teasing him, Cosmo said seriously: 'Well, Horatia Geldschmidt, for one. He's all right at her place, but I have to shut him in another room when she comes here.'

'How dreadful.'

He suddenly laughed. 'The sound of her voice drives him into a frenzy. He took a great piece out of her ankle once. Here's your drink, love.' He knelt at her feet, to give her the glass. 'God, your hands are freezing. Shall I turn the heating up?'

'I'm fine.'

'Bugger off, Pilot. Down you get, boy – '

'Leave him, I don't mind.'

He was very close to her now, his face on a level with her own, his heavy hand cupped round her knee. She smelt him, mingled with the fumes of the whiskey. His sweat was sharper and muskier than Vinny's. He had a slight Irish accent lying under his actor's RP vowels. On one or two drunken company occasions, Hester had heard him unleash a vinous, unintelligible brogue, but she had never noticed that it was there all the time, clinging stubbornly like a cheap scent. Micks, Paddies, potatoes and poteen. Dull plays, peat floors, alcoholism, bombs and The Nolan Sisters. Oh, what a snob I am, she thought. There's nothing wrong with being Irish.

'Cosmo, what on earth are you and Faith doing in that photo?'

'What? Oh, that,' Cosmo glanced over his shoulder. 'I'm holding her legs while she kisses the Blarney Stone.'

'Is it in Ireland?'

'Are you *serious*?'

'Oh. I couldn't work it out. When was it taken?'

'About eight years ago. We were on holiday. Not that she needed to kiss any stone – the woman has a tongue on her like a yo-yo. It should've kissed her.'

Hester smiled, to cover her mystification. She felt every one of his fingers through her skirt, and the ridge of the worn gold ring he wore on his right hand. Their positions oppressed her. She was being forced into responsibility, and that was not what she had planned at all.

'You don't mind me smoking, do you?'

'No, love, how could I? I'm on thirty a day since Faith walked out. I hadn't touched one for two years.'

'Two years!' Hester echoed respectfully. There was apparently no end to the woman's iniquity. Her mouth began to go dry. What she had done had inevitable consequences. Why did he not get on with it? With a pang of dismay, she realised he was going grey. His silver hairs trapped the light when he shifted his head. Mentally, she begged him not to become pathetic.

'I nearly went demented,' he said. It had begun, and Hester struggled against the weight of his confession. His slow, melancholy voice and his naked, solemn eyes filled her with dread.

'Yes, it must have been hard.'

'It put ten years on me.'

Stop it, she wanted to say. Don't tell me. 'Cosmo, you have been nice. I haven't even thanked you, have I? It was stupid of me to make such a fuss – '

'No, not at all,' he assured her. 'I cried my eyes out when it happened to me.'

'Did you?' Hester hoped she was keeping the horror out of her voice. Once his secrets were out in the open, they would trap her. 'But it was different for you, you had an excuse. I mean, you lived with Faith for years, and I only had Vinny for

126

four months . . .' Suddenly, she longed for Vinny so intensely that the tears rushed back to her eyes. For the next few seconds she was overcome with bleakness, but the attack had one beneficial effect. Cosmo's own ponderous woes dropped to the back of his mind.

'Don't start again, darling –' He plucked Pilot away, and the springs of the sofa sagged and groaned under his weight as he sat down. Hester flopped against him and he circled her with his arm. 'For Christ's sake, Hester, nobody deserves that many tears.'

She was thinking. Emotionally, she was far too tired to listen to an embarrassing recitation of his miseries. As long as he held her like this, it was fine. Why didn't he start making love to her? She waited, leaning her head against his collar bone. Her eyes were swollen and her hair wild, but she knew she was desirable. Strangely, although Cosmo's breathing was feverish, he seemed reluctant. She pulled his face towards her. His lips were cold and tasted of whiskey, but his tongue was hot and wet, cramming her mouth uncomfortably. He wanted her desperately, there was no doubt about that. His pelvic writhing and urgent, smothered yelps made Hester eager to get rid of the sharpest part of her physical longings. If only he would be firm with her, so that she could shut her eyes and be certain someone was there. Piercingly, she recalled Vinny, and her insides unfolded ready for a man, Cosmo or anyone.

He drew away from her, stammering: 'You're not angry, are you? You don't think I'm forcing you? I didn't invite you here just so I could –'

'Let's go to bed,' she whispered.

His eyes widened. 'Are you sure?'

'Yes, of course.'

'Let me look at you. I don't believe it, I don't believe how beautiful you are –'

Hester smiled. She had heard this speech before, but it was always nice to hear. Cosmo stood up, pulling her with him, and the thing was done. She wondered if she had made a ghastly mistake. 'Stay, Pilot,' he was saying. 'Stay in here, that's a good boy. He – he usually sleeps with me,' he explained sheepishly.

'Oh.' This was another poignant personal detail Hester did not want to know. Cosmo hurried her out of the room and shut the door on the wailing, rejected spaniel. Obviously he hated doing it – he even shot her a reproachful look – but what was she supposed to do? She was not doing it with a dog in the room, and that was that.

They went upstairs, Hester gripping Cosmo's wrist. There was now a large bulge under his flies, and she wondered curiously if she would be big enough to take him. She seemed to have shrivelled such a lot since Vinny's departure. Cosmo pulled the bedroom curtains shut before he switched on the lamp beside the bed. The duvet was twisted back untidily. He heaved it into place and a chewed plastic bone clattered to the floor. Both of them were awkward, waiting for some sort of rhythm to carry them along. The first time Hester went to bed with Vinny, it had been exactly as a first time should be, with clumsy groping, sweaty endearments and clothes torn off in a frenzy.

Cosmo massaged her neck with his lips. Oh, get on with it, she thought. He was mumbling. 'Hester, listen – I can't – I ought to – I can't – you're so incredibly beautiful – ' It tickled. She twitched away from him. He began to unbutton his shirt, with straining trousers and a face which suggested he was about to be guillotined. Hester took off her jersey, taking it for granted that he was goggling at her breasts. She was not going to look at him until they were both nude. Nudity was somehow more decent than underwear. He lay on his back, raking his eyes across her body with gratifying awe. She admitted that he was quite splendid, an excellent specimen. She got into bed quickly so that he would not see how she stared at his penis, lying massively among the hairs on his belly, with the veins standing out and the skin retreating from the tip. Absurdly, she felt the way she gazed at it was intrusive, and not quite polite. Cosmo drew the duvet over them, and the whole bed smelled of him, like the lair of a beast.

After tentatively kneading her buttocks, he rolled over on top of her, taking his weight on his elbows. His face was choked and pleading. Hester, with a nervous itch for contact, wrapped her legs round him.

'No,' Cosmo muttered, 'No.'

She ignored him. One impatient wriggle and the tip of his penis was inside her.

'No!' he shouted. With an expression of agony, he thrust mightily against her womb and immediately squirted, groaning with despair as he came, and mashing the pillows with his fists.

Hester lay dumbfounded as she felt the spasms contending in his body. She had had indifferent experiences in bed, but nothing as mortifying as this. It was a kind of disease, she believed, with a medical name she could not remember. The embarrassment was appalling, and she closed her eyes, wondering what on earth one was supposed to say. Something warm dropped on her shoulder – a tear. When she was able to look, she saw Cosmo propped above her, his back rigid as he tried not to cry, his wet eyes betraying him. Hester's stomach froze. She was deeply sorry for him, knowing now why he had been so reluctant to jump on her when he evidently fancied her, and why he had kept saying 'No'. If only she had listened, but men spoke such peculiar gibberish between the sheets.

'Cosmo.'

'Don't talk to me!' He snatched himself out of her so violently that she was whipped on the thigh with a dribble of semen, and presented her with his back. The bed bucked and tossed as he moved.

'It's all right, Cosmo, really.'

'Don't say a word to me. Oh, Jesus Christ.'

Hester raised herself on her elbow. His shoulders were tight and still. Full of pity, she touched his arm. He shook her away, but knowing she must persist she stroked him gently, until his knotted muscles relaxed a little.

'I'm sorry,' he said angrily.

She guessed what humiliation the anger must cover. 'Don't be,' she coaxed. 'It doesn't matter.'

'Course it fucking matters.' And of course, it did.

Hester blinked owlishly at the unfamiliar stripes of light on the ceiling until she remembered where she was. Cosmo had jolted her from her doze by getting out of bed. She saw his shadowy figure by the open door pulling on a towelling dressing gown, trying not to disturb her. Through her lashes, she observed him going across the landing, switching on the light in the bathroom. She listened to the jets of his urine falling into the lavatory bowl in loud bursts, with pauses in between. When he pressed the flush she quickly shut her eyes again, but he did not come back into the room. He was creeping downstairs. Below, a door banged, and there was a fretful bark from Pilot, hastily stifled.

Properly awake, Hester switched on the lamp, shading her stinging eyes until she was used to the light. A tartarous film had settled across her teeth. Her thighs were welded together with old sperm, and the fishy smell gusted up at her from under the duvet when she moved her legs. Stiffly, she got out of bed and left the room. Casing Cosmo's bathroom, she yearned to be at home among her soothing creams and gels, but she was less fussy than people supposed. The materials at hand were a flannel, soap and a comb. She used these to rub up her misted beauty until it shone, working the comb through patiently until she had tamed her hair back into its remarkable blonde curls. When she had finished, she went to the top of the stairs, crisp and restored, supposing she would have to find Cosmo. She put on her jersey and padded barefoot to the kitchen.

Cosmo sat at the table, clutching Pilot in his arms. He was silently crying, a wash of tears dripping off his nose and chin on to Pilot's resisting head. Gravely, he looked at Hester in the doorway.

'Oh Cosmo, honestly, what a pair we are. First me and now you.' She smiled at him.

'I didn't mean to wake you.'

'Oh that's all right. I had to get up, I felt so ragged. I used your toothbrush, I hope you don't mind.'

'No.'

'I'm going to make some tea. Would you like some?'

'Yes, yes please.'

She plugged in the kettle. 'I think Pilot wants to get down. I think you're squashing him.'

Cosmo gawped at her stupidly before he understood. He put Pilot on the floor and the dog scuttled to his basket, looking at Hester over the edge. Now she had two great pairs of eyes pinned to her.

'I'm incredibly hungry, Cosmo. Do you have any biscuits?'

'I – I don't know.'

'Well, I'll look, shall I?' She flicked open the cupboards, which mostly contained Fray Bentos steak and kidney pies and tin upon tin of Mr Dog. 'May I open these fig rolls? Are they terribly ancient?'

'Help yourself.' Apologetically, Cosmo stole the sleeve of his dressing gown up to his eyes. Hester was touched, and felt fond of him.

'I always get hungry if I wake up this time of night,' she said, with her mouth full. 'It reminds me of fire practice at my boarding school. I never could get back to sleep afterwards.'

She made two mugs of tea with tea bags, and sat down opposite Cosmo.

'I'm really sorry about what happened,' he said.

Hester looked studiously down at her tea. His voice was polite and normal, but his male tears were dreadful. 'It doesn't matter. You were tired.'

Shaking his head, Cosmo crammed a biscuit into his mouth. 'This isn't the first time.' He took another biscuit, broke off half and tossed it to Pilot. 'Lately, I – well, you're sweet. Faith used to give me hell.'

'What a cow she sounds,' said Hester warmly. 'That can't have helped you much.'

'No, it didn't.'

'Do stop going on about it. Drink your tea.' His staring made her uncomfortable.

'I should have told you,' he said. 'I feel worse because it's you. You've no idea, Hester, how I worship you, and now, when you're being so kind – ' He sighed, and sniffed deeply, reaching for another biscuit.

'But anyone would – '

'No!' He was vehement. 'You're not like the others. I might have known I'd mess it up, and I should never have brought you here, but I couldn't resist. You being here is like the moon come down from the sky.'

Hester dipped a fig roll into her tea, fascinated.

'It isn't just your beauty which sets you apart,' he continued. 'I've watched you, and you couldn't be so beautiful on the outside if you weren't pure and good on the inside.' The tears were drying on his heated, eloquent face. 'You're an angel. Vinny must be blind to let you go. He must be without a soul.'

'But I'm not good!' Hester interrupted. 'I'm no better than anyone else.'

'I've seen you,' said Cosmo, 'like the Blessed Damozel, leaning out from the gold bar of heaven. Her eyes were deeper than the depths of water stilled at even.'

Hester shivered. He was vomiting up his soul, and in the tainted, half-digested lumps of poetry she recognised a distorted image of herself.

'Darling, are you cold?' he said eagerly. 'Can I fetch you a blanket, or something?'

'No, but Cosmo, I do wish you'd stop.'

'Let me, please let me, I'll never have the courage again. Shall I tell you what I thought of, when I first saw you?'

'Don't, please – '

'No, let me. There's a fisherman's church in Brittany with a carved altarpiece. It's a storm, all in dark wood, the sea churning, the boat overturned. The men are all in the water with their hands raised, pleading, like this – ' He clasped his hands and cast his eyes upwards, to show her. She looked away, blushing for him. 'And in white wood, gleaming, shimmering, stands the Blessed Virgin, Hester, the Star of the Sea – she's gazing down at them, with such an expression on her face – just like you. And I'm like them.'

Hester felt obscurely ashamed, as if she had acted out some stupendous lie, forcing him to get this impression of her. 'Oh Cosmo, for goodness sake – '

'All right, I won't say another word. I won't bother you ever again. You won't even have to notice me. I shouldn't have taken advantage of you, bringing you here. I certainly shouldn't have coerced you into making love with me.'

'But I wanted to!' Hester insisted.

'I'm a wreck, I'm an impotent old drunk. I should never even have dared to look at you.' He covered his face with his hands.

For one moment, Hester's perceptions swung round to take in the two of them from his point of view. She, shining and unattainable, the moon come down from the sky, the star of the sea. He with a heart bursting for her, ridiculously grateful for any crumb she threw him. Vinny had cast her off as if she had been a very ordinary sort of woman, and her first fall had made her feel very small and inadequate. The sensation of holding Cosmo in the palm of her hand, and having the power to blow good or evil over his life, soothed her bruised vanity. She knew she was not the goddess he had invented, but she really was a kind girl, with a conviction that suffering should not proceed from her if she could prevent it. She was miserable because Vinny had left her, but there was no reason why Vinny's action should set in motion a chain of misery. 'Nonsense. All that's the matter with you is that you're unhappy. That's no crime.'

The wretched man was sobbing behind his hands, and she got up to put her arms round him, pitying him from her soul. They were alike, the two of them, and it was fitting that they had found each other. He bored his head into her stomach.

'Don't, oh, please don't – don't be good to me unless you mean it!'

She caressed his hair. 'Of course I mean it.'

'I love you badly enough as it is. If you're any kinder to me now, I'll die when you leave me!'

Hester remembered how Vinny had repulsed her when she made a similar appeal. She would be merciful where he had been mean. 'I'm not going to leave you.'

'Let me see you again – give me another chance – '

'Don't be silly, Cosmo. Of course you can see me again. I'm not going anywhere.'

'Really?'

'Really and truly.' At the back of her mind, she imagined Vinny witnessing this poignant renunciation and being suitably chastened.

Half laughing, half crying, Cosmo got out of his chair and took her in his arms. 'Oh, my darling – '

Suddenly realising all over again what she had lost, Hester clung desperately to what she had just gained. The Blessed Damozel, reeling from the bar of heaven, clasped her hands behind the poet's neck. Cosmo kissed her face all over, brushing her mouth gently. His hand went up her jersey to squeeze her breasts. She felt his erection and found herself concentrating fiercely, praying there would be no repetition of the previous débâcle. Under his hands, she became deliberately limp and passive. His pelvis was butting gently, rhythmically at hers. Gradually the action became harder, until he was grinding into her flesh. Pilot leapt to his feet in his basket, and barked in nervous staccato.

Cosmo lifted Hester on to the edge of the kitchen table, parted her legs and speared her. He was so triumphant he looked almost diabolical, until, plunged up to the hilt inside her, he suddenly laughed. Hester laughed too – it was all right, she had cured him. Her own power made her dizzy. Pilot barked himself backwards, and retreated into the space between the refrigerator and the stove. Still laughing, Cosmo slid in and out of her, until his gathering speed wiped the smile off his face, replacing it with a frown of intent. Hester shut her eyes. Shudders of physical pleasure jarred her spine. She had been afraid that she would blurt out Vinny's name, but when it came to the point he had never seemed further away. Cosmo was sweating and gasping, his thick sinews knitting, as different from Vinny as it was possible for a man to be. 'I'm going to come,' he needlessly informed her. 'I'm coming – ' He did so, charging into her entrails so hard that it hurt, and bellowing: 'Oh, Jesus, Jesus!'

She held his head while he went through the symptoms of a man who has just ejaculated, spluttering and tottering like someone plucked out of the water, nearly drowned. Then the endearments began, the renewed professions of love, blissful sighs of release, face-splitting yawns.

In bed, he lay folded round her, his hairy stomach tickling her buttocks when he breathed. Hester, wakeful, watched the darkness being slowly diluted by the dawn. She felt careworn and anxious, no longer rejoicing in her power or her glorious sacrifice. At first, she had used making love to suppress his pathetic outpourings, but she had not been allowed to get away with it. He had forced her to hear, and by freeing him she had turned the key on herself.

Twelve

Hester made a new beast of Cosmo Brady. She squared his shoulders, opened his suspicious countenance and satisfied his hungry soul. Love stripped away his crusted bark, and he emerged green and tender – handsomer than ever, in a swaggering, stagey fashion. Hester changed the diet of meat pies, banishing his incipient paunch, and sent his shabbiest clothes to Help the Aged. She made him wear aftershave and cut down his smoking. His greying hair was darkened and trimmed for the part of Ludolph, and he grew a small Ronald Colman moustache to highlight the glare of his dazzling teeth. Once more, groups of schoolgirls he passed in the street began to misbehave to attract his attention, but his eyes were fixed upon his Blessed Damozel, and he wafted round the theatre in a blissful cloud of Hammam Bouquet and happiness.

Hester put her own flat on the market and moved into Corsica Street. She had set herself the task of pulling Cosmo's ravelled edges together, and was so successful that the rest of the company was lost in wonderment. The affair caused intense speculation at first, and there were many predictions of doom, but Cosmo's star continued to rise and the sensation became history. The sight of the two of them going home arm in arm, as contented as a pair of nesting doves, became familiar.

Paul's production of *Otho the Great* was now nearing completion. The company had spent five tedious weeks in a black-painted, subterranean rehearsal room, with the daylight hours charging past unseen above their heads. The play, though undoubtedly interesting, proved obstinate, and pencils had been driven through the blocks of verse which resisted performance. Keats's sense of theatre was poor, and large tracts of luminous poetry had to be trampled like grapes to extract some sort of meaning. Paul had tried ludicrous experiments where bold cutting failed, but with the first preview staring him in the face he suddenly became inspired. Ideas poured from him in an unending firework display, and the understudies stopped going to sleep under their newspapers. The whole process made everyone as weary and begrimed as labourers on a building site, but they had a production at last, and the sages of the theatre predicted success.

Every department in that vast medieval fortress hummed with industry. There were thrones in the paint shop, swords in the armoury, ringlets in the wig room, and uniform jackets pinned to stout calico dress-forms up in wardrobe. Morag, the designer, had made a model of the set, like a Pollock's Toy Theatre, perfect and complete down to a little pasteboard figure on a wire, to show the scale. There was to be a floor of varnished parquet, hideously expensive, and a semicircle of grey gauzes. Through these, the actors were to materialise and vanish, figures in a mist. Additional scenery was to descend from the flies. There were heraldic banners artfully scorched and tattered, garlanded pillars, coats of arms, and two immense portraits of Cosmo and Sir Freddie, in the style of F. X. Winterhalter.

Against this twentieth-century restraint, the costumes were to blaze with Victorian splendour. The actors had all been up to the fourth floor for fittings, standing passive in an airless cubicle while Morag draped them in swatches of dyed silk and pulled kid gloves over their fists. Sir Freddie Brough, as Otho, had shaved off part of his beard, and was dressed to look as much like the Emperor Franz Josef of Austria as possible. He would have preferred his usual fur robes and crown, and he shouted that it was all a lot of bloody nonsense. In his day, he said, if a play was historical, you did it period – you didn't frig about setting it wherever you fancied. His bad knee was giving him hell, his court breeches cut off his circulation, and he utterly refused to carry a sword. However, when he saw the F. X. Winterhalter portrait, he became entirely reconciled. He made a private arrangement with Morag to buy it at the end of the run, and told everyone he meant to hang it in his dining room.

Vinny discovered he could not act with a monocle unless he glued it to his eye, and it left a permanent eczema of gum arabic on his skin. Both Vinny and Cosmo had to wear sabres, and they learned the peculiar, groin-thrusting stride which would prevent them from tripping over. Cosmo had the perfect build for uniform, now that his stomach no longer bulged, and he looked magnificent in everything Morag designed for him.

The women dragged round pounds of ruched and bustled taffeta, laced so tight that the whalebone left red welts across their stomachs. Hester had a set of imitation sables hired from Bermans and Nathans, which looked tawdry in daylight but glossy and splendid on stage. Horatia was sour because the style of the clothes did not suit her attenuated frame. Morag had padded her white court dress with enough stuffing to fill a sofa, but her collarbones jutted above it, and the sheen of the material made her look weazen and sallow.

Kitty had been given the part of Cosmo's page. The smallest dress-form was wheeled out for her, and a scaled-down hussar's uniform contrived. For the second act she had a white sailor suit, and she looked so charming that Morag called all the dressers in to admire. Lately, however, the relish had gone out of such things for Kitty, and only one compliment pleased her. Cosmo walked into the fitting room to have the epaulettes tacked to his tunic, and when he pulled her hair and said he could eat her, Kitty's cheeks reddened with gratitude. She did not mind that he turned away immediately to frown at himself in the mirror, because she was training herself to exist on crumbs now that he lived with Hester. Kitty alone thought Cosmo was wonderful as Ludolph. The others complained that he barnstormed, messed around with the blocking and spat in their faces when he spoke. Horatia said all he needed was a couple of 'Arr Jim lad's and a parrot on his shoulder. The problem was that Paul let him rampage at will. Kitty saw what the others did not – that there was a certain power in Cosmo's unleashed energy, and that the slightest snub would quench it entirely. His confidence was too newborn to sustain a breath of criticism, but Horatia and Vinny were tired of being used as whipping posts for his artistic misdemeanours. Paul nagged the rest of the cast into excellence, and used their talents to cover the bald patches in Cosmo's scenes.

Paul had been eau-de-nil for a week when Cosmo began his affair with Hester. It had been thought best to break it to him gently, and Madge and Horatia, for once in accord on this errand of mercy, did so at a special supper in a dark corner of Francesco's. To see the colour draining from his lips, as Madge told Hester afterwards, was perfectly ghastly. After wearing the willow for a few days, Paul began to enjoy his unrequited state. It fed a touching strain of sentiment in his austere production, and sparked off a series of poignant images. He moulded the actors into postures which felt artificial but looked lovely, he assured them, from the front.

'Sob louder!' he called from the back of the stalls, on the day before the technical run-through. 'I can't hear you. This isn't a film, you know!'

Kitty and Sir Freddie, in whose arms Cosmo lay, were good at sobbing. Bill Duckworth and the man playing the priest were not, and their constipated snivels sent Horatia into agonies of suppressed laughter as she lay dead upstage. Madge and Alice, kneeling over her, felt she was wicked, and stared into the distance to disassociate themselves. 'Horatia Geld-schmidt, keep your feet still!' shrieked Paul. 'I won't have buggering about!'

They were rehearsing on stage, on the set of *The Caucasian Chalk Circle*, which was playing in the theatre that evening. The front rows of the stalls were littered with bags, overcoats and the prone, bored bodies of the understudies. Malcolm Snelling sat in a plastic chair stage left, with the prompt copy of the script.

'Well, it's awful,' said Paul. His voice fell flatly across the auditorium, which looked dingy and unnatural under the working lights, there being no definition between it and the stage. He hurried down the aisle and climbed the temporary wooden steps, with Patsy at his heels. The dead bodies sat up and rubbed their heads, and the crouching figures furtively massaged their cramped tendons.

'Better,' said Paul, 'but still awful. There's something the matter, I don't know what. If only it didn't look so much like the last act of "The Student Prince". The critics will make jokes about Mario Lanza, I know they will. Not that I ever read reviews. Jim, where were you sitting?'

'The other side of the slips,' said Patsy, 'and I'm afraid I couldn't hear. You all have to watch the ends of your sentences.'

'Not you, darling.' Paul placed himself next to Cosmo's recumbent body and squeezed his neck. 'The critics never understand my approach. They'll deliberately overlook the German simplicity of "Otho". Not one of them will have the intelligence to compare it to Schiller or Kleist. Alice dear, what on earth were you gawping at? Please try to look more distressed. I can't tell you how eerie it looks otherwise. Madge, keep holding Horatia's hand, but look through the door at Cosmo.'

'But I can't see him because Hester and Bill — ' began Madge.

'Just pretend,' said Paul. 'Handkerchief, Hester, otherwise fine. Don't do it any worse than that.'

Hester grimaced to herself, for she always forgot the right moment to produce the handkerchief. It had to come out just after she had drawn off her glove for Cosmo to kiss her hand, but not too soon, because then it looked as if she was about to sneeze.

'Stop giving performances,' Paul ordered. 'This is meant to be a tableau, like a narrative painting. The focus is on Cosmo's death, and nobody will look at you unless you're looking at him. Bill, stay down on one knee, and keep leaning over him, but cheat it back a little – you're masking his feet. And why can't you sob? Harry, the same applies to you. It's no good just looking mildly sorry, is it?'

'Gersa's a soldier,' Bill protested. 'He's seen men dying before.'

'I want resounding sobs. Jim, go up to the circle and see if you can hear him next time. Now Kitty – Kitty Ashbourne. Where is she?'

'Here, Paul. Was I late again?'

'No, no, darling. Come here.' He took her hand, pulling her downstage and rattling through her lines. ' "Alas! My lord, my lord! they cannot move her! Her arms are stiff – her fingers clenched and cold." Now, when Cosmo falls forward, take his whole weight. It doesn't look natural at the moment. And really hold him.'

'I'm too heavy for her,' said Cosmo.

'Hmmm.' Paul meditatively drew his hand across Cosmo's forearm.

'Freddie, run forward earlier, to help her.'

'I do try, you know,' said Sir Freddie, in an injured voice, 'but my bad knee makes it jolly difficult. I can be further downstage to start with if you like.'

'Yes, try it.'

'He weighs a ton, you know. I shall probably get a hernia.'

'Just try it.' Fretfully, Paul returned to the stalls. 'We'll go from "Tomorrow, son, be your word law." '

'We've got to clear in ten minutes,' Malcolm called down. 'They're waiting to set up for the Brecht.'

'Where did he say?' boomed Sir Freddie, as the other actors milled around him.

'Tomorrow, son,' said Malcolm, glancing down at the book, and taking a half-finished cigarette Horatia thrust at him as she passed.

They had been going over and over this scene since lunchtime, and Kitty was the only person besides Cosmo who was not soured and disgruntled. She loved acting Cosmo's death, for she cradled his head in her arms and felt the warm weight of his body crushing her legs.

'Tomorrow, son,' began Sir Freddie, 'be your word law; forget today – '

'I will when I have finished it!' said Cosmo, in his mad hiss, which rained saliva into Sir Freddie's beard. 'Now – now, I'm pight, tight-footed for the deed!'

'Alas! Alas!' Hester said, rather flatly, struggling to remove her tight rehearsal gloves.

'What angel's voice is that?' exclaimed Cosmo, stopping short and rolling his eyes. 'Erminia!' She managed to pull the glove off in time for him to kneel and kiss her hand. 'Ah! gentlest creature, whose sweet innocence was almost murdered; I am penitent. Wilt thou forgive me? And thou, holy man, Good Ethelbert – ' Harry Tafflin, the priest, stepped forward to sprinkle him with holy water, the cue for all the onlookers to cross themselves, 'shall I die in peace with you?'

'Die, my lord?' enquired Hester.

'I feel it possible.' Cosmo dropped from mad hiss to tragic croak, and Hester conscientiously wrapped the handkerchief round her nose.

There was an aching, unnatural pause, followed by Sir Freddie saying violently: 'Oh, fuck, fuck! It's me! I'm dreadfully sorry – '

'Physician,' prompted Malcolm. They were all quite used to Sir Freddie's attacks of amnesia.

'Physician?'

'I fear', said the doctor, 'he is past my skill.'

'Not so!' Despite his difficulty with the lines, Sir Freddie managed to invest his famous voice with a thrilling pathos.

'I see it – I see it – ' Cosmo shouted. He leapt to his feet, and strode stiff-legged to the front of the stage. 'I have been wandering! Half mad – not right here – ' he tapped the side of his head, 'I forget my purpose. Bestir – bestir, Auranthe! Ha! Ha! Ha! Youngster!' He suddenly seized hold of Kitty, who had been told to tremble at his unwonted harshness. This she did well enough to draw a murmur of 'Lovely' from Paul.

'Page! go bid them drag her to me! Obey! This shall finish it!' Kitty shrank back in horror as Cosmo, with a wild laugh, pulled a wooden rehearsal dagger from the belt of his jeans, and brandished it aloft.

'Oh, my son! my son!' wailed Sir Freddie, shuffling towards him. 'This must not be!'

'Am I obeyed? A little talk with her – no harm – ' Cosmo directed a hideous smile of lunacy at the dress circle, so they could be in no doubt as to his intentions. 'Haste – haste – haste!' he barked, and Kitty pelted away upstage.

'Set her before me – never fear I can strike.'

Several voices: 'My lord! My lord!'

'Good Prince!' cried Bill Duckworth emotionally.

Cosmo staggered away from him, saying, 'Why do ye trouble me? out – out – away!' with a large gesture, as if shooing hens. 'There she is! take that! and that!' He lunged at the air. 'No, no, that's not well done – where is she?' He retired downstage, and clasped his forehead despairingly.

This was Kitty's cherished moment, and she wondered if she would ever get through the play without her whole hide tingling with anticipation. She was to throw open the doors, displaying Madge and Alice bent over Horatia's dead body, and run to Cosmo's side.

'Alas! My lord, my lord! they cannot move her! Her arms are stiff – her fingers clenched and cold.'

'She's dead!' bellowed Cosmo, and he cast his whole weight into Kitty's arms, with such force that her knees buckled under her and the breath was nearly driven from her body. Sir Freddie dived forward in time to prevent her collapsing, and they laid him downstage centre, in his final position. Kitty embraced his head and shoulders, while Sir Freddie knelt over his body, clutching Cosmo's nearest hand to his breast and frequently kissing it as he wept. Once he began, everyone else wept too.

'Take away the dagger,' said Harry Tafflin.

'Softly; so!' Bill plucked it from Cosmo's nerveless grasp. He did it sternly, for this was his cue to start sobbing.

'I fear it could not harm him,' said Sir Freddie.

'No!' groaned Bill, as heartrendingly as he could. 'Brief be his anguish!'

Kitty held Cosmo's perspiring face near her own, and wept piercingly. Her fresh, high, childish keening sounded a chord

143

of human grief in the midst of the sombre spectacle, as Paul had intended it should. In the stalls, his eyes misted over, and his beautiful creation danced.

'She's gone! I am content. Nobles, good night!' As Cosmo spoke, Kitty felt his buttocks contracting with the effort to project his voice. 'We are all weary – faint – set ope the doors – I will to bed – tomorrow – ' His head lolled heavily to one side, glassy-eyed. Sir Freddie closed them gently, and there was no more movement on stage, and no sound except the scattered crying. Bill and Harry, seeing Patsy's tiny figure marooned among the mauve plush seats in the circle, sobbed with all their hearts.

'And curtain,' said Paul, wiping his eyes. 'Much, much better.'

The group round Cosmo collapsed with groans of relief.

'Okay everyone!' shouted Malcolm. 'Ten o'clock tomorrow.'

Cosmo playfully swept Kitty into his arms. 'Well? How was that?' he asked her, laughing.

'Lovely, darling,' Horatia said behind him. 'Dazzlingly adequate. At a couple of points, I almost thought you were going to act.'

Thirteen

At six o'clock on the first night of *Otho the Great* the theatre smelt of festivity and fear. The principal actors tenderly nursed their exposed egos, carrying wan faces above churning bowels. Vinny was vomiting out his terror in the second floor gents, and the trestle table inside the stage door was piled with facetious cards and flowers, in strict observance of the tribal ritual. Sir Freddie had sent the entire company sprays of white heather in miniature pots. Horatia had irises from Tommy, Kitty had carnations from her parents, and there was a sheaf of creamy pink roses in cellophane for Hester, from Cosmo. Everyone knew they were from Cosmo because Madge had managed to get the little card out of the envelope to look.

Fright made Horatia grim and unusually silent. She sat in her cubicle with the curtains drawn, painting a peachy bloom on her thin cheeks. Madge had been made up for an hour and, now that she had finished Blu-tacking her cards round the mirror, she was at liberty to sit on the divan in her corset and petticoat, talking to Kitty.

'I took poor Alice some of my Estée Lauder cover-up. If she puts it on under her base, it'll never show.'

'Poor soul,' said Kitty. 'Colin again?'

'Yes, wouldn't you know it. He went on one of his benders, and a policeman brought him home. And he wouldn't go to bed but kept hitting her, and apparently the policeman kept saying Will you be all right Madam? because at one point he had the cheese knife. Oh, it sounds dreadful.'

Alice had arrived at the theatre that morning with a black eye. Nobody referred to it in front of her, but they were all sorry, and tried to show it in small ways.

'I told her to come down here in the interval.' Madge gestured towards Horatia's cubicle, and mouthed: 'Will she mind?'

'No, of course not,' Kitty assured her. 'But there's only one bottle, Madge, so don't go telling the whole building.'

Madge rubbed under her arm, where the whalebone was biting into her flesh. 'I bumped into Vinny just now. In fact, he almost knocked me over.'

'Going to throw up, I suppose?' asked Kitty.

'Yes, as usual. I told him not to have that pot-roast. I said, you know how you get.'

'Do stop wittering, Madge,' Horatia snapped, from behind her curtain. Kitty and Madge raised their eyebrows at each other meaningfully. 'If you can't keep quiet for two minutes, bugger off and let me get ready in peace. Where's the bloody dresser with my frock?'

At six twenty-five, there was a settled atmosphere of concentration and nerves.

'Otho company,' Malcolm's voice said blithely over the Tannoy. 'Good evening, ladies and gentlemen. This is your half-hour call. Half an hour, please, and jolly good luck to you all.'

'This is the bit I loathe,' Vinny said. 'The waiting. I feel as if I was about to be executed.'

'Hmmm,' said Cosmo. He was trimming his moustache with nail scissors, and striving not to show how irritated he was by Vinny's behaviour. Vinny was roving hyperactively round the dressing room bare-chested, in high, polished boots and hussar's breeches.

'Why the fuck do we do it, eh? Times like this, I wish I was a chartered accountant, or something. Don't you?'

'Hmmm.'

Vinny flung open the window, and began to sing Buddy Holly's 'Rave On' in a loud voice.

146

'Shut the window,' Cosmo said crossly, snatching at a card as it blew off the table. Vinny obeyed, and stopped singing.

'It's the half,' said Cosmo. He meant 'Shouldn't you be ready?'

Vinny flung himself into his chair in front of the mirror, and said in a clipped voice: 'It is a far, far better thing I do than I have ever done. It is a far, far bigger prat I make of myself than I have ever been.' He glued in his monocle and began to apply paraffin wax to the ends of his false moustache. While he was fixing it to his lip, he looked slyly aside at Cosmo, who was frowning as he arranged his turban. In the first scene, he was supposed to be disguised as an Arab, and his costume was a deliberate copy of Lord Byron's Albanian dress. Vinny knew perfectly well that his singing was annoying. He longed to reach across and cram the turban over Cosmo's eyes; he longed to shout 'You pompous, boring old fart' into his ear.

Astonishment was too weak a word for what he had felt when he heard Hester was sleeping with this man. What on earth did she see in him? Even his good looks were ridiculous. The Albanian dress made him into a flashy parody of a silent film star. Shades of Douglas Fairbanks, Vinny thought, or Rudolph Valentino in *The Sheik* – all glittering teeth and white knuckles. How could any woman take it seriously?

'My desert is waiting,' sang Vinny, delighted with the way Cosmo's suspicious eye rolled towards him, 'Oh, come there with me!'

'Otho company,' Malcolm's voice said. 'The house is now open. Please do not cross the stage. Thank you.'

Cosmo lit a cigarette, without taking his solemn eyes off his reflection. What does he say to her? Vinny wondered. In a way, he supposed he was jealous. He was perfectly happy with Rosamund, but he had got used to the idea that he had broken Hester's heart – everyone had told him so at the time. And yet, in a matter of weeks, that heart had mended sufficiently for her to move in with Cosmo Brady. He had always known that Hester would not survive on her own for long – she was not the type. Obviously, she had gone for Cosmo on the rebound, but that did not explain Cosmo's vast contentment. Surely he knew that he had got her half-price in the sales? Vinny considered that Hester's charms were wasted on him. She's not the woman I took her for, he thought.

'You and Hessie are coming to Francesco's tonight, aren't you, Cos?' he asked.

'Yes.' Cosmo looked belligerent. He did not care for the apellation 'Hessie'.

'I don't know where Rosamund gets the energy,' Vinny remarked, 'organising a first-night binge at two days' notice.'

'We still think ten quid a head is rather steep,' said Cosmo. Yes, you would, you arsehole, Vinny thought. He thumped Cosmo between the shoulder blades, as hard as he dared, and said: 'I haven't wished you good luck yet, have I? Knock 'em dead, Cosmo.'

Cosmo smiled at him, a slow, shy smile. 'Thanks, same to you.'

Vinny itched to hit him again. He went to put on his tunic. 'Oh, I'll be fine, if I can just get the first line right. Apparently, if I drop the end of the sentence, the whole show dives.'

'You always sound okay.' Cosmo shifted nervously in his chair. 'Paul's hardly said anything to me at all. Do you think – do you think he likes what I'm doing?'

Vinny no longer wanted to hurt Cosmo. He was not a kind man, but he had an odd feeling stirring in his vitals which he recognised as pity. 'He loves you to death,' he said. 'You know that.' They paced out the rest of the waiting time together in comparative peace.

'Otho company, this is your Beginners' call. Your calls please, Miss Geldschmidt, Mr Bliss, and all concerned in the opening of Act One. Stand by please, Mr Chambers and Sir Frederick. Thank you.'

Vinny found Horatia, bloodless under her paint, smoking a last cigarette in the quick-change room. He kissed the side of her wig. 'Give us a drag, mate.' She gave him the cigarette, and he manoeuvred it carefully under his moustache.

'Are you feeling all right now, Vinny darling?'

'Oh yes, love. It's good luck when I park a custard.'

'I've got nineteen pins in this fucking tiara, I'm so terrified it'll fall off again.'

They hovered in front of the mirrors, strangers to their new costumes, still trying to reconcile themselves to their startling appearances, and live up to them.

'How's poor Cosmo?' asked Horatia.

'Geldschmidt, this will break your heart. He asked me if Paul likes what he's doing.'

They both snickered unkindly.

'Don't be too anxious about him, darling,' she said. 'He's convinced that he's the greatest actor in the world. One of these days, he'll get found out.'

'Not tonight?'

'Oh, stroll on, Vinny, the critics will eat all that John Barrymore stuff.'

Vinny began to fiddle with the pot of gum arabic that had been set for him in case his moustache came unstuck. He let the glue-brush drip patterns across the white formica table. 'I know I'm hardly the person to say this, but I can't help wondering what Hessie sees in that wally.'

Horatia looked delighted. 'I've been trying to guess what you thought about it. You've been awfully quiet.'

'Yes, well, it's not my place, is it? She deserves better, that's all.'

'I believe he's quite good-hearted,' said Horatia.

'I daresay. I couldn't give a toss. All I know is he's a bore, and a pompous one – the kind that knows it all. She can't be in it for the conversation. It's probably sex. Hessie likes her oats, so he must be dynamite in bed.'

Horatia cackled, her pagan eyes kindling with amusement. 'Shall I tell you something?'

'What?'

'Something about Cosmo.'

'If you like.' Vinny replaced the lid of the glue pot and ground the cigarette under his heel. He had begun to think about going on but, when he started to preen in the glass, Horatia put her hand on his arm and made him look at her.

'Well. I've slept with him.'

'Ha ha. Pull the other one.'

'No, I really have.'

'What? You mean you fancied him enough to – when was this?'

'Two years ago. We were on tour together. And Vinny darling, let me tell you, it was hopeless.'

'How do you mean?' He shifted his feet uncomfortably and tried to shrug her bony fingers off his sleeve. Her face was inches away from his own and her scent was stifling him.

'It was a shambles. I can't think why I bothered – he had a tremendous crush on me, and perhaps I was flattered. He used to get these erections when we were on stage. I used to see his codpiece swelling, I kid you not. And he followed me round like a puppy, so eventually I thought Why not? And darling, it took me two solid hours to get his clothes off. There I sat in my hotel room, listening to him droning about God, and wishing like anything I'd brought sandwiches and a thermos.'

'Couldn't he get it up, then?'

'He had a stonker you could have hung your hat on. But when we finally got down to it, he came in two seconds flat. Premature ejaculation. I'm told it happens to Catholics all the time.'

'The poor old bastard.'

'So Hester's certainly not in it for the sex, take that from one who knows.'

'Well,' Vinny said thoughtfully. A charge of power shot through his own loins. This explained a great deal. 'Well I never,' he said. 'I say, Horatia – '

'What?'

'Remind me never to sleep with you. God almighty.'

Malcolm came to the door with a torch. 'On you go. Have a good one.'

They walked round the back of the black backdrop, listening to the audience, and picturing the big guns of Fleet Street ranged against them. Vinny settled his clanking sabre against his leg, and Horatia coughed furtively. Silence fell upon the auditorium, a terrible, expectant hush, as the house lights faded. There was a long, throat-parching wait, during which Vinny and Horatia stared at the cue-light. When it flashed green, they parted the curtains and walked on in blue darkness.

Vinny, with a bad taste lingering in his mouth from Horatia's unsavoury revelation, took up his position, with his dry heart knocking in his chest like a nut in a drum. The lights blazed, and the audience saw him downstage centre in his white uniform, while Horatia's still figure posed behind the gauze.

By the interval, the unpleasant part of the tension had evaporated. The evening was going well. Vinny whooped and danced along the corridors, raising the dull echoes, and the applause crackled out over the backstage relay. On the stairs, he saw Hester, quite alone, manipulating her heavy skirts as she turned on the landing. The long train on her dress made her as slender and graceful as a reed. Dreamy and unhurried, she was sweeping out of sight through the fire doors.

Vinny ran to catch her up, grabbing her hand. 'Hello, sweetheart. You look fabulous – can't get over you in that costume.'

She was taken by surprise. 'Vinny – hello. I – it's going well, isn't it?'

'How are you?' He could not help thinking about Cosmo's sexual inadequacy, and searching her embarrassed, reproachful face for signs of dissatisfaction.

'I'm fine,' she said.

'What are you doing down here? Visiting Cosmo?'

'No – Horatia asked me. She's got a bottle of champagne.'

'Oh, she has, has she? That's the first I've heard of it, and we're right next door.'

'How's Rosamund?'

'Great. You'll see her at Francesco's later. Why won't you ever talk to me these days?'

'Don't I?'

'Come off it, Hess,' he said urgently. 'You know you've been avoiding me.'

'I'm not – I haven't – '

'I thought we were going to be friends.' Vinny knew he was causing her pain. He was selfishly glad that he could still do so.

She walked on, her hand loose and passive in his. 'We are friends, aren't we?'

'Yes, of course.' Playfully, he swung her hand backwards and forwards. 'I told you you'd find someone else, didn't I? Although I must say, I nearly shat a brick when I heard it was old Brady. Did you always fancy him? You certainly kept it quiet.'

'Shut up, Vinny,' Hester said mildly, 'shut up.'

'All right, okay, I'll shut up. If you like him now, that's all that matters.'

'You – ' she began. They stared at each other when they halted outside Horatia's dressing room. Suddenly shy, Vinny pushed open the door and shouted: 'Where is it, then? Where's my champagne?'

Several female voices cried: 'Go away!'

Hester hurried into the room, and Vinny sauntered after her. 'Garçon! A glass of champagne, please.'

'Oh Hester, why did you tell him?' demanded Horatia. She was leaning over the divan, pouring warm champagne into paper cups for Madge and Alice. Vinny snatched Kitty up in his arms.

'You'll give me some, won't you, my little dumpling?'

'Put me down!' cried Kitty, laughing and trying to kick his shins. 'Oh Vinny, please put me down – I'll bring you some if you go away.'

'This is women only,' said Horatia, 'so you bugger off. You shouldn't be drinking during a show anyway.'

Vinny gently set Kitty down. 'You'd like me to stay, wouldn't you, Alice?' He remembered the black eye and bent down to kiss her hand.

Madge shrilled, 'No she wouldn't!' and tittered inanely. Alcohol always upset her system.

'Go on – oh please – I'll show you my cock – ' He made as if to open his flies, and even Hester laughed.

'Oh, for God's sake,' said Horatia, 'put the tired old thing away.'

'Out you go.' Kitty pushed him into the passage and shut the door on him. He rattled the handle and hooted at them through the keyhole.

'I suppose I'll have to give them some,' said Horatia, filling two more paper cups. 'You take it, Kitty.'

Kitty took the cups to the room next door, pleased to be asked. Outside, she listened to Vinny's voice and Cosmo laughing.

'Room service!'

Vinny let her in, unbuttoning his tunic to air his scrawny chest. The atmosphere in the room reminded Kitty vaguely of her brothers' bedrooms at home. There were the same mixed flavours in the air of feet, school changing rooms, athlete's foot powder and dirty talk. All masculinity impressed her. Cosmo lounged beside the mirror, resplendent in a blue uniform barnacled with gold braid, flushed and grinning.

'Doesn't she look a duck, Cos?' Vinny tweaked her sailor collar as he took the champagne.

'Like Ganymede, cup-bearer to the gods,' Cosmo said. 'To what do we owe this honour?' His dazzling crescent of teeth gleamed at her flirtatiously.

'It's from Horatia.'

'How kind.' He downed the drink in one gulp, and crushed the cup. 'Say thanks, won't you?' To Kitty's mingled shame and pleasure, he drew her on to his knee. He was so large and solid that it was like sitting against a wall, except that she could feel the heat blasting out from his stomach and groin. She inhaled the healthy smell of his sweat, and the exotic tang of the Hammam Bouquet shaving lotion Hester made him wear.

'Oh, you dirty old man,' said Vinny, combing brilliantine into his hair, 'you filthy old sod. Let the poor little thing alone.'

'Is Hester next door with you, Kitty love?'

'Yes – shall I fetch her?'

'No, just tell her to lay off the drink, there's a good girl. She's got to drive me home – I intend to get splendidly pissed tonight.'

'Okay.'

He squeezed her waist and released her. 'Thank you, darling.'

At the door, Kitty lingered to say hesitantly: 'Is it going well, do you think, Cosmo? How do you feel?'

'Fantastic,' said Cosmo, 'fan – tastic.'

'Good luck for the second half.'

'Just watch me, love.'

'You might learn something,' said Vinny, winking at her.

Kitty leaned shivering against the wall in the corridor, smelling Cosmo on her clothes, and imagining licking the salt off his damp flesh. She did indeed watch him during the second act, hidden in the wings, waiting for the moment she would take him in her arms, in a fever of carnal anticipation. Cosmo thundered through the rest of the performance like a storm, on a thrilling, upward spiral of energy. He heard the words forming patterns of meaning he had never dreamt of before. His muscles and nerves were straining, but he rode the many-headed beast of the audience effortlessly. Horatia whispered to Vinny that he was really almost good, and Vinny, surprised, agreed.

It was one of Paul's maxims that a great story should be inevitable, but never predictable. Inevitably, Prince Ludolph raved and died, and Keats's hoary old tragedy reached its romantic climax. Kitty, with Cosmo's sweat trickling into the crook of her arm, sobbed out real tears as the lights went down but, although they dropped on to his wet face, Cosmo was too dazed with exhaustion and triumph to notice.

The applause broke like a wave while the actors were stumbling back to the wings in darkness. There was hasty hugging and wringing of hands as they formed the lines for the curtain calls. Malcolm flashed his torch round their euphoric faces.

'Well done, my brave little Thesps. Don't forget to lock up your swords before you leave, will you?'

Cosmo searched for Hester, bending absent-mindedly to accept Horatia's kiss.

'Oh darling, that was brilliant – listen to that! Can you believe it's over? God, I'm a rag. It felt like being fed through a mangle.'

The understudies and bit players trooped out in a long line. Out came the principals, two by two, ending with Hester, on the arm of the man playing Albert. Cosmo watched her, aching with love. If this is it at last, he thought, if this is my success, she shall have everything. Vinny ran on to bow with smiling self-deprecation, as if he was really too democratic to care for the attention. Then Horatia, all gracious charm, looked boldly into the eyes of the people in the front three rows as her satin skirts billowed in a deep curtsey. The critics were running up the aisles like ants, as the ushers pinned back the doors. When Cosmo stepped out, the applause swelled, and there were actually shouts and whistles. He savoured the moment, loose-limbed and panting, as if he had been engaged in some brutal sexual act. Sir Freddie made his way down to the front with imperial slowness, and his bow was deep and dignified. There were yells of 'Bravo!' from the cheap seats. The whole company joined hands to bow together, then filed back into the wings. The applause rolled on, and Sir Freddie said in his loud voice that he was all for milking it for another go. It was finished. They swarmed, kissing and congratulating.

'That's the best it's ever gone – '

'Listen to them – '

'They were standing up in the slips!' Sir Freddie roared. 'Bloody nearly a standing ovulation!'

Hester waited on the stairs, holding the bannisters to steady herself against the tide of people dashing past, wrenching off clothes and false hair as they went. Vinny and Tommy were wrestling, and kicking each other's behinds. She fought her way back to where Cosmo stood, submitting to Sir Freddie's whiskery kisses. Cosmo had changed. There was a shimmering mantle of success around his shoulders.

'This is the lad, eh, Hester?' Sir Freddie was saying. 'I'll buy you a drink, old darling, just as soon as I remove this Ruritanian garb.'

'Well?' Cosmo grabbed her hands, imploring. There was only one opinion he wished to hear. Hester clasped his sweaty head in her arms, nearer to loving him than she had ever been.

Fourteen

The notices, for Cosmo in particular, were excellent.

'Brady's deeply-felt performance endows the character of Ludolph with a tragic intensity only hinted at in the text.' (*Guardian*)

'This heroically built Irish actor plays Prince Ludolph as a loner, whose eventual madness springs from his refusal to acknowledge the treachery of those around him.' (*The Times*)

'Cosmo Brady's musical Hibernian voice never allows us to forget that Keats is, first and last, a poet.' (*Independent*)

'When the bitter truth dawns, Brady's fist closes convulsively round the hilt of his sword. It is a moment to be treasured, and there were few who did not feel a thrill of genuine theatrical magic.' (*Daily Mail*)

Cosmo found himself one of the bloods of the theatre. His jokes were laughed at, his opinions sought, and even his agent treated him with respect. Horatia sourly advised him not to let the queues at the box office and the repeated curtain calls turn his head, but he only laughed at her and told her she could go to hell. He seemed to think she had lost her power to deflate him.

Two weeks after the opening of *Otho the Great*, Horatia invited Kitty out to lunch. Kitty was flattered, but apprehensive. Horatia apparently held her in high regard, but there was no ignoring the woman's reputation as a troublemaker. Paul often said she could set the angels in paradise bashing each other over the head with their harps. When he heard about the lunch, he told Kitty to find out what she wanted right at the start and spare herself trouble. There was bound to be something, he said, since he had never known such a woman for scheming. He added that Kitty should take care, as Horatia was in one of her rages – it was quite obvious why.

It was not obvious to Kitty. Why should she be in a rage? Here she was, genial and eager to please, plying Kitty with innocent questions about her family. Kitty was drinking dry Martini over a plate of smoked salmon. Being unaccustomed to alcohol at lunchtime, she was very slightly tipsy, with an oiled tongue, and numb, velvety fingers. As she talked, she stepped out of her tight new shoes and stretched her pinched toes on the carpet. Rather strangely, Horatia had chosen Simpson's in the Strand for their rendezvous, and she had dressed for the occasion in an explosive, speckled tweed, as if she was going beagling. At first, Kitty was daunted by the masculine pomp of the surroundings, and the fact that the only other female in the upstairs dining room was one ancient crone in furs, having her meat cut up by her grandsons. Horatia, however, was so humorously intimate, so sinuously persuasive that she made the panelling and sporting prints seem comforting instead of oppressive. Smells of dark porter and thick gravy fought with Horatia's bal à Versailles, which Kitty thought she must apply with a crop-sprayer, as it snaked its way into the tulip-shaped glass of white wine pressed on her when she had finished the Martini.

Horatia's eyes were black as olives, ironic and disdainful under long, heavy lids. Her profile was a roman bronze, filed down to sharp bones. For the first time, Kitty noticed a slightly foreign intonation in Horatia's voice; a staining of certain vowels, and an exotic emphasis at the ends of sentences.

'I heard you telling Madge', she said, 'that you wanted to leave your Summer Garden.'

'Yes, I'm thinking about it.'

'And I know why.' She speared a pathetic, wrinkled little potted shrimp with her fork. 'It's because you think you're in love with Cosmo Brady, isn't it?'

'No!' Kitty protested naively. An alcoholic flush dyed her from ears to ankles.

'Oh, for goodness sake, don't get embarrassed about it. Did you imagine I hadn't noticed?'

'I do quite fancy him – ' Kitty began.

Horatia smiled indulgently. 'Nonsense. You'll be kissing his shadow soon. You watch him from the wings, for God's sake. Such a give-away – nobody else can be bothered these days, not even Paul. And you quote the utterly unremarkable things he says as if they'd been handed down on tablets of stone. You've been the colour of a brussels sprout ever since he took up with Hester.'

'That's not true. You know how much I like Hester. I'm glad they're so happy.'

'That's what amazes me,' Horatia said, elegantly buttering a shard of toast. 'You're being so noble.'

'I haven't any choice,' Kitty pointed out.

'Why didn't you make a pass at him when Faith left? He was so desperate, he'd have slept with anybody.'

'I did sort of try,' Kitty admitted.

'Fluttering your eyelashes at him gets you nowhere,' stated Horatia. 'He's as thick as a post, darling. Nothing short of a hand down his flies convinces him you're serious.'

'You know him terribly well, don't you?' Kitty asked respectfully.

'None better. That's why he can't bear me – I know how he slags me off behind my back.' She leaned forward. 'But I'm really fond of him, no matter what he says. I can hardly bear to see him making such a fool of himself over Hester.'

'But she loves him – '

'Oh, it can't last.'

'Poor Cosmo. I hope you're wrong.'

'Do you? Do you honestly?' Horatia looked sceptical. 'I don't think you're really in love with him at all.'

'I wish I wasn't.'

'Bullshit,' said Horatia sharply. 'You're revelling in it. You don't know the meaning of a real passion. His meaty body makes you think naughty thoughts, and because you're such a good girl you feel you have to wrap it all up in a lace doiley. You wouldn't be sublimating poor old Cosmo so desperately if you'd had any sort of experience with men.'

Kitty picked up her knife and fork, and began to eat again. 'Do I sublimate him?'

'Nobody is as divine as all that. As soon as you leave home, and stop having fantasies in your frilly little bedroom, you'll get over him. Mark my words.'

This was very rude, but Kitty could not help laughing, although she reddened again.

Horatia laughed too, suddenly relaxed. 'Anyway, he's years too old for you, and he's such a boring fart most of the time. You'd get awfully tired of waiting for his occasional flashes of sex-appeal.'

Kitty was still giggling tipsily, despite knowing that when she recalled this conversation later she would be mortified.

Horatia refilled their glasses. 'Have you found anywhere to live yet?'

'No,' said Kitty.

'Why don't you move in with me? I'll only charge you a pittance – I do so hate living on my own.'

'With you?' Kitty was amazed.

'Why not? We get on wonderfully well.'

'Do we?'

'Kitty, I've been sharing a dressing room with you since September and we haven't fallen out once. That, for me, is an absolute record.'

Two pictures presented themselves to Kitty. One was the Summer Garden, her sentimental gingerbread house, afloat in a lake of rustling boughs. The other was the house in Betterton Street, dark, jumbled and exotic, with Horatia prowling inside it, closing the heavy curtains against the spring sunlight as if afraid its rays would crumble her to dust. Probably, like everyone else, she shopped, washed, peeled potatoes and unblocked drains, but Kitty doubted it. She imagined her in evening dress, lying in a satin-lined coffin with her hands folded across her breast and her eyes glassy, like a vampire in an old film. It should have been a straight choice between black and white but, mesmerised by Horatia's worldliness and glamour, she was tempted.

'Do consider it, Kitty. I'm sick to death of my own filthy company.'

'But what about Tommy?' Kitty asked cautiously, unsure how matters stood between Horatia and her 'village idiot'.

'Oh, he doesn't live with me. The sex is great, but the table-manners are revolting. I generally call a taxi for him and he goes home to Camberwell. Sometimes he sleeps over, if I'm feeling kind.'

'You are horrible to him,' said Kitty.

'Darling, he can barely read. And when he writes a cheque – which is the nearest he'll ever get to literary composition – it looks like he's used a carrot dipped in tar. You never saw such a peasant's scrawl.'

'He's fond of you.'

'Yes, I know, poor love,' Horatia looked sober. 'Perhaps I'd be nicer to him if I had someone like you around.'

'Look, do you mean a word of this?' demanded Kitty. 'Are you teasing me?'

'No! If you were there, my damned soul wouldn't be nearly such a burden. It's sometimes just awful to be me. I know I'm nasty, Kitty but it's only for effect. When I feel attention slipping away from me, I have this compulsion to chuck a couple of people on the fire. It's sheer perversity, and it's never quite so strong when I'm with you.'

'You're with me at the theatre,' Kitty said, 'and it doesn't stop you being nasty to Madge every single night.'

'That's what you think. I'd have killed her by now, if it hadn't been for you.'

'Poor Madge,' said Kitty piously.

Horatia sighed, 'Oh, all right, poor Madge. But aren't actors terrible fools?' Her contemptuous pronunciation of the word 'fool' reminded Kitty of the Biblical warning that whoever shall say to his brother 'Raca' shall be in danger of the council, but whoever shall say 'Thou Fool' shall be in danger of hell fire.

'What, the whole profession? Including us?'

'There are no grey areas,' Horatia said. 'Actors are either all surface intelligence and delight, or foaming nutcases who howl at the moon.'

'Why do you do it, then?'

'Oh, it all stems from the parties my mother used to give when I was a child. As soon as I stopped being amusing, I was packed off to bed. It made a performing monkey out of me. My sister was always dragged out howling after half an hour, with her mouth full of cocktail cherries. She grew up perfectly normal.'

An octogenarian waiter brought their main courses. While her beef was being carved at the trolley, Kitty leaned back in her chair and surveyed the room.

'Horatia!' she exclaimed suddenly. 'Look!'

'Well, I never,' said Horatia, glancing at the doorway. 'It's Hester.' She squeezed lemon over her river trout.

'But what an extraordinary coincidence!'

'Yes, it's a small old world, isn't it?' She was smiling to herself, in a thoughtful, private way.

'Won't she die when she sees us?'

Hester's hair was neatly woven into a thick plait and tied at the end with a taffeta ribbon. She wore a new navy coat with gilt buttons and looked most unlike herself. A grey man in a dark suit clasped her arm protectively and said something to a costly-looking woman who had halted to settle her dainty morsel of a handbag.

'Parents,' said Horatia, with her mouth full. 'Isn't Lady S. a stunner? You can see where Hester gets her looks.' She watched the door ravenously.

Kitty laid down her fork with a piece of roast beef impaled on its prongs. Cosmo came in, stiff and preoccupied, wearing a suit and tie. On the threshold, he turned and beckoned impatiently. In came a bulgy, elderly woman in a purple coat with a fur collar and a matching fur hat. Over her arm, she carried a large patent leather bag with a vicious clasp. Her patent leather shoes stretched painfully across her bunions, and her ankles were swollen and puffy above them.

Horatia let out a triumphant hoot of laughter. 'Isn't she gorgeous?'

'What? Who is she?' Kitty murmured in confusion.

'Can't you tell? That's old Ma Brady.' She rolled back in her chair and laughed fragments of trout into her napkin. 'Poor old Cosmo!'

Kitty laughed too, with a flaming face. Mrs Brady, looking accusingly round the room, was seated at the table, in a tremendous state of confusion over her handbag, coat and scarf. She had sat down with the coat still on, and went into a series of contortions as Cosmo and Hester's father tried to get it off her.

Sir Oswald Stretton was idly scanning the room when he met the bold black gaze of Horatia. Puzzled, he turned to speak to Hester. She saw them, nudged Cosmo, and waved delightedly. Cosmo's mouth fell open in astonishment, then he drew his brows together in a thunderous scowl.

'Come on.' Horatia leapt up briskly, brushing the crumbs out of her lap.

'Horatia, we can't – I don't think we should – '

'They've seen us now.'

Horatia approached their table with a sparkling, predatory smile. Kitty hastily fumbled on the floor for her new shoes, and hurried in the downwind of Horatia's scent, trying to telegraph apologies to Cosmo. She had never seen him so furious. His murderous glare did not soften when he finally tore his eyes off Horatia to look at her, and she wished she knew what she was supposed to have done. Just as she reached the table, her new shoes betrayed her. The unscratched soles skidded, and she fell on her bottom with a bone-racking thud. Cosmo, being nearest, was obliged to get out of his chair to help her. For a second, his face, remote with anger, was inches away from her own. He whisked her up and dropped her on her feet so roughly that Kitty was left with the sickening impression that he would have liked to shake her.

Resisting the urge to massage her throbbing buttocks, she

waved off the solicitous chorus and tried to efface herself behind Horatia. 'Fancy seeing you here,' Hester was saying happily. 'I'd never have guessed this would be one of your haunts. Daddy spotted you – don't you think that was clever of him? You've heard me talking about Horatia and Kitty, haven't you, Mummy?'

'She never stops. I feel as if I know you.' Lady Stretton smiled at Kitty encouragingly.

'Hester, you're absolutely radiant,' said Horatia, 'and what about you, Cosmo? Don't you look smart? Doesn't he look smart, Mrs Brady? I bet you're proud of him.'

Mrs Brady replied with a carbon copy of Cosmo's belligerent glare. She knew Horatia as the wanton woman who had showed her bosoms on the television – Cosmo had reported her outrage at the time.

'Mary's staying with us until Saturday,' Hester said. 'Isn't that nice?'

One of her sweet blue eyes narrowed in a suspicion of a wink. Kitty managed to smile through the scarlet agony in her bottom.

'No wonder Cosmo's looking so happy,' said Horatia suavely. 'Well, we mustn't keep you from ordering. We only popped across to say hello.'

'Glad you did,' said Sir Oswald. 'We always love meeting Hester's theatrical friends. Are you drinking anything, Cosmo?'

'I'll wait for the wine, thanks,' Cosmo said, in a clenched voice.

'Er – Mary?'

'I never touch the stuff,' announced Mrs Brady.

Hester looked away from Horatia, and bit her bottom lip, in an effort not to laugh.

'You don't have to have alcohol,' said Cosmo testily.

'Well, what have they got, then?'

'How should I know?'

'Don't you drink at all, Mrs Brady?' asked Horatia, edging closer. 'Goodness, how awfully wise of you – '

'We must get back,' Kitty interrupted hastily. 'Come on, Horatia, our food's getting cold.'

Final courtesies were exchanged and they returned to their table. Horatia's tallow-coloured face was flushed with excitement.

'I wanted to stay!' she complained. 'Why did you have to drag me off in such a hurry? Hester's father was about to ask us to join them!'

'Honestly, Horatia, how could you?'

'How could I what?'

'The way you were looking at Sir Oswald Stretton – as if you were going to rip all your clothes off – and making poor Hester corpse. And what on earth is the matter with Cosmo?'

'Oh,' Horatia was suddenly distant. 'He's always in a paddy about something.'

They ate their congealing food. During coffee, Horatia openly stared at the group across the room, and kept up a rude commentary on Mrs Brady. 'She's putting on her glasses to read the menu. Wouldn't you know she wears glasses with little blue bits at the top? Her complexion looks like a mildewed flannel – that's the way Cosmo will end up, Kitty, so you're well out of it. Now she's having to squint at the trolley. God, she looks suspicious. You'd think they'd asked her to eat a boiled Carmelite nun.'

Kitty laughed, but mainly from nerves. Horatia was making no attempt to keep her voice down, and her demeanour was openly insolent. The more resolutely Cosmo ignored her, the more she misbehaved. By the third cup of coffee, she was almost snarling.

At the other table, a waiter was removing the dirty plates. Cosmo rose, saying something to Hester. She looked surprised, and rather uneasy, but she nodded and turned to her parents with an explanatory smile. A ghastly heaviness settled across Kitty's stomach. Cosmo was striding towards them, aggressively buttoning his jacket.

'Shit,' said Horatia. The aggravating glitter died out of her face, leaving it gaunt with dread. 'I'm beginning to wonder if this was such a good idea after all.'

'What?' Kitty squeaked. 'If what was a good idea? Oh my God, Horatia, don't tell me you knew they were going to be here!'

'Forgive me, Kitty, forgive me – ' Horatia mumbled, rapidly and almost inaudibly, 'I shouldn't have – '

Cosmo lunged at Horatia, snatching her wrist. 'What the fuck do you think you're doing?'

'Oh Cosmo, language, language!'

'You've gone too far this time, you treacherous bitch!'

'God, that hurts.' Horatia's eyes were vitriolic. 'Let me go.'

He flung her arm back at her. 'You'd better have a bloody marvellous excuse for this. Come on, let's have it, before I smack it out of you with the back of my hand – ' His voice was a suppressed roar, and he was trembling in his effort to control his rage.

Horatia nursed her wrist sullenly. 'It's a free country.'

'How could you do this to me? You knew how difficult it was going to be with my mother and Hester's parents – you knew it was important to me – that's why you wanted to bugger it up, isn't it? For Christ's sake, what have I ever done to you?'

'Cosmo darling, sit down. Everybody's looking. I only wanted to get a glimpse of your mother, and when you so meanly refused – '

Cosmo slammed his fist down on the table. Coffee slopped into the saucers and Kitty jumped like a hare. He turned on her violently. 'And what about you?' he demanded. 'I suppose you thought it a terrific fucking joke, coming along to spy on me – I bet he makes a dick of himself – very bloody funny, and I hope you're satisfied!'

Kitty, rigid with terror, began to sob. Unable to bear his blind, furious face, she fixed her eyes on the plate of macaroons in front of her, and her tears made sepia blots on their gleaming white domes.

'Now, look what you've done!' whispered Horatia passionately. 'Leave her alone. She didn't know anything about it – she thought she was just having lunch with me. She wouldn't have come if I'd told her!'

'Don't you give me any of your bullshit – '

'Just lay off her, Cosmo. Can't you see for yourself it's true?' She whipped a pungent handkerchief out of her bag and handed it across the table to Kitty. 'Poor little thing, she's never seen you in one of your tantrums. It's an unsavoury sight, isn't it, darling?'

Cosmo gave a high groan of frustration. 'Why do you always do this to me? Why do you want to ruin everything I do? If you hate me so much, why don't you just come out in the open and say it?'

'I don't hate you,' said Horatia. 'Stop dramatising. Piss off back to the Strettons.'

He pressed his hands into his face. 'I'm sorry, all right? Kitty, listen love, I'm really sorry.' He bent down to plant an angry kiss in her hair. 'You're never going to get the chance to do anything like this again, Miss Horatia Geldschmidt. You've had it this time. No more getting round me with invitations to that pretentious fucking morgue you live in – this is it, do you hear me? I am never – never – going to speak to you again. Kitty, for God's sake stop crying, sweetheart. I should have known it was all her fault.'

'If you could see what a silly turd you look,' said Horatia. 'Everybody's staring at you.'

'Before I sever relations entirely,' Cosmo said, 'you might as well know that Hester and I are engaged. It'll spare us the trouble of telling the rest of the theatre. We're going to be married in August, as soon as the season's over.'

Kitty's last hopes were so feeble that they died with scarcely a pang. 'Oh Cosmo, how lovely!' she sobbed. 'How beautiful – I know you'll be happy – '

Cosmo looked taken aback, then suddenly smiled. 'Darling, what a sweet thing to say.' He crouched down beside her chair. When his face was level with hers, Kitty saw the distilled fury drying on his lashes. 'And I was such a bastard, yelling at you like that. What on earth can I do to make you forgive me?'

'Nothing – just send me an invitation, so I can come and dance at your wedding.'

'All right.' He embraced her, and gently kissed her cheek. Kitty put her arms round his neck and wept into his shoulder, trying not to get snot on his suit. Cosmo rubbed her back affectionately.

'Congratulations,' Horatia said. Her face was haggard and ghastly.

'Kitty,' said Cosmo, 'will you please tell that bitch I don't want her congratulations. And will you please tell her that if she ever uses you to do her dirty work again, I'll tear her hair out.'

Horatia's eyes were opaque, and her pallor corpse-like. 'You prick,' she said. 'You bogtrotting Irish prick.'

Cosmo unlocked Kitty's arms. He straightened, gazing studiously over Horatia's head, rammed his tie inside his jacket, and returned to his table, to assure Hester untruthfully that everything was fine. Kitty mopped her face and blew her nose, ashamed of herself for crying – it seemed a bad omen for a betrothal.

Fifteen

Hester sadly decided that it was no use worrying about being such a captive when she had nowhere to escape to. Cosmo's unnerving nightmares always brought home to her how securely she was netted in his frightening love. After apologies and whimpers of relief, he usually dropped quickly back into sleep, while she lay tense and resentful, eyeing the digital alarm clock as it bled out the hours in a ghostly green halo of light.

The nightmares oozed through the gaping holes in the myth Hester was trying so hard to sustain. They were Cosmo's subconscious messages to himself, urging him to see by what a glass thread his whole happiness was suspended. He imagined she sensed when his dreams were turning bad because their minds were in mystic communion, and the horrors appeared in her own dreams like warning angels. Hester, feeling this was probably how it ought to be, played down the fact that she could not help waking because he shouted aloud and wrenched off the duvet. She had a brisk, governessy way of switching on the bedside lamp and prodding his shoulder to wake him, which Cosmo found comforting. Despite being clammy with terror, he was fascinated by his own complexity, and usually asked her what he had said. His own memories were confused. Presumably they were so horrible that his mind refused to dwell on them. Hester edited her replies, because the subject of the nightmares was pitifully obvious to her. He called her name, or implored mysterious people to bring her back. There were sinister undertones, too – prayers which were hammered to fragments by the words 'bitch', 'cunt' and 'whore'.

Now, as he clutched her in his sleep like a talisman against evil, half-stifling her with his possessive embrace, Hester renewed her vow that he should never guess. It was hard work but, now Vinny was lost to her, what did it matter? A passable imitation of contentment was the most she had left to hope for, and she was training herself to swallow the daily dose of disappointment without choking. Cosmo had many excellent qualities. She recited them to herself as a rosary of justification: he was kind, he was unselfish, he lived to please her. It was not his fault that she still pined for Vinny. It's not my fault either, she thought. I've tried to love him. Cosmo deserves to be loved, but I just can't do it.

Once or twice, by terrific efforts to suspend disbelief, she had nearly loved him. He had proposed to her most beautifully in the candlelight behind the trellis at Francesco's, holding a diamond ring in the palm of his great hand. The picture he had painted of their safe, rose-embowered future had been so attractive that, for once, Vinny's watchful phantom faded. Later the same evening, however, that poor illusion fell apart when she saw Cosmo on the edge of the bed, clipping his toenails. If she wanted to preserve her pretence of fondness, she had to see him laundered and on parade. The smallest reminder of his human functions filled her with disgust. Sometimes the sight of his shaving things on the bathroom shelf was enough to distress her. A debilitating nausea gripped her if she found a hair of his in the sink. It was all right when they were eating together, or making love, but the traces and smells he left around the flat were sickening. She polished and scoured round him, dousing him with scent and hanging pungent lozenges above the lavatory. It really was not fair, when she had gladly endured the stench of Vinny's feet, the brown skidmarks on his Y-fronts and his lurking, unflushable turds. Cosmo's dirty underwear was whisked into the washing machine as if it had been a pile of dressings torn off a gangrenous wound.

Everyone, including Cosmo, interpreted this domestic

slavery as a sign of absolute adoration. Her parents were too blind with satisfaction to see that their only child was drowning. Hester tried not to blame them for failing to hear her silent cries for help. She had been very quick to introduce them to Cosmo, knowing how critical they were about her lovers and half expecting them to talk her out of it. When Sir Oswald and Lady Stretton instantly approved of him and took him to their hearts, she had been bewildered and confused. She listened to their assessment of his character and thought she must be wicked not to have noticed the points they raised. Her father declared him mature and intelligent; her mother said he was considerate and had beautiful manners. Handsome too, she said – what a pair they made. The twelve years between him and Hester meant that his wild oats were well and truly sown. He was ready to take his responsibilities seriously and settle down. There had been talk of marquees in the garden, of true lover's-knots done in flowers by a very clever friend of Lady Stretton's, of a lace veil turning yellow in a drawer upstairs. Nobody noticed Hester's silence. Her mother said: 'I'm glad you've got over that desperate character you were seeing before Christmas. Daddy and I never liked the sound of him.'

What she was building, at such cost to her soul, evidently had value in the eyes of the world. Hester did penance for her barrenness of heart by transforming the forlorn flat in Corsica Street into a lover's paradise, a cosy nest straight out of the pages of a magazine. There were fresh curtains in the sitting room. The two 'Troops Out' posters in the hall, a legacy from Faith, had been replaced with flowery pastels in coloured wooden frames. She heaped the sofa with bright chintz cushions and put the old, depressing batik ones in Pilot's basket. Geraniums bloomed on the kitchen window sill, and the air was fragrant with baking, ground coffee and clothes warm from the iron. She was giving Cosmo the home she had meant to build for Vinny.

She sighed, and tried to ease her cramped legs into a more comfortable position. Cosmo's slumbrous arm lay across her like the trunk of a tree. He was snoring slightly, and sleep had washed the years off his face. Not for anything could she hurt him. His character was always bursting out in guilt-inducing rays of sweetness. Sometimes he apologised after making love, because she seemed to want more than he could give her. When this happened, Hester was humbled into the dust. She recalled the Saturday after the opening of *Otho*, when she had dragged him round the Tottenham Court Road branch of Habitat. He had patiently wheeled the trolley while she loaded it with lamps, blinds, towels, plates, cutlery – all the contents of a maiden's hope chest. She chose a 27-centimetre carving knife, lethal and gleaming, to replace the existing one, the handle of which was tied to the blade with string. Cosmo had filled in the Access form with great good-nature – nobody could call him mean – but he had made her pay him one penny, the lowest coin in the realm, for the carving knife. If he gave it to her as a present, he explained, it would cut their love.

Sixteen

In the first week of April, Paul Fletcher's company took *Otho* and *The Miser* up to Manchester for a fortnight. The draughty, gilt-encrusted old theatres of the provinces were standing empty, and the Arts Council had put out a decree that the big companies of the capital must tour if they wanted their subsidies increased. Sets, lights, wigs, props and costumes were sent ahead by road, in vast pantechnicons the size of Noah's Arks. The actors were crated up like geese and dispatched in a reserved second class railway carriage.

They had moaned a little about the inconvenience, but a carnival atmosphere prevailed when they gathered on the platform at Euston station on the Sunday afternoon. Actors on tour are positively expected to behave like noisy, drunken, oversexed rabble. Away from spouses, mortgages and children, their responsibilities were minimal. A hotel in a strange city provided the perfect setting for debauchery and intrigue, and anything was permitted, as long as they turned up sober at the Palace Theatre in time for the half-hour call. People without lovers nourished hopes of acquiring one, or at least the temporary use of one. Those who had left lovers behind covertly sized up the available talent and wondered if they dared risk a small fling. Sour spirits, with no prospect of any sort of lover, went round reminding everyone that the *Measure for Measure* company had all caught crabs in Bath the previous year.

They descended on the Midland Hotel in a rapacious hoard,

rupturing the Sabbath calm with demands for drinks, ironing-boards and porters. They thundered and shrieked along the quiet, carpeted corridors, they loudly criticised the restaurant menus, and they harassed the switchboard operator by tele-phoning each other's rooms. Madge Worsnip plugged in her heated curlers and began embalming herself with creams and oils, intending to cut a dash at dinner. Alice Knowles and Sir Freddie Brough sat on Alice's bed, sharing a plate of ham sandwiches and reminiscing about the good old days of touring in a wicker basket. They agreed that the younger generation, with their loutish manners and uncouth plays, could never have endured it. We had stamina, Alice was saying. Oh, those horrible 'combined' digs. A shilling extra for use of cruet, and you always had to share with the company nympho-maniac. Supper on a tray at half past ten with the poodle act playing at the working men's club, and woe betide you if you were caught smuggling food into the bedroom. 'All the big London shows used to try out in Manchester,' Sir Freddie said nostalgically. 'No cheap previews in those days. If they pelted you with eggs, you had a chance to save your arse before you got to Shaftesbury Avenue. Oh, Alice darling, Ivor Novello made a heavy pass at me in the lobby of this very hotel. I was loved once.'

Vinny parked his rucksack and switched on the television, enjoying this opportunity to think his own thoughts without Rosamund strip-searching his brain. He was very fond of her, but she was chief of the mind-police, and dreadfully difficult to deceive. She knew him up and down, front and back, from the crown of his head to the seams in the palm of his hand. He was beginning to get the measure of her now, and she was no fool, not in any department. He had lived with clever women before, but they had all committed the silliest blunders where he was concerned. Rosamund had coolly selected Vinny as the father of her planned baby, and she patrolled the waters round him like a piranha fish.

Bing Crosby was singing on the screen. Vinny watched him blindly while he mulled over the problem of Hester's engagement. He had not yet had the chance to consider it properly, because Rosamund had been observing him, and all his energies had gone into the required display of indifference. Now, he took out the anger he had been hiding and looked it over. Hester was throwing herself away. Was this, he wondered, the ultimate cry for help, was it some obscure female form of revenge, or did she really want to marry Cosmo Brady?

Vinny knew what she was like when she was happy. He could not fail to see that she was miserable now, and he was savagely pleased. Her beauty had become wistful and tender, and it haunted him amazingly. These days, she seemed withdrawn and etherealised, hedged about with tantalising reserve. The love she had lavished on him was buried deep in her heart, and there it would stay until the last judgment, unless Vinny raised his finger to summon her back. Stretched out on the counterpane of his hotel bed, Vinny smiled to himself. Cosmo was too thick to notice that he was missing something. He possessed the shell of Hester without the essence, and he probably had no idea how animalistic she could be underneath the refinement, how she could fornicate with delicious abandon and climax in a fever of raw emotion. Vinny could not help regretting the days when he had lived in her atmosphere of unquestioning adoration. Not that he had ever allowed her to voice any criticisms, poor girl. He had found her pliable enough to mould into the perfect woman, and when he had finished his Galatea she turned out to be tiresome and clinging. Rosamund did not cling. She would drain his active loins to the bone in her endeavours to get pregnant, but caresses tended to skid on her worldly varnish. With pleasurable sadness, Vinny dwelt on Hester. What a delightful, romantic affair it had been; what a sweet, summery paradise he had lived in until he got so bored; what heights of decency he had almost reached.

In the room next door, he heard her singing. She was on the other side of the wall, and he would sleep with his head six inches away from hers. 'Early one morning, just as the sun was rising, I heard a maiden singing in the valley below.' He dwelt upon this charming image, and the familiar harangue which followed it: 'Oh, don't deceive me! Oh, never leave me! How could you use a poor maiden so?' Poor maidens could never bring themselves to believe that love grew cold. By the very tenacity of their passion, they set themselves up as martyrs. Leaving and deceiving them was almost a kindness, since it permitted them to fulfil their destinies, so celebrated in song and story. He knew that Hester still loved him, although she was managing her life with a toughness and resilience he had never suspected in her. Still, he did not doubt he had made the right choice. He was not cut out to be the other half of a pair of Dresden figurines – too old and too addicted to sleazy pleasures. All the same, he was desperately curious to know what was going on in Hester's mind, and he found himself wishing he could break down the ashy crust of her reserve just once more, to warm himself on the embers underneath.

On the other side of the wall, Hester was flitting about between suitcase and wardrobe, her arms full of clothes. Cosmo stood by the window, watching her and trying not to get in her way. She was humming, and this rare liveliness made him feel unwanted. She enjoyed all the social idiocies that went on among the actors, and she was good at joining in. He was not, and if he tried to keep up with her he felt like a lumbering bear on a rope. Rowdy groups became restrained when he sat down among them, and he was always sure he heard sighs of relief when he took his sombre presence away. Hester had done wonders for his relationships with his colleagues, but he was not sure he could stand living in their pockets for a fortnight.

There was worse than this. As soon as the door closed behind them, he had recognised the room, and while Hester admired the fittings in the bathroom, the contents of Cosmo's stomach had turned to cold cement. It was the room in which he had had his ghastly experience with Horatia Geldschmidt. Every inch of it had been stamped on his memory during that long sleepless night. The anguish, guilt and humiliation rushed back to him, fresh as the morning when he had scuttled away down the passage with his limp tail dragging.

'Look, Cosmo, what's the matter with you? Why are you so cross?'

He would never tell her about Horatia. The whole affair was too shameful and grimy for Hester's pure ears. However, he had no trouble finding an answer. There were plenty of grievances in his collection.

'Well, it's these fucking beds.'

'I asked at the desk,' Hester said placidly, shutting a pile of jerseys into a drawer. 'They're very sorry, but they haven't any doubles free.'

'Oh, for God's sake – '

'Don't shout, darling. It won't hurt us to sleep in single beds for two weeks.'

'It's the principle of the thing,' he said crossly. 'I took the trouble to ask Malcolm in advance and he's cocked it up. Or perhaps it was deliberate. Perhaps he thinks I'm so old and boring that I don't have a sex life. Vinny's got a double bed and Rosamund's only coming for the weekend.'

'Never mind,' said Hester, in an absent, smoothing-down voice, 'we can always push them together.'

'Don't be ridiculous,' Cosmo was crosser than ever. 'We'd have to pull them apart every morning, wouldn't we? Do you really want to go through such a ludicrous ritual?'

She stopped what she was doing and looked at him. 'Oh, you funny old thing – I suppose you're worried about what the chambermaid might think?'

Was she laughing at him? For one fraction of a second, Cosmo felt a twinge of resentment. What servants thought never mattered to posh girls like Hester.

'Honestly, Cosmo, you must stop being so self-conscious. Anyone would think the Russians had a satellite trained on you, the way you behave.'

'Bog-Irish, you mean?' he asked. 'Is that it? The oaf from the land of navvies and stableboys, who doesn't know how to carry on in a hotel?'

'No – you know I don't mean that – ' Her eyes widened with dismay, and Cosmo repented.

'I'm sorry love,' he said. 'You know how I hate leaving home.'

She kissed him fleetingly, on the way to the bathroom with her vanity case. 'Cheer up – it'll be fun.'

He tried to cheer up, thinking that perhaps the haunted room would not be so bad if Hester was beside him. He followed her like a sheep, and wrapped his arms round her, smelling her hair and longing to make love.

'I'm going to have a bath,' she said.

He let her go. 'Why?'

'I feel like it.'

'Suit yourself, then.' He left the bathroom in a sulk, and sat down on one of the beds, feeling redundant.

'Cosmo,' Hester said patiently, 'stop it. Stop worrying. Other people manage to cope with leaving home occasionally. They even manage to put their dogs in kennels without the world coming to an end.'

Cosmo had, to his embarrassment, shed tears on leaving Pilot at the kennels that morning. He could not help it. There was so much wire netting, and Pilot's head had looked so round and vulnerable.

'I hope he's not pining,' he said. 'Maybe I should give the place a ring?'

Hester strangled a laugh, and Cosmo said: 'What? What?'

'I just had a picture of Pilot on the phone, saying "Mustn't grumble".'

He laughed. 'I do adore you, Hester. What would I do without you?'

'Why don't you ring down for some tea?' she said. 'You can watch the end of "Going My Way".'

'Christ, no – I hate that film.'

He took *Earthly Powers* out of his suitcase and began to read, trying to ignore the wallpaper with its unpleasant associations, and smelling the fragrant clouds of steam coming out of the bathroom. He would lick her damp, perfumed breasts when she came out, and exorcise his former failure on one of those problematical single beds.

'Darling,' Hester said, from the echoing bath.

'Yes?' Cosmo lowered his book hopefully. From where he sat, he could see one of her pearly arms hanging over the side. She was divine with the warm water running off her, like Venus rising in her scalloped shell.

'What's the time?'

'Twenty to.'

'Oh dear,' said Hester ruefully. 'Oh, I'm sorry. I forgot to tell you.'

Cosmo did not like being apologised to in advance. The way she predicted his anger seemed to prove what a boring and bad-tempered old fart he was.

'Forgot to tell me what?'

'Oh dear. I told Kitty we'd meet her in the bar at six. And Madge, of course, and Alice, and probably Horatia.'

It was impossible not to be angry. From now on, their private life would be dominated by the movements of the herd. 'Don't we see enough of this bloody company? Why don't we just take them to bed with us?' He wondered if she was making a wincing face to herself, as Faith used to do when he shouted.

'Everybody will be there.'

'I daresay.' He picked up his book, gripping it aggressively with both hands.

'Cosmo.'

'What?'

'Would you please speak to Horatia?' This was asked in a small, polite voice. Hester had a passion for reconciliation. Both she and Kitty had been working on him since the incident at Simpson's.

'No,' he said adamantly. Hester was an angel, but there were elements in the case she could not and should not understand. Horatia was obviously waiting to betray him, and what a hilarious joke she would make of it. He wished he could wrench out her evil tongue.

'But darling, it's such a silly quarrel.'

'No! Look, she's not to be trusted.'

'Don't you think – ' Hester was even more polite, 'don't you think you're being just the tiniest bit – pompous?'

'No, no, no!' shouted Cosmo. 'Will you and Kitty please get off my case?'

'Don't you think it might be rather awkward, while we're on tour?'

'I couldn't give a toss.'

The bathwater sucked and gushed. Hester had got out. She came to the door looking small and childlike, swamped in his dressing gown. 'Is it all right if I talk to her? I won't, if you really mind.'

Cosmo stood up, holding out his arms. Poor little creature, it was incomprehensible to her. She came to him, hot drops falling from her ankles, and he embraced her. Surely even Horatia would think twice about saying something to hurt this seraph. If it came to it, nothing that oozed from her cobra's tongue could smirch Hester's inviolable goodness. 'My sweet girl,' he said, 'of course I don't mind.' He cupped his hand protectively round her golden head for a moment, before he released her to get dressed.

When they went down to the lounge, they found Vinny, rolling a cigarette with his feet resting on the low table. Beside him, Madge was dressed in a semi-festive ensemble which had just missed its mark and come down on the wrong side of formality. She was wagging her sausage-like curls coquettishly at Vinny, and sipping a tiny glass of sweet sherry. Her eyes raked the room, terrified of missing something.

'Evening,' said Vinny, smiling at Hester.

'Hello,' she replied.

Cosmo was glad to note that her eyes glazed into distant courtesy and looked straight through him. It was a pity, he thought, that Vinny had been placed in the room next door to theirs. God knew what they would have to listen to for the next fortnight. He imagined Vinny making love with sordid, yowling noises, like a cat in a gutter.

'Don't sit there!' Madge shrieked at him. 'I'm saving it for Simon! He did say he'd be down, didn't he?'

'Yes, love,' Vinny said kindly.

'You did tell him six, didn't you?'

'Yes,' drawled Vinny, still kind. Cosmo could see how intensely she bored him.

'The other chair is for Alice,' Madge lowered her voice reverently. 'She's just gone to ring Colin. They're keeping him another week at the clinic.'

'Oh, dear,' said Cosmo.

'Poor Alice,' said Hester.

They sat down, refreshed now that they had nodded to the shrine of Alice's misfortunes.

'Don't mention it to her, if you can help it,' Madge said. 'I'm trying to keep her mind off it. If she talks about it, I'm as positive as possible. I mean, let's look on the bright side. At least he's not roaming round hitting policemen.'

'Yes, that must be a great comfort to her,' said Vinny, with a sly glance aside at Hester. She absorbed it without reaction.

'The amount of crap she takes from that man is disgraceful,' announced Cosmo. 'She should divorce him.'

'But she loves him!' Madge was shocked by this unromantic viewpoint.

'She doesn't,' said Hester thoughtfully. 'I don't think she knows herself why she stands by him.'

'Because he's there, and he's hers,' declared Vinny. 'One drunken old arsehole of a husband in a clinic is better than none.'

Cosmo thought this remark was in poor taste. He tried to stop the expression of disapproval creeping across his face. Vinny often had this effect on him.

'Over here, mate!' Vinny called to the waiter. Across the room, three elderly ladies in petal hats turned to stare. 'What's everyone having? This is on me.'

Cosmo stifled a groan. He could see how this would go on. For two whole weeks, they would all generously vie with each other to provide alcohol for larger and larger crowds of people. At the end, they would have to settle disproportionately large bills, having subsidised the drinking habits of the women, who hardly ever paid for anything.

'I shouldn't,' said Madge. 'This is my second.'

'You'll never get a leg over Simon with that attitude,' Vinny told her. Madge and Hester thought this amusing, but Cosmo could barely force a frosty little smile. He wondered why he was finding Vinny so offensive, so much more threatening than usual. Watching Vinny flirt with Madge, he realised it was because there was no Rosamund. She was in London, performing *Don't Know Nuffin* at the theatre's Studio until the weekend. It seemed a long time since Vinny had been at large without her. Cosmo considered her a fool for trusting him, but it was one of her more fearsome qualities that she affected not to care what her lovers got up to behind her back.

'Listen,' Vinny was saying, 'anybody know what happened with Horatia and Tommy? Are we supposed to say anything about it?'

'They're not sleeping together,' said Madge. 'Tommy asked the desk for a single room. He told Simon in the lift that he'd just had enough.'

'White to the lips, I'll bet,' said Cosmo, without thinking. The conversation limped for a moment, and he caught Vinny looking at him, knowing and amused. A little shiver blew through his veins.

'Yes, she's a harridan all right,' said Vinny.

'Well, I'm sorry for her,' said Madge. 'She manages her love affairs so deplorably. I think she's rather a pathetic figure, in spite of being so rich. Paul says she's not right in the head. He says one of her aunts is locked up in a home, stark raving bonkers. The way she treats men − '

Horatia arrived, diffusing perfume and elegantly swinging the key to her room. Madge pursed her fuchsia lips round the rim of her dainty glass. Cosmo scowled and looked at his hands. He was angry with himself because this was one of her good days, and he had decided she was looking her best before he could stop himself. She wore her plain, expensive clothes with a sort of careless magnificence. The russet tints were out in her short hair, and she had formalised her appearance for dinner by attaching huge, misshapen bronze clods to the lobes of her ears − she never wore delicate jewellery. After a bout of destruction, her angular face fell into softer, more contented lines. Like a boa constrictor that's just had its tea, Cosmo thought. The miracle was that Tommy had managed to sleep with her for so long. Possibly, he had the innocent courage of the very stupid. How that nice child Kitty Ashbourne could live with such an acidulous bitch was beyond him.

'Want a drink, Geldschmidt?'

'I'll get my own, thanks.' Vinny had asked out of ritual, to include her. They all knew that Horatia rarely drank anything at the moment except champagne, and she saw no reason for contracting her habits to fit those of her poorer colleagues. She ordered a bottle of Mumm's and two glasses.

'All right, what's this I hear about Tommy?' asked Vinny.

'He's gone and left me,' Horatia said, with impenetrable cheerfulness. 'Isn't it desolate? You'd better lock your door, darling, or I might come creeping in to take liberties with your slumbering body. Are you speaking to me yet, Cosmo?'

Cosmo was unable to stop his limbs freezing into an instant sulk.

'Don't,' murmured Hester. 'Don't tease him.'

'Hester, you must admit he's being unreasonable. God knows, I apologised. He's being grossly unreasonable, isn't he, Vinny?'

'No good appealing to me.' Surprisingly, Vinny came to Cosmo's defence. 'I'd love to have an excuse not to talk to you.'

Horatia laughed. Vinny was nearly always in favour and could insult her as much as he liked.

'Did you see Simon on your way down?' interrupted Madge.

'No,' Horatia said, in an insolent voice. 'Did you want him for something?'

'I just wondered what had happened to him.' Madge was offended.

'Well,' said Horatia slowly, 'there was a terrible crowd round the laundry chute on my landing, Madge, and when I pushed my way through they were saying something about a poor man who'd hurled himself down with a wild cry.'

Vinny and Hester giggled. Cosmo wrestled with his own desire to laugh, keeping a poker face because he knew Horatia was watching him.

'I only asked,' grumbled Madge.

'Here he is,' said Hester.

Madge's joy was qualified, for Simon had made the mistake of having Kitty on his arm. 'Just look who I've got next door to me. Are you sure you won't share, sweetheart? Ever so much cosier.'

'Away on tour and trying to get laid,' said Vinny. 'Oh, you slut.'

Madge assumed her bright straining smile. 'I've saved a chair for you, Simon.'

As if he had not heard, Simon took the seat next to Vinny. 'What about you, eh? Rosamund must want her head examined, letting you off the leash.'

Cosmo laughed savagely. This seemed so true.

'Oh, it's all right for some,' Vinny said to him. Cosmo was furious at this implied cheapening of his relationship with Hester.

'You know where you can come on a cold night,' said Madge archly, 'if you don't mind climbing a flight of stairs. Number four-one-four.'

'Got that, chaps?' Horatia picked up Madge's key and showed it round the table.

'Horatia Geldschmidt.' Kitty was stern. 'What have you done to Tommy? I've just had him on the phone. He's incredibly upset.'

'Oh God, Kitty, you should have heard what he called me — absolutely the Tower Hamlets lexicon.'

'You probably deserved it. Go and give him a kind word. He's pining for one.'

'Why should I – ' Horatia began, outraged.

'Go on, a kind word won't hurt you. Go and do it now.' She was standing her ground, not in the least afraid. 'Or I won't speak to you. Nobody will, in fact.'

'Isn't she strict? You see how easy I am to handle? I'm putty in her hands.' This was said to Cosmo, and he very nearly replied. 'A kind word is the limit, darling. Open the suds when it comes. I got a glass for you.' Horatia glided gracefully away towards the lifts.

Hester exclaimed: 'I don't know how you do it! Will she really apologise, do you think, or will she make it worse?'

'She'll apologise. She honestly is fond of him.'

'But how do you dare?'

'It's not hard,' said Kitty modestly. 'The great thing is to get her in front of an audience. She's not as terrible as she likes people to think,' she added, appealing to Cosmo.

'No, no, a thousand times no,' he said. 'Don't you ever give up?'

Kitty looked so crestfallen that he felt obliged to kiss her. He had never forgiven himself for the way he had shouted at her at Simpson's. She sat happily on the arm of his chair, leaning on his shoulder, and exchanging shrugs of regret with Hester.

'Four-one-four, eh?' said Vinny. 'What about tonight, Madge?'

'Whips and thongs,' screamed Madge. 'I know what you like, you pervert.' She adored smutty banter.

'You come in here with your knickers all tattered and torn,' intoned Simon, quoting a venerable company joke, 'and you try to tell me you found ten bob in the gutter.'

'God, is it going to be this vulgar for a fortnight?' wondered Kitty.

Alice came stalking back from the telephone, with heavy tread and blank, expressionless face, and the vulgarity ceased.

Seventeen

The company played *Otho the Great* for their first three nights. On Thursday, *The Miser* joined the repertoire, and a full dress technical rehearsal was called for the afternoon. On stage, the action staggered from cue to cue, with long, chaotic pauses in between. The stage hands were raising clouds of dust with the heavy black curtains, as they tried to block stray shafts of sunlight which were seeping into the false gloom. Patsy, deputising for Paul, sat in the stalls, wrestling with the tawdry confusion. The actors lounged on the set in a trance of resignation, staring at the dizzy tiers of seats, the boxes, galleries and fat plaster mouldings. Upstairs, those waiting to be called sat over tea and Mars Bars in the canteen, with towels under their chins to protect their costumes. The dressing rooms were strewn with knitting, novels, crossword puzzles and Teachyourself books – the litter of people used to sitting out long tracts of boredom.

Hester sat in the dressing room she shared with Horatia, powdering over the ravages in her exhausted face. She had hoped that, without Rosamund, Vinny would feel free to make some sort of friendship out of their old affair. Instead, he ignored her. Perhaps this was just as well, since the days were more manageable when she could only glimpse his back through a forest of other people. At night, however, when there was no such need to keep up appearances, her craving for his attention drove her almost mad. She would lie tensely coiled in her single bed, straining her senses beyond the wall which divided them. The memory of his lovemaking made her writhe against the mattress, silently masturbating to the relentless rhythm of Cosmo's gravelly snores. Afterwards, she usually wept. Cosmo's happiness was ticking away in her hands like a time-bomb. If only he knew how the inside of his white and gold seraph was rotted through with love for another man.

Hearing her name on the relay, Hester applied a little more foundation to the bluish smudges under her eyes, and trailed her long skirts down the narrow, drably-painted stairs. She flattened herself against the exposed hot water pipes as the commedia characters surged past, smiling out of their ghastly white faces.

'What a fucking job for a grown man,' Simon Gartner said.

In the wings, Hester picked her way through the tangled ropes and gaping property baskets. Sir Freddie and Harry Tafflin were on stage, sweating under their low-comedy wigs. Alice stood like a patient cow, chewing wine gums. Vigorous hammering issued from the flies, and two stage hands with cigarettes between their teeth were oiling a squeaky door. The lights changed rapidly over the whole scene, going from dusk to brilliant noon and back again in a matter of seconds.

'Cue sixty,' Patsy shouted. 'Is Hester there?'

'Yes?'

'We're jumping straight to your entrance. Quick as you can, please. Isn't that frigging door fixed yet?'

'No,' said one of the stage hands, 'it'll have to come off its hinges before we go up.'

'Not now,' said Patsy crossly. 'Oh Jesus, can I please remind everybody that we have to break at five? Will people not in the scene please clear?'

The lights went into one more convulsion and settled into their proper state. Malcolm wandered across the back of the set, muttering into his walkie-talkie. Knowing nothing would happen for ages, Hester did not hurry to her place. Behind the thick, soft curtains, the thumps and shouts in the rest of the theatre were muffled.

Vinny was ahead of her, down on his knees searching for their cuelight.

'Here,' she whispered, pulling back a fold of curtain. 'We'd better ask Malcolm to tape it up higher. Awful if we lost it tonight.'

'Yes.' He stood up stiffly, without looking at her. When they performed the play in London, he always managed to avoid waiting alone with her for this entrance. He would plunge through the blacks at the last possible moment, smelling faintly of lager because he had pelted all the way from the greenroom. He was only here now for professional reasons, and he tilted his head away from her, to emphasise the fact. Hester gazed at his profile, and the heat of his body stirred the very roots of her hair. Their breaths mingled in the furred darkness. The dim blue bulb above them bleached Vinny's bones and filled the hollows between with inky shadows. She sensed that he was spinning out a thread towards her, and was almost stifled with suspense. His hand found hers, and he pressed her fingers gently. It was a tentative gesture, most unlike him. When he did finally turn to look at her, Hester became intensely still, terrified that one careless movement would spoil everything.

Vinny circled her corseted waist, roughly pulled her towards him, and slid his tongue into her mouth.

A great pang of love shuddered through her, and she mumbled: 'Oh God, I'll die – I'll die – '

They sucked and licked ravenously, gasping for breath and stumbling against the curtains.

'Hester and Vinny!' wailed Patsy from the stalls. 'Where the hell are you?'

They sprang apart, scrubbing at their smeared faces. The cuelight at their feet was flashing green.

'Sorry Jim,' called Vinny. 'Didn't see the light. We've found it now. Shall we go back?'

'No! Just come on! Jesus Christ.'

Flushed and guilty, they made their entrance. Vinny would not meet Hester's eye during their exchanges on stage. She was too giddy with happiness to care, clumsy and euphoric in the sudden lightness of freedom. Cosmo, standing in the wings with his arms folded, was nothing but a shadow.

At five o'clock, the whole company rehearsed the curtain call and were dismissed until the evening performance. Whooping and jostling, they tore back to the dressing rooms, unhooking their clothes as they went, to extract the maximum amount of time for tea. Sir Freddie resolutely elbowed up the narrow stairs. On the landing, he collided with one of the wig girls, who was carrying a tray of pins, combs, hairspray and spirit gum. In one hand, like Hamlet with the skull of Yorick, she held a wig block made of solid wood and weighing several pounds. Sir Freddie's bulk overbalanced her. She dropped her tray, and the wig block went flying over the banisters. It landed on Vinny's head with a nauseating crack, and he crumpled silently to the floor. Hester, before she knew what she was doing, screamed – the scream of her life, which sent diminishing echoes all the way up the stairwell.

The next few moments were a tumult of shrieks, exclamations, feathers, coloured tights and skidding satin pumps, as those who were already halfway up the stairs swarmed back to see what had happened.

'Look what you've done!' roared Sir Freddie. 'Don't you know how lethal those things are?'

The poor wig girl leant over the rail and saw Vinny stretched apparently lifeless below. She burst into tears, and Sir Freddie immediately clasped her to his padded bosom, saying: 'There there, darling, it was all my fault, clumsy old bugger that I am – '

'Stand back,' ordered Cosmo. 'Let him have some air.'

The other actors shuffled back, as obedient as a flock of sheep. Horatia knelt down and laid Vinny's head across her knees.

'I don't know them,' Tommy Inchbald murmured. He clutched Simon's arm in anguish. 'I don't know his lines – my mind's a fucking blank!'

Harry Tafflin tripped over a rolling can of hairspray and put his foot into a glutinous puddle of spirit gum.

'Is he dead?' Sir Freddie bellowed ghoulishly.

'Hold up a mirror and see if he's breathing,' someone suggested.

'Don't be ridiculous.' Cosmo unfastened Vinny's embroidered waistcoat.

'Oh my good God, if he's dead, I'll never forgive myself – ' moaned Sir Freddie. 'I'll retire – I'll never step on a stage again – '

Cosmo looked up, frowning. 'Where's Malcolm? Has anyone called an ambulance?'

'He's only stunned,' said Horatia, 'but he's going to have a lump on his head the size of a hand-grenade. Vinny, can you hear me, darling?'

An eddy of profound relief went through the spectators as Vinny showed signs of coming round. They had all been seeing themselves in the coroner's court, and then perhaps at a memorial service in St Paul's, Covent Garden, reading the lessons in a choked voice and listening to affecting tape-recordings of Elgar's 'Nimrod'. The atmosphere brightened now that they had permission to enjoy themselves.

The first thing Vinny saw when he opened his eyes was Cosmo's earnest face, a few inches away from his own. Cosmo smiled encouragingly and said: 'Don't move. You'll be all right.'

'What?' Vinny croaked.

Cosmo picked up one of his hands and patted it kindly. 'A wig stand fell on you. Just lie still for a second.'

'Will he be able to go on tonight, do you reckon?'

'Shut up Tommy,' said Horatia, 'you selfish little bastard.'

'My fault, my fault,' mourned Sir Freddie. 'Oh, do buck up, Jessie. Nobody's blaming you.'

The wig girl was now having real hysterics, and Sir Freddie and Harry had trodden glue all over the stairs in their efforts to console her. She was eventually led away by two of the dressers, and doctored in quick change with brandy from the pub next door.

'Okay everyone, break it up.' Malcolm Snelling pushed his way through the ranks, with the air of someone who knows he is terrific in an emergency. 'Right, Vinny, there'll be a doctor at the hotel in fifteen minutes. I'll drive you back as soon as you're ready. How do you feel?'

Vinny managed to form the words: 'Like shit.'

'He's concussed,' said Cosmo. 'Don't rush him.'

Vinny sat up and his nose began to bleed, as it always did in a crisis. Even in his queasy and tottering state, he was careful to avert his face so that he did not bleed on his costume. The scarlet drops splashed on the concrete floor, until Malcolm produced a handkerchief.

Madge had turned the colour of putty under her white make-up. 'Blood!' she quavered. 'Oh, I can't look!'

'Don't, then,' said Horatia.

Cosmo pulled Vinny's arm across his shoulders, and dragged him to his feet. The rest of the company gathered to watch Vinny's shoes scrambling for a foothold, as Cosmo effortlessly whisked him up the stairs. The sensation was over and they dispersed to change, chattering and excited.

'Well, wasn't that thrilling?' demanded Horatia, slamming the door of the dressing room behind her. 'I always adore it when someone misses death by inches. You should have seen Cosmo's face just now, when he suddenly realised he was speaking to me. We've finally exchanged the kiss of peace – Hester?' Horatia paused in the act of stepping out of her petticoat. 'What's the matter?'

Hester was perched on one of the wicker costume hampers, with silent, mascara-streaked tears running down her face. Horatia made explosive noises intended to be soothing, and sat down beside her on the creaking basket.

Hester blew her nose briskly. 'Don't take any notice, I'll be all right.'

'Well, of course, it must have been worse for you than anyone,' said Horatia. Her long nose sharpened as she caught the scent of scandal. Like a squirrel with a nut, she was looking for a way to crack Hester's soul and feast on the secrets inside. 'One forgets, now you're with Cosmo, but naturally you haven't stopped caring about – '

'No.' She could not let Horatia get away with this. 'It was the revolting noise when it hit his skull – it absolutely turned my stomach. That's really all it is. I thought you and Cosmo were incredibly brave.'

'Oh, Cosmo's being wonderful – absolutely saintly. I wish you could see how sweet he's being to Vinny. It's so touching, when you consider how much they hate each other. Vinny will have to be civil to him now, won't he?'

'The merciful shall obtain mercy,' said Hester.

'Eh?' Horatia was perishing with curiosity, and Hester was frightened. She had something to hide, and sensed that Horatia was her enemy. 'Hester, are you sure you're all right? I'm rather worried about you.'

'Yes, I've always been a coward,' Hester said firmly. 'When I was little, I had to give up riding in gymkhanas, because I cried so much when I fell off my pony.' She stood up, and began to take off her dress. 'So, Cosmo's talking to you now, is he?'

'Yes.'

'I'm glad.' She was not glad. 'Don't tell him you found me crying, will you?'

'Why not?'

'He'll only make a fuss. He's always trying to protect me.'

'Rather tiresome for you, I should think,' suggested Horatia.

'Oh no, it's lovely, but don't say anything, will you? I don't want him worried.'

'I shouldn't dream of it.'

When they got back to the hotel, they found Vinny in the lounge, holding a polythene bag of ice cubes to the swelling on his head. The wig girl, still hiccuping, was on his knee, and he was cheerfully telling his circle of admirers how he had vomited all over Malcolm's car.

'He says he's going on tonight,' Kitty told them. 'Isn't he marvellous?'

'I'm glad you're not dead,' said Horatia. 'I would have missed you.'

'That's handsome of you, Geldschmidt,' he said.

'Oh, I do feel so dreadful about it!' The wig girl succumbed to another attack of remorse, and Horatia said, with hectoring kindness: 'Now Jessie, for the last time, it wasn't your fault.'

'Don't think about it.' Vinny gave her waist an affectionate squeeze.

'I nearly shat a brick when I thought I'd have to go on for you,' Tommy said.

'Yes,' said Horatia, 'we all noted your incredibly gallant behaviour.'

'Lay off, Geldschmidt,' ordered Vinny. 'I'm not complaining, am I?'

Malcolm Snelling joined the circle, saying breezily: 'Well, thanks a lot, Vinny. Thanks awfully. Anyone who wants to know what he had for lunch, just come and look at my dashboard.'

'Sorry, mate.'

'Are you sure you're okay to go on?'

Vinny was, and his actor's courage was the great theme of discussion in all the dressing rooms that evening, from number one, the 'Bridal Suite' shared by Sir Freddie and Harry Tafflin, to the large communal changing room occupied by the commedia dell'arte. The accident had cheered them all considerably, and *The Miser*, which had lately been rather pallid, was received by the Manchester audience with gratifying roars of laughter.

After the show, Vinny went straight to his room. Hester would have liked to stay in the hotel bar for a drink, but she made no objection when Cosmo suggested they should go to bed. She was particularly anxious to be as obedient as possible to his smaller wishes until she had worked out a way to leave him. It might be possible, she thought, with careful planning, to break his heart in just one or two places, instead of shattering it to fragments. As Vinny always maintained, nobody ever died of it.

Cosmo was restless and disturbed. She watched him pacing about the room, picking up small objects without seeing what they were and tugging at the lobe of his ear. He was struggling to put something difficult into words – she recognised the signs and waited.

'Hester – '

'Yes, sweetheart?'

'No, don't take your dress off for a minute. Listen, I'm worried about Vinny.'

'What?'

Cosmo did not see her surprise, or her twitch of fear, because he was pacing again. 'He shouldn't have gone on tonight, you know. He's not as well as he makes out. He threw up in the sink during the interval. I just wonder if he's all right next door.'

Hester could not think of anything to say. He was obviously leading up to requesting a favour, and she could not imagine what it would be.

'The thing is, love,' he said unhappily, 'someone should go and see, and I think it ought to be you. No, listen, he doesn't like me. I always seem to irritate him. And I can't help thinking, Hester, how different – I mean, if it had happened to me I'd have you to look after me, wouldn't I?'

Hester's eyes filled again. It was all quite hopeless, when Cosmo insisted upon having these attacks of goodness. He misunderstood the tears.

'I know what I'm asking, but just for tonight, if you could, you know, forgive him – '

'Yes, I'll go now. How nice of you to think of it,' said Hester dismally. 'He doesn't deserve it.'

'Oh well,' said Cosmo, smiling shyly, 'there'd be no world unless people sometimes got favours they don't deserve. I don't really deserve you, but here you are.'

Give me a gun and I'll shoot you, Hester thought. It would really be a lot simpler and kinder than what I'm planning. 'I shan't be long, then.'

A moment later she was knocking at Vinny's door, shivering and tender, as if she had lost a layer of skin. There was no reply, so she called his name softly and tried the handle. The door was unlocked and she went inside. Vinny lay on the bed like a corpse. His eyes were closed, and he looked drawn and colourless. Without his bright hues, he was older, and the lines around his mouth showed, fretful and uneasy. The light from the lamp on the bedside table made fan-shaped shadows under his sandy lashes. She stood over him, taking in all the vulnerable points that women love to discover and men hate to have observed. Touching his shoulder, she sat on the bed.

'Vinny?'

He opened cloudy, bloodshot eyes, and hoarsely said: 'What are you doing here?'

'I came to see if you're all right. Can I do anything for you?'

'Cut my head off, and chuck it out of the window.'

'Does it hurt?' She felt his forehead timidly, waiting for a sign from him that would allow her to become intimate.

'Agony.'

'Did the doctor give you something?'

'Paracetamol,' he said. 'I didn't take it.'

'Why?'

'I didn't want to fill my system with toxins.'

'Oh Vinny, what a time to get herbal. I've never understood why you won't take aspirins and Rennies and things, when you snort such tons of coke. Where are they?'

'Table.'

'I'll fetch them.' She went to the bathroom for a glass of water, and recognised his shaving things with affection – the lidless can of foam, and the safety razor, with unwholesome grey froth clinging to the blade. While Vinny swallowed the tablets, she stood awkwardly with her hands behind her back. They were both embarrassed. The seconds went by; still he gave no sign. He lay back against the pillows, massaging his eyes and groaning. Perhaps it was unfair to expect anything when he was in such pain.

'You'd better take your clothes off,' she said. 'You can't sleep like that. I'll help you.'

'No, I'll do it presently.'

'For God's sake,' she said, offended, 'I've seen it all before. Lift your foot.' She took off his shoes.

'Hess, please – '

'It won't take long.' She had in the past undressed him on several occasions, when he had been too drunk or stoned to do it himself, and she stripped him naked with great efficiency, folding his clothes carefully. When she had pulled the covers over him, she could not leave. He watched her, shading his

194

weak eyes. Hester's breasts ached with love for him, he looked so sad.

At last, he said: 'He's waiting for you, I suppose?'

'Yes.'

'What a mess. Look, I'm sorry.'

'Sorry for what?' Her little hands folded into fists.

'You know – this afternoon. I don't know what makes me do it. You're furious with me, aren't you?'

'No,' said Hester flatly.

'Rosie will be here tomorrow.'

'Yes.'

'We couldn't do anything, even if we – maybe it's just as well. Does Cosmo know you're in here?'

'He sent me as a matter of fact,' she said. 'He was worried about you.'

'So that's why you came?'

He was offering her back her pride, and she thought she had better take it. 'Yes. I hope you'll feel better tomorrow. Goodnight.'

'Hess, I'm glad you came but – you know – '

She was not convinced. Vinny never half-wanted anything. He pursued what he wanted with his whole soul, and he had kissed her. It was not much, but she still hoped.

'Goodnight.' She switched off the light and left him.

In the room next door, Cosmo was sitting up in bed, watching television. He was eating a cheese sandwich and wearing the maroon pyjamas he had insisted on bringing for decency's sake, in case there was a fire.

'How's he doing?'

'He'll be all right.' Hester pulled her dress over her head to hide her face. 'I made him take some painkillers.'

'Oh good,' said Cosmo. 'Switch off the telly, will you?'

Lying in bed, Hester waited until his snoring started, and then she cried herself to sleep.

Eighteen

The pattern was nearly complete, and the eldest of the Fates whetted her shears to cut the thread. Vinny had lied to Hester in a feeble attempt to ignore the impulses which were about to complicate his life. He owed it to Rosamund to try, but it was useless. Through the biting pain in his head, he could feel a hormonal storm brewing. It broke while he slept, illuminating his concussed dreams with lightning-flashes of revelation.

When he opened his eyes in the thin spring sunlight, and lay listening to the sound of running water on the other side of the wall and Cosmo's sweet voice waking the plangent echoes in the bathroom, Vinny realised that for the first time in his philandering life he was genuinely in love. Finding a soft place somewhere in his toughened hide, love had made an incision. He saw the thousands of opportunities he had missed when he lived with Hester. His instantaneous possession of her had made him complacent, and he had failed to look properly at what he had won.

Luxuriously, he gave himself up to his desire. It was Rosamund's fertile period, and she was due to arrive in Manchester that evening for a weekend of intensive fornication. Cosmo trailed after Hester like a ball and chain – the situation ought to have been impossible, but it was not Vinny's custom to let other people stand in his way. According to his laws, the feelings of other people were never his responsibility. However, while he was planning his strategy, he discovered that his philosophy was not as clear-cut as usual. Possibly the falling wig-block had walloped his conscience like a meat-tenderiser, for the identities of Cosmo and Rosamund pressed upon him uncomfortably, and there was a crack somewhere, through which doubt was creeping. This itch of guilt was unpleasant, but too weak to divert him from his purpose.

When Rosamund came, Vinny devoted himself to deceiving her. She was so intent on procreation that she had relaxed her usual vigilance, and she did not notice that his displays of affection were far too bright and insistent. On Saturday night, after the performance, Vinny sat at her feet in the hotel bar, and she sifted his hair with her coral nails, never dreaming that he could betray her while he was actually in her hands. Across the room, Hester was talking beside Cosmo, who dozed morosely in an armchair, unwilling to go to bed without her. Over the heads of their lovers, Hester and Vinny carried on an intense telepathic courtship. In the small hours, Vinny made fierce love to Rosamund, meanly praying that her elderly womb was too mummified to conceive, and tormenting himself with the idea that Hester and Cosmo were making love in the room next door. His feelings for Cosmo swung between virulent dislike and an anxious compulsion to propitiate him. On Sunday, he chafed and burned over the arts pages in the *Observer*, cooling his thirsty eyes on Hester whenever he dared, and reading his own frustration into all her gestures. On Monday morning, while Rosamund was packing up the possessions she had strewn all over his room, it was all he could do not to toss them into her suitcase with one violent sweep of his hand. They met Cosmo and Hester on the way down to Rosamund's taxi, and Vinny conversed politely with Cosmo, feeling all the time like a flayed Laocoon shouting impre-cations at heaven. Only when Rosamund had gone did he take in what Cosmo had been saying. The woman in charge of publicity had selected a party of actors to speak to some drama students at the University, and Cosmo was among them. They departed after lunch and, as soon as the minibus had turned the corner, Hester and Vinny broke their agonising silence in the deserted lounge.

'Oh, what a mess you've made of it,' said Hester. 'Just think how simple it might have been.'

'You didn't have to take up with Cosmo.' Vinny was always surprised by the depth of his resentment. 'That hasn't made it any easier.'

'Vinny really, really!'

'You don't love him, do you?'

'No.' Hester seemed amazed that he needed to ask.

'Give me another chance, sweetheart. I'll never run away again.'

'Famous last words,' she said wanly.

'Okay, you don't have to believe me, Hess – I know I don't deserve it – but I love you. I can't live without you, it's as simple as that. I know it sounds a bit worn out, because you've heard it before, but I mean it this time.'

'I'll take you anyway.' She was extremely calm. 'I haven't stopped loving you for a single second, and I never will. I'll take you back, whatever you do to me. My God,' she added impassively, 'you're crying.'

He shrugged, and wiped his nose on his sleeve.

In the same quiet voice, she said: 'Who's dramatising now?'

'If I can't have you now, I'll die.'

'The world seems awfully full of people who'll die if they can't have me,' she said, with a bitterness he had never imagined in her.

Vinny sniffed back his tears. 'Why are you acting like this?'

'I don't know. I'm scared.'

'Scared of what?' He laughed shakily through a bubble of snot. 'Of too much Bliss?'

'Let's go upstairs,' said Hester.

'Now?'

'Don't you want to?'

He was angry. 'You know bloody well I do – but that's not it – ' He crushed her fingers in his hot palms. 'You have to see how different it is!'

'I don't care.'

'I care! I fucking care! You'd better realise, you're going to be

198

my girl now. I'm going to ditch Rosamund, and you're going to break your engagement to that prick Cosmo Brady.'

'Don't shout,' she said tremulously. 'I'll do anything for you. I should have thought that was obvious. Please darling, let's go upstairs. The others won't be back for hours.'

In the lift, she startled Vinny by saying: 'Oh, it's such a relief to be my real self again. I'm only real when I'm with you.'

A plush-lined afternoon hush lay over the hotel corridors. Vinny hung out the 'Do Not Disturb' sign and locked his door, and they fell upon each other's open mouths.

Horatia could be great fun when she chose, and her whispered comments during the afternoon had kept Cosmo in an un-usually lively state. Mellowed by the adulation of the drama students, he found himself agreeing to share a bottle of cham-pagne with her when they got back to the hotel. He had been misled before, but it seemed to him that he was finally learning to control her and extract the enjoyment from their relation-ship without activating her nasty temper. Since their last reconciliation, he had been allowed to take huge liberties.

'You don't have to keep up this champagne attitude in front of me, you know,' he told her.

'It's not an attitude,' she said amiably. 'Why should it be an attitude?'

'Because it's such a waste of money, love. We all know you've got it, so what are you trying to prove? Some of the others think you're doing it to show them up.'

'Do they? What else do they think about me?'

'No, Geldschmidt, you're not going to draw me out. I haven't the strength for another quarrel.'

'Oh dear, I must be pretty well loathed.' She was smiling and bristling with delight. 'Cosmo, you're beyond price.'

Cosmo, thinking he sensed respect for his opinions, expanded. 'I shouldn't go on about this champagne thing, since I'm drinking it – '

'No,' she interrupted softly, 'you certainly shouldn't.'

'But it's just the latest in a long line of poses, isn't it? There was the Zionist pose – ' he had been laying down the law all afternoon, and now could not stop, 'There was being upper-class and going out with that titled bloke. Then you went to the other extreme and started picking up guttersnipes. And now there's this "Darling, I only drink champagne" stuff, and making people in transport caffs run out to the off licence so you can have it with your eggs, chips and beans. And I know it's simply not true. I've seen you drinking ordinary wine. I've even seen you down a pint of beer.'

'When?'

'Right here in this very bar, darling, if not at this very table. That was during your radical actress pose.'

'It was also during my Cosmo Brady pose,' she reminded him slyly.

He held up a magisterial finger. 'That was not a cue for a stroll down memory lane.'

But it was too late. 'You do realise you're in the exact same room? I nearly died when Hester told me the number.'

The familiar fear blew across Cosmo's blood. 'You didn't say anything?'

'No, of course not. Please don't go all stuffy on me. I haven't told a soul. Look, I regret it as much as you do.'

'I doubt that,' he said warmly.

'Oh, thanks a lot.' She appeared highly amused, always her way when he was particularly offensive.

'Sorry, Horatia. You know what I mean.'

She refilled their glasses. 'It doesn't reflect well on either of us, let's face it. It was like some dirty joke about a Catholic and a Jew.'

'Jesus Christ, stop going on about it.'

'Why? Nobody's listening. You must admit, I've been very good. I could have put it round the whole theatre.'

'That would kill me,' he said.

'I know it would, you funny old egg. That's why I kept quiet – I don't want to hurt you. I'm sorry about it, because it stops us talking properly. You and I were born to be friends, only we ruined it by trying to be lovers.'

'Born to be friends, eh? Then why are you always getting at me?'

'I'm trying to reach you,' said Horatia coolly.

He was cautious. 'I'm always willing to be friendly. It's difficult sometimes, working out what you want from me.'

'Oh, here we go again!' exclaimed Horatia, laughing. 'For the last time, I'm not trying to slice off your testicles. What would I do with them?'

Cosmo laughed too, but in parentheses. He did not want his attention to falter.

'I'm good for you,' she insisted. 'Look at you now, you haven't sulked once all afternoon. Why can't you be like this all the time?'

'Well, if it comes to that, miss, why can't you? You haven't been nearly such a pain in my arse lately.'

'I'd venture to say, Cosmo, that I know you better than anyone. I'd even venture to say I know you better than Hester.'

'Crap.' He was not having this. 'I've told her things I'd never dream of telling you.'

'She only sees your best side. I've seen you angry, I've seen you absolutely foul. Hester thinks you're a sweet old thing who wouldn't hurt a fly. My guess is you're capable of almost anything.'

He put down his glass, beginning to feel uneasy.

'If we'd ever got it together properly', she continued, 'you'd be a different man.'

'A nervous wreck,' he suggested.

'You had the wrong attitude, darling. Never mind love. If we tried again, we'd get it right.' She leaned towards him. 'Why not? A quick tumble, just as friends. Enormously liberating.'

She leaned in close to him, and the sudden exhalation of perfume heated Cosmo's blood. For one reeling moment, he saw himself in the hotel bedroom on top of Horatia, splitting her with violent, furious thrusts, and his groin ached with desire. He would tear out her insides, and pay her back for all the humiliation she had caused him in the past.

'I – I couldn't – ' he began.

Horatia leaned closer. 'Do you know what I'd like to do to you?'

Brushing the rim of his ear with her lips, she told him what she would like to do to him. Cosmo had never heard such a stream of pornography issuing from a female mouth, and he turned scarlet.

'No! I can't!' The spasm passed, and his limbs contracted in a palsy of shame. She had opened an abyss of obscenity, and all the buried filth in his soul had surged to the surface. He was disgusted with himself, and with her.

'You're tempted,' she said.

'I am not! It's out of the question.' He drew away indignantly. 'You know I can't cope with infidelity. That was my problem last time.'

'Ironic, really,' said Horatia acidly, 'when the woman was Faith. She never thought twice about cheating on you.'

'Only with Dom.'

'That's what you think.'

Cosmo flinched, but he no longer cared about Faith. Besides, as soon as he saw how angry his refusal made her, he expected to have all sorts of horrors thrown at him, and he armoured himself accordingly. Like Perseus, he avoided the eyes of the Gorgon, and conversed instead with her reflection in his shield.

'Anyway, I'm with Hester now, and I could never deceive her, not for anything.'

'What would you do if she cheated on you?'

'Don't be ridiculous,' he snapped, outraged by this blasphemy.

'Sure of her, aren't you? I don't think she's quite got over Vinny, so I'd watch her.'

'Crap.'

'Well, when that wig stand fell on him, I found her in floods of tears in the dressing room. She made me promise not to tell you.'

'Then why are you telling me? God, you can be a bitch sometimes.'

'She still makes eyes at him — I've seen her do it.'

Cosmo was very angry on Hester's behalf, but for himself he found he was sorry for Horatia. If this pitiful attempt at slander was the best she could do, he must have hurt her more than he realised.

'I know her,' he said, firmly but kindly. 'There's not a single part of her that's false or bad. She's the living essence of truth.'

'Yeuch!' said Horatia. 'You're soaking wet.'

'She's utterly pure – yes, go on and laugh. I certainly wouldn't expect a woman like you to understand. There are depths of goodness in her. She never puts herself first – it's always for me, what I want, what's best for my comfort. It's cruelly easy to take advantage of someone like that, and I'd never think of doing so. I make bloody sure I pay her back with the same consideration – I'd cut off my right arm to make her happy. Yes, sure, she had a tough time getting over Vinny – it goes deep with her. Now she's mine, I'd die for her, I honestly would.'

All the animosity had faded from Horatia's face. Poor thing, thought Cosmo, bolstered by his eloquent declaration. Poor sterile thing.

'I don't want to foul it up for you,' she said. 'She's lucky, darling. I hope she knows it.'

He smiled at her magnanimously. 'I suppose you wouldn't let me sign for the champagne, just this once?'

Hester and Vinny dozed on a sheet creased with activity and blotted with patches of congealing semen. Their legs were tangled and their stomachs welded together with sweat. In the corridor outside, Hester heard heavy, measured footsteps, and someone whistling. She listened idly, until the steps halted and a key clattered in the lock of the room next door.

'My God!' she whispered, jerking Vinny's head off her breast. 'What's the time? It's dark, it's nearly dark!'

'Get up quietly and put your clothes on,' Vinny mumbled sleepily. 'He doesn't know you're in here.'

Hester sat up in the sticky bed and pressed her hands to her flushed face. 'Oh, what have I done?'

Nineteen

A torn scrap of cloud blew across the sun, and a leaden chill momentarily extinguished the sweet, lemony April light. The grass on Parliament Hill was new and wet, growing in thick, juicy blades which licked Hester's stockinged shins. Her hand was curled in the pocket of Vinny's leather jacket as they trudged upwards, their heads bent against the battering wind. This was their first meeting as lovers since their return from Manchester.

'Please don't send me any more notes,' Hester was saying. 'What if Cosmo found one?'

'How else am I supposed to communicate with you? You don't have to leave them lying around.'

'I think you want him to find one.'

'Maybe.'

'Don't drop me in it, Vinny – we have to wait for the right time.'

'Oh, yes? And when will that be?'

'When you've told Rosamund, for a start.'

'Shit,' muttered Vinny. 'Why is it so difficult?'

The clandestine letters he had been pressing into her hand at the theatre were his only outlet, when the frustration became too much to bear. They were usually penned in the dressing room, right under Cosmo's unsuspecting nose. Vinny wondered what it was about Hester the second time around that aroused such violent passions in him. Sometimes she looked so patient and withdrawn, so wistfully grieved, that he wanted to shake her.

'Let's not quarrel,' she said.

At the summit of the hill, they stood breathless, taking in the view. London lay at their feet in a blue haze, misty and untidy, with shining tower blocks piercing the sky. Above their heads, two scarlet kites dived and curveted, the clear air hissing through their tails. The long grass sloped away beneath them, shivering like the surface of a lake.

'It's lovely, isn't it?' Hester's eyes were glassy and euphoric. Vinny kissed her cold mouth, and a gust of wind lashed her long hair round his neck.

On a bench near by sat an elderly man in a Homburg reading *The Times*, folded very small to prevent the pages flapping. A slack, stout woman in a wheelchair, his wife perhaps, stared wistfully over the city with her mittened hands in her lap. Her gaze was riveted to a farthest point of the horizon, as if the distance was a luxury, and she hoped to see the ocean beyond the Kentish hills. The feet of the boys flying the kites thudded across the turf, and the wind snatched their calling voices. Hester and Vinny sat down on a bench facing away from the city, towards the unseen chimneys of Kenwood House. The valley was dotted with clumps of trees and sliced about with hedges and ditches.

'I'm so happy,' Hester announced placidly, huddling close to him. 'If you'd never left me, and we'd just carried on as we were, I'd never feel as wonderful as this.'

'You haven't been looking particularly happy lately.'

'I haven't been contented,' she corrected him. 'It's not the same at all.'

She was quite calm. Vinny had come prepared for high drama, but it was not needed. Sitting up in the rafters of London, with the kites tossing above him and the plumed boughs waving below him, he felt strong and serene.

'We've got to decide what to do,' he said, 'since we both know what we want. All right, there are other people involved, but we shouldn't let them stand in our way. Why should four people be miserable when two people can be happy?'

'Cosmo's not miserable,' said Hester. 'That's just the problem. Two people are perfectly happy at the moment, Vinny. We're the miserable ones.'

'You've got to tell him, Hess, or I will. I can't share that dressing room with him much longer the way things are. He keeps talking about you as if you lived in his fucking pocket – it's driving me insane.'

'I know, I know, I know,' she said irritably. 'But you've got to see how awful it is for me. I can't leave clues, because he never gets suspicious. If only he'd guess something and confront me – but he thinks I'm so perfect.'

'You are,' Vinny kissed her warm throat. 'You're absolutely peerless.'

'I mean, he genuinely thinks I'm like an angel. Nobody could be kinder, or more sensitive – '

'How can he be sensitive?' Vinny asked, with a nasty inflection. 'A second ago, you said he was thick.'

'I didn't. You don't know him.'

'You're sorry for him, aren't you?' he demanded angrily.

'Yes. He's a nice man. I don't look forward to hurting him.'

'You don't mind hurting me, though, do you?'

'Don't, please.' She looked pained and weary, but he could not repress his desire to own all of her.

'How long are you going to make excuses? How do I know if you intend to leave him at all? Perhaps you do love him, and you're trying to have your bloody cake and eat it. Perhaps you're messing me around because it makes life more bloody interesting.'

'Stop it,' she said wretchedly. 'What's the matter with you?'

As soon as he was sure he had the power to make her unhappy, he relented. 'I'm sorry, love. I'm jealous. I've no right to lecture you about leaving him, when I'm in the same situation with Rosie.'

'Has she guessed anything?'

'No,' he said, sighing. 'And I haven't the heart to drop any hints. She wants that kid so much, Hess, and she's thirty-six, so there's not much time.'

'Why does it have to be yours?'

'Because she loves me.'

'So you're still trying?' she asked coldly.

'Darling, I have to fuck her, don't I? You're still doing it with Brady, I presume.'

'That's different,' she insisted.

'For crying out loud, what do you expect me to do – slip a contraceptive pill into her muesli every morning? They haven't invented an invisible condom yet, as far as I'm aware.'

'You're being amazingly short-sighted, Vinny. One day she'll get pregnant. Then what will you do?'

'I don't know,' he said crossly. 'Leave her, I suppose. She wants that kid more than she wants me.'

'I don't believe you.'

'That's because you're so young,' he explained. 'You don't understand how strong the urge gets when time is running out. Everyone tells her it's normal to wait up to a year, but she's already booked herself into a clinic for tests.' He added sheepishly: 'I have to go too.'

'What for?'

'Sperm count. I'll have to wank into a jam-jar.'

The worried crease melted out of Hester's forehead, and she laughed. 'What, in front of everyone?'

He was laughing too. 'Of course not. Bill Duckworth had to do it, and he says they shut you in a cubicle with a dirty magazine. He says he had to knuckle away for half an hour before he could produce anything. I'll think of you – I get a hard-on just hearing your name.'

She felt his flies. 'You've got one now. Give me a jam-jar.'

'I've had a stonker for ten days, sweetheart. Leave it alone, or I'll come.'

She became sober again. 'You'll have to say something before she gets pregnant, Vinny. I don't want her to have your child. She'll soon find someone else.'

'She'll have my goolies, Hess. She's got loads of friends, and they'd all pull the knives out. You'd be living with a pariah.'

'Oh, I don't mean to make you criticise her,' said Hester. 'I'm in the same position with Cosmo, more or less.'

They kissed again, feeling noble as they forgave their respective partners for being in the way.

'Come on,' said Vinny, in a burst of confidence, 'why should it be such a big deal? Neither of us is married – not yet. We don't have any children to think about – '

'Yet,' Hester interrupted.

He ignored this. 'All we're going to do is split up with Cosmo and Rosie and shack up together. I'll marry you eventually, but you're not getting a ring until you take that bit of shit off your finger.'

She surveyed her diamond. 'Poor Cosmo.'

'Poor Cosmo my arse.'

'There you go again!' she cried. 'For the last time, you don't realise what would happen to him. He scares me to death sometimes.'

'Why? Why? What does the bastard do to you?'

'Nothing. But I look at him and I can't bear the idea of hurting him.'

'Bloody emotional blackmail,' snarled Vinny, childishly furious that he had no monopoly on Hester's sympathy. 'Just scribble out a Dear John and leave it on the mantelpiece.'

'You know I can't do that,' she said. 'We have to work with him, you share his dressing room – '

'The man is a drip,' declared Vinny. 'He couldn't do a thing to us.'

'Darling, if we could just wait until the end of the season – until we've finished "Otho" – '

'But you've agreed to marry him at the end of the season,' he pointed out. 'If you wait that long, you'll have all the invitations out, and your Dad will have paid for a striped marquee. If you want to be kind to him, you'd better tell him before he rents his morning suit, hadn't you?'

'I don't know what to do.'

'Don't panic,' he said. 'It can't be that bad.'

Unexpectedly, she said: 'He has nightmares. He won't say what they're about, but I know, because he talks in his sleep. They're all about me leaving him, or being spirited away.'

'Shit,' Vinny was disgusted. 'He ought to see someone.

You've got to get out, my love. You can't go on sleeping with a weirdo. Shit. He should be in a home.'

'I don't know why I told you. You've never liked him.'

'That's why you took up with him in the first place, isn't it?'

'Piss off,' she whispered. She tried to shrug away from him, but Vinny caught her.

'This is ludicrous. Our only chance of a meeting in days and we keep sniping at each other. It's only because I want you so much.'

Their tongues writhed together, and Cosmo and Rosamund were blown into oblivion, as if they had never existed.

'I'll take you into the woods and stick you up against a tree,' Vinny mumbled into her lips. 'I'll kneel down in the mud and suck you off. You'll go home with your arse all covered with dead leaves – '

'Where can we go?' Hester pleaded. This was, after all, the reason they had met.

'My place.'

'We can't!' She drew away from him, horrified.

'It's okay. Rosie's in Paris – she won't be back till Tuesday.'

'It's not right!' she said, with unusual vehemence. 'You said you'd find somewhere, Vinny. I didn't mean Rosamund's house.'

'It's my house too, the amount of rent she makes me pay.'

'I thought you'd find a hotel or something.'

'Sweetheart, you'd loathe that kind of place.' Vinny recalled a dismal, orange-curtained establishment in Victoria, where he had once tumbled a married woman, and shuddered. 'Come back with me, please, I'll go crazy if you don't – '

'But it's sordid!'

'What we're doing is sordid anyway,' he said. 'May as well be hanged for a sheep as for a lamb. Oh, Hester, please, please!'

She could not resist him. They walked down the slope and across the footbridge, their stomachs churning with anticipation. On the floor of Rosamund's sitting room, they made violent love, with a towel under Hester to catch Vinny's copious secretions. Afterwards, she said she felt dirty. He gave her tea, and some of Rosamund's oatmeal biscuits. While he put the stained towel into the washing machine, she sat wiping her eyes, drinking her tea with her coat on, like a visitor.

Twenty

The two couples sitting at Cosmo's table in Corsica Street seemed admirably contented. The lamps were lit, the curtains drawn, and the casserole dish scraped clean. The dirty plates were stacked in front of Hester, and on the top one she had piled soggy, discarded crusts of wholemeal bread, jagged fragments of Hovis crackers, waxy cheese rinds, and the skeletal remains of grapes. Cosmo, the founder of the feast, was smoking a cigar and pouring Cointreau. He had invited Vinny and Rosamund to dinner partly because he felt it was time to be civilised, and partly because he was about to play Rosamund's husband in a television series called 'The Wearing of the Green'.

Hester and Vinny conversed with distant amiability, as if they had not been having a passionate affair for two months. Vinny admired the new loose covers on the sofa, as if his naked buttocks had not pressed against them the previous Monday. Hester's hand lay passive on the cloth. Cosmo placed his hand over it, blotting it out, and she smiled at him.

'Not for Rosie,' said Vinny. 'It's her turn to drive.'

'He's right, I'm afraid. I'll have to wait for coffee. No, sit down, Hester, that wasn't a hint.' Rosamund was languorous and relaxed. 'I'm sorry, Cosmo?'

He was in the middle of a quotation. ' "It's the most distressful country that ever yet was seen, for they're hanging men and women for the wearing of the green." That's where it comes from.'

'Oh, how stupid of me.' The lines round her mouth tautened intelligently. 'And there I was, combing through Yeats. The shameful fact is, I don't know a damn about Irish history. And I'm relying on you to help me with the accent, since you're the genuine article.'

'It's not difficult to pick up,' he said. 'It's just difficult to get rid of, once you've got it.'

'I think it's beautiful,' said Rosamund reverently. 'You'll have to endure me hanging on your every word. The only other Dublin accent I have access to at the moment belongs to an old wino who hangs about outside Gospel Oak station. All he ever says is "Give us fifty pence for a cup of tea" and I can hardly build my characterisation round that.'

Cosmo laughed. 'I'll take you down to one of the Irish pubs in Camden Town, when they've got the fiddlers in. You can have a drink and puke in the gutter afterwards – I'll instruct you in all the social niceties.'

'Honestly, Cosmo, I wasn't implying – I wasn't being – well, I suppose we all have preconceived ideas. What do you think of the scripts? Are they accurate?'

'The background seems pretty sound.' Cosmo swelled graciously, as he always did when his opinion was earnestly sought. 'I like the parallels with "Ulysses", but I suppose they'll make the usual concession to an American audience and cut them out in the final draft.'

Vinny, who had been picking at the crumbs on the cloth, raised his head to give Hester the faintest shadow of a wink. She hastily took a sip of Cointreau.

'But I don't suppose literary cross-references transfer well to the small screen,' murmured Rosamund. 'I thought the Easter Rising sequences read marvellously. Have they cast Parnell yet, do you know, for the early episodes?'

'Does anyone want more cheese?' asked Hester. 'Someone's got to finish the Brie, or Cosmo will guzzle it for breakfast.'

'I will not!' He was not displeased.

'You're disgusting. You'll lose your figure, and then what will Paul say?'

Cosmo's smile was somewhat forced. He never could see it as a joke.

'Just let yourself run to seed,' advised Vinny. 'Bill always says he got on much better with Paul after he started going bald.'

'How you all exist in that hothouse atmosphere, I'll never know,' said Rosamund. 'I'm awfully fond of Paul, but he'll never employ me – I've made it clear I won't play. May I steal one of your cigarettes, Cosmo?'

'Of course.' He pushed the packet towards her. 'Or a cigar, if you prefer. I thought you'd stopped.'

She lit a cigarette. 'Oh, that was part of my healthy conception programme. No fags, no booze, no additives in food. But I'm sick of it. I still haven't bloody well conceived.'

Hester allowed her hair to fall across her face as she dropped cutlery into the empty casserole dish. The scarlet tip of one of her ears was visible to Vinny.

'You'll be earning a packet with "Wearing of the Green", Cos,' he said. 'I nearly shat a brick when Rosie showed me her contract.'

'Don't be vulgar,' she said, smiling. 'Cosmo and I are far above the considerations of mere money.'

'Oh yes, like fuck. You told me you were only doing it so you could buy an olive grove.'

They all laughed, and Hester raised her head slightly.

'All right,' said Cosmo, 'I'll admit, the money's better than a poke in the eye. We've been discussing buying a house. The woman downstairs is driving us mad, and we could do with more space.'

'A garden,' suggested Rosamund. 'Go and have a snoop round Kentish Town. I nearly bought there. Just the place for young marrieds.'

'Not so young,' Cosmo lifted Hester's hand to his lips. 'I need a sinister gothic pile, where I can imprison my child bride.'

'I had a look at the scripts for the series,' Vinny said quickly. 'Quite up-market stuff. Not as many "begorrahs" as I expected. You must be sick of doing stage Paddies, Cos.'

'Pity we have to be called Flanagan, though,' commented Rosamund. 'It's such a Dave Allen sort of name.'

'Could have been worse,' said Cosmo, with a rare flash of playfulness. 'Could have been McGinty. Or O'Reilly.'

'Or Brady,' offered Vinny.

Cosmo laughed. 'Ah, go and fuck yourself,' he said Irishly.

'It really is a lovely accent,' remarked Rosamund. 'I was thinking of going over to Dublin a couple of weeks before we start shooting, just to get my ear in.'

'Don't miss our wedding,' said Cosmo. 'It's going to be quite an event. Hester's mother is a frustrated Cecil B. de Mille. Three months filming will seem like a nice rest after that.'

'Have you chosen the dress yet, Hester?'

Hester was busy stacking the tray. She replied with a wavering, uncertain smile.

'Not so simple,' said Cosmo. 'It's got to match the family wedding veil. Christ knows what my mother will make of it all. The Anglican ceremony will be enough to kill her.'

'Pilot's scratching, darling,' Hester said. 'Shall I let him in?'

'What? Oh yes, I'll do it. Poor little beast, he hates being shut out, but he's such a scavenger.' With heavy, satisfied movements, Cosmo got out of his chair and opened the door. Pilot jumped on him ravenously, barking and worshipping his shoes. 'All right, calm down, no need to go mad. Thought we'd forgotten you, didn't you?' He stooped to rub the spaniel's head. Pilot's teeth snared the cuff of his shirt, and Cosmo's face became gentle and preoccupied as he tried to pull it free. 'Stop that Pilot, or out you go. Do you hear?' He returned to the table. 'Nobody minds him do they?'

'I do,' said Vinny. 'The little bugger always tries to bite me.'

Sure enough, as soon as Pilot picked up the scent of Vinny, he stiffened, and bristled all over like a nail-brush, growling deep in his chest.

'Pilot!' Cosmo exclaimed reproachfully. 'He's normally so sociable, isn't he, Hester? Come on, you know Vinny – '

He did indeed know Vinny. Cosmo snatched him up, just before he got at his ankle.

'I'll get out of the way,' said Vinny, standing up. 'Give me the tray, Hess. I'll help you with the coffee.'

'Oh, I'm all right.' She was awkward. 'You don't have to – '

He took the tray from her and they went to the kitchen together. Hester closed both doors behind them.

'She looks stunning,' said Rosamund, who knew how to get round Cosmo, and had professional reasons for wishing to do so. 'I've never seen her look so lovely.'

Cosmo caressed one of Pilot's long ears. 'Yes, that dress suits her.'

'Oh, come on.' She smiled conspiratorially. 'Who cares about the dress? If she wore nothing but a barrel held up with bits of rope, like Mrs Crusoe in the pantomime, she'd still look fabulous. You've fallen on your feet, haven't you?'

'I'm happy,' Cosmo said. 'For the first time in my life, I'm really, really happy.'

Behind the kitchen door, Vinny had pulled down Hester's dress to expose one of her shoulders, and was in such a state of agitation that he stood with one foot in the dog's basket.

'God, oh God,' he murmured thickly, fumbling to pull up her skirt, 'I'm desperate for you.'

'Stop it – Vinny, we mustn't – not here – don't – I've got to talk to you – ' Her voice faltered and dissolved as his hand scrambled down the top of her tights.

'Can't leave you alone.' His face was scarlet, and his hot fingers were working frantically in her pubic hair. Hearing Cosmo's laughter across the hall, she remembered to switch on the coffee machine while she shuddered and sighed her responses. Vinny unzipped his flies and guided her hand to his hard penis. She suddenly withdrew.

'I can't,' she whispered. 'Please listen to me.'

'Hess? What's up?'

She had turned away from him, and her tears were splashing among the opaque smears of gravy on the dirty plates. Vinny took her in his arms, striving to be restrained and protective in defiance of his savage erection. 'Hester darling, what's happened?'

'I'm pregnant.'

'What?' His hand froze in the act of stroking her back. 'Shit. You're not. You can't be.'

Hester wriggled away from him and wiped her nose on a discarded paper napkin. Vinny, after blinking helplessly and looking all round the kitchen, took his foot out of Pilot's basket and fastened his trousers. He began to pace, and a crease appeared between his eyebrows. When he spoke, his voice was tight and angry.

'Might one ask whose it is?'

'Yours.'

'How do you know? Look, I thought you were on the pill. This has to be a mistake.'

'I – I changed to a diaphragm when I moved in with Cosmo,' Hester said. 'I've always put it in religiously, if he so much as looks at me.'

'A diaphragm! But you – '

'I haven't been using anything with you. Please don't be angry – I know it seems like I did it on purpose – I mean, I obviously did – but I wanted to be close to you – it gets in the way – ' She was becoming incoherent. Vinny embraced her again.

'It's all right, I'm not angry. Just tell me how late you are.' He had had conversations like this before.

'Six weeks.'

'Six days, you mean?'

'No,' she sniffed into his shoulder. 'Six and a half weeks.'

'Jesus Christ, Hess, why on earth didn't you tell me?'

'Maybe I hoped it would go away or something. And I was so terrified of spoiling everything.'

'Did you think I'd chuck you again? Or make you get rid of it?'

'Yes. Oh Vinny, I want it so much. Sometimes I'm so thrilled about it that I forget everything else.'

Vinny's hand moved round to her stomach. 'What do you reckon it is?'

'It's a boy,' Hester smiled back at him blearily.

'Shit. I wanted a girl. I get on better with women.'

'Too well. You're not furious with me, are you?'

'No, I'm actually pleased.' He was thoughtful. 'My first child. How do you feel? Are you sick?'

'I feel wonderful. Complete and happy – all the clichés. Not sick at all, and a good thing too. Cosmo's a bit dense, but even he'd smell a rat if I started throwing up every morning.' They both laughed. 'Will you still fancy me when I've got a huge fat belly?'

Vinny squeezed her against his genitals. The shock had taken some of the starch out of his penis, but it was hardening again rapidly.

'I've never fucked a pregnant lady. You'll be all sensuous and earthy, and continually randy.'

Their sighs became laboured and throaty, and the coffee machine began to gargle behind them.

'We must get back,' said Hester.

Vinny opened his trousers again. 'Bring me off.'

'Are you mad? Cosmo could walk in any second. No, I certainly won't. You'll have to wait.'

'I can't,' he hissed. 'Go on, Hess, jack me off. It won't take long – I'm about to shoot – '

Hester felt the muscles in his back knotting and tensing. She was aware of the foolishness of their position and the terrible danger of discovery, but her heart was melting with love for the father of her child. She closed her hand round his penis and held out a piece of kitchen towel to catch his semen. He stood with his mouth slack and his eyes half closed, his imbecilic gaze fixed on the Tate Gallery calendar on the wall opposite.

'Hurry up, can't you?'

'Don't rush me – aah, aah – I'm co – oh! oh!'

'Quiet! Do it quietly!'

He missed the kitchen towel and squirted up her sleeve. 'Shit,' he said breathlessly, leaning forward with a hand over his racing heart. 'Sorry.'

Hester was at the sink, scrubbing away at her dress, while the coffee overflowed and spat on the hot plate. It seemed to her that the whole room stank of illicit sex.

'Sorry about that.' Vinny pulled up his zip and switched off the coffee machine, laughing.

'It's not funny,' complained Hester, sniffing her sleeve cautiously. 'We must get back. There's no time now, but we must talk.'

'We do nothing but talk, sweetheart. We've really got to make that break. Now that you're pregnant, it's absolutely imperative.'

'I know, I know.'

Feeling an uncomfortable twinge of decency, he said: 'It's got to be soon. He's bound to notice, and you can't let the poor sod think it's his.'

'It's a question of finding the right moment,' said Hester, as she always did. This was not the place to quarrel, so Vinny swallowed his irritation, and helped her to load cups on the tray.

In the sitting room, Rosamund and Cosmo were talking shop. Cosmo lounged splendidly, elated by Rosamund's artful assaults upon his ego. She was smoking one of his cigars and drinking Cointreau. Pilot was dozing in Cosmo's lap, his jaw resting on the edge of the table. Briefly, he cocked an eye open when he sniffed Vinny.

'I'll do the driving, Rosie. You're sloshed.'

'I know.'

Hester paused in the act of pouring coffee to stroke the back of Cosmo's head.

When the front door had closed behind Vinny and Rosamund, Cosmo stretched and scratched his stomach.

'She's quite pleasant, when you get to know her. I think living with Vinny suits her. Softens her corners a bit.'

'Yes,' said Hester faintly.

'You look tired, angel. Leave the washing up. I'll do it in the morning.'

'Okay.' She was tired. She dragged herself up the stairs, clutching the bannister, listening to Cosmo whistling as he switched off the lamps and wondering sadly how she would feel about her child if it was his.

Vinny had driven halfway up the Holloway Road before he registered that Rosamund was crying. At the traffic lights outside Jones Brothers, he glanced aside and saw two wet silvery tracks on her cheeks. 'Rosie?' He was glad he was driving. It meant he would not have to focus all his attention on her. Rosamund's tears were rare, and carried ominous implications.

'I drank too much,' she said, with a genuinely brave smile. Her instinct to hide her misery harrowed him.

'Come on, what is it?'

'Oh, I'm just so sick of not drinking and not smoking when it's all for nothing. I'm never going to have a baby, Vinny. I'm too fucking old.'

'Don't be stupid,' he said uneasily.

'I want it more than anything in the whole world.' The last word was dissected by a violent sob, which she gulped back impatiently. 'I never imagined I could want anything so much and not get it.'

'You've only been trying a few months,' said Vinny, trying to sound sturdy above a stomach contracted with fear. 'Give yourself a chance. You know it takes time.'

'I haven't got any time!' Rosamund wailed. 'You want a baby, don't you Vinny?'

'Yes, I've told you a million times.'

'Darling, you don't have to stay with me if I can't give you one. I'd hate you to go – you know how much I love you – but I'd understand. I'd accept that as a reason.'

At the next lights, he patted her thigh, and said: 'Shut up, you silly bitch. I'm not going anywhere. You're plastered – you'll be embarrassed to think about this tomorrow.'

She laughed, and briskly blew her nose. 'I love you, Bliss. And if you did leave me to get a baby, I'd have your guts for garters.'

Vinny pretended to find this amusing, but secretly he was in despair. What a night he was having. He had had to reassure two women, one because she was pregnant by him, the other because she was not. And he had promised them both the earth.

Twenty-one

Several days later, Hester amazed Horatia by calling in un-announced at Betterton Street. Kitty was away, and Horatia knew her own attractions were few. She wants something, she said to herself. But what did she have that a lovely creature like Hester Stretton could possibly want? Horatia scented a ripe scandal, and her nose sharpened to a rapier's point. Hester sat at the kitchen table with a sordid shaft of afternoon sunlight falling on her fairy masses of hair, as inviolable and majestic as an angel. Horatia, bitter-tinged and sallow, banged about among the cupboards, producing tea and slices of cake, trying not to let Hester's extravagant grace make her feel inferior. She had been marinading her bony body in a bath, and was hastily dressed in an orchid-splattered kimono, tied at the waist with a pair of tights. In Kitty's absence, the washing machine spewed out damp clothes, there were flecks of ash in the butter, and the fridge smelt like a sour fart. Hester created a little kingdom of tidiness round her chair, as if her beauty shamed the various dirty objects into order. It is an illusion, Horatia reminded herself: a physiological freak, an arbitrary distribution of muscle and bone, a fact beyond Hester's control. She was not doing it on purpose.

'Well? Has Cosmo decided to accept Paul's apology?'

At the mention of Cosmo's name, Hester's face became so poignant that Horatia sat on hot thorns of curiosity.

'Yes,' said Hester, picking the fruit out of her piece of

cake. 'It – it was all due to you. I couldn't budge him.'

There had been an unpleasant scene when Cosmo told Paul he was leaving the company to do 'The Wearing of the Green'. Betrayal had made Paul vicious, and he had accused Cosmo of being a bad actor. He was now contrite, and miserable because Cosmo refused to speak to him.

'You can do anything with him,' Hester said, looking at Horatia with pleading eyes. 'He sets such store by what you think. He's going to let Paul take him out to Francesco's, just the two of them. I can't imagine how you persuaded him.'

'It was only a question of stroking his ego. Let's you and I, who love him, admit that he is pathetically vain.' Her words had a false heartiness, which irritated her. 'Look Hester, what's the matter?'

'Nothing,' insisted Hester, but she meant Horatia to see that she was lying.

'It's Cosmo, isn't it?'

'Yes.'

Horatia drew in a long breath of exultation and became business-like, lighting a cigarette and planting her elbows on the table. 'Is he stepping out of line?'

'No.' She hesitated. 'It's me. I – I've been seeing Vinny again.'

'I knew it!' Horatia crowed. 'I guessed! It was in Manchester, wasn't it?'

'Does anyone else know?' asked Hester.

'No, darling. I was operating on pure instinct. When did you do it?'

'When you were all at the University, talking to those drama students.'

Colour crept into Horatia's cheeks. She shrieked with high, dangerous-sounding laughter. 'God, what a scream! I was making a pass at Cosmo at exactly the same time. I needn't have felt so guilty, need I? Not that he was having any.'

'He doesn't fancy you,' said Hester. 'He never fancies women with brains.'

Horatia's face was now the colour and texture of ancient

221

candles. 'No,' she agreed, smiling, 'he does go for the silly types. Faith talked a lot, but she hadn't a brain in her head.'

'He makes dolls of us,' said Hester, 'or idols. Vinny says it's all the same.'

'Well,' Horatia said, in an intimate voice which made Hester's flesh creep, 'you are a dark horse. There we all were, thinking butter wouldn't melt in your little mouth, and all the time you're having a bit on the side. I suppose Vinny can handle you now there's no danger of a commitment?'

'We're in love,' said Hester simply. 'He's asked me to marry him.'

'God.' Horatia was laughing again. 'You are in a mess. Cosmo will have a fit when he finds out – I wouldn't be you for anything. Have you ever loved him?'

'No.'

'I didn't think so.' Breathing smoke, Horatia began to devour cake. 'I always smelt a rat. I did try to warn him – perhaps I should have tried harder.'

'I wish you had,' said Hester. 'He would have listened to you.'

'You do amaze me, Hester. You've certainly got guts. You must have known from the start that some day or other you'd have to dump him, but on you went, letting him get in deeper. You don't pay much attention to other people's feelings, do you? I suppose because everything comes so easily to you.'

'That's what you think,' muttered Hester.

'Of course, it will virtually kill him.' Horatia extinguished her cigarette with such righteous force that the crockery on the table rattled. 'He worships you, whether you deserve it or not.'

'I never asked him to.'

'Look, you let him do it. It all comes to the same thing.'

'I didn't promise anything – ' cried Hester, 'he just assumed – you know how he is – I was lonely – '

'Of course you were,' Horatia said suavely. 'And you knew that he was lonely too. Who can blame you for wiping your nose on him? Why waste a Kleenex?'

Hester clumsily jogged her cup, slopping the tea. 'It wasn't like that.'

'Oh, I'm not passing judgment, Hester, goodness knows. I just find the whole thing rather a hoot. Cosmo goes round telling everyone you're Little Miss Perfect, so it's quite refreshing to hear that you've been knobbing Vinny on the sly, just like an ordinary human being.'

'We're in love,' quavered Hester.

'You're as bad as Kitty, always trying to dress up good honest lust and elevate it into romance. Why should Vinny suddenly have become trustworthy? He's probably fooling round with you because he's bored. I'd be bored, living with that praying mantis.'

'He's leaving her,' interrupted Hester. 'He's going to live with me!'

'So what? He'll be off again in a few months.'

'He won't!' Hester shouted. 'He's changed! And I'll tell you why – because I'm having his baby. I positively know it's his.'

'Hold on, hold on – ' Horatia, astonished, turned this information over. 'Are you sure? What if it's Cosmo's?'

'It's not.'

Horatia cheerfully cut herself another slice of cake. 'Oh darling, I give up. You're quite beyond me. If you're so sure it's not his child, how can you possibly go on living with him?'

Hester groaned. 'How can I tell him?'

'You'll think of something.'

'Horatia,' Hester said humbly, 'you've got it all wrong. I didn't set out to use him. You know how impossible it is to tell him things.'

'I've never heard anything like it outside a Russian novel,' said Horatia, with a narrowing of her eyes which made Hester squirm. 'You'd better drown yourself.'

'I shouldn't have gone home with him,' Hester said wretchedly. 'I shouldn't have slept with him. But I only meant it to be that one night.'

'A mercy-fuck,' Horatia suggested.

'Sort of – he was so kind to me. But he cried – it was awful. I never saw a man cry before. I'd already made him unhappy, without doing a thing. He told me he was unhappy just because I existed. It threw me into a total panic. How was I to

223

know how it would turn out?' Her voice was shaking. 'Please stop making out that it was all my fault.'

'No,' said Horatia levelly. 'Stop shoving the blame on Cosmo, and admit it – you behaved like an absolute bitch.'

She pronounced the last word with smacking relish, and Hester started to cry. Horatia watched her sobbing, and trying to scoop away the tears with her wrists. That marvellous beauty of hers had brought her nothing but trouble. Thinking of this gave her a feeling of satisfaction, and made her kinder. She put the tea things in the sink, and took a bottle of champagne out of the fridge.

'I'm sorry, Hester.' The cork came out with a brisk report, and expensive mist wafted from the neck of the bottle. 'You'd better have a drink. I know it's early, but it'll do us both good. Take no notice of my nasty tongue.'

'I deserve it,' Hester sobbed.

'Stop crying, for God's sake,' Horatia sat down to fill the glasses.

'I love Vinny so desperately, Horatia – I didn't mean to be a bitch, but I can't live without him.'

'Oh, I believe you. What are you going to do?'

Hester blew her nose and took a gulp of champagne. 'I don't know.' She looked at Horatia hopefully.

'You'd better go home and do it now.'

'No! No! I can't!'

'Get it over with – this is quite a good time. He'll have two days to pull himself together before the next show, and I can ring everyone up and warn them not to say anything – '

'No!' wailed Hester, starting to cry again. 'I've nowhere to go.'

'You can come here.'

'Horatia, I just can't face him.'

'Write him a letter.' Horatia brightened. 'I'll tell you what to put.'

'He wouldn't believe a letter. Wherever I went, he'd come and find me. If I came here, I'd spend my whole time listening for him, and the sound of his feet coming up the stairs would kill me.'

'Hester – ' Horatia was surprised, 'you're surely not afraid of him?'

'Not because he'd hurt me,' Hester assured her hastily. 'I know he'd never do that.'

'He's an emotional blackmailer,' declared Horatia. 'A master of the art. Meek people can be so domineering.'

'If only – ' Hester blurted out, 'if only you'd talk to him first! I know you could make him see the truth – he always listens to you!'

The entire reason for her visit was unfolded in a moment. Horatia, after a stunned pause, laughed softly.

'Hester Stretton, you take the biscuit. I can't have heard you properly. You want me to tell Cosmo you're pregnant by Vinny?'

Hester hung her head, but still seemed hopeful. 'Yes.'

'Can't you see that it just wouldn't work?'

'It would,' Hester insisted. 'You could do it.'

'Of course I could. But is that the point?'

'But it would make things so simple!'

'Things are not simple. Are you off your head? Cosmo has a right to hear it from you. The point is, Hester, it's not my problem. Why should I be the one to break the poor man's heart? He'd never forgive me – I'm the last person in the world he'd take it from. No, you're a big girl now, and you must take the responsibility for your own actions.'

'Oh, what have I done?' Hester moaned. A plainer woman would have sounded foolish, but she was genuinely tragic.

'You won't get rid of him as easily as that, darling. You'll have to eat your shit sandwich. It comes to us all.'

'Horatia, please – please – save me – you can do it. Make him see I'm not what he thought – you could do it so he wouldn't hate me – '

Horatia let her go on, enjoying the drama. The unfortunate fallen angel was at her feet, with human tears swelling her celestial eyes.

'And make him hate me instead? No thank you. Naturally, I'm awfully sorry for you, but you'll have to handle it yourself. If Cosmo comes to me afterwards, that's his affair. I shall pretend to know nothing about it.'

This was her last word, delivered with iron certainty. Hester left crestfallen and, after seeing her to the door, Horatia caught her reflection in the hall mirror. Her eyes were wild and unfocused with excitement. As she went upstairs to get dressed, she wondered if she should have warned Hester that Cosmo would not submit to the cuckold's horns as meekly as she imagined. He had, after all, hit Faith when she left him, and Hester meant worlds more. The revelation had been trembling on her tongue, but she had forced it back. Why should I tell her, if Cosmo hasn't? she thought. A good working class black eye would serve her right. Horatia had had black eyes herself, and reasoned that they had never done her any harm. Spoilt bitch, it might knock some sense into her.

Twenty-two

Pilot was ill. He languished in his basket, shivering, and would not leave the folds of his tartan blanket when Cosmo shook the lead.

'It's probably nothing,' said Hester.

Cosmo knelt down on the floor. 'He hasn't touched his food. What is it boy? What's the matter?' He shook the lead again, as if to conjure up tempting vistas of trees and green fields, but it was no use. Pilot feebly licked his hand, making it clear that it was the flesh, and not the spirit, which failed him. He seemed humble and apologetic, as if he expected to be deserted, now that he could no longer amuse. Very gently, Cosmo stroked his head with the backs of his fingers.

'Poor old Pilot,' he murmured, 'poor old thing. What's the trouble, eh? Have you eaten something?'

As if he could answer, Hester thought impatiently. What's the bloody point of talking to him? Damn that dog – he would be ill now.

Cosmo ran his hand along Pilot's spine. 'He must have picked something up in the Fields – they're always full of rubbish.'

The worn gold ring on his little finger became the only hard point in a wavering, nauseous mirage. Hester sat down on one of the kitchen chairs, gritting her teeth against the faintness. Her unborn child was reacting aggressively to being kept a secret. She had imagined pregnancy as a dreamy sojourn in a rocking-chair, looking down at a fecund belly under a swelling smock. Nobody had prepared her for this pulverisation of her nerves, and there was nobody she could talk to. Shivering with loneliness, she watched Cosmo contracting his limbs still further, so that he could gaze levelly into Pilot's round brown eyes.

'I'll give it chance to pass through, before I call the vet,' he said. The words 'pass through' made her gorge rise, and when Pilot started being sick Hester was in despair. Cosmo spread newspapers on the floor and sat through the whole day with the suffering spaniel in his arms. It was Monday, and they had a performance of *Otho the Great* that evening. Hester waited, in dumb wretchedness, beside the front door, while Cosmo gave instructions to the woman downstairs and showed her how to feed Pilot milk and water with an eye-dropper.

The July weather was blazing hot, with air as thick and still as jam. The car had been roasting in the sun for hours, and as soon as Cosmo strapped himself in he filled it with the odours of regurgitated dog-food and canine diarrhoea. Hester hung out of the window, tense as a board in her efforts not to retch.

'It breaks my heart,' said Cosmo, sternly watching the road. 'He looks at me so trustingly, as if I could explain everything. I think he thinks I could cure him, if I wanted to. But he doesn't blame me for not curing him. It's as if I was God and he was Job. The Lord giveth and the Lord taketh away. Blessed be the name of the Lord.'

He lurched round a corner, and sour sweat broke out on Hester's upper lip.

'He's terribly dehydrated,' he continued, blind to the way her knuckles whitened round the edge of the window. 'Did you see how runny his shit was? Practically liquid. Don't lean out too far, sweetheart.'

Inside the stage door, he fell into a detailed discussion of Pilot's symptoms with Bill Duckworth, who was another dog-fancier, and he barely registered Hester crashing through the double doors as soon as she had signed the book. Her stomach was in heaving rebellion, and she tore past Vinny, who was holding out his arms to her in the blank, dusty corridor. When she got into her dressing room, she vomited into the sink.

Vinny found her on the floor, shuddering and weeping, with porridge-like gobbets clinging to her hair. He lay on the carpet beside her, holding her while she gasped out how ill and miserable she felt. The half was called over the Tannoy, and he made her sit on the divan under the open window, with a glass of water. Neither of them cared that the blinds were up, or that Madge Worsnip was squinting at them curiously from her own window across the quadrangle.

'I'm all right now.'

'I could kill that bastard for making you so sick.' Vinny ran the taps, to clean the basin.

'In my condition,' she said lightly, but he did not smile.

'Why doesn't he notice? How can he be so stupid? This is the man who's supposed to be so fucking sensitive. This is the man who's keeping you away from me, because his delicate feelings mustn't be wounded. You're too soft about him, Hess. He doesn't give a toss.'

'I wish that was true.' She took a final gulp of water, and lit a cigarette. Her body was limp and debilitated, but calm. The sensation of not feeling sick any more was almost better than being well.

'You shouldn't be smoking. It cuts off the baby's oxygen.'

'Oh Vinny, for God's sake – '

He took the cigarette away from her and crushed it out. 'It's not good for you to be around Cosmo, either. Secondary smoking is just as bad.'

She was amused. 'You're really getting into the idea of having this baby, aren't you?'

'Yes, why not? It's my claim on you.'

'And mine on you.' Quite restored, she stood up to embrace him.

'When?' he demanded, as he always did now, every time they met.

'Soon, very soon.'

'Bullshit. That's what you always say. I don't want that man near you when you're carrying my baby.'

'I said soon,' she snapped. 'Don't nag me.'

Cosmo, meanwhile, had wondered vaguely why Hester had sprinted away from him, but he was preoccupied with Pilot. He was also hungry, and Bill Duckworth had informed him, as a friend, that he smelt of shit. He had spent his first half hour at the theatre cramming down a sausage sandwich and a cup of coffee, and taking a shower, with Bill's towel and bar of Lifebuoy. Ten minutes before Beginners, he sat, damp and fragrant in front of the dressing room mirror, applying Yardley's brilliantine to the hair at his temples. Bill had been reassuring about Pilot. It was undoubtedly something he had eaten, and it would be out of his system in a few hours. Cosmo began to feel more sanguine, and his thoughts meandered over the performance ahead. The house was sold out, and there was a queue for returns – not bad for a Monday.

It took him some time to realise how abnormally quiet Vinny was being. His thoughts were not usually allowed to rove about so peacefully. Vinny, half-dressed in breeches and riding boots, was on the divan, turning the pages of the *Evening Standard* but eerily contemplating Cosmo's back. As soon as he became aware of this unfaltering stare, Cosmo was unnerved. Vinny's moods were a worry to him – it actually felt safer when he was being noisy.

'Are you okay?'

'Oh, *I'm* fine,' said Vinny, with peculiar emphasis.

'Good.' A moment later, Cosmo put down the jar of brilliantine. 'Look, is something wrong? Are my flies undone, or what?' He laughed a little, hoping that facetiousness would lighten the atmosphere.

Vinny's thin skin flushed. Lungeing forward, he grabbed a handful of Cosmo's hair and pushed his nose down into a drum of face-powder. Cosmo freed himself with a mighty wrench of his shoulders, and retreated to the window, sneezing with such violence that he covered them both with a film of dust. He was astonished. Vinny faced him, fiercely at bay, with his arms twitching at his sides.

'Serves you right.'

Cosmo spat. His mouth tasted of scented ash. 'What are you talking about?'

Vinny went for him again, but he was on the defensive now and managed to slap most of the blows away. 'Stop it, will you? What have I done? Look, lay off, will you?'

'You don't know, do you, you piece of shit?'

'Know what, for Christ's sake?' Cosmo blundered about the room, overturning the bin and bruising his legs against chairs, holding up his forearms to shield himself. His moustache was full of powder and he sneezed again. Vinny shoved his knee into Cosmo's groin. He bellowed, and hit back as hard as he could, before he knew what he was doing. Vinny's varnished hessians left the floor, and he landed in a sprawl. Silence fell, as if a radio had been switched off. Cosmo's heart was galloping under his ribs. Wiping the hot drops of agony out of the corners of his eyes, he tenderly felt his scrotum, and lowered himself into a chair.

Vinny's arms were wrapped round his diaphragm, and he was keening in a reedy, plaintive voice which had had all its lower register shot away. Blood seeped from his nose and dripped off his chin, spattering his bare chest.

'Oh, Jesus Christ,' groaned Cosmo. Turning his head aside, he surrendered himself to an explosive fit of sneezing, which all but jerked him off his chair. Each detonation sent a charge of pain through his smarting testicles. When the prospect cleared, he was too bewildered to be angry, and too obscurely guilty, without knowing why.

'I never touched your nose,' he said.

'Starts by itself.'

'Oh.' Cosmo recalled suddenly how he had feared and envied Vinny, in the days when they first shared the dressing room. Beside that light, self-assured figure, he had felt ponderous and hopeless. Now, Vinny was as pale and vulnerable as a skinned hare, and Cosmo felt he had crushed something valuable. He was disgusted by his own coarse brutality. Cautiously, because of his aching loins, he got up and soaked a wad of tissues under the cold tap. He applied them to the back of Vinny's neck, which was youthful and exposed, with bluish veins; so repellent that he wanted to touch it. His vertebrae stood out along his back like piano keys.

'Should I do anything else?' he asked, retreatingly defer-
entially.

'No. It's stopping,' Vinny said.

'Good.'

'God, you whacked me hard.' He drew in a couple of
experimental breaths.

'Harder than I meant to,' said Cosmo. 'I'm sorry.'

Vinny bared his teeth viciously. 'I bet your bollocks hurt.'

'I'll live,' Cosmo said.

'Pity.' Vinny put his hand to his nose and began to laugh.
Cosmo watched, fascinated, as a ribbon of blood trickled
across his wrist.

There was a rap at the door, and Norman, their shrivelled
dresser, walked in with Cosmo's tunic hanging over his arm.

'Sorry I'm late, my loves. Oh ye gods, Vinny, ye gods – ' He
grabbed Vinny's shirt off the divan, and examined it for spots
of blood, his dyed quiff wagging.

'Never mind that!' shouted Vinny. 'What about me? I'm on
in ten minutes!'

'All right, dear, panic not, here I am. Bend over the sink.'

'No way.'

'You should be so lucky. I only want to run the tap on your
neck.' He left Vinny doubled up over the sink and went to the
telephone. 'Jessie, could you dash down to 204 with a bag of
ice cubes? It's an emergency.' Replacing the receiver, he added:
'She'll think we're mixing cocktails. What has been going on in
here? This floor's all over powder.'

Cosmo turned away, blushing warmly, as if he had been
detected in some sexual aberration. It was one of those
moments when he was sure of nothing in himself, and terrified
of what would be thrown up from the black mire of his
unconscious.

Vinny stood like a lay figure, holding a wet towel to his face,
while Norman buttoned his tunic and buckled on his sabre. He
was finished by the time the ice cubes arrived.

'Don't you dare get a mark on that frock.'

'Thanks, Norm.'

'I'll bring you a cup of tea when I come to change you.'

Cosmo hurried over the last details of his dressing, anxious not to be left alone with Vinny. When Norman had gone, Vinny mumbled: 'Sorry.'

'Why on earth – '

'Forget it. I'm not going to tell you. You'd better forget it.'

But Cosmo was too disturbed to forget it. He could have wept and begged Vinny's pardon – but for what? The old terror of being found out, in all his inadequacy and unworthiness, froze him. Then a thought germinated, no more than the ghost of an idea. Hester lay somewhere at the bottom of all this. He had always known that Vinny would some day regret what he had thrown away. Their positions reversed as Cosmo, realising that poor Vinny was jealous of him, decided to be kind. 'It's okay,' he said. 'Don't worry about it.'

He went up to the stage victorious, and immeasurably relieved.

Pilot was worse when they got home. Cosmo gave a long groan as he knelt down among the unwholesome vapours of decay. Hester thanked and dismissed the woman downstairs, feeling the stench defiling her clothes.

'She might at least have changed the bloody newspapers,' Cosmo complained. He snatched up the stained and blotched pages of that morning's *Guardian*, and Hester averted her eyes. Fortunately, she was not expected to do anything, as the dog was his territory.

'Cosmo, are you going to stay up long? Only I'm so desperately tired. It's not that I don't want to help – '

His face cleared for a moment as he leaned forward to kiss her. 'Go to bed, love. You look worn out. I'll come later.'

'What are you going to do?' She did not want to lean on him too heavily. The idea of having the bed to herself, without his great body pitching against the mattress, was heaven.

'I'd better stay with him. He looked so thrilled to see me just now. I didn't desert you really, did I, boy?' Taking a pile of 'Wearing of the Green' scripts off the table, he lowered himself to the floor beside Pilot's basket, with effortful, settling grunts. His resignation touched Hester.

233

'I'll make you some tea,' she said.

'Thanks, darling.' Cosmo was already absorbed, with the script open in his lap, and one hand resting lightly on Pilot's back.

On Tuesday morning, Hester woke alone. She went downstairs and found Cosmo asleep among the bowls of rancid milk, with Pilot lying across his stomach. She climbed over his legs to open the window and noticed with a slight shock that Pilot was looking at her through swollen slits of eyes. An irrational sense of terror took hold of her. Cosmo, when he woke, gazed at her stupidly, as if he did not know her. She had to kiss him, for reassurance, when the sensation passed.

The vet called before lunch, and told Cosmo that Pilot had picked up parvovirus. The animal was obviously suffering, he said, and he hinted that it might be kindest to have him put down. Cosmo was not having this. Red with obstinacy, he bullied the vet into admitting that Pilot might have a chance, and he started to curse the man loudly before he was out of the front door. It was not the vet he was angry with, as Hester very well knew, but the squat toad, Death, waiting in the house to make his execution, like a bailiff. Cosmo defied him.

There was no show that evening and the day wore on very heavily. Hester sat watching Mary Berry stuff a chicken on afternoon television, listening to Cosmo's patient voice as he entreated Pilot to take some nourishment from the eyedropper. At intervals, she heard him thundering upstairs to the bathroom, yanking the flush impatiently, and thundering down again, determined not to lose a moment. Pilot was weak and rasping, his leaden tongue drooping from his parched mouth. His round eyes, patient in their swollen sockets, oozed thick drops of moisture. They were very low, the two of them. Pilot was getting feebler, and Cosmo was trying to pull him back from wherever he was drifting to. It cut his heart to see his plaything, who had been bred to mop up any affection he had to spare, continually surprised by pain.

Hester, battling with nausea, made salad for supper – it was too hot for anything heavier – and watched Cosmo chewing watercress like an old horse leaning over a gate. She hated him, and the oppressive house, and went to bed alone again. Cosmo put the sofa cushions on the kitchen floor, and sustained himself through the long hours of darkness by taking swigs of Martell straight from the bottle. Pilot's eyes were drowning, and he was so dry that his bones seemed to scrape and clatter beneath his skin.

On Wednesday, Hester could endure no more. Indifferently, she told one of her lies to Cosmo, and went out to meet Vinny for lunch at Mon Plaisir. A heavy slab of heat lay across the city, and sweat trickled between Hester's breasts, but she felt better with every mile she put between herself and Corsica Street.

'It's catching,' said Vinny. 'All that fucking doom. No wonder you're depressed.'

Hester poured herself some mineral water – she was not allowed alcohol, since Vinny did not want his child to become a dipsomaniac while still in the womb. 'Where will you go, when you leave Rosamund?'

'Simon Gartner's place. He's just bought this flat in Clapham. What's so funny?'

She was smiling. 'Nothing. I was just remembering him at that party at Francesco's. God, he was drunk. Does he know?'

'No, but he's a good sort.'

'I'm going to Horatia's,' said Hester. 'She doesn't like me, but she did offer. It won't be so horrendous with Kitty there.'

Vinny frowned. 'Is this a game, or are we really making plans?'

She was serene, and rather distant. 'I'm going to do it today.'

'What?'

'It's time. I told you there'd be a right time. I've got it all worked out.'

Vinny pulled his bread apart nervously. 'I'll tell Rosie.'

'You don't have to. I'll tell him this evening, and take a suitcase round to Horatia's. I was lying in bed last night, imagining what I'd take.'

'Jesus God, Hess. Shall I meet you?'

'No, I'll see you at the theatre on Friday.'

'Why not?' He was hurt.

'It's just a couple of days, to sort myself out. Can't I be alone for a couple of days? One or other of you is always on at me. And anyway, you'll still have to deal with Rosamund, won't you? Let's do it neatly.'

'We'll meet on Friday,' he said, 'free as air.'

They joined hands across the plates of empty oyster shells.

Rosamund had a matinee of *Don't Know Nuffin* and was safely imprisoned in the theatre. Vinny took Hester back to her house in a taxi, and they made love on the spare bed, damp and flushed with the heat of the afternoon. Hester made them iced lemon tea, garnished with sprigs of fresh mint Rosamund had left out on the chopping board. They drank it naked, in the dim light behind the drawn blinds, and Vinny made her laugh by describing his fight with Cosmo, and Cosmo's hysterical sneezes.

'This will all seem pretty silly in a couple of years,' he said.

'I think your philandering days are over,' said Hester. 'You won't have the strength.'

'You're right there, Hess. Too old and weary for any more of that. Golden boys and girls all must, as chimney-sweepers, come to dust.'

Forgetting the time, they fell asleep. The shadows were lengthening when Hester left and the midges danced in the hall light when Vinny switched it on. As he watched her running down the path towards her taxi, he impulsively called her back, although he had said goodbye and wished her good luck many times.

Her fair head turned in the summer dusk, and he embraced her once more.

'It's all my fault, love, but I'll make it up to you, I really will.'

She leaned out of the taxi window as it was pulling away, and called: 'Vinny, next time you see me, I shall be quite transformed.'

The house in Corsica Street was stuffy and hot when she returned. Dirty-looking flies had gathered from miles around, scenting a carcass, and they droned in columns round the light fittings. The windows were wide open, and now that it was evening a breeze set the sitting room curtains ballooning gently over the sill, but the air that blew in was London air, laden with the smell of diesel and the dust that gathers in the cracks of city pavements. The street outside was grimy and exhausted, having scorched in unremitting sunshine for the last twelve hours. The light was wan now, but the sky was still harshly blue, and the sinking sun had a filmy, unhealthy look.

Hester nerved herself to snatch her freedom. It had all seemed easy when she lay in bed with Vinny, but when it came to the point her heart ached for poor Cosmo. She realised she could never cut herself off from him entirely. All her life, she thought, until she was an old lady, she would suddenly drop what she was doing and wonder guiltily how he was. He had claimed her for eternity, and she had to get away. Harshly or kindly – it did not matter how.

Cosmo was still in the kitchen, where she had left him, with Pilot in his lap. His vigil had aged him, and the stubble on his cheeks and chin was noticeably sprinkled with grey. As soon as he raised his pleading eyes to her, she knew that her argument had been blown to atoms. She could not do it tonight, when he had been sitting alone all day, working out the puzzle of Pilot's mortality.

'Darling, I'm so sorry I'm late. Is he any better?'

'No,' Cosmo said hoarsely. 'I can't do any more. I'm just waiting.'

She knelt down on the floor beside him, and pushed his hair away from his sticky forehead. 'Why didn't you ask me to stay?'

Pilot was as parched and withered now as a dead leaf flapping on its brown stalk, but the drops still ran from his sore eyes as he fought for breath. Cosmo murmured: 'I can't bear it. He looks as if he's crying.'

They waited. Hester furtively flexed her cramped knees. The twilight thickened round them.

One more stirring of the bones in Cosmo's lap, one almost human sigh, and the last drop fell from Pilot's round eye. Cosmo felt the stillness beneath the sharp ribs, and laid the dead animal carefully in his basket. Hester hardly dared breathe.

'He loved me,' said Cosmo, bursting into tears. 'He loved

me so much!' His head landed on her shoulder with the weight of a cannonball. Hester stroked and soothed, staring at the indigo sky outside the window. He could not stop crying. His great fists churned in his wet eyes as he wept for the one creature who had loved him unreservedly – this implication was not lost on Hester. After half an hour, or perhaps longer, she became aware of the smell winding past her nostrils from Pilot's basket. A fly settled greedily on his leg and began rummaging in his black and tan pelt. When Hester brushed it away, it did a slow circuit and dived down upon Pilot's glazed eyeball.

'Cosmo,' she whispered, 'we ought to bury him.'

'No!'

'My darling, we must. I'll do it, if you let me go.'

In a ghastly dream, she watched herself disentangling Cosmo and putting Pilot's remains into a black plastic bag. Cosmo lay on the floor, howling with anguish. She had never carried anything dead before, and the bag felt horribly heavy and slithery as she bore him downstairs to beg a spade and the garden key from the woman in the flat below. Digging a hole in the cindery, neglected flowerbed took much longer than she had expected. Night fell, and she worked in the square of the light thrown down by the kitchen window, almost choking in the syrupy heat. She tipped the end of the bag, and Pilot tumbled into his grave in an ungainly huddle of limbs. Shovelling the earth on top of him was the hardest part of all. Earth to earth, she thought, with the sweat pouring off her. Ashes to ashes. And she left his little bones to the worms.

Cosmo had fallen asleep over a glass of wine at the kitchen table, fondling the chewed slipper which had lain at the bottom of Pilot's basket since he was a puppy. Hester was extremely relieved that she did not have to talk to him. The disappointed flies were hovering on the ceilings, like mourners after a funeral, waiting for a ham sandwich and a glass of sherry. Hester killed them all with Flit, and went up to the bathroom, to scrub her hands raw. The house was too full of death to admit a drop of anything else, but her parting speech could wait until tomorrow.

Tomorrow, she really would be free.

Twenty-three

Like Ahasuerus taking up his wanderer's staff, Cosmo left his house on Thursday knowing he had to walk, but with no idea where he was going. He had just been forced to spew up his past and then eat it again, in a new and disgusting form. There was a man who built his house upon the sand, he was thinking, and the rains descended and the floods came, and the winds blew and beat upon that house. Somewhere inside him was an unimaginable pain.

He was aware of himself as a trailing rag-bag of confusion, with two heavy wet hands, which he kept holding up to check that they were normal. Each time he tried to organise his thoughts, he was distracted and beguiled by the things he saw. Despair had washed his eyes so clean that all he could see was a vivid chaos. Without his blinders on, the thrusting clarity of everything bewildered him. The blades of grass tufting the pavement were unexpectedly rich and fat. The magenta sari worn by the woman in the corner shop had graduations of shadows in its folds which were quite beautiful.

It was six o'clock, and the bold colours of the hot July day were fading into pastels. In the builder's yard beside the railway, the concrete nymphs slung their urns upon their plump, hard shoulders, and looked cruelly away from him at their own shadows on the gravel. Cosmo left Corsica Street and stood by the zebra crossing on St Paul's Road, feeling the traffic stir his clothes. The string of shining cars and towering, scarlet buses girdled the roundabout like animals in a circus.

Across the road, the woman who dealt in second-hand books was carrying in the cartons marked 'All in this box 25p'. The cases in the window behind her gleamed with tarnished gilt, and looked as if they would smell of cupboards in a mouldy vestry. Next door, the ironmonger in his green dust-coat was moving his riches, which decorated the pavement in all weathers. He had flowerpots, plastic bowls, brooms with blue nylon bristles, and bunches of sink-plungers, tied up like strange utilitarian bouquets. Cosmo watched him stooping to pick up a pile of dinner-plates, printed with sepia coaching-scenes. He was so fascinated that, for a quarter of a second, he forgot what had happened to him. Then the impressions became too much for him, and he covered his aching eyes to shut out the gaudy maelstrom. He wanted to shout Hester's name so loudly that he would summon her back – the old Hester he had believed in, who had never existed outside his imagination. How could he have been so mistaken?

Crossing the road, he threaded his way through the crowds of men with briefcases who were tramping homewards, loosening the knots in their ties. From the open door of 'The Hen and Chickens' he caught the soapy, yeasty smell of the leavings at the bottom of pint glasses. Outside the primary school, he suddenly wondered where on earth he was going, and sweat burst out under his arms. There was an immense force of life to be found in everything – the sparrow hopping in the deserted drinking-fountain, the plastic bunting flutter-ing above a cohort of used cars, the dusty foliage of the trees. Every stick and stone insisted on its own vitality, assuring him that any sort of life was a triumph. A charge of violence shot through him as he waited to cross Canonbury Square.

The Georgian fabric of Canonbury Road had been rent with holes, then patched and darned with Victorian churches, and sour blocks of council dwellings. On the blank side of a pub ahead of him, he saw the words 'Take Courage' in fiery letters, and wondered for a second if he had projected them there himself, in a subconscious attempt to organise his scattered wits. Blowsy women trundled pushchairs loaded with shopping. Babies with knowing, aggressive faces ate potato crisps, and were indiscriminately shouted at and smacked.

On the Essex Road, he stopped suddenly in front of a magnificent Edwardian funeral parlour, the litter licking at his ankles in the summer breeze. Its marble and gilding hinted genteelly at the grim mahogany boats on sale inside, ready to carry loved ones across the river Styx. 'Cremations, Memorials, Embalmings.' Cosmo tried to move on, but it was no use – his attention was trapped by a shop near by, which dealt in stuffed animals.

They were displayed as a collector's joke, but he found their useless ferocity pathetic. A puma sprang at him, with wired claws outstretched. A fox snarled, but the moth had got at its red pelt. There were large flat fish in glass cases, with dates written on them, and the names of the men who had caught them, all that long time ago. The proud anglers had all mouldered into dust, but the fish lived on, in a peculiar way. Cosmo considered the Last Judgment, when people's bodies, so he had been told, would rise from their graves entire. He imagined the light beginning to gleam in the dull eye of the fox, and the fiery tints returning to its shabby coat. The mouth of the puma would redden and stretch, and the whole dead shop would be a riot of living colour, as fresh as the day of Creation.

In a glass case in the opposite window, sitting on mock grass under a false tree, were two little mouse deer, posed for all time in their vulnerable solemnity. They were each perhaps a foot high, animals as beautiful as anything God ever made: gentle, meek and charming. Cosmo had to stop looking at their tender glass eyes, because they reminded him of Hester, and it was more than he could bear. How could he have been so deceived? The pain shot through him, piercing layers of feeling he had never known he possessed. Dizzy with humiliation, he stumbled on, feeling his pockets and trying to recall where he had left his cigarettes. They were on the sitting room table in Corsica Street, beside an ashtray with two crushed stubs, and an empty coffee mug. Fortunately, he had remembered to take his wallet. Seeing a small shop in a side street, 'V. Polanksy, Delicatessen', which displayed cigarettes beside the window, he went inside.

Lights, sounds and colours dazed him. Music was playing somewhere, with a jolly, insistent beat. 'There's a brown girl in the ring, tra la la la la, and she looks like the sugar in a plum.' Out of sight, voices clamoured and feet thumped up and down stairs. At the back of the shop, there was a bead curtain, hooked back across an open doorway. A young woman, slender in a backless summer dress, paused there with a plate of sandwiches to pull up the strap of her high-heeled shoe. Cosmo saw the thin covering of flesh moving across her shoulder-blades, and the pink plastic combs holding up her dark hair. Behind her, in a room crowded with cardboard boxes, an older, stouter woman was washing plates at a stone sink. Two tiny children were chasing each other inanely round the shelves. The young woman in the doorway held out her hand and the smallest child staggered towards her. The shop was an Aladdin's cave, so crammed with goods that Cosmo had to keep reminding himself what he had come in for. Bruised nectarines breathed out a sweet smell at his feet, and he smelt the reddish earth clinging to the Cyprus potatoes. Salt-encrusted salamis hung in a pungent row above the meat and cheese counter. Dark rye bread and shiny plaited loaves were stacked beside bags of sugared pretzels and dry-looking foreign biscuits with pictures of luscious apricots on the packets. A smiling girl clutching roses was reproduced end-lessly on the labels of the Balkan jams. Cosmo heard a burst of laughter from three elderly female shoppers at the till, and saw a half-empty wine glass standing forgotten in the chilled cabinet, with the sweet-cured hams and the canary-coloured lumps of Cheddar. Nobody was hurrying. It was like a dream. The stocky, grizzled man at the till picked up objects one by one, stared at them narrowly, and punched in the prices. He licked his finger, peeling off a brown paper bag, and wrapped a muddy cauliflower. The festive atmosphere puzzled Cosmo, until the three ladies suddenly began to laugh and exclaim.

'Here she is, then – let's have a look at you!'

'Aren't you a picture!'

'Quite the little bride!'

A fat little girl, with tight dark curls and black button eyes, had come to the doorway. Smiling and squirming under the attention, but accepting it as her due, she stepped into the shop very carefully, to display herself. She wore a tight white dress which resembled net curtains, and a wreath of white nylon flowers. The expression on her blob of a face was a smug, self-conscious parody of extreme virtue. As soon as Cosmo saw her, he turned cold. He knew at once that the child was the reason for the party upstairs, and that she was got up in her plastic virgin's garb for her first communion. It was the repudiation of her pagan innocence, her first step to adulthood. She was old enough now to communicate with the saviour of her soul. Angrily, he refused to look into the eyes of someone who had just received the body of Christ. You're a little cannibal, he wanted to say, eating carrion. The frilly hem of the child's dress brushed his foot as she came past him to show the gold cross round her neck and the silver bangle on her plump wrist.

The man at the till turned to look searchingly at Cosmo, and he felt his bowels loosening with panic. But all the man said was, 'Yes sir?' and Cosmo heard himself reply, 'Twenty Silk Cut.' He was unbearably hot. Outside, he opened his jacket to let in the limp breeze and lit a cigarette, walking on to Islington Green.

Islington's Angel had fallen almost as far as his own. The pavements were jagged and smirched, and the shops vomited tawdry wares. He turned into the Pentonville Road, past a collapsing fence held together by the rags of flyposters. A tainted breath of wind stirred the grass mound covering the reservoir. In Claremont Square, he followed a sign which said 'Merlin Street Baths', because he felt dirty and was vaguely attracted by the idea of water. But the dirt reached down below his skin, and he knew that all the baths in Merlin Street could never wash him clean.

A solitary traffic warden passed him in Amwell Street, swinging her hat in her hand. She went briskly, as if she was on her way home. Cosmo walked briskly too. Through his confusion, he had a scrambled instinct that he was hurrying towards something important. A shop called 'Getting Married' drew his eyes briefly. Some people, apparently, did get as far as the altar. 'Let Us Take Your Photographs', begged a placard propped against a plaster wedding cake. The pictures on display showed brides so red and grinning that they looked like honest milkmaids.

The old-fashioned chemists on the corner had a stand of Leichner stage make-up in its window. 'Casualty Simulation. General purpose blood.' Was there more than one purpose for blood? Cosmo panicked as he ran up against a memory of Vinny in the Manchester dressing room, the day the wig block fell on his head. Dreamy with concussion, he had sat with his hands cupped under his nose while the blood dripped into his palms.

'Oh, oh, oh,' Cosmo whispered aloud to himself. 'I do feel so very sick.' He recovered himself by touching walls and lamp-posts, and tugging at the leaves which spilled through the netting round Lloyd Square gardens. Then he stared at the mossy dustbins and skeletons of motorbikes in Lloyd Baker Street, until he had managed to reduce the world to a series of nonsensical objects. On King's Cross Road, he turned towards Mount Pleasant and Exmouth Market, wondering about the lives of the jowly men he glimpsed in the pub on the corner, and whether they were happy dragging their beer-bellies and wagging their mottled red gills. The light was paler now, and the crowds were thinning. The vast advertisement hoardings in Farringdon Road dwarfed him. A giant tin of beans and a monstrous packet of detergent reduced him to a speck. Afraid of being left there alone, he followed a knot of men with briefcases down Farringdon Lane. Talking loudly, and laughing, they jostled into the Café St Pierre, and Cosmo was left loitering. He gazed through a plate glass window at the old Clerk's Well. It was covered with a wooden lid, warped and veined with age.

'The parish clerks of London, in remote ages, annually performed sacred plays,' he read. 'The water was greatly esteemed by the Prior and Brethren of the Order of St John of

Jerusalem, and by the Benedictine Nuns of the neighbourhood.'

Once, the city had teemed with the cowls and wimples of God's slaves. In those days, there had been less distinction between the two callings of actor and priest. It was all pretence and ritual. The Mass was no more sacred than a long-running West End farce – the 1,987th side-splitting year! The same old lines, night after night and twice on Wednesdays and Saturdays, the same old rituals among the actors, to keep the meaning of the words fresh. Cosmo massaged his fingers, and watched a man in an apron crossing Clerkenwell Green, wheeling a trolley loaded with quires of paper. A pub sign jutted out in a narrow lane – 'The Three Kings'. Three moorish gentlemen in mauve turbans and flashing earrings followed their star in the direction of the saloon bar, where they were invited to help themselves from the cold table. A cold table we had of it, thought Cosmo.

Behind the railings, there was a sooty eighteenth-century parish church. Graves like boxes stood beneath the trees, their inscriptions obliterated by the weather. Time was slipping away. There was no need to think about the future, or the wretched betrayed past. The famous clock-makers of Clerkenwell were probably buried here, he thought. Having dealt in the commodity of Time all their lives, they were taking their pleasant retirement, until Time itself shall end. On that day, they would be glad enough to wake and find themselves redundant. Except that Cosmo knew there was no Judgment. People's actions, good or bad, could not be registered by a heaven that did not exist. They were thrown away into the black pit of the past. A man was not connected to his sins for ever. He walked on, and in Smithfield Market his feet squelched on the bleeding scraps of rotten flesh in the gutter. An open-sided van was collecting the soiled sawdust and fatty, mortifying litter, and the stench of the grave was overpowering enough to make the eyes water. Other passers-by clamped their hands to their noses and looked quite green at this reminder of decay. Cosmo remembered coming here once at five in the morning, after a party. In the pallid dawn, he had watched the burly meat-men in their bloody aprons swinging great frozen carcasses on their backs.

On he went, towards Gray's Inn. In each street, he expected something to change, and nothing did. His immense desolation was catching up with him. Somewhere at the back of his mind, he had assumed he could go on indefinitely, until he disappeared, and the traffic ran over his empty clothes. The confusion was less intense now, and he tried to think. He was as homeless as the tramps huddled on the church steps in Kingsway.

Then he suddenly thought of Horatia, and in this extremity he faced at last the one element in their relationship he had always managed to avoid. If he had burned his own eyes out, he could not have been more wilfully blind. Searching for the reasons behind her malignity, he had sometimes thought it as pure and impersonal as God's love for the world; existing merely for its own sake. Now, he knew that she was driven by the strongest and simplest motive of them all – she was in love with him. Horatia Geldschmidt was in love with him. The realisation took his breath away. Here was the key to her talent for reading his soul – passion had sharpened her natural cleverness into supernatural penetration. She was always insisting that she knew him, and she certainly did; better than he knew himself. Since she had guessed, she should damn well help him now – that would be a fitting prize for having scored the bullseye. In fact, as matters stood, she was his only hope, and he loathed her for it.

Her house in Betterton Street was less than five minutes away, and he plunged dangerously across High Holborn towards her.

I can't do it, he thought, when he stood gazing up at her inscrutable windows. His heart bounded with fear – if he was really lucky, she would be out. But as he pressed the Entry-phone button, there was a bitter drizzle of sweat on his upper lip, and he struck the front door with his fist, muttering: 'Be there! Be there! Be there!'

Twenty-four

Cosmo's mouth went dry, and for a moment he was dizzy. He stumbled on a loose fold of the haircord carpet, and sent a dog-eared Yellow Pages hurtling down towards the street.

'Hester, is that you? What happened? Who's there? Oh my God, it's Cosmo – what on earth are you doing here?'

'Horatia?' He was in a terrible dream, where friends turned into strangers just as he reached them.

'No, I'm – I'm afraid she's out,' stammered Kitty. 'She's in Shrewsbury. At a regimental dinner.' Her hand went nervously to her mouth, and she scanned Cosmo's face with appalled, guilt-stricken eyes. At the top of the gloomy staircase, she stood like a figure in a stained-glass window, edged with silver from the lamp behind her.

'I mustn't – I'll be off, then.'

'No, don't go, Cosmo. Come in,' Kitty said urgently, holding out her hand. 'It's all right. There's nobody here but me.'

He closed his eyes, but she was printed on the inside of his eyelids, leaning forward, rimmed with light.

'Come up and have a drink.'

Cosmo wearily climbed the stairs, catching hold of her outstretched hand, which felt dangerously insubstantial. She drew him inside and shut the door, as if she was afraid he would sprint away.

'You look exhausted. Sit down on the sofa.'

He stared at the thin gold ring she wore round her middle finger, and imagined those bird bones snapping under the lightest pressure.

'Cosmo?'

Dropping her hand, he stumbled down the hall and shut himself in Horatia's lavatory. Cursing herself for her blunder, and wondering why on earth Cosmo had turned up instead of Hester, Kitty listened to the silence. Presently, she crept along the drugget, straining not to make a noise, and put her ear to the lavatory door. There was a long, hoarse breath, then some indistinct muttering. Absently, she gnawed her nails, and she winced when she heard the sound of vomiting. The three heavy splashes in the bowl tugged at her stomach. I wish Horatia was here, she thought. She'd know what to do with him. That afternoon, packing her net evening dress into a cardboard box, Horatia had said: 'He's got a Master's Degree in self-pity. He'll go to pieces. If you try to be nice to him tomorrow, he'll spit in your eye.'

There was another unnerving spell of silence. Kitty tentatively rolled her hand into a fist. She was about to knock on the door when a liquid, despairing moan began another burst of vomiting. She decided to risk going in, and the door jammed against Cosmo's back. He was kneeling on the floor, fervently embracing the lavatory bowl.

'Let me in.'

The room was tiny and reeked of sick. Kitty slid through the gap and stepped over his abject feet. Positioning herself against his shoulders, she held his wet, ghastly forehead, and wished she was braver. His head was heavy, and every time it jerked forward she felt her arms being yanked out of their sockets. Breathing through her mouth, she listened to the jets of bile hitting the water. It seemed to last for ages. Cosmo spewed passionately, until he brought up a dribble of greenish mucus and went limp. A fat bead of sweat dropped off the end of his nose on to the seat.

'Sorry,' he said breathlessly. 'What a disgusting mess.'

'Don't worry, I'll deal with it. How do you feel?'

'Clean,' he gasped, 'purged.'

'What?'

'Purged, I said.'

'Oh. Could you give me some room?'

They pressed and scrambled together in the confined space, and Cosmo crawled out into the hall on all fours. 'I'm so light, I could fly!' he exclaimed. 'It's like a dream.'

Kitty pushed the window open, and bathed her face in the warm night air. Be strong, she ordered herself, he needs you. There was a device in the cistern which turned the water blue, and this made the swimming gobbets look infinitely worse. The sides of the bowl were coated with what looked like lentil soup, and she had to wipe the speckled seat with wads of tissue. She pressed the flush repeatedly, working the brush under the rim, and using up half a bottle of Harpic. When she had finished, she found Cosmo propped against the wall outside. It was worse than she had imagined. He looked so sad and puzzled that the task of sympathising seemed enormous. Something inside him was utterly beyond her understanding. He's wondering how much I know, she thought. Why did I have to blurt out Hester's name like that? He'll never trust me now.

'Shall I make some tea?' she asked brightly.

'I'd like a drink.'

'Do you think you should? Well, there's gin, wine – she's got everything – you know her.'

'Something strong. Gin.' He surprised her by gripping her knee. 'You're very sweet, Kitty. Very kind.'

'Come into the sitting room.'

'I will in a minute,' he said.

'Okay.' Kitty went into the kitchen, and had a little frantic, fist-clenching session of silent panic. Oh God, tell me what to do! Should I go back? Holding her breath, she listened as he dragged himself to his feet and went back into the lavatory. This time, he locked the door. Slashing his wrists? Taking an overdose? Drowning? As soon as she heard the perfectly ordinary sound of urinating, she banged the cupboard doors, so he would not think she had been eavesdropping. The lavatory flushed again, rather feebly this time, and he went into the sitting room. When Kitty carried in the tray, he had taken off his jacket and was standing beside the fireplace, earnestly examining his face in the glass.

'You're hurt!' she cried. 'You should have told me!'

'Eh?' He shrank back suspiciously.

'There's blood all over your sleeve. You must have cut yourself.' She set down the tray. 'Honestly, you're in such a state.' She touched his arm, but he twitched it away from her. 'You're shaking,' she said patiently. 'Let me look at it.'

'Don't.'

Kitty traced the edge of the large brown stain. 'It's dry. Whatever it is, it's stopped bleeding, so it can't be all that bad.'

Cosmo hastily rolled up his sleeves, and disagreeably said: 'You don't have to fuss over me.'

Humbled, Kitty handed him his drink, and took hers to the large armchair. Cosmo sat down on the high nursery fender, which creaked under his weight.

'When will Horatia be back?'

Of course, he doesn't want me, Kitty told herself pitifully. I'm less than nothing to him. When I'm sympathetic, I get accused of making a fuss. 'Some time tomorrow,' she said. 'She'll probably go straight to the theatre. Some man is driving her down.'

'You don't have to pretend,' said Cosmo harshly. 'Social niceties are rather out of place when I've just puked all over you. You're dying to get rid of me.'

'No!'

'Bullshit. You expected Hester just now, didn't you?'

She turned scarlet, and her ears rang with embarrassment. 'Yes, but – '

'Why?'

'She telephoned this afternoon, to say she was coming.'

'To stay?' demanded Cosmo.

'Well yes, Horatia invited her.'

'I see.' He swilled gin round his mouth, washing away the taste of sick. 'It's all coming out now. You had me nicely sewn up, didn't you, you three?'

'I didn't have anything to do with it!' Kitty hotly insisted. 'When Horatia told me, before she left, it was the first – '

'Told you what?' he interrupted.

'That – that Hester was leaving you.'

'And what else?'

He looked so fierce that Kitty retreated into the cushions. 'To put sheets on the spare bed.'

'What else?' he roared at her.

'That she – that Hester was going back to Vinny,' whimpered Kitty.

Cosmo made a visible effort to control himself. 'Very neat and tidy. Always take the side of the person who behaves worst.' He went to the table to refill his glass. 'What's the matter?' he asked irritably, looming over the armchair. 'Why are you goggling at me like that – have I got two heads, all of a sudden? What do you think I'm going to do to you?'

'Nothing. I just feel so sorry for you.'

'You've all been plotting against me.'

'Cosmo, that's not true,' Kitty's voice became firmer when she sensed that he was willing to be persuaded. 'I'm on your side.'

'What's your opinion, then?'

She hesitated between loyalty and love. She chose love.

'She's been rather cruel to you.'

This satisfied him. 'Yes, you can say that again. She was cruel, all right.'

'But she didn't mean to be.'

'Oh please, Kitty, do me a favour. Bloody fool I must have looked. She was laughing up her sleeve all the time.'

'She wasn't.'

He sat down again. 'Nothing I've ever had in my life has been real. I'm always being deceived.'

After a short silence, Kitty dared to ask: 'So what happened? Where's Hester now?'

Cosmo did not reply.

'She must have gone to meet Vinny.'

'No,' he said.

'Well, where then?' she persisted. 'Didn't she tell you where she was going? Perhaps she's at her parents'.'

'Look!' he yelled. 'Look, will you stop interrogating me? I don't know, and I don't care!'

Kitty was on the point of tears. 'Don't shout.'

'Sorry. I've been demented all day.' He rubbed his hair with a weary gesture. 'Do you know, she didn't even care about Pilot? She was out all day yesterday, while he was dying in my arms. She was out with him.'

'Oh, is Pilot dead?' cried Kitty. 'Oh, poor little thing!'

'It seems ages ago now.' He looked old and harsh. The flesh was sagging away from his fine bones, and there were deeply incised lines round his eyes. He held himself awkwardly, as if he was lost inside his body, but Kitty, who usually set so much store by his grace, only loved him more. Never mind what Horatia said about self-pity – she was not going to leave him to be eaten by the starlings. She went over to him, and knelt at his feet. 'You'll miss him terribly, won't you?'

'It's all falling apart. Every single thing I had.'

'What can I do for you, Cosmo, darling?'

'Nothing.'

'Come and eat something. You'll feel better afterwards, I know you will.'

Obediently, he shambled into the kitchen behind her and sat at the table, watching her break eggs into a glass bowl. The outline of her nipples showed beneath the white T-shirt she wore. She pushed her dark, curling hair behind her ears with stumpy, bitten fingers, and her neat, staunchly-placed calves reminded him of the legs of a child in an impressionist painting. He shovelled down the scrambled eggs, warmed-over shepherd's pie and coffee she provided for him, unsettling her with the way he kept his eyes glued to her. He stared so because she was floating away, and her sweet, soft face was melting into the distance. Out of the depths he reached for her, like Dives seeing Lazarus cradled in Abraham's bosom. Separated by an unbridgeable gulf, and for all eternity. Send Lazarus with one drop of water for my parched mouth. He snatched Kitty's hand, which was still clutching a fork, and pressed it to his lips thirstily. Smiling, she gently tugged her hand away and carried the coffee cups to the sink.

Cosmo jumped up after her, grabbing a handful of her skirt. Under the flowered material, her flesh was warm and supple. Her T-shirt moved slightly over her breasts. He touched her ribs, to feel her heart beating there.

'What are you doing?' she laughed uneasily.

'Let me feel you.'

'If you want,' she said hopefully. 'If it will help. But you mustn't think that just because I cooked for you and everything that I expect – '

'I've changed my mind,' he interrupted. 'I don't want to die any more, Kitty, please, please – I want to live – '

Her feet whisked off the floor as he lifted her up. When her face was on a level with his own, he kissed her desperately, as if he would suck immortality from her mouth.

Blood ran warmly into the dusty channels of his dried veins. He dropped her and began to unbuckle his belt. Kitty coughed and rasped, holding her side – he had squeezed her too hard. Her face was varnished all over with his saliva. He ripped open his flies, and she ducked behind the table before he could lunge at her, saying: 'No, wait a minute – '

Unwilling, he waited, wrapping his fist round his penis.

'I want you to know that I understand,' Kitty announced solemnly. 'I don't expect anything. I can guess how you're feeling now, and you won't owe me a thing afterwards.'

Massaging his shaft, he realised there was a password. He racked his brains, and came out with: 'You're beautiful. I want you.' Even in his own ears, it sounded feeble, but it seemed to satisfy her.

'Oh Cosmo,' she whispered reverently, 'I've dreamed about this so often. I never imagined it might really happen.'

She led him upstairs ceremoniously, turning to smile at him from a pale, beatific face. In her bedroom, she stood back to let him see her domain. Cosmo, still fisting himself rapidly, had the vaguest impression of new paint, Horatia's second-best pictures, a fleecy dressing-gown flung across a chair, a pair of tights looped over the doorhandle. She flitted about, turning down the bed, twitching the blinds, and switching on lamps. Finally, bracing herself, she stepped out of her clothes, revealing an under-developed little body, white as an egg. With his free hand, he pushed her down on the bed and parted her legs.

'Aren't you going to undress?' she asked shyly.

Cosmo flung off all his clothes except his blood-stained shirt. When he knelt above her, she trapped his face between her hands and kissed it lightly all over. A picture flashed into his mind of the old Hester, in her loved, angelic form, and he shrugged her away.

'I do understand,' Kitty whispered.

He plunged into her so hard that she drew in a sharp breath and tried to wriggle away. Taking one of her downy buttocks in each hand, he sawed himself into the tight passage. He had assumed that he would shoot in a couple of seconds, but there was a blockage somewhere. Silently, he bashed his pelvis into hers, gathering speed. Eventually, she stopped resisting and crooned with pleasure, murmuring endearments. These died away, and still he laboured. The pressure inside him built until he was nearly frantic, and his sweat blotted the pillow.

'Now! Now!' he grunted, and the orgasm of his life turned him inside out, from the soles of his feet upwards. He came and came, until it was almost too much to bear, and plummetted into sleep as heavily as a stone.

Twenty-five

'Cosmo, will you please listen while I tell you something?'

On that grievous Thursday afternoon, Hester had been strained taut, and the cuffs of her jersey were pulled down over her hands – a sure sign that she was nervous.

Cosmo always liked to finish what he was saying. 'I've lost an inch off my waist since the last time I was measured.' Hester was being a little insensitive, he thought. She had been trying to interrupt him ever since he returned from his costume-fitting at Morris Angel's, and she knew perfectly well how it upset him to have the flow of his mind disturbed. 'Do you realise, I haven't been this size since I was twenty-one?'

'Will you listen to me?'

'Yes, all right love.' He broke off part of his digestive biscuit and looked around the floor for Pilot. The dazzle of his teeth diminished. 'I keep forgetting. I'll never get used to it.'

'Cosmo!' shrieked Hester. He noticed with surprise that she was quivering with agitation. 'Why don't you ever listen to anything I say? It all gets edited before it reaches your brain – I might as well be talking gibberish! You only hear the things you think I ought to say!' Cosmo was astounded. This was a long speech for his delicate, withdrawn white gardenia to make, and it was the first ever to contain criticism of himself.

'Sorry darling,' he said meekly.

Hester forced herself to breathe more steadily. 'Oh God, I'm messing it all up – I knew I would, I knew it – '

'Messing what – '

'Cosmo, could you please sit down? Please could you? You look so dreadfully big.'

He was on his guard. 'What've I done?'

'Nothing. I didn't mean to sound as if I was accusing you.'

'Well, good,' he said, relieved, 'because I haven't – '

'I'm begging you!' Hester wailed, in a frenzy of irritation. 'I'm imploring you!'

'Look, sweetheart – '

'Sit down! Sit down and listen for once in your life!'

'Jesus Christ Almighty,' he plumped down in a chair. 'Can I eat a biscuit, or will that put you off your stroke?'

Hester stole a glance at his injured, righteous face, and muttered: 'God, I'll never do it.'

'Hester, are you all right?'

'No, I'm not,' she said. 'Haven't you noticed anything about me lately?'

'No.'

'Don't just say no like that, Cosmo. Think about it properly.'

'Like what?' He knew he was very bad at this kind of conversation.

'For instance, that everything between us is wrong, and that I'm totally miserable.'

If she had picked up the kettle from the draining-board and bashed him over the head with it, he could not have been more stunned. 'What?'

'I know you've been just fine,' she said, with sudden bitterness. 'As long as you're all right, you don't give a toss how I feel.'

'But – but that's ridiculous,' he whispered. 'You know I'd – I'd walk through hot coals to make you happy!'

Hester snorted rudely. This gallant declaration seemed to enrage her. 'Oh, I know, I know. And you'd cut off your right arm, and you'd be strung up by your ears, and you'd be burned at the stake and shot and boiled in oil to save a single hair of my head – '

He was dumbfounded to hear his tender words flung back at him so ungratefully. 'Yes – I – you know I'd die for you – '

'Oh no you wouldn't! You'd die to stop anyone else getting at me, but you don't give a shit whether I'm happy or not. Vinny was right, and I didn't believe him at first.'

'What's Vinny got to do with this?' Even Cosmo was suspicious by now.

She was in full flood. 'I've been in despair for weeks. I've been ill and lonely and frightened, and not once have you asked – '

'I said, what's Vinny got to do with it?'

She avoided his eyes. 'I'm very, very sorry, Cosmo. I'm sorry about everything.' And she began to cry.

Though he had a ton weight sitting on his chest, and an icy fog in his ribs, Cosmo was softened. 'Take me through it slowly, love. I'm miles behind. Why were you in despair?'

'It wasn't my fault!' she wept.

'Hester, I'm not clairvoyant, you know. Should I understand what you're talking about?'

But it was written on her guilty face. He watched in horrified disbelief the withering of his pure camellia japonica, the woman who carried all his hopes on her shoulders.

'You've been cheating on me,' he said.

When she nodded, he actually felt his face change colour. If ever a man's heart could be said to break, Cosmo's broke at that moment. All his blackest horror came gushing through the cracks.

'I hated deceiving you,' Hester said, 'but you were so difficult to tell – it wasn't only that you were so good to me, but all the time you were making those threats about what would happen if I left you – and it wasn't fair. Nobody should have that responsibility. I was very vulnerable when I met you. You knew I was, and you took advantage. You squeezed promises out of me. Yes, you did – and you can't blame me for breaking them.'

Cosmo said, very quietly and distinctly: 'You are a whore.'

Her face hardened obstinately. 'I might have known you'd say that. Well, all right then, I'm a whore. I've committed the unpardonable sin of loving someone more than Cosmo Brady. And let me tell you, Cosmo, it's a bloody relief not to be an angel any more. All that Blessed Damozel stuff – it was blackmail – a few threats to make sure I didn't step out of line. Other men would have beat me round the head with a bottle, but you were smarter.'

'You sound like him!' he cried in anguish. 'That's not you!'

She had, at least, the grace to blush. 'I think it too.' She wiped her face. 'This is such a relief – I should have done it weeks ago. Vinny was right about that, too.'

The nightmare closed in around Cosmo. 'How long?' he demanded.

'Does it matter?'

'Yes – I've a right to know how long I had you. How soon did he try it on again?'

'I slept with him in Manchester,' said Hester. 'But you never really had me.'

'When?'

'When you were doing that workshop at the University.'

'You never could resist him, could you?'

'No,' she said sadly, 'I never could. Don't ask me what it is about him. You can either blame him or thank him, depending on your point of view. If he'd never left me in the first place, none of this would ever have happened.'

'Oh my Christ, you treacherous, lying whore!'

'That's right, Cosmo. You get it out of your system.'

Cosmo was in an agony of humiliation. His head went down on the table, among the butter and the sugar, and the brown paper bags full of fruit, and he began to howl.

'I'm getting used to it now,' Hester remarked. 'I simply hated it at first. I thought men never cried.' But she was still weeping herself, and he knew he was distressing her. He wanted her to suffer.

With a trembling hand, she lit a cigarette, and said, 'Oh, this is ghastly!' as if she thought it was nearly over.

'He doesn't love you,' Cosmo managed to gasp out, between sobs. 'He – can't love you like I do!'

'It's too late,' said Hester. 'I'm pregnant by him. I'm going to have his baby.'

It was odd that even as he reeled under this supreme blow, he took particular notice of the objects on the table: the prim attitudes of the salt and pepper pots, the exhausted appearance of the bag of plums, the drooping state of the butter.

'It's mine,' he said.

'It's Vinny's.'

'You want it to be his.'

'It is his.'

'Why can't it be mine?' he screamed at her.

She held her ground. 'Don't you yell at me.'

Cosmo grabbed the edge of the table and began to rock it violently. All the objects toppled and crashed to the floor. 'That's my child, and I won't let it near him – you have a blood test! I want my child!' There was a soft, insistent thudding under his feet. The woman downstairs was banging her ceiling with a broom. Cosmo leapt up, overturning his chair, and went to the place by the hot water pipes, from which she claimed she could hear all their conversations. 'Yes, you bang away, you nosey old bitch!' he bawled. 'You warped old virgin – this is my house and I'll do what I like – if you want to move, you fucking well move!'

The thudding ceased. Cosmo wiped his forehead and turned back to Hester. She took a step away from him.

'Have you got proof?' he asked.

'No, but – '

'Get it. You're not going anywhere until you know for certain.'

'You can't stop me!'

'If it's mine, I'll forgive you. We'll start again.' He meant to forgive her so savagely that she smarted under coals of fire for the rest of her days.

'It's not yours, Cosmo, for the last time. I fucked him without my diaphragm.'

Cosmo struck her hard across the mouth. She staggered under the blow, but he had not knocked the wickedness out of her.

'You – you – ' she shouted breathlessly, 'if I was carrying – if I was pregnant with triplets – and they were all yours – I'd rather die than stay with you!' She wiped her lip, and looked at the blood on her finger. 'I hate you! I'm sick to death of your snivelling and your dreary fucking and your incredibly boring obsession with God, and the way you think everyone is trying to cheat you, as if they could be bothered. You were too stupid to notice you were living with a woman who hates you, but everyone else knows, and they've been laughing at you – ' The children of Bethel were slaughtered by bears, because they mocked Elisha. Cosmo picked up the carving knife.

Hester, clenching her fists, began to scream and scream. She was a demon, hideously ugly, with a swelling, bloody mouth. She was the embodiment of dirt and evil.

'Stop that noise,' said Cosmo.

Still screaming, she made for the door. Cosmo got there first, and put his whole weight against it. 'Oh no you don't. You can stop complaining about my snivelling, Hester, because I'll never cry for you again.' He took a handful of her hair and jerked back her head. As he raised the blade of her knife, she stopped screaming, and there was a look on her face of recognition, as if she had suddenly spotted him in a crowd. He plunged the knife into her throat, and her eyes widened in astonishment. Again and again he thrust it in, with such force that a thin, warm spray of blood squirted into his face. Her little starfish hands stopped grasping at the air, and she was limp in his arms. He knelt over her on the floor, digging the knife into her stomach and breasts, hearing the blade scrape against her ribs, until his mighty fury was spent.

Sounds came back to him first, as he knelt there. He heard the tap dripping into the sink, and a van slowly driving past outside. There was a piping bird among the stunted shrubs in the garden. Then came physical calm, as his galvanised muscles relaxed one by one. This was not an unpleasant feeling. He was breathless, and his pulse galloped as if he had just been making love. Then his sense of touch returned. Something was turning cold and sticky on his hand. The knife slipped from his grasp

and fell on the lino with a homely clatter, as if he had dropped
it while washing up. He raised his hand to examine it curiously, surprised how weak his arm was. It was covered with
blood, and dripping. His other hand was behind Hester's
neck, and he gently plucked it away, because the blood was
running down his wrist. He stood, on legs which were miles
away and kept buckling at the knees. They carried him out of
the kitchen and upstairs to the bathroom, where the quiet was
blinding. What really amazed him was how normal everything
looked. The towels were hanging on the rail, the soap was in
the dish, and the bottle of dandruff shampoo was still on the
side of the bath, with the cap off. He washed his hands and face
hastily under the cold tap, watching the water run pink down
the plughole.

He rolled up his sleeves in a businesslike way and hurried
back downstairs. All that was left of Hester was a red carcass, a
collection of still, heavy limbs, and a matted sheaf of flaxen
hair. Blood wrapped it in a shining mantle – breasts, throat
and stomach were all stained a vulgar scarlet, deepening to
brown. There was a gory stain spreading on the crotch of its
grey trousers. Its hands and feet were lying at extraordinary
angles. Cosmo stood astride the object, staring gravely down
at what had once been the face. Gingerly, he picked up the
knife and threw it into the sink. Unable to think of anything
else to do, he went to Pilot's basket and took out the tartan
blanket upon which the poor little dog had lain in state. It
unfolded to a good size, and he nudged the body aside so that
he could spread it out on the floor. The object was wet and
unwieldy, but with many grunts and curses he managed to get
it on the blanket, lying on its back.

The blanket was predominantly red, and he tried to decide
whether this made the object look better or worse. Slightly
better, he thought. After standing back to consider, he pulled
the corners of the blanket so that it was in the exact centre of
the room. Then, across the tattered breast, he placed the hands.
The feet had a sickening tendency to loll in ridiculous attitudes,
but he placed them as best he could.

All this had tired him. Surveying his work, he rolled down

his sleeves, put on his jacket, and picked up his wallet and keys from the floor. Closing the kitchen door behind him very quietly, he plunged out of his house, and prepared to lose himself in the city.

Twenty-six

The word 'murderer' stamps a man through and through, like the word 'Southend' on a stick of seaside rock. When Cosmo woke on Friday morning, he had dropped through the bottom line of humanity and was crawling in the pit, with wolves and witches for his brethren. Any redeeming qualities he might have had were now irrelevant. The bare fact that he had committed a murder was enough to characterise him for all time.

Kitty was standing, already dressed, beside the bed, holding a cup of tea. He became acquainted with the murderer's terror of discovery. Yesterday, he had been too anguished to care what happened to him, but now he had an overwhelming longing to save his hide. What did Kitty know? What could she have guessed? Her face was awe-struck and troubled, and when she put the tea down on the bedside cabinet she unmistakably shrank away from him. Perhaps she knew it all – perhaps the men from the Yard were already waiting downstairs. *Miss Ashbourne, we have reason to believe that you know this man. I must caution you that anything you say may be taken down – Cosmo Brady, I arrest you for the murder of Hester Georgina Stretton – that on Thursday the twenty-third of July you did wilfully and with malice aforethought –* all this tumbled through his mind in the fraction of a second. His animal instincts sharpened.

Raising himself on his elbow, he asked: 'What's the time?'

Kitty was plucking nervously at her earrings. 'Nearly half past eleven. I thought I'd better wake you.'

'Thanks.'

'Do you want some breakfast? The water's hot, if you'd like a bath.'

'I'd love one.' The whole room stank of sex and fear.

'And I could wash your shirt.'

Sweat prickled under his arms when he realised he was still wearing his shirt. The jagged bloodstains on the right sleeve screamed to heaven – he had to get rid of it.

'No thanks, I haven't time.'

'But it's so dirty,' Kitty protested. 'You can't possibly wear it like that. Look here, why don't you borrow one of Rupert's?'

'Who?'

'He's the one Horatia went to see in Shrewsbury. He keeps some clothes here.'

'Oh, fine.'

'I'm sure he won't mind. He's more or less your size, too.'

'Kitty, I'm sorry about last night.'

She looked distressed, and covered it with a bright manner. 'Oh, you needn't be. I – I was glad.'

How glad would she be when she found out she had offered her body for the comfort of a murderer? Would she pity him then, or would she shudder, to think that he could have killed her as easily as pulling the head off a canary? Once a man had committed one murder, he was popularly supposed to acquire a taste for it.

'Why are you staring at me like that?' he demanded suspiciously.

'Well, well, it's your hair – '

'Eh?'

She was embarrassed. 'It's changed.'

Cosmo swung his legs off the narrow bed and went to the dressing table mirror. 'Oh, my Christ!' Overnight, death had withered him with a frosty breath. His whole head was as grey as ash, and the stubble on his face was like volcanic dust. He touched it wonderingly. His temples had been dyed for the part of Prince Ludolph, and the dark patches looked like rouge upon a corpse.

'It was like that when I came in this morning,' Kitty was saying unhappily. 'It did give me such a turn. I didn't sleep with you, because you were thrashing about so – I went to the spare room. And when I came to get some clothes – well.'

Cosmo could not organise his thoughts while he kept catching gusts of his guilty sweat. 'Can I have that bath?'

'Yes, of course, I'll get the shirt.'

'Does this Rupert have anything to shave with?'

'Sorry.'

'Shit.' He strode into the bathroom next door and ripped off his repellent shirt.

Kitty followed him. 'I thought people's hair turning grey overnight only happened in books and things.'

Go away, Cosmo thought. Haven't you seen enough yet? He managed not to say it.

'Shall I get you something to eat, Cosmo darling?'

'Lovely.'

She left him in a cloud of steam. The water was scalding. His face creased into a silent scream as he sat down. The tip of his penis was smarting – he had really given it a walloping last night. Kitty must be cut to ribbons, he thought. Poor little creature. The old Cosmo would have been mortified to recall such venery, but it hardly mattered now. He scrubbed and scoured himself vigorously, and when he felt clean he lay back, boiled scarlet and tender. The first thing he worried about was Kitty. At that very moment, she could be on the downstairs phone, looking fearfully over her shoulder and cupping her hand round the mouthpiece. Don't get carried away, he thought. She only knows that Hester's left me, and that there's a bit of blood on my shirt. There's no earthly reason why it should ever occur to her that I'm a murderer.

Panting in the heat, he levered himself out of the bath and took a towel off the rail which smelt of Horatia's scent. I ought to leave, he decided. They'll have a list of all the addresses – it's only a matter of time. He emptied his bladder into the departing bathwater, wincing as the urine stung his sore nut. Kitty had put the shirt on her bed. It was clean, but it savoured of another man. He thanked providence for this Rupert person – if not for him, Horatia would have been in last night and he would have spilled the whole story in five minutes. He had been out of his mind to come here.

When he went into the kitchen, his stained shirt rolled tight under his arm, Kitty was in a domestic flurry, straining to please him.

'It's practically lunchtime, so I opened some soup.'

'Oh yes, thanks.'

'I like your hair, now I'm over the surprise. It's rather distinguished.'

He grunted at her rudely, and shovelled down the lovingly-prepared meal with his ears cocked for a sound at the door.

Leaving was difficult. Kitty's eyes were full of tears when she kissed him goodbye, and she clung to his lapels. He listened impatiently to a pathetic little speech about how she understood and expected nothing from him, and at last managed to get in with: 'You've been tremendously sweet, love. Bless you.' He fled downstairs, just as her face was beginning to pucker. What a crown of delicious martyrdom women put on when they had been fucked by men who did not love them. They seemed to prefer love when it was one-sided – perhaps romance was more controllable when it all went on inside their own heads.

Out in Betterton Street, Cosmo gulped the free air. It was cooler than the day before, and the sky was pearly grey. The lunchtime crowds were weaving about the pavements – jaunty Covent Garden types, spilling into the gutter outside the pub. He made towards Long Acre, marshalling his thoughts and deciding that he might yet have a chance. If only he had not made so many mistakes. With a little forward planning, the whole thing could have been undetectable. An accident – everyone would have been so sorry for him then. Suppose he had hired a car, in disguise, and under an assumed name. He could have followed her to one of her meetings with Vinny, struck her down, abandoned the car. Yes, then he would have gone back on the Underground as far as the Angel, shedding his disguise on the emergency stairs, and walked back along Upper Street as himself. He imagined himself at home, the doorbell ringing, the blue serge outline and peaked head of a policeman through the frosted glass of his front door. What an obliging, innocuous face he would have presented to them. 'Yes officer, can I help you?' One of them would be a woman, to make the tea and put an arm round his shoulders. 'Please try to pull yourself together, sir, we have to ask these questions.' Hester's infidelity would come as a dreadful shock – what a performance he would give. 'She wasn't alone, sir. No, Mr Brady, she wasn't with her mother. Are you acquainted with a Mr Vincent Bliss? With a Vincent Titmarsh Bliss?' Cosmo marched down Bow Street, dreaming up ludicrous middle names for Vinny. 'With Vincent Sniggardly Bliss? Vincent Cruet Bliss? Vincent Weinsock Shatley Bliss?'

If only he had found a way of pinning it on Vinny altogether. Cosmo unconsciously made snapping movements with his mouth, as he assumed the character of Vinny being dragged screaming from the dock. 'I'm innocent, I tell you! I loved her!' Several passers-by regarded him charily out of the corners of their eyes, and Cosmo realised he was muttering to himself. He was turning into one of those men who shout on station platforms, causing decent folk like his former self to shrink behind their newspapers. With his sprinkling of grey stubble, he was admirably cast for the part. He scratched his chin aggressively.

I must get shot of this shirt, he thought frantically. At the top of Wellington Street, in the shadow of the Royal Opera House, there was a rubbish bin pinned to a lamp-post, but it was too conspicuous. Someone would notice and remember it when his face came up on the news. He crossed the Strand beside the old Lyceum Theatre, and lost himself in the narrow streets which touched the water's edge. His own fiendish nature was beginning to horrify him. Death was at the ends of his fingers – ordinary people did not know what a tightrope they were walking between awareness and oblivion.

Through an opening, he saw a tumble of old houses, crouching in the shadow of a slab-like American Bank. He ran through the archway into a forgotten alley, where the windows were blind with dust and the cramped house-fronts plastered with the brass plates of lawyers. Looking all round rapidly, he dropped his shirt behind some railings and hared back to the Strand, his heart beating in his mouth. Nobody had seen him, but he could not get over the feeling of being watched.

He had to appear to walk purposefully, but had not the ghost of an idea where he was going. A fugitive and a vagabond shalt thou be in the earth. Calling his nerves to order, he forced himself to assume a brisk, preoccupied expression – it was like trying to look normal in front of a camera. When he caught his reflection in shop windows, he looked absolutely ghastly, and deeply suspicious. He dug his hands into his jacket pockets, to hide their trembling. Men in business suits were hurrying through the revolving door of Simpson's restaurant. Recalling Kitty's tearful face, and her hands on his lapels, the chill of his stomach began to thaw. I mustn't think about it, he thought, or I'll give way. He saw the dark brown moles on her white arms, and her spread legs before he gored her. The vicious pain returned. He should go back to Betterton Street and take the poor girl in his arms – all she wanted was a kind word or two, and who should know better than him what it was to suffer for kind words? But he paced on, dodging the crowds and trying to stay alert in case he ran into anyone he knew. His agent's offices were in Villiers Street, and the West End was always swarming with actors. The food he had just eaten burned the lining of his stomach, and there was a firework display going on in his large intestine.

A knot of American tourists, dressed in foolish nursery clothes as if visiting Toytown, were photographing Nelson's Column. Cosmo tilted back his head and made out the silhouette of the great Admiral, lonely against the pale, damp sky. A flock of greedy pigeons soared up from one of the fountains, with a great rushing sound like a round of applause. Insolent-looking Italian girls straddled the balustrades of the National Gallery, studying maps through shocks of carefully disarranged hair. Cosmo went inside, thinking that here, at least, he could loiter, without seeming too shady. He stood on the Boris Anrep mosaic in the hall, and all around him the slow, considering footsteps of the visitors dropped like stones in a well. In his first year at drama school, a foreigner in London and desperately shy, he had often taken refuge in here on Sunday afternoons, because it was one of the few places where you could put up a good show of being too absorbed to be lonely. He knew every single picture, from Monet's 'Water-lilies' to the Wilton diptych. This time, he started at the Monet. Across the wide expanse of parquet, people strolled with curious, frowning faces, pausing to consult guidebooks and catalogues, or stepping backwards to take a reflection out of the varnish. A cerebral hush lay over the place, broken only by intelligent murmurs and the creaking of the security guard's boots. Cosmo paced conscientiously through each room, but paid little attention to the paintings. The airy, echoing galleries opening out of each other into the distance made him think of the antechambers of a Royal Palace. Suppliants, petitioners and courtiers strolled in the antechambers, talking in reverent, muffled voices. Behind the door of the throne room, God sat at his assizes, in a sunburst of terrifying splendour. He had heard the clamouring of Hester's blood and was preparing to deliver a thunderbolt of Justice.

But, from a muddy canvas, Christ's sad face looked past him, half-shadowed by the light of a candle on a table. The picture was Honthorst's 'Christ Before the High Priest', and the Messiah stood with his hands tied like a common criminal. The fact was, he had been judged himself, and the flesh had fallen from his bones two thousand years before.

The afternoon was wearing away. He left the National Gallery and threaded his way through the crowds on Charing Cross Road. At Cambridge Circus, he turned into Shaftesbury Avenue, passing Morris Angel's where he had been at his costume fitting not twenty-four hours before. For the first time, he thought of his work, and realised there would be no 'Wearing of the Green' now. They would have to trim down those homespuns and Donegal tweeds to fit someone else – and how that other actor would dislike standing in such cursed clothes.

On High Holborn, Cosmo sauntered, gazing into shops and telling himself he must escape or he was lost. The question was, where to? Soon, the world would know what he had done, and there would be nowhere left to shelter him. If I'd really had my wits about me, he thought, I'd have taken my passport and buggered straight off to Heathrow. What did I imagine I was doing, frigging about walking to Horatia's? Why didn't I take the car?

He turned into Chancery Lane, and choked back a spasm of panic when he almost overbalanced a policeman. Don't look round, he commanded himself. If he wants you, he'll come and get you. Most probably, he had heard nothing at all, but Cosmo longed to find out, by accosting him and asking him the time in a German accent, or pretending he had lost his way. He darted down a side-street on his left, and followed another party of American tourists into the London Silver Vaults.

Glancing upwards, he saw dozens of grey-haired, fish-faced Cosmo Bradys gawking at him from convex security mirrors. The Americans were happily submitting to searches by the two guards at the desk, offering their bags and camera cases with garrulous charm. Cosmo slipped past the desk and joined the people who were already walking downstairs. The stairwell reminded him of the tiled entrance to a swimming bath – it had the same lingering institutional smell of slops and disinfectant. He stepped into the gentlemen's lavatory on the landing, and when he came out five minutes later the Americans had gone. Somewhere beneath his feet, he heard them, like a flock of amiable geese. Far below street level, he found himself being pinned by the red eye of a security camera, which watched the reinforced glass cases like Almighty God. In the cases were unwieldy silver epergnes supported by scantily-clad angels, silver elephants balanced on crystal rocks, and antique silver bracelets in bald velvet cases. Cards bristled among the slabs of precious metal. 'N. Zuckerman. No. 65', 'Z. Konig. No. 38'. Notices everywhere urged visitors towards two rows of shops, in all the languages of greed.

Cosmo's scalp became several sizes too small. He was walking through a prison door, massively thick, barred and bolted. The dizziness came back, and the rigid lines of the corridor in front of him sagged and buckled, as if he was seeing them through water. It was open day in the jail, and each thick door was pinned back. The tiny cells were crammed with silver, and the pallid lighting was reflected dully in great tubs and urns, punch bowls, bunches of cutlery, and coy miniatures of piglets and mice, over which the American ladies exclaimed. A young man in a skull cap was holding up a coffee pot for a leathery American man. 'But it's new,' the American was saying. 'I want an old one.' His wife was taking out her other glasses to squint at the scent bottles and decanter labels.

Cosmo staggered from cell to cell, drowning in the nightmare. For the first time that day, he had totally given in to his panic, and nobody noticed. Choking with claustrophobia, he touched the cold wall. His ears were rushing, and any second now he would start screaming: 'Let me out! I can't spend the rest of my life in one of these!' It was a cemetery, with rows of family vaults where green bones were stacked on the shelves in mouldy coffins. His pulse slowed, and he was able to fill his lungs. He took out his handkerchief and wiped the rank dew from his face. Slowly, the objects and people around him hardened into reality, and he became light and calm. Afraid that he would be stared at, he began to saunter among the cases, careful to drift away before anyone asked if he wanted to buy something.

There was a display of mourning trinkets jumbled together under a glass frame – black enamel rings and bracelets, with wreaths of willow cleverly fashioned from human hair. The largest piece was a hinged gold locket, showing on one side a daguerreotype of a heavy-faced Victorian infant, and on the other a tuft of faded baby hair. It was engraved in Gothic letters: 'Jesus Called a Little Child Unto Him. Matt 18:2'.

The woman pressing in behind him called over her husband to look, but when the vendor asked if she would like him to take it out of the case she laughed and shook her head. 'I don't know who'd buy something like this,' she said. 'Mourning jewellery is so unlucky.'

Cosmo, looking studiously at an arsenal of fish-knives,

began to cry. The hard iron bands which had been constricting his breathing ever since the murder dissolved, and he could no longer protect himself from his dreadful grief for Hester. It was no good trying to recall the evil woman who had squirmed on the blade of his knife. She was before him now in all her gentle beauty, transformed at last into the angel he had cast her as all along. The sting of betrayal was cancelled out by the suffering he had caused her, and for one more glimpse of her he would have descended into the Underworld, like Orpheus, and risked unimaginable torments. The tears rushed down his face faster than he could wipe them away, and he dashed through the vaults with his head down and his chest heaving.

On High Holborn, he ran through the crowds, knocking against people without feeling them, and ducked through an archway into Staples Inn, which was deserted. Putting his arms round a tree that grew out of the worn cobbles, he wept and wept. He thought of Hester's unborn baby, also slain, of her parents, who had lost their only child, even of Vinny. There was nothing he would not have done for one crumb of forgiveness.

This was absolute despair, so thick and deadly that he hardly registered the embarrassed glances of the people who occasionally trotted past. The boughs of the tree shivered and rustled above him, and he prayed for something to come out of the chaos and save him. Oh, have mercy, he begged, and he was so desperate that he did not even wait to see if his voice echoed back at him from an empty universe. Leaving the tree with a salty patch on the bark where his cheek had been, he stumbled back on to the main road, and watched his feet pounding the dusty pavements. The cars and buses tangled at Holborn Circus. Brakes screamed and music pounded out from open windows. Cosmo stood on the extreme edge of the kerb and, through the storm in his head, he heard a still voice at his elbow.

'Excuse me, would you be so kind?'

Cosmo did not believe that anyone would dare to address him when he obviously had the tomb stamped all over his face.

'Excuse me, would you be so kind?' he heard again.

Turning, he saw that the man next to him was blind. His blank eyes, half shut, squinted over the bridge of his nose, and his head was tilted back as if he did not fear the dangerous world he could not see. His long white stick probed the gutter fastidiously, like the tongue of a butterfly.

'Excuse me, would you be so kind?'

This was a chant he must repeat a hundred times a day to the empty air, always in faith that someone in the invisible crowd would be kind enough to help him. He could not afford to wonder whether the man next to him was a murderer. Since there was nobody else on the kerb, Cosmo silently offered his right arm.

'Thank you. Thank you so much.'

When they crossed, Cosmo remembered, like a sign, how blind Bartimeus had sat by the highway begging and, when he heard that Jesus was passing near by, had shouted into his darkness: 'Jesus, thou son of David, have mercy on me!' The people round him had tried to silence him, but he went on bellowing at nothing, so great was his faith, until Jesus stopped. 'Lord,' he said, 'that I might receive my sight.'

Cosmo found his own darkness unbearable. He knew that all his life he had missed things and got things wrong – he was as blind as Bartimeus, but he had never shouted loud or long enough.

'Thank you,' the blind man said, and strode away with his chin up, tapping briskly with his stick.

I'm back at the same point, thought Cosmo, on the same road, despite all the twists and turns I made. At last, after his desolate wanderings, he had a destination. He went past the little gatehouse which sealed Ely Place from the main thoroughfare, glancing at the man who sat inside boiling his kettle and eating biscuits off a plate. The smart eighteenth-century houses were bright with window boxes of scarlet geraniums, and there were tubbed bay trees, carefully tonsured, to prevent them flourishing like the wicked.

St Etheldreda's stood back from the trim terraces, a small patch of city land that had been bled upon, burned and bombed during seven hundred years. Through the door at the side, Cosmo walked in, and the odour of incense, faint beneath a reminder of the mashed potatoes and fishcakes which had been cooked for lunch, whisked him straight back to his seminary on the outskirts of Dublin. There was a wooden display case for Catholic Truth Society pamphlets, priced one shilling and dated 1955. There were pleas for funds – Christ's poor, the Clergy House, St Peter's pence. There was a notice board, with badly-printed invitations to money-raising barbecues. Xeroxed sheets gave details of obscure and eccentric lectures about phenomena in Guadalupe, Walsingham, Fatima and Garabandel. 'Why is the Madonna weeping? The Australian Friends of the Rosa Mystica invite you to share her tears and listen to a message of global importance. Maria, Rosa Mystica, ora pro nobis.' St Etheldreda herself, in painted plaster, stood high up on a bracket, opposite the glassed-in cloister.

The quiet was dreamlike, emphasised by the clanking of pans in the pantry, and the sudden snatch of laughter behind a closed door. Cosmo bathed in it luxuriously, making his way slowly along the stone-flagged passage, past the graphic photographs of the church's structural defects, past the entrance to the crypt, where the steps dropped down into rimy gloom. He went up the stairs, past rows of dusty collecting boxes which suggested threepenny bits, bent sixpences and very small spiders, and up the shallow stairs with his heart thumping fit to stifle him. He rediscovered the peculiar stillness of an empty church; the impalpable atmosphere of expectancy; the ominous look of the shrouded safe which held the sacrament. Votive candles were guttering before a side-altar to the Blessed Virgin Mary. The English martyrs watched him from the stained glass window above: a silent, eager, soft-robed huddle. Cosmo knelt on the cold stones before the picture of the Virgin, crossed himself, and unlocked the words.

'I confess to Almighty God, to Blessed Mary Ever Virgin, to Blessed Michael the archangel, to the holy apostles Peter and Paul, to all the saints, and to you, Father, that I have sinned exceedingly, through my fault, through my fault, through my most grievous fault.' He struck his chest three times – the sign of contrition – and waited. The stone floor made his knees ache. He felt nothing, but the blankness was exquisite after the pain and he had not come expecting a miracle – he was hardly in a position to issue such requests to the Almighty. The miracle was that he was here at all. He was utterly exhausted, and all he could do was start again. He sagged forward until his head rested on the floor, and he spread his palms on the stones. *Soliditas Cathedrae Petri.* Now let me die, since I have seen thy face.

It was like suffering with a crippling toothache, he thought. His attitude to it changed, but the pain itself did not. In the taxi on the way home, he had made himself visualise Hester's body, and when he turned the key in his front door he decided that he was calm enough to face it without being afraid. But he was only calm enough to face what he had nerved himself to expect.

Holding his breath in the deathly silence, he turned the handle of the kitchen door. It jammed against something heavy, and Cosmo got a shock which all but killed him.

The body had moved.

Pilot's tartan blanket, which he had spread so meticulously, was creased and twisted, as if she had writhed upon it. Clots of congealed blood daubed the lino.

'Oh Hester, no, no – '

She lay stiffly curled under the table, her eyes grey and opaque, with one arm clutching her mutilated stomach and the other clutching at the air. Her face still wore its final expression of surprise, which the passing hours had stretched into the beginnings of a crazy smile. The telephone receiver hung down over the edge of the table, and there were bloody fingerprints on the wire where she had vainly pulled it.

He carefully replaced the receiver, and knelt down beside her, taking her outstretched hand. The diamond in her engagement ring shone in a setting of frozen blood. He pulled down her eyelids, and the skin resisted him like chilled Plasticine.

Then, like the voice of Judgment, the telephone rang. Dazed, still holding her hand, Cosmo picked it up.

'Hello? Hello – Cosmo, is that you?'

'Yes,' he mouthed.

'Hello? Is that Cosmo Brady?'

He cleared his throat. 'Yes.'

'What the fuck are you doing there? Did you forget about the show tonight? I called the half ten minutes ago, and your fucking phone's been busy every time I tried – ' It was Malcolm Snelling, in a Stage Manager's Frenzy. 'I suppose Hester's with you?'

Cosmo stared down at the wrinkled eyelids. 'Yes.'

'Well, what are you waiting for? Get in the bloody car – it is working, isn't it – I'll just have to hold the show till you get here, and, my God, you'd better have a good excuse for this, or I'll have your arses, the pair of you – '

Cosmo wetted his lips. Out came his voice, surprisingly neutral and polite. 'I'm afraid we won't be coming. You'll have to send the understudies on.'

'What!' The earpiece vibrated to Malcolm's shriek of outrage. 'Are you out of your – '

'I'm terribly sorry, Malcolm, I'm going to have to hang up on you,' Cosmo said. 'I have to call the police.'

'What?'

At the stage door, Malcolm held the telephone away from him and turned to Vinny, who was waiting anxiously behind him.

'This is unbelievable – he's gone barmy. He says Hester's dead.'

Twenty-seven

Before anyone had a chance to verify the story, the actors, like a hive full of bees, sensed a death in the house and swarmed. The long dusty corridors backstage were full of dishevelled, half-clad figures, running to and fro in restless agitation. Voices shrilled, feet drummed on the linoleum, fire doors swung crazily on their hinges.

'Oh Christ,' said Malcolm. 'Bloody nice this is going to look on my show report.'

Out in the foyer, the 'House Full' cards were up, and the girl who played Cole Porter songs on the flute was finishing, to feeble, preoccupied applause. The audience were already stubbing out cigarettes, tipping back the last of their drinks, and stowing their belongings under the mauve plush seats. Malcolm, in the middle of his professional nightmare, heard them over the relay, criticising the set in loud, curious voices. It was too late to turn them away without causing administrative chaos. It was too late to print slips for the programme. The front-of-house manager, who announced all the fire alarms and bomb scares, wrote down the details on a scrap of paper and prepared to clamber up on the apron with his whining microphone.

Derek Hooey hastened out of the greenroom, and crashed into Rosamund Jaeger's dressing room, damply clutching a bottle of lager.

'Get out,' she said.

'Oh, you've heard, have you?'

'Yes.'

'Bloody amazing, the way news gets about in this place. You know who's behind it all, of course?'

Rosamund had just come from her fertility clinic with a poisonous snake in her heart. She was obsessively painting her lips, until they looked as hard as enamel in her grim face. 'Who?'

'Well, Vinny Bliss, obviously. So much for your great love affair that shook the world.'

'You're drunk,' said Rosamund, 'and you smell. Get out.'

'She was pregnant, apparently.' Hooey smacked his lips appreciatively. 'What a sordid little tale. Jealous lover hacks pregnant girlfriend to pieces. What a tasty snippet for the Sunday papers. We'll all be wrapping our chips in it for weeks.'

'Get out!' Rosamund screamed. 'Get out! Get out!'

'Oh, I'd write a play about the actor's ego,' Hooey said, when he was back in the bar, 'if I thought anyone would bother to go and see it.'

Upstairs in Wardrobe, Simon Gartner caught the scent of Cosmo's sweat on the Albanian costume, and a sickening fart of terror hissed between his clenched buttocks. As Cosmo's understudy, he was now the living incarnation of bad luck, and the others shunned him as if he had had an albatross tied round his neck. Two dressers were ramming his feet into a pair of borrowed hessians. He had often wished he was in Cosmo's shoes, but when it came to the point they were too big. 'Carve it on my tomb', he muttered, 'That when I rest beneath, men shall confess, this Prince was gulled and cheated.' The lines were crumbling away into nothing, and when he tried to visualise entrances and exits he saw only Cosmo in the last scene, holding his dagger aloft, with silver flecks of saliva drizzling in the light round his head.

Simon stared out of the window at a jagged row of ventilator shafts, thinking: it's exactly like a dream – a ghastly dream. His mind wandered over the events of a normal evening. At that moment, he should have been comfortably awaiting his call in the dressing room he shared with Tommy Inchbald and three lads from *Measure for Measure*. A routine had evolved, which he could go through with only half his brain. Canteen supper. Get dressed, and read the small ads in *City Limits*. A mug of tea brought in by the dresser at about eight. Half of Bass in the interval, another half after the curtain call, then home to Clapham. Folded into the routine were small, depressing bursts of acting.

At a certain point in the second act, he always climbed the off promptside stairs and met Hester. It was printed in his mind like a photograph, though he had taken it completely for granted until now. The door was pinned back by a stage weight, and empty glasses were lined up on the ragged carpet against the wall. This was where Hester stood between her entrances, smoking delicately so she would not spoil her lipstick. In the dingy overhead light, her hair was dark gold and her elaborate make-up a gaudy mask. A gilded lily, Simon thought. He never liked to see her beauty coarsened. The long velvet train of her dress flopped down the stairs behind her. When she saw Simon, she always smiled in the gloom and took her cigarettes and lighter from the muff. Simon always accepted one, with the words: 'Thanks darling, I shouldn't. I owe you millions.' His costume hadn't any pockets.

'No, what rubbish, you don't owe me,' was the ritual reply. There were slightly darker rims round the blue of her eyes, and her lashes were moist and thick with mascara. For a few minutes they smoked and gossiped idly, in whispers, about the progress of the show. Then they crushed out the cigarettes in the hollow of the stage weight and went through the door to the stage. Hester solemnly manipulated her skirts, and Simon gallantly effaced himself to let her pass. She acknowledged this as a right, like a queen, but if he looked under the paint he always saw that her face was amused and friendly.

But she was dead. He felt she was dead when all these images lost their animation and became enshrined in marble. The taste of death was in his mouth: ashy, frightening, somehow exciting. When his body reacted, quite unconnected to his brain, by starting to cry, the actor in him stood aside and marvelled.

Vinny was too hysterical to cry. 'She was supposed to come to you!' he was shouting. 'She was on her way to you last night! You must have seen her!'

'Go away.' Madge, trembling but defiant, blocked his path. Her blue nylon wrapper was buttoned in the wrong holes across her tremendous bosom, and her hair was pin-curled beneath a wig-stocking, making her look as if she had had the top of her head sawn off. 'Can't you see what state she's in?'

'She' referred to Kitty, who was weeping into Hester's muff on the divan. Horatia, also weeping, was huddled into the corner by the telephone, with her bony shoulder blades working painfully against the top of her corset.

'She's not going on,' warned Vinny. 'If she puts a toe on that stage in Hester's costume, I'll kill her!'

'Stop acting as if she wanted to go on, poor little thing!' cried Madge. 'It's not her fault.'

'If it's anybody's fault, it's yours,' said Horatia's voice from the corner.

'Mine!' Vinny turned crimson and rudely shoved Madge aside. Horatia came out to face him, with a broad stripe of eye make-up down each cheek. The tendons in her neck stuck out like piano wires.

'If you hadn't behaved like such a shit this never would have happened!' she screamed. 'Why couldn't you have left her alone?'

'Don't you go sticking up for that evil bastard!' Vinny roared back at her.

'He's not! He isn't! It's all your fault!'

'Oh, it's mine, is it?' Vinny's broken veins were an unhealthy purple behind the youthful flush in his cheeks. 'What about you? You might have saved her, but you didn't, did you? You were so fucking jealous, you just told her to piss off! You knew what was going to happen, and you didn't lift a finger to stop him!'

Horatia's thin face crumpled, and she began to snivel uncontrollably.

'She told me all about it.' He pursued his advantage. 'She went down on her knees to you, and you knew perfectly well you were the only person who could help her.'

'I – how could I tell what was going to – oh please don't blame me, Vinny! I did help her – I told her she could come to my house! Didn't I, Kitty?'

'You said she'd have a black eye,' said Kitty thickly.

'I didn't! I didn't!'

'Yes you did, and you were looking forward to it. You said so.'

Vinny grabbed Horatia's shoulders and shook her so hard that the pins flew out of her wig. Dull, heavy coils of corpse's hair fell across his hands.

'What are you doing? Stop it! Stop it at once!' Madge managed to grab the back of his military collar, and she pulled at it energetically until he let go of Horatia.

'Nobody's going on,' he said, breathing hard. 'There isn't going to be a show.'

Hester's velvet dress, brought down for Kitty, was lying across the divan. Vinny picked it up and ripped it from hem to waist. 'There. You can't wear it now.'

As the door slammed behind him, Kitty wailed: 'But I don't want to go on for her! I can't!'

'I don't see why not,' Horatia aggressively wiped her nose with the back of her hand. 'You managed to stand in for her last night.'

Madge let out a little squeal of horror. 'Oh Horatia, how could you?' She bounced down on the divan and scooped Kitty protectively into her arms. 'Don't you listen to her.'

'You stupid little cow,' said Horatia. 'In he comes, covered with blood, acting like a lunatic, he vomits all over the house, and all you can do is make a pass at him.'

'You're just jealous,' Kitty sobbed into Madge's shoulder, 'because he slept with me and not you.'

'Who the hell do you think he came to see in the first place?'

'He wouldn't have touched you!'

'Bloody right he wouldn't,' Horatia sobbed back, 'because I wouldn't have let him – he was probably in the mood to shag any old thing – you were an absolute fool to go along with it. Oh, why wasn't I there? When I think how he must have felt, wandering about, all alone!'

'Don't you go blaming Kitty,' Madge said, unable to resist taking advantage of Horatia while she was in a state of misery. 'You never liked Hester – you were always saying horrible things about her. I wouldn't live with your conscience for anything.'

'The thing is,' Kitty said despairingly, 'I did know it was wrong. He looked so ghastly, Horatia. It would have broken your heart.'

Horatia wept. They all three wept in concert, until Madge blearily handed round a box of tissues.

'Look at the time,' she said. 'We should have gone up five minutes ago. Why haven't we had Beginners?'

In the dressing room next door, Malcolm was fighting it out with Vinny.

'I've got a theatre full of punters. What the hell am I supposed to do with them?'

'Tell them to fuck off. Give them their money back.'

Douglas Binyon, the Equity Deputy, was sitting in Cosmo's chair, with a nylon poloneck over his *Measure for Measure* trunk hose. 'Since the understudies haven't been rehearsed according to the agreement,' he piped up, 'technically, the company would be well within their – '

'Do me a favour, will you, Dougie?' snapped Malcolm. 'What are you doing here, anyway?'

'I called him!' shouted Vinny, hurling his tunic across the room and pulling his jersey over his head. 'He's my union representative!'

Binyon was mocked and ignored by his fellow actors when they had nothing to fear, but when there was trouble he was wheeled out like a battle standard.

'He's my representative, too,' Malcolm said. 'I've got to get a show on, and you're the only thing standing in the way. You're on a report, Vinny, do you hear?'

'What do you mean, the only thing?' Vinny demanded furiously. 'What about Hester – isn't anyone thinking about her? That's just the trouble with you, and people like you. Actors are disposable, aren't they? If one of them drops out, you can always fill in with another. Don't give me all that shit about the show must go on. Send on Tommy, if you're so worried.'

'It can't be done,' Douglas Binyon put in. 'Not with three understudies.'

'Listen, Vinny,' Malcolm aggressively stabbed at the air with his finger. 'I'm not having any prima donnas from you! If I don't see you in costume in the prompt corner in two minutes, you're fired!'

'All right then, I'm fired.'

'I don't think you can – ' Binyon began faintly.

'You've got a bloody bare-faced nerve!' shouted Malcolm. 'You've stirred up enough trouble already – '

'Meaning what?'

'Get dressed and get up on that stage!'

'No!'

'Doug, is there anything I can do with him?'

'Well, to be honest, I just don't know,' Binyon said. 'I've never had an actor refusing to go on before.'

In the end, it was Sir Freddie who settled the question. He came into Vinny's dressing room with stately tread, fully dressed and made up. A stout cheroot was burning between his fingers – the only sign that everything was not normal. The room immediately became small and claustrophobic.

'Good grief,' he said, 'of course you're going on. Never heard such nonsense in my life.'

He was so magnificent in his Franz Josef costume, so genuinely amazed at the thought of not going on, that Vinny was cowed.

'I'm not thinking about me,' he mumbled, 'it's wrong, after what's happened. It's immoral.'

'Immoral my arse,' said Sir Freddie. 'As for what's happened, I don't believe a word of it. That Cosmo Brady always was barking mad. Now get dressed, there's a darling. No point in fretting. She'll turn up safe and sound.'

'She's dead,' muttered Vinny. He seemed to realise it for the first time, and he sat down on the divan as limp as a marionette.

'Don't you think', rumbled Sir Freddie, 'that you owe it to

her to go on? She'd want you to go out there and show them what a real pro is made of.' He uttered this cliché so sincerely that they were all impressed. To Sir Freddie, 'The Show' was a great unstoppable juggernaut, as crushing and impersonal as the tide. Allowing oneself to be crushed by it was the highest form of virtue. It did occur to Malcolm that Hester would have wanted to live far more than she would have wanted the Show to go on, but Sir Freddie's huge presence and mellifluous voice knocked this rebellious thought to the back of his mind. 'Oh, I know what I'm talking about,' the great man said. 'I was bombed out of three theatres during the Blitz.' He extinguished his cheroot in Cosmo's ashtray. 'Someone run down to the bar and get him a nip of brandy. Where's his dresser? Never around when you want them.'

Vinny clumsily pulled off his jersey, and reached for his tunic. Walking down the corridor with Malcolm, Sir Freddie said: 'Well, now I've seen the lot.'

'What do you think, Freddie? Do you think Cosmo really did it?'

'I haven't the foggiest, old darling. Nothing like this would ever have happened in my day. These young actors – I blame the Fringe, I seriously do. When you look at plays like that piece of crap in the studio, full of violence and bad language – and I blame the repertory system. Popping in for three shows a fortnight, twiddling their thumbs the rest of the time on full pay. That's not a life for an actor. Eight shows a week and they wouldn't have the strength to run round killing each other.'

'It won't be much of a show tonight.'

'Oh, my dear boy,' said Sir Freddie imperturbably, 'it'll be a total disaster. We'll be lucky to get out of this building in one piece.' He shook his hairy jowls, and added: 'Hope she's all right, though. Nice little thing. Pretty, too.'

Malcolm called Beginners, and the loose threads of the show were hastily gathered together. The front-of-house manager, in his burgundy velvet dinner jacket, went out to silence the impatient audience and announce the cast changes. Simon was in the wings, looking like a bundle of dirty washing in Cosmo's Albanian costume, which was much too big. 'Break a leg, old lad,' Sir Freddie said, patting his shoulder. 'We'll busk it somehow.'

This was the first kind word Simon had had since he put on the murderer's cursed clothes, and his lip trembled. 'I'm going to make such a dick of myself.'

'Well, never mind, never mind. Not your fault. If you forget the words, make 'em up. That's what I always do.'

Vinny, very pale, stole into the quick change room. The tide of his popularity had turned, and he had run a gamut of filthy glances from his colleagues on the way up. Horatia was already there, skewering her tiara to her wig. Her red, puffy face had been freshly crusted with make-up, and looked dreadful under the pitiless lights. Their eyes met in the mirror as Vinny glued in his monocle.

'I'm sorry,' she said.

'What've you got to apologise for?'

'I mean, I'm sorry for you.'

'I know what you're thinking, so you can save it.'

Malcolm came to the doorway, 'Okay, we're off. Just get through it, that's all I ask. I'm on the book tonight. Do what you can for the understudies, poor sods.' He whispered into his walkie-talkie: 'Ready, Harriet, house lights down.'

Behind the gauze, Horatia pressed Vinny's cold hand. 'We're in the same boat, darling. Nobody's talking to me either.'

'Piss off,' said Vinny.

This would normally have turned her tongue to vitriol. He hardly recognised the small, sad voice that came out of the darkness beside him. 'Oh Vinny, forgive me, darling.'

It was a dismal performance. Simon stuttered through his lines and stumbled over Cosmo's sabre. Sir Freddie hauled him in and out of his key-light by the back of his cloak, and nudged him hard when his cues came up. In the second act, Kitty appeared, all of a tremble, in Hester's dress, which had been tacked together so that she was not quite falling out of it.

Malcolm had been in touch with the Islington police station, and it was now generally known that the remains of Hester were in a hospital morgue waiting for official identification.

Sir Freddie went on acting, as he would have done if the last trump had sounded and the Lord God of Hosts had materialised in the stalls, but juicy tears were rolling into his whiskers.

'My injury is all my own!' shouted Simon, his borrowed boots skidding on the parquet. 'And so is my revenge, my lawful chattels!'

In the wings, Horatia plucked at Vinny's sleeve. 'Are you all right, darling?'

'Leave me alone,' he said.

They ran on together, while Bill Duckworth disentangled Simon's cloak from the main gauze, and hustled him away into the darkness. The lighter-minded portion of the audience laughed. Audiences always love a shambles. They watched with rapt attention, so they would not miss a single mistake.

'Go no further,' began Horatia, 'not a step more. Thou art a master plague in the midst of miseries. Go – I fear thee! I tremble, every limb, who never shook before. There's moody death in thy resolved looks! Yes, I could kneel to pray thee far away!' A rim of vermilion appeared round one of Vinny's nostrils. He sniffed hard. Two streaks of blood crawled down his upper lip. 'Conrad, go, go!' Horatia cried. She leaned in close to him, and whispered: 'Your nose is bleeding.' He turned upstage to wipe his nose, and his hand was covered with blood when he drew it away. 'There! yonder, underneath the boughs I see our horses.'

'Aye,' said Vinny, 'and the man.' Blood was dribbling from his fingers, and he held his arms stiffly away from his white costume.

'Yes, he is there! Go – no blood! no blood!'

A fat red drop splattered on to the stage, and there was nervous tittering in the front three rows.

'Go gentle Conrad – Farewell – and for this Heaven pardon you!'

Normally Horatia kissed him, but she decided against it and dashed away into the wings. Vinny, with his back to the audience, mumbled his last speech and plunged after her.

'No blood, indeed,' whispered Horatia, pushing a bundle

of tissues into his hand. 'Right idiot I felt. God, Vinny, you're bleeding like a pig.'

Vinny begged a cigarette from Malcolm and went out to the stairs. It was very quiet, except for the show, grinding away on the relay above him. Sitting down on the top step, he tried to understand what had happened. After the phone call from Cosmo, he had left his body, and floated round in a dimension of shock. Infinite pain was about to sweep over him and kill him but, since there was nothing he could do to avert it, he sunk his bloody head on his knees and waited. Over the crackling relay, Simon yelled at Horatia: 'She is the world's chief jewel and, by heaven, she's mine by right of marriage! She is mine!'

He shut his eyes, but failed to summon up a picture of Cosmo. It was odd, he thought, that he was not consumed with hatred, or thirsting for revenge. He had always disliked Cosmo, and a twinge of this familiar dislike was all he felt now, tinged with a sense of defeat. He had won after all; he had kept Hester from his rival. Vinny was fathoms down, with his nose bleeding in thick drops on the stairs, as if it had been his heart.

'I wonder what we'll do now?' mused Alice Knowles, after the curtain call, 'Will Paul recast?'

'What'll happen to Cosmo?' someone demanded.

'He'll be inside for years, I should think,' said Tommy Inchbald. 'And a bloody good thing too. I'd like to pound his head to jelly.'

'Yes, you would, you odious little thug,' snapped Horatia, who had recovered some of her sharpness. 'Shows what a great big man you are.'

'Fuck me standing, she's actually sorry for him!'

'Yes, I am. And I'm going to help him. I don't suppose he's got a solicitor, or anything – ' The prospect of interference had given her strength. She was hurrying along the corridor, ripping the pins from her wig.

'I expect you know a marvellous little man,' jeered Tommy after her, 'and don't forget the food parcels from Harrods – you know how the poor love 'ates porridge!'

Sir Freddie wiped his eyes and trumpeted into a handkerchief. 'The pity of it all', he said, 'is that he'll never step on a stage again, not after this.'

Rosamund was waiting for Vinny at the stage door, as she always did when their shows played on the same night. He had assumed she would be there, but he was suddenly shocked when he saw that she was. Outwardly, her demeanour was perfect, because she knew that they were being watched, but Vinny recognised the squareness of her shoulders and knew he was in for a hard time. He did not care.

'My poor darling,' Rosamund said softly. She put her arm round his neck and kissed him, clinging to him for a moment afterwards, all melting sympathy.

'Let's go,' he said. How like her, he thought, to keep up appearances. The worst thing you could do to Rosamund was to injure her pride. He had made a fool of her – a pitiful fool – which she never could or would forgive. To the other people hanging about beside the desk, she was giving an admirable performance of a civilised woman, a woman who had known all about her lover's affair with someone else and was his best comforter in this tragedy. The slight snarl at the corner of that sweet smile, visible only if you were close, betrayed how furious she was.

'All right, sweetheart,' she said. 'I'll drive – you look awful. What happened to your nose?'

'Just started bleeding,' he said.

'My poor Vinny, what a night you've had.' And it hasn't even started, she added silently. Vinny heard this clearly, as he let her take his arm and lead him out of the theatre. 'Goodnight, Peter!' she called to the stage door manager.

Rosamund kept hold of him all the way down to the underground car park. 'You do look wretched, Vinny. Just as if someone's smacked you in the face.' There was a little steely edge to her voice now, but she was still in character, and he knew this meant there was a tremendous storm brewing. Still he did not care, and wondered why he had been so scared of her rages in the past. Her Oscar de la Renta scent filled the car with femininity, and her varnished fingers searched confidently in the glove compartment for a tape. Vinny hated her for being alive, when Hester was dead. Very coolly, as if expecting to be challenged, she put on the Bruch violin concerto, and they drove away, the whole car throbbing with soupy, heart-wrenching glissandos. At Russell Square, Vinny began to cry.

'Are you all right, darling?'

He did not reply.

'You mustn't be ashamed to cry for her,' said Rosamund. 'She was a nice girl, and she loved you. Of course you must cry. Only don't sniff, there's a love – it sets my teeth on edge. Take a Kleenex out of my bag.'

Vinny sniffed angrily and wiped his face on his sleeve. He was trying not to remember drinking iced tea with Hester, two days before. His loins twitched, but that hunger could never be satisfied again. Vinny, next time you see me, I shall be quite transformed. Leaning out of the taxi window to blow kisses to him, and he had let her go. Why, why, why hadn't he stopped her, or followed her?

By the time they reached Gospel Oak, he was sobbing uncontrollably; crying for Hester as he had never cried for anything in his life.

Rosamund wrenched his door open. 'Out.'

'I'm not staying,' he said.

'I'm not asking you to stay.' She let them into the house. 'But I'm not expecting you to spend the night on the street. You can have the spare bed.'

Vinny sat down at the kitchen table, sinking his head into his arms.

'You've slept there before, haven't you?' demanded Rosamund. 'Well, of course, I've been a complete fool, but for some reason, for some amazing reason, I trusted you.' She slammed her keys down. 'I can understand you not telling Cosmo, but why didn't you tell me?'

'Leave me alone.'

'Like fuck I'll leave you alone. You're going to pay for what you've done. You brought her here, didn't you? Answer me, Vinny.'

'Yes.'

'When was I meant to find out?'

'Tonight.'

'Oh. All packed up, are you?'

'Yes,' said Vinny. He had stuffed the rucksack before leaving for the theatre.

'I see. God, I've seen you do it with so many women! All the time we were talking about our future, you were having furtive little love-ins with Hester Stretton.'

'Don't you dare say a word against her!' he spluttered.

'Let's get this straight, Vinny. We're not talking about Hester, or Cosmo. We're talking about you.' She sat down opposite him, and folded her hands deliberately on the table. Her voice was brisk and businesslike – she might have been an analyst in consultation, but her eyes were chips of ice.

'You knew what I was like,' Vinny said. 'You're just the same.'

'I'm not a liar. Do you know what you've done?'

'Don't keep saying that! I haven't done anything!'

'Of course, you think it's perfectly all right to muck about with other people's lives. If you'd stayed with Hester in the first place, she'd be alive now.'

'You made me leave her!' shouted Vinny.

'Oh, come on. If it hadn't been me, it would've been someone else. You can't shift the blame. You're also responsible for that poor wretched man. He wouldn't have done it if someone had bothered to tell him the truth.'

Vinny raised his head, and the two of them stared at each other with intense loathing. 'He's a maniac. He's sick.'

'He should have killed you,' said Rosamund.

'I wish he had.'

'Very gracious of you.'

'She was – she was pregnant.'

'Yes,' said Rosamund, 'I wondered when we'd come to that.' She tensed, ready to spring.

'Now you see why I couldn't tell you,' said Vinny. 'You'd have hated the idea of another woman carrying my child.'

'Your child!' screeched Rosamund, slamming her fists down on the table. 'Your child? You really fancy yourself, don't you?

Mr Big Prick, shooting your wad all round London – well, you're not such a wonderfuck after all. I went down to the clinic today. Want to know what they said? There's nothing wrong with me – I could have a dozen children any day I like. It's you! You're the one who can't do it!'

Vinny gaped at her, stunned into silence.

'You've got an abnormally low sperm count. You can look at the results yourself if you don't believe me. That was Cosmo Brady's baby inside Hester, and you made him kill it.'

'I – I didn't – ' whispered Vinny.

'Oh yes you did. This is all your fault – what use are you, you piece of shit? Why should I keep you in my house? You don't love me, you can't keep your willy dry for five minutes, and you can't even father a child – what fucking use are you anyway?' She pressed her hands into her cheeks, suddenly shocked by her outburst.

Vinny was too ruined to cry any more. He sat at the table, massaging his elbows. Rosamund was the one who cried.

'Oh, for God's sake, Vinny, what shall we do?'

She really did love him, and it occurred to Vinny, shattered as he was, that something might be salvaged. There was no reason why Rosamund's life should be ruined too.

'Rosie,' he said, 'please don't heave me out.'

She sighed heavily, as if relieved, or resigned. 'No love, I won't.'

Cosmo was sitting on a hard plastic chair at Islington police station, under a harsh fluorescent light. He was not in handcuffs. Someone had even brought him a cup of tea. Two policemen were sitting opposite, with jackets unbuttoned. They were the second pair, the first having gone off for supper. One of them had a *Daily Mirror*. The other sat with legs sprawling and arms folded, gazing at the posters on the wall above Cosmo's foggy grey head. He would not speak to either of them. He was ready to accept any sort of punishment, but their heavy-handed kindness broke him.

At first, he had been desperate to confess. Two policemen had come round to Corsica Street ten minutes after he called.

They had had to break open his front door, because he would not answer it. He was on the floor, stroking Hester's face, knowing that the last seconds of his real life were ticking away. The younger policeman had retched when he saw the blood, and when he accidentally stepped in some he rubbed at his boot frantically, like Bluebeard's wife with the key to the forbidden chamber. The older policeman had seemed kind, and Cosmo began his full confession, but the policeman was far more interested in making him let go of Hester's body. He knelt on the floor beside Cosmo, assuring him that he could say everything he wanted at the station. There was an ambulance waiting in the street, and the younger policeman stood out in the hall to block the intense curiosity of the woman downstairs. Everyone was embarrassingly kind, but they avoided looking him in the eye. He knew they all thought he was a basket case, but there was no point telling them he was not. Nothing looks madder than a person insisting over and over that he is not insane.

Cosmo shifted in his chair, and the two men opposite twitched. They looked bored, but their eyes were pinned to him. For the first time, he realised he was a captive. If he had tried to make a run for it, he would not have got as far as the end of the passage. He stared at the policeman with the newspaper and idly wondered what his life was like, where he lived, whether he was married. His body was exhausted beyond belief, and he thought how much better he could have endured this if he knew that his own bed was waiting at the end of it all. But he could never go back to that flat again. Oh, Hester.

He must have muttered it, for one of the policemen said: 'What?'

'Nothing,' Cosmo said, in his rusty voice. He coughed, and looked down at his shoes. He would have given worlds not to have done what he had done, but the murderer was the old Cosmo, whose skin he was already shedding. It was not that he had comfort, but he had been feeling, ever since he knelt in the church, that there was a possibility of comfort somewhere, if only he could be granted the ability to find it. Lord, that I might receive my sight.

Once, in a catechism class at school, he had been asked, 'Cosmo Brady, what is God?' and the immensity of the concept of God had smitten him into silence. What was God? He had wanted to say that God was the hundreds of rainbow shades contained in a drip of water about to fall off a tap; that God was the gaudy, oleaginous streaks which moved so slowly across the surface of a soap bubble; that he was the white chalk dust which swirled with such grace in the rays of sun sloping through the high windows. The teacher waited, leaning on Cosmo's desk, with the wings of his black soutane slipping over his shoulders, and Cosmo wondered how he could ever find words to explain that the glass was not always dark – God could be met face to face, for a fragment of a split second, in any shining thing. The priest took Cosmo's silence for ignorance, and he was handsomely whacked on both ears for not knowing that God is Love.